DIGITAL

Magic

Philippa Ballantine

Dragon
Moon

Digital Magic

ISBN 10 1-896944-88-4 Print Edition
ISBN 13 978-1-896944-88-3

Dragon Moon Press is an Imprint of Hades Publications Inc.
P.O. Box 1714, Calgary, Alberta, T2P 2L7, Canada

Dragon Moon Press and Hades Publications, Inc. acknowledges the ongoing support of the Canada Council for the Arts and the Alberta Foundation for the Arts for our publishing programme.

The Alberta Foundation for the Arts
COMMITTED TO THE DEVELOPMENT OF CULTURE AND THE ARTS

Alberta
COMMUNITY DEVELOPMENT

Canada Council
for the Arts

Conseil des Arts
du Canada

Printed and bound in the United States
www.dragonmoonpress.com
www.chasingthebard.com
www.pjballantine.net

Save a Tree Program

At Dragon Moon Press, our carbon footprint is significantly higher than average and we plan to do something about it. For every tree Dragon Moon uses in printing our books, we are helping to plant new trees to reduce our carbon footprint so that the next generation can breathe clean air, keeping our planet and it's inhabitants healthy.

DIGITAL

Magic

Philippa Ballantine

www.pjballantine.net

www.chasingthebard.com

Beggar that I am, I am even poor in thanks,
but I thank you; and sure, dear friends...
-Hamlet Act I, Scene II

Dad, you showed me the magic in the world from the beginning.

Mum, your delight in my success was a light that kept me going.

Gabrielle, your patience as both comma and apostrophe threatened to overwhelm me amazes me.

Tee, you love to take credit for my podcasting and writing, but eventually the banter stops, and I just have to admit, you are right.

For my family, the ones I was lucky enough to be born into and the ones I found along the way—without you there would be no magic, digital or otherwise.

CHAPTER ONE
Awaken

The great shadow crept the length of the roof as silent as a prayer; each paw finding its way unerringly to the path of least noise. The half-eaten moon made its dark fur dance and for a moment it was haloed in silver light. At this momentary disturbance, the black lip curled back revealing a creamy expanse of fang. An unvoiced growl rumbled within the deep chest.

Shoulders scything, the panther resumed his ascent. On either side the roof sloped sharply away into the unlit manor's garden and though he could not hear them yet, he knew that the guards would soon be reaching the front door. Even his feline power and silence were no protection from night-scopes and high powered splinterguns. Stealth and the darkness were his only allies in this shape.

Curved dark ears twitched this way and that, tracing even the faintest noise to its source for the danger it might bring. Nothing was stirring in the distant wing of the house where the owner lived, but the northern wing that housed the art collection was humming with barely concealed activity. The best prizes were always worth the risk.

He reached the small window; the sort that was used for ventilation in those days before central heating. The older the building, the better, as far as a twenty-first century thief was concerned. The cat paused again, sniffing the rim of the window. Good, no recent scents. Perhaps if he was lucky the window was so unremarkable from below that it drew no attention. His stealthy paw made short work of the fragile ancient lock and without pause he slipped into the room.

It was museum-like — thick with the scents of beeswax and age. Moonlight ran in faint streams through the still evening air to glitter momentarily on the glass-topped cases below. Inside were mementos of lost ages, cleaned, dusted and displayed for tourists to gape at. It was there that his target lay. The cat's eyes narrowed and his posture stiffened as if sensing prey. The smell of well-varnished wood made his nose twitch, but his keen sense of scent also brought him more important information. The guard had just passed here, his half-eaten salami sandwich tucked into his back pocket and his boots just recently cleaned of mud that reeked of dog. Yet the cat's nose was the least of his advantages.

A flicker of cool mist enshrouded the beast, hiding his form for a heartbeat; when it cleared, a far different one had taken his place. The tall dark-haired man was already moving along the walkway, ducking his body low against the windows, moving with the same graceful economy as the cat. He was better equipped; his dark leather hushsuit dropped his thermal temperature to that of a passing moth, and strapped to his hip was the darkest and ugliest of pistols.

No normal shapeshifter would have been able to retain clothes and equipment, but he had never been anything like normal. Magic ran pure through his veins and the pesky details of logic and physics did not intrude.

But this world had not left him completely unchanged either — money, for example, had already exerted its power. He was not here for random violence; he was here for something far more interesting and profitable.

Others in his trade sacrificed flesh for metal and soul for machine, but he disdained all of that; his natural talents more than made up for a somewhat traditional approach to thievery. His body, after all, was the only thing left to him from a dangerous and tragic past, and he was not about to cut into it merely for fashion.

He reached the end of the walkway. After a momentary pause on the varnished handrail, he lightly dropped the three floors down onto the stone floor. It was a fall that would have broken the legs of any other. His dark eyes scanned the shadows. Something about this place felt wrong. A prickle of fear ran on hot feet up his back and he knew better than to ignore his instinct.

Yet his prey was only an arm length away. The glass-topped display case seemed little protection indeed for such a prize.

He'd seen many beautiful things in his time, acquired them by fair means and foul for his customers. This was different. He knew that immediately.

It was a mask — simple and elegant. The empty eyed female face looked back at him and seemingly into him at the same time. The mouth rested slightly open, caught in the act of speaking while the full white lip trembled. It was a face beautifully familiar; it spoke of his childhood, when he had thought those times long forgotten. This mask, with the hint of spiraling curls framing it, had captured the form of two people: both had captured him when he had been young and foolish.

It was run through with such a delicacy and power that it could mean only one thing. No other place could have created such a frail thing of pale stone and infused it with such spirit.

This was the moment when any other person in his line of work would have smashed and grabbed. And yet the man waited; his breath warm in the chill air and almost fogging the glass, nostrils flaring wide. Far off, outside the walls of the mansion, a dog barked and a guard's stiff curse followed. Still, he did not move. He was part of the world — quiet but awake. Simply waiting for it to whisper its mysteries to him. Dark eyes never left the velvet-couched mask; tracing it, trying to find its meaning.

He suddenly remembered to breathe and the scent of jasmine plunged into his body. It was like a hammer blow across the face. Something so vastly unexpected that he almost cried out. It resounded through his bones like nothing had for centuries, a dreadful ache lodging itself under his ribs. The smell of it flooded his nose and mouth, sweet and heady like a summer wine or a field choked with flowers — made all the more powerful simply because he knew what it was.

How could this part of home be merely another possession, stared at by mindless tourists who could never understand its true meaning? The desire to hold it and feel the cool stone was intense. Every fiber of him ached to reach out and take it. His mouth twitched. The pain was sweet and terrible and he wished it both gone and eternal.

It was mead and madness to senses deprived for so long. In that one heady instant all that he had become since the last time he had sensed this, had been swept away. Knocked back to childhood, he couldn't help it. "Home," he whispered against the night, longing stretching his voice out into the friendless darkness.

The security system picked him up straight away. He might as well have stood up and shouted his name to the world. The moment was broken. The sliver from his past vanished while the scent dissipated into reality. The mask had reclaimed its mystery and now he was in real trouble. The rattle of metal against the window told him the security system was rapidly blocking any escape. Harsh technology was locking the intruder into the hall until the guards arrived with guns blazing and questions left to the morning.

Still faintly dazzled by what he had seen, habit nonetheless got him to his feet and running. He bounded back the way he had come, changing mid-air to his faster form. The pale feline claws now sunk deep into the wooden floors. Below him the room was flooding with murky-gray gas, illuminating the red criss-cross of infrared beams. As he leaped and bounded past them he felt a vague fuzziness steal over him. And then cat ears picked up the whine of sentrybots powering to life.

The powerful panther's haunches bunched and hurled him along the walkway, ears flattened and mouth held in a silent snarl. From behind came the snap of electricity as the air jolted alive with electronic fury. Every section of his dark fur rippled with it and his rational mind told him he didn't have long. Ahead, the small window that had allowed him entry was chugging relentlessly shut behind a security screen. The thin bar of moonlight it allowed in was too narrow even as he leapt the last few feet, but the cat barely missed a beat.

Now the dark man dropped to one knee and smoothly unsheathed the blunt ugly weapon he carried at his hip. Two sharp blasts ripped open the descending metal between him and freedom.

Cat form carried him free of the hall even as the guards were responding to the alarm. He scrambled along the roof, leapt ten feet into the trees and galloped away just as the men were opening the doors. The only hint they had that he even passed was the rabid barking of their dogs.

The panther retreated to the quieter, deeper shadows. He stared fixedly at the huddled mound of the great house, yellow eyes half-hooded. A few quick licks across his shoulder assured him that he was alive. Though the incident was humiliating, he had at least survived. Still, neither domestic cat nor leopard likes to fail.

Huddled under a thick yew tree, he shifted back to his human shape, the better to think. The urge to swear and punch something was powerful, perhaps a hangover from the feline rage that still pumped in his system. However, the remembrance of that scent quieted him a moment. It called him back to a time when he had been quite another thing; when his world had been something different, something far more beautiful. He half-laughed to suddenly realise that tears were running down his cheeks. Thrusting them aside with the back of his hand, Ronan knew it was a foolish thing and one that he had thought himself long past.

"Bloody fool." He reprimanded himself. The weapon on his hip felt suddenly heavy and ugly. He couldn't help thinking that he would have had no need of such a thing once; indeed, it would have been a humiliation and a travesty to carry one.

But he was quite used to this life now, settled almost. It was just stupid to yearn for what could not be. It would only drive him mad. And yet….

The sigh would not be contained. It was a mystery that had to be unraveled. Until it was, he couldn't simply travel on. It would itch at the back of his head forever. This little village must hold the answer to that glimpse and he could not rest until he found it; as coveted a prize now as the mask itself. Still, this task too required patience and care. He would wait till morning. Then he could get the lie of the land and work out just what sort of mess he had stepped into.

From the shifting shade of the oak Ella watched the cat's figure enter the bushes and the man's emerge a few minutes later. How strange, her sleep befuddled brain thought. But then, this dream had been strange right from the very beginning.

Ella couldn't even recall having fallen asleep in her little cottage, but Qoth had been curled on her feet and the fire had been blazing, so she must have. Looking down, she saw that she was dressed, but her bare feet were damp in the wet grass. That confirmed the dream; she couldn't feel the cool metal of spinebridge against her back and without its digital signal her legs would normally be useless.

Still, she was not far from home. Obviously dreams were not all distant alien landscapes — this was Penherem Manor. She'd watched the cat fleeing the sudden blaze of light and half expected to see Tania Furlion's elegant shape in pursuit. The Lady of the Manor would never have done any such thing, but then, in dreams anything was possible.

Ella leaned against the elm that sheltered her as the man loped further away from the scene of the crime. She felt sure it was a crime. At this distance he was more silhouette than reality — all lanky frame and nice long legs.

In the manner of dreams, she suddenly realised she was not alone in watching. The back of her neck prickled and a wash of fear flooded through her. With an empty heart, she turned to face the other woman. Ella's dream throat was suddenly dry and she swayed slightly now, relying on the tree to hold her.

The other woman was more frightening than she should have been, so Ella concentrated on looking very hard at the physical. A pale mist wafted from her shoulders, giving the appearance of near nakedness but somehow managing to swallow form as well. The face turned toward Ella as if suddenly aware of her presence. The line of the jaw was perfect, sharp and unforgiving. The hair was bone white and long enough to mingle with the mist. But then the ruined eyes lifted. There was nothing there. Only a grim, wrinkled expanse.

That broken face was no accident. Ella felt her own eyes burn. No car accident, no fate of birth had denied this apparition her eyes. She had taken them, like some mythical Cassandra, sacrificing sight for deadly powers. She couldn't say how she knew, she only did.

The blankness was watching her; it saw what she was, measured her and was perhaps interested. But Ella did not want to be interesting. She wanted to be bland. She wanted to melt into the landscape.

What are you? Why are you here? Where are you from?

That voice was peeling her apart, revealing her hollow inadequacy, laying her naked in the dark.

I'm not here, I'm nothing. The broken sobs in her throat finally woke the shaken woman to her living room, but the sudden warmth of home could not thaw the chill of fear that had lodged in her heart. Nothing could erase the void that had seen her. She burrowed into her pillows and tried to hide herself from the memory of the nightmare.

But the woman and the man-cat were not the only things awakening into the night. Neither could know what else was stirring in the darkness.

Something more had felt the brush of power and Art. It responded as the man had — with longing and memory. The earth stirred and cracked as the man-sized seed gave up its long hidden spawn, ripe with hatred and plans. Foxes and night owls fled the ancient scent, rustling the half dead leaves of autumn while even the smallest mouse followed after; prey and predator united in terror.

This newborn monster unfolded in the dimness of Penherem's plastic perfect forest, a dark purple putrid flower that was just beginning to bloom. The trees, unable to uproot themselves, still pulled back in horror. A dark nightmare stepped out on sticky feet ready to find its target. Within the smooth skull ideas bubbled and seethed as it pushed its infant powers out into this new world, sucking up all the knowledge from it. With a sigh its lips pulled back from teeth in pleasure.

Tourists traveled from all over this festering globe to walk in the footsteps of their ancestors and they got what they imagined, rather than what had actually been. It knew. It had seen. It had been there. Nearly six hundred years it had waited, a fungal spore looking for the first hint of rain.

The Between gates were still closed, the Nexus changed. That, it could feel well enough, but the taste of that other realm had stirred it awake. A chance was all it needed and perhaps there would be only one. It had to proceed cautiously, for the world was changed from when it had last stalked the fields and forests. This new woodland of technology, of steel and shared hallucinations, was unfamiliar. It would have to find a guide, someone's lead to follow until it knew its way.

But mankind could not have changed that much in six short hundreds of years, and if there was one thing it knew, it was people. It could hunt out the best-hidden weakness, even those that a human himself did not acknowledge, and use them to its Master's gain.

It pulled its shadow-thin legs free of the casing and shook its many-eyed head in anticipation. If the Art was here it would find it, and if it was the time of the Healer, even better. The mere thought of rejoining with its beloved Master sent a hiss of delight rippling out from its pierced carapace. Ancient wrongs would be undone.

It stretched in a curved sickle of darkness and made its way off on tender and strangely delicate feet. Time to be about. Time to shake this new millennium up.

Ella woke with a gasping breath, the world spinning around her. For one dreadful moment she didn't know where she was, what her name was, everything was superseded by panic.

But then, she was used to panic, used to the sound of her heart thundering in her throat. Two nightmares in one night were bad even for her. First the eyeless woman and then the razor sharp image which she couldn't quite remember, except for the terrific fear it had brought with it. She lay very still on the couch, letting her breathing return to something near normal.

Like she had a thousand times before, Ella repeated her mantra to still the fear. *I am home; I am not in London.*

Any day when that was true was another good day — better than those she'd fled. She'd left that life and Nill behind. She was Ella and that was how it was going to stay.

But even to think of him and those times was to give them power over her. With a resolute tightening of her jaw Ella reached out and grabbed the spinebridge from where it lay on the coffee table. It resembled nothing so much as a glittering silver bug, only a cascade of green lights on its outspread legs and central column showing it was more than a hand-sized sculpture.

Ella didn't know how to feel about the bridge. Had it been a generation before, she would have been confined to a wheelchair, suspended in that curious state where people either looked at her with extra scrutiny or not at all. But on the other hand, it was old technology. The bridge had to be removed while sleeping, as there was a limit how long wiring and the human nervous system could be connected at a stretch. And it did not shield her totally from sympathetic eyes; she still walked oddly and under thin shirts the curved dome would have been clearly visible even without its flashing lights.

Ella counted her blessings, though, and slipped the cool metal under her shirt to lie against her T11 injury. The steel device snapped audibly into the array of sockets and sensation returned to her legs. One day, she might be able to afford the astronomic price of biomelding and consign the bridge to the past.

Still with a hint of caution, Ella levered herself out of the couch. The morning light had already crawled across the carpet toward the floor to ceiling bookshelves, to rest lightly on Tolkien and Lewis.

But Qoth had not waited for the sun to reach her. The chocolate cat was perched on the window seat and, even though her back was to her mistress, Ella could imagine the expression of contentment on her face. The feline lived for warmth and it was her ritual to watch to make sure the sun returned. It had already clambered above the rolling green hills and was slowly washing over the thatched and cozy roofs of Little Penherem. It would be filtering down the narrow streets and running in long swathes across the village Green.

Ella leaned her head against one overstuffed chair and watched the cat with lazy amusement. Every day it was the same. As if the chocolate tabby needed to see the dawn to make it happen.

Ella could only dream of having the same kind of lifestyle— there were already three deadlines blinking from her notepad and her own personal goal of another three thousand words hanging overhead. The freelance work took priority as always—it did, after all, pay the bills — but the novel had to be done by the time summer rolled to a close.

Ella had just managed to turn her mind to filling her notepad with at least some perfunctory words when someone began banging on the door.

Qoth gave her a yellow-eyed glare from the window that might have been reproach, but her human had already accepted the offer of procrastination.

Limping slightly, Ella went down the hall to answer the unremitting thumping. When she finally yanked the door open with a small growl, she found Bakari leaning against the doorframe, one hand already raised ready to give another battering.

He looked at her through golden eyes and flicked back one of his dreadlocks from his shoulder. Bakari was too exotic for Penherem; he looked like was made out of beautiful deep wood that someone had spent many loving hours polishing. Few believed he was in fact an English librarian.

Then again, she was almost certain that librarian was not all her friend was. The faint musk of him reached her, and like every other female in Little Penherem she couldn't remain totally immune. In morning light he almost gleamed and as always he made her feel more than a little dowdy.

"Weren't napping, were you, Mouse?" He smiled enough to excuse the use of that terrible pet name he had for her. "You'd better watch out or someone might think you have a social life."

"Cheeky bugger," she replied without malice and ushered him in. "You know that you have the social scene all wrapped up round here. There's none left for the rest of us."

He shrugged while prowling around the edges of her domain — too hyped up to sit down perhaps. "Perhaps if you bothered to go outside now and then…"

Her notepad was blinking determinedly so she replied distractedly. "I do go out."

"Playing maid to the Furlion woman twice a week doesn't count. Writing a book isn't an excuse to become a hermit you know." Bakari gave Qoth such a firm stroke it made her blink in surprise.

Sometimes Ella wished that Bakari would try and fit in more. If he were more accepted by the rest of the villagers, the two of them wouldn't be forced into each other's company all the time.

The man was a delight to look at and smarter than was healthy in this day and age, but sometimes he had a way of prodding her with her own inadequacies. That was probably why she alone was unmoved by his charms.

Bakari folded his dark form into the wing backed chair by the window and smiled disarmingly. "Don't pout, Mouse. I just wanted to check on you."

Ella sighed and waited for the lecture; this was familiar territory. She'd made the mistake of telling Bakari some of why she'd moved to Penherem, just the bit about Nill. Somehow he thought this qualified him as her guardian. Easing herself back into the chair by the fireside, she watched as he scanned the bookcases that lined her parlor with professional interest.

"You can tell a lot about people by what they read." He muttered, "You know, some people have gotten rid of their paper editions altogether..."

She stiffened defensively, "I don't like plugging into all those gadgets — gives me the willies messing with your brain like that."

Bakari flicked back the hair behind his ear revealing the tiny silver IO plug. "Lining makes life worthwhile."

"But you work in the library — you need it. Me, I prefer the classics. Reading may be slower but it's more satisfying."

He snorted, "I didn't get this thing put in for pleasure, Mouse. Nothing but a business tool. After all, it's all about information. Who has it, who doesn't, who wants it and who is willing to pay for it."

She wondered not for the first time what sort of business he'd been involved in. Someday he might share his reasons for becoming the librarian of such an insular village. He wouldn't be the first to think that it was a good place to hide.

Little Penherem was one of those darling satellite villages, orbiting around the not-so-distant planet of London. It catered to tourists, local and foreign, that wanted a taste of England. They demanded an England that only existed in a plastic, no-crap, no-dirt place like Penherem. It was history watered down and made palatable for the masses — and not a history that anyone who had lived then would be able to recognize. Rape, spitting and bigotry were filtered out. Mass hallucination and feel good atmosphere poured in. Penherem was a pretty cardboard cutout.

However, the danger that Ella sensed hanging around Bakari tasted all too real. It seemed almost familiar, perhaps because Nill had shared that, too.

"In fact," he pulled out the hair-width silver cable from one of the pockets in his trousers and waved it in her direction, "mind if I check my messages?"

Ella had seen him at the business end of a Line in the library. Not the dusty front of house where the books were mere window dressing, but out the back where the information centre pulsed with a more modern beat. Bakari was a real lion there, prowling the corridors of information that had replaced the motorway in importance.

Trying not to show her discomfort, she shrugged. "Sure."

Bakari pounced on her Line, attaching the monofilament and then inserting the other end into his head IO. Just like that he was in and gone. Those golden restless eyes drooped a little as Bakari concentrated on that far off world. Very few were brave enough to go for the full head gear — most retained some residual fear of having hardware implanted directly into the brain. In Ella's eyes it was a very reasonable concern.

She hadn't worked out exactly where to look when someone was running the Line — was it impolite to stare or was it worse to ignore them as if they weren't there at all?

"It's alright, Mouse." His voice was soft and slightly slurred as if he'd had one too many beers down at the Green Man. She realised that his irises had swallowed up the whole of his eye. "I'm not doing anything illegal. I just need to speak to a friend and I'd rather not have the book squad interrupt."

Ari's sarcastic comment on the dozen or so local ladies that occasionally helped run the library still made her smile a little. They carried on that ancient tradition of the interfering village wife with great vigor.

Still, Ella couldn't really see why he would be worried about what they thought — he certainly had never shown much regard for it up until now. He finished while she was still deciding if she believed him or not. The speed of that other realm was another unnerving thing about it.

He had already removed the cable and tucked it away somewhere. "Thanks Ella... it's just a pain wondering who's going to come into the library when I'm busy like that."

Surely it was over so swiftly he could have found some time to do it. Whatever it was he'd found, he didn't look too happy about it.

"I better move and so should you, Mouse."

Resisting an urge to bark back, she shooed him to the door once more. "I'm on my way."

"Maybe you'd come over to mine for some breakfast tomorrow." He embraced her swiftly and had released her before she could muster a complaint. "You know how much you love my French toast."

"Well, if that's on offer I guess I can manage it."

"I'm holding you to that," he grinned before trotting down the steps and vaulting over her picket gate.

Ella waved him off from the doorstep while her mind worked in little circles. Despite his cheerfulness, there was something wrong with her friend. The smile on his lips was not reflected in his eyes. He was hiding from her. And Ella was somewhat afraid that she had worked out the emotion that she had seen on her friend's face. Fear — and what could make a lion afraid, she hated to think.

Ella was about to go back inside when a giggle sounded from just beyond her garden wall. For one confused minute she thought it could have been Ari. Then the jasmine that climbed the broken down brick wall shook and Penny Two Dolls emerged. Her wide blue eyes gleamed with mischief and she completely ignored the twigs that had caught in her hair.

Ella bent down to the girl's height and for the second time that morning tried not be angry. "Have you been peeking in the window again, Penny?"

That gap-toothed grin spread across her face was impossible to be annoyed with, but Penny tucked her battered Two Dolls into her pants pockets just in case Ella meant to take it out on them. The broken-eyed toys wobbled as she shoved them further down into her tiny overalls.

Looking over her shoulder Ella hoped to see Alice Thorn. She had yet to quite work out the relationship between child and older teenager. She could have been sister or young mother, but whichever she was, she was the only person who seemed capable of getting Penny Two Dolls to behave anything like a normal child. But there was no sign of Alice's ragtag bone-thin form.

Ella sighed. Much as she liked Penny, there was something vaguely worrying about the way she managed to get into anyone's house, and that innocent blue-eyed look didn't mean she would think twice if something she liked took her fancy. Ella had very few possessions, but the ones she did have, she treasured.

Ella rolled her eyes skyward. She couldn't stand out here all day exchanging words with a little girl who had so far shown no signs of having any of her own. By the time she looked back the girl was gone.

Chapter Two

Avenge

It was in bred in every soldier: never accept defeat. The New Zealand military forces had a long history of bravery and daring far exceeding their size. And yet at this moment no one could see a way out. General Seddon looked around the briefing room, hoping for one his comrades to suggest something — anything but the recommendation that was lying in front of him. It was a hasty report but he didn't doubt that it contained all New Zealand's available options. And it was painfully thin.

Seddon had been trained for heavy decisions, to send men to death and battle, but this... this was far beyond the parameters of his training. The remains of the nation's leaders both military and civilian around him were worn as narrow as the report on the desk. He would have asked God, prayed on his knees down in the little church on the waterfront not far from where he and Jessica had their home, but he could not for two reasons. The enemy had bombed the church along with the base two days ago. And Seddon had ceased to pray once Jessica was gone.

Even that pain, though, would not save him from this decision. He couldn't slink off and leave the hard part to others.

Six hundred kilometers away, Aroha sat with her Nana podding peas in the sun porch. The day was hot, making her cotton dress stick to the back of her legs as she swung them backward and forward inches from the wooden floor. She didn't speak, her eyes watching the drift of clouds while her mind locked to that terrified one so far away. She didn't tell Nana what she heard in the wind, for even if she believed her there was nothing to be changed.

It was only a few miles to the city of Wellington where the enemies' warships were pounding the last of the population to dust. She'd already tasted the death and fear of thousands in the last few days — it scared her and destroyed the beauty of the day.

The General could feel the heavy looks from around the table and he resisted the urge to wipe the trickle of sweat from behind his neck. This wasn't the war for a solider. They couldn't hope to give the enemy even a break in stride. They hadn't expected to be in this position, naked and alone against a world that had always come to their aid. But their allies had more these days to worry about than a tiny country at the bottom of the world. They might miss the lamb, but they'd cope, he thought bitterly. But it was not for any of those things that the country was lost. It was for their other more precious resource — water. All over the globe, that which had been taken so lightly was now a cause to die for. And it was something New Zealand had plenty of. And she had grown complacent in the strength of her allies. But to the enemy, the water was worth the risk, and for them it had paid off.

We've got to look after ourselves, Seddon reminded himself. He might not have had many weapons to defend his home with, but he wouldn't be afraid to use that last one.

Aroha's mouth twitched. She flicked back her brown hair and looked askance at Nana through it. Could she not feel the man's anguished thoughts? Even though they all knew about what was happening and had taken the shots, there was still a strange normalness to the day. Shouldn't they be hiding rather than preparing vegetables?

Aroha looked down the valley to where the little village of Makara lay cupped in the greenness of fern and toi toi grass. They'd heard the bombing of the city even though it lay beyond the hills and the village had reacted swiftly — perhaps a lingering racial memory of guerilla warfare. Adam Tohai had taken his tractor and plowed up a large section of the sealed road. The farmers had driven their stock into the bush until whatever happened, happened.

Seddon was thinking of children like her, ones that had grown up with the pohutakawa as their Christmas tree and hearing the tui call in its branches. What would their world be like after this?

He twitched, scooped up the report and looked across at his lieutenant,
"It's been ratified?"

"Yes sir," Rawlings blue eyes didn't flinch. "Public approval of
ninety percent. We're a go."

"God," Seddon whispered to himself and it wasn't a prayer, "Then
give the order, release Utu."

Even now the earth mother Papatuanuku was keening so loud
that Rastas the ginger tom hissed loudly. Nana raised her head as
he ran off, but her hand went out to her granddaughter, "Finish
up Aroha. I think we better head in — it's getting dark."

Utu — the word filled up Seddon's mouth and he wondered if it
had done the same to Maori warriors of old. But it'd been different for
them; blood and revenge, yes — but also honor. It was a consequence to
action. Here and now, for them, it meant nothing more than survival.

Rawlings turned away from the others. She tapped her code into
the console, submitting her eye to the retinal scanner attached. Then
she slid the device across the table. The officials all did the same. Some
hesitated briefly, battling with thoughts of what would no doubt come
back to haunt them, but Seddon was proud. Even if they all looked like
fanatics and lunatics to the rest of the world. When it was his turn he
didn't waver. The people had spoken. He completed the code, scanned
his retina and it was done.

The little huddle of leaders did not move, suspended in the moment.
As if thinking that if no one moved, if no one went outside, it would all
prove to be nothing but a bad dream.

Nana was right. Aroha shivered. It was indeed getting darker.

All over the country, from the chilly beauty of the fiords to
the near tropical beaches of the north, the virus was released into
the fresh water. The one thing the enemy wanted was poisoned
against him. From the water it would spread like wildfire and
all those humans not inoculated would die. Blood would boil
from nose and mouth, internal organs broken apart by utu's
onslaught.

Seddon leaned back in his chair feeling less a soldier than he had
in thirty years. But there would be no winning by the enemy today, not
unless they wanted to die on foreign soil. Then there would be no easy
path for New Zealand either.

Looking around the faces at the table, he could see they understood. No foreign aid for them now, no exports and no tourists — they had made themselves a pariah. The scientists said it would take two generations for utu to run its cycle. Two generations before the children of New Zealand could go anywhere. He'd already sent notification to all their allies and enemies, and he knew that when he returned to his desk, there would be horrendous quarantine restrictions in place.

Pushing himself back from the table, he went to the cabinet and produced a bottle of scotch. "There won't be any of this coming in from now on — we'll have to make do." He poured them all a generous glass.

To the south, Nana was pulling the curtains and locking the doors. Aroha stoked the fire in the coal range and watched the flames leap. She didn't need to hear Seddon's voice to know it was now all different. The air, the water and the earth herself, said it. Nothing would ever be the same.

Ronan sat, contentedly sipping a tangy pale ale at the Green Man. What a curious time this early twenty-first century was. Over four hundred years since a young powerful Bard had broken the Nexus and sent the Fey world, the font of all magic, drifting away from this one. So long ago that he'd thought the echo of it was almost gone.

Yet despite Industrial revolution, information revolution, wars of all types, over land and water and some just for fun, he still was here — ever the wanderer. His emotions on that piece of luck fluctuated.

This village was something new to him, though. He scanned his surroundings with an unthreatening smile on his lips. The beer was certainly better than the place that had made it. This typical English pub was so typical it rang very untrue. Little snugs, blazing fire, buxom wenches serving trencher bread; the Green Man struggled to prove itself authentic and yet was not. Public houses, Ronan recalled, had only recently become pleasant enough for him to contemplate spending any time within their walls.

He leaned back in his well padded chair with a contented sigh. This was far more comfortable than the period they were trying to cultivate. Why couldn't they simply enjoy their era instead of aching for something that had never been and thus was certainly beyond recall?

Not then for its own comforts and beauties did Ronan admire the Green Man, but rather for the broad range of humanity it seemed to have trawled up. The room was full of wide-eyed tourists talking in loud voices about the atmosphere and the beauty of the spot. A little collection of locals were gathered around by the bar chatting to the affable publican and his smiling competent looking wife. Such people were the kind he had a real affection for.

The drone of the combined noise was beginning to make his head ring a bit, though. Ronan tried to tune them out, concentrating on the good beer. Amazing how humans still intrigued him even after all this time. The intricacies of their expressions, their insatiable desire for the transient things in life and not least their incredible taste for the most marvelous food, all held his attention. They were, in fact, what had made over four hundred years bearable, with their tangled web of brawling and loving.

Ronan eased back in his chair some more but resisted the impolite urge to prop his feet up on the table. The fact that he was drawing a few sideways glances was not unusual and by now he was used to it; perhaps it was the hushsuit or the wide smile he had never learned to control. Ronan grinned into his beer once more. This body had many advantages — which was just as well really, all things considered. It was one of the few left to him.

"Excuse me, I hope I'm not interrupting." The sweet sounds of Virginia drew his attention.

He'd enjoyed his time in that state two decades before, and so beamed his widest smile up at the woman standing next to his table.

"Certainly not." How unfortunate that in this age men no longer wore hats. He would rather have liked something to doff.

The perfect replica of all-American beauty almost dazzled him with row upon row of perfect white teeth. "I was just wondering if you could point me to the VFT Station? I left my map-pilot in the B and B."

19

The corners of his smile turned down. "Unfortunately, you've mistaken me for a local. I'm just a traveler here myself."

A hint of a forming pout on those far too perfect lips. "I'm sorry. I just thought…"

Ronan held up his hand, "None of that — I just wish I could help." He suddenly wondered exactly how his voice sounded to her — what ideas his accent formed in her pretty little head. He'd been told before that his habit of mimicking the accents around him was rather unnerving.

"Me, too." A small coy look. "I kind of wish I was staying now."

He dropped her a meaningful look. "A great pity."

Blushing, the young American scampered back to her group of friends huddled in a nearby snug. Despite himself, Ronan found himself staring after her. Well, that was a surprise; he could have sworn he had become bored with the fairer sex. It had to be last night's taste of the past. Old memories had not been the only thing that stirred.

"This is called laying low, then?"

Ronan turned and smiled easily at the dark and handsome face of his contact. The only name he had to go with it was a quick tag, which was all people in his business were comfortable with: Vortex. This man's golden lion eyes were not just reproachful — but also tinged with a little fear. He was darting little sideways glances out from under his dreadlocks as if he expected an assassin to leap out from behind the bar.

Ronan was not displeased, though. A little fear was always an advantage in their profession. Even while he had never met Vortex in the flesh before, he was immediately pleased with what he saw. In truth, part of him had been dreading some rural amateur.

He gestured his contact into the chair next to him. "This is what *I* call laying low."

"Well, why we couldn't have met somewhere less public? I mean… I know these people."

Something about the local seemed vaguely familiar, but after so long with humanity that wasn't unusual. Ronan tried to figure out what it was over another warm sip of beer. The trouble was that there were just too many damn memories to sift through. He hid his confusion beneath a slightly antagonistic frown.

"And I don't know you — yet." Ronan let the obvious sink in. Vortex had to understand who he was dealing with, and trust was something that was hard to come by in this business. It was earned or exchanged through a complex web of contacts. You got a name for yourself for getting things done and keeping your business quiet. Vortex's voice was bordering on the range where they might well be overheard.

The other's jaw worked a little as his eyes sized him up. Finally the tension oozed out of him like coffee from a broken cup. He shrugged. "It's no drama I suppose. The village thinks I'm a drug peddler as it is. That's probably what they think you are too — they wouldn't know anything about you being Panther."

Ronan's tag was getting alarmingly well known, but that was something he was willing to accept when the consequence was that some of the better jobs came his way. Vortex was a long-time Line pal and a friend of a friend, but something about him was triggering ancient instincts. This realm had very little in the way of friendships to offer — and even Ronan needed friends.

Leaning across the table, he offered Vortex his hand and his name. "Ronan Rymour." It wasn't his true-name, but it was the one he'd used for more than a hundred years and that was still worth something to this near-stranger.

"Bakari."

The atmosphere was easier after that. Having stepped over that first hurdle they were a bit quieter, more relaxed. Bakari didn't even ask what had gone wrong last night. But Ronan didn't need his long-gone powers to know that was exactly what was on his mind.

"This job is more than I thought. Not as rural. I'll have to scope things out, so I'll need some inside info." Rymour drained the last of his ale.

Bakari nodded. "Sure thing, but not here, eh?"

Nothing alarmed him about this man, nothing made his hairs rise, or his pulse quicken. With an ease born of someone used to going on instinct, Ronan rose. "Certainly."

"There's just one thing I gotta know." Bakari was suddenly very close, his golden wide eyes effectively pinning Ronan, "You've felt it too — right? When you saw it?"

An emotion not unlike grief welled in him, the memory both sweet and painful. He didn't need to ask what Bakari meant.

"Oh yes," he replied softly, "I felt it." The language didn't have the right words to convey how well and how deeply he had been affected by his encounter the night before.

The other gave him an odd appraising look as if he could see beyond the human face Ronan wore, "I knew you would, Panther — you have an old soul, like most of us here."

It should have shocked him, this human's sharp perception, but he was beginning to suspect the very same thing.

Ronan flashed him a bone-white smile. "Quick wits are what we will need, my friend." He drew him out of the Green Man where curious ears could not reach. "I've found an old soul doesn't get you nearly as far as it used to."

Bakari, despite all his best intentions, found he was relaxed as he walked back with Ronan to his cottage. It wasn't like the villagers would think it strange, he occasionally had visitors up from London, but all the same it felt just wrong to be chatting with this man in broad daylight. He'd lived enough to know such dealings went on in the dark and usually with more nervousness than he was experiencing now.

Every member of a crew he'd ever dealt with in his life made his hair stand up and his shoulders tense. He was a Liner, after all, used to the buzz and burn of the virtual world. His kind usually got on with Crew like Rottweilers and Siamese cats — but not this guy.

As they strolled off High Street away from the Green Man they talked about tourists and architecture and the worth of places such as Little Penherem. It was like he had turned some sort of switch that demanded Bakari have no fear of him. He'd heard that such things were possible in the Line, but not in the fleshworld.

The reached the tiny cottage Bakari's position earned him in the village and he couldn't help smiling when Ronan complimented him on the granny's bonnets and lamb's ear in the front garden. Bakari's London friends never noticed the flowers.

Inside was not as pleasant, for he had as yet to develop any interior decorating skills. But Ronan made himself right at home, flopping down on the woebegone couch and flicking one leg over its arm.

"I'm not going to take it out on you," he said affably. "You didn't scope the target well enough, but then again I didn't behave very... professionally either."

Bakari held back any sarcasm he might have felt. Truthfully, he'd been too excited about making contact with Panther and he'd taken it for granted Tania Furlion hadn't changed security since he'd checked it out a month earlier. He hid his embarrassment with a slight cough. "Well I would Line in and..."

"Be my guest. It would be good to know what I'm up against in there — but," he paused, perhaps sizing up how much further to trust Bakari, "I'll need to do a bit more reconnaissance of my own."

"What more could you want?" Bakari hid his surging panic as he fished out his Line from his pocket.

"There was something about that mask," Ronan's face had tightened. "Something unusual. I thought this would be a twenty-four hour job, but it isn't. I won't charge you extra if I can doss down here for a couple of nights."

That was exactly what Bakari didn't want, for there was too much about Penherem that might draw his suspicions. But what could he say — Ronan was the only one able to do this particular job.

"Sure thing," Bakari smiled, "if you don't mind the couch."

"I've slept in worse," Ronan replied.

This was going to be tricky. Bakari knew his new houseguest was unfamiliar with the Line, but he had probably picked up the basics.

"Gimme a few minutes then," he said. "I should be able to hack the Hall's security system easily enough — long as they haven't altered that too."

"Take all the time you need," Ronan tucked his legs up in the couch. "I like to nap during the day anyway." His eyes were already shut, but that didn't fool Bakari.

The Liner rose and walked back into the dimly lit recesses of the bedroom. It was Spartan like the rest of the house, but it contained all he needed; a bed, a lamp, a dog-eared poster of the

23

African savanna as his ancestors might have known it, and his own heavily encoded node. He didn't know if he could trust that anymore, hence wanting to use Ella's that morning. But he'd look like a right idiot in front of Ronan if he went off now.

Bakari sank onto the rumpled but spacious bed. Some preferred the perennial lotus position while they were Lining, thinking it made them look like religious gurus, but he had always preferred to return without strain in his muscles. So, lying flat out on his hedonistically comfortable bed, Bakari plunged into the Line.

As always there was that flickering moment when the body reluctantly surrendered control of feeling and gave over to the mind. It was a white and gold retina slash that reminded Bakari of looking foolishly into the sun. Rather than phasing into the Second Step he chose to plug straight into Third. Bakari opened his avatar eyes onto the digital world.

He now wore dark feathers and saw through bright raven eyes. Why exactly his avatar was a bird of death he had never worked out. When he had first walked the Line this was the form his brain conjured.

The foothills of the local Line rolled away beneath him. Simple looking turf concealed streams of information and consciousness that the initiated could mine. Right now, that was not what Bakari needed.

Having got his bearings, he dropped back to Second Step. Here, not being fully immersed in the avatar, he was able to access the more mechanical side of Lining. While keeping an eye on the lie of the land, he sketched a control cube. He had his little box of tricks preloaded into this avatar. He selected a seek-and-report bot, a tightly bundled reel of code which was more than enough to break through most government Line security — let alone that of Penherem Hall. He sent it darting on its way, confident it would bring back what he would need to give Ronan.

That task accomplished, he sketched another cube. This one was to complete his primary purpose for this visit, summoning his contact.

He re-routed signals through all the channels that he could think of, attempting to outwit any Liner that might be trying to trace him. Bakari was not surprised to find several waiting traps, but they were slap up jobs and his signal easily avoided them without even alerting their controller. None, though, were the dreaded Infinity Rose — a particularly bad Crew he'd ruffled the feathers of two years back. They were known for having long memories when it came to grudges.

A nano later, the signal was successfully routed and Bakari moved back to Third Step and peered once more out the raven's eye.

It only took four nanos for his contact to reach him.

It appeared over the horizon, a very fast moving object like a long silver dart; not an avatar, but a remote. He'd not expected any different; these people were very careful about revealing their code or their name. They were quite happy to have him out there taking all the risks while they lingered in the shadows.

The remote, about half the size of his raven avatar, hovered a few feet away with its cherry-red sensor blinking rhythmically atop it. "This communication is outside the designated time interval agreed on."

Bakari's beak snapped. "When something comes up, it's difficult to stick to a schedule."

Whoever was at the other end of the remote took a nano to digest that little acorn of information, perhaps deciding if he or she really wanted to know what was happening. "You have the mask?"

"Not yet, but I should soon."

"And Panther?" the remote bobbed up and down as if it was getting mad.

"He got close. He did feel the effect."

"Then perhaps you were right, Vortex."

"So you can cut me some more slack."

"You've already had as much 'slack' as we can give."

Bakari the raven twitched his wings, making feathers rattle. "If you want results, you've got to give me more time."

The remote bobbed, for a moment silent. "As long as you remain undetected, that is acceptable. Continue with the plan."

He had no choice in the matter — there was no pulling back now. Unfortunately, the devil he'd made his bargain with knew that all too well.

CHAPTER THREE

Moments

The man's voice was gone. Aroha woke the next morning and felt the emptiness.

She lay still in the warm cocoon of her bed and listened to Nana quietly moving around the kitchen. It could have been any day, but it wasn't. As the New Zealanders had slept, utu had invaded quietly and more cunningly than their previous enemy. It was already lying curled and waiting in their bodies. A frightening ally if ever there was one.

Fighting back an urge to cry, she slipped out of bed and got dressed quickly. Then, rubbing her eyes, she trotted down the worn carpet to the kitchen. Nana had her back turned while she washed something in the sink but she had anticipated her granddaughter's arrival; a jug of milk, a plate and spoon and the box of cereal were laid out, ready for her meal. Aroha slipped into her customary chair and began arranging breakfast in her usual ritual. The trick was in the timing. Pour the milk on and wait too long, and the cereal went soggy. Eat it too soon, and it was just too crackly in the mouth.

Nana was watching her, she suddenly realised. The sun was streaming in through the window behind her grandmother, outlining her in a halo of silver. Aroha grinned through a mouth of cereal. Nana's hair was the prettiest. Once it had been long and brown but it had turned into a wonderful concoction of gray and silver. It was almost pure white around her forehead and ears. Aroha loved to watch Nana brushing it out at night after releasing it from the bun she always wore during the day. She supposed it was Nana's one vanity — though she'd never admit it.

"You better enjoy that cereal today, Aroha. I have only so many packets put away." Nana sighed. "There might not be anymore after that. Who knows if the factory survived…"

Aroha contemplated her half-finished bowl.

"Still, we're lucky," Nana had turned around and was once more scrubbing vigorously at some unfortunate dish in the sink. "Those poor people in the city… Lord knows what they're going through. At least we have our own garden."

Communication lines had been the first thing the enemy had cut, and no one knew if they would ever have the raw materials to repair them again. Aroha could catch a few of Nana's surface thoughts, but as always her inner self remained hidden. Her granddaughter caught images of people screaming, running riot through once bustling streets. Aroha had been to Wellington a couple of times and she could overlay her memories of steel and water with Nana's imaginings. For once Aroha wished she could tap deeper into her grandmother's head. She wanted to find out if she was scared or hopeful — only then would she know what she should be feeling.

Aroha finished her cereal, chewing slowly, enjoying the taste of something that might not last long.

She'd been half thinking of asking if she and Sally could go into the bush. She chased the remains of her cereal around the bowl trying to find the right words.

But if Aroha was unable to read her Nana's mind, perhaps the opposite wasn't true, for Nana turned and fixed her granddaughter with a piercing gaze. "And don't think of running anywhere outside the village. Plenty of soldiers could still be around."

Aroha made a face, but knew better than to argue. Instead she trotted after as Nana took the bucket out from under the sink. She followed through the kitchen and the sun-porch to the water pump. Nana was such a little woman, small to the point of frailty, but there was strength in her arms. The water gushed out all icy and fresh with a hiss. It contained utu, but the taste had not been affected.

Nana's thoughts were now of those who had not taken the shots, those who objected to such things. They might have accepted utu, but they also accepted the consequences. Right now they would be dying; screaming in agony, or perhaps praying mute and silent to a God that no longer cared. The blood would hopefully choke them

27

long before their internal organs failed. Some people had left to take their chances in the wide Pacific. Yet they would be in just as much pain, leaving all they loved behind. *It's not mine, but I love this land.* This was what Nana was thinking.

"Me too," Aroha said softly, though she knew her grandmother heard.

Nana pulled the bucket up the stairs and onto the porch, ignoring Aroha's offers of help. Following on her heels was a little shadow. Barely had the fly screen door banged shut behind Nana than Sally was pushing it open again and sticking her head around it.

Nana sighed but gestured her in, realizing that the child would only loiter in her garden until she did.

Sally's scarlet red hair was its usual mess, with tough little biddy bid seeds and broken fern in it. The girl's mother had another six children to look after and Sally, being the most elusive of her brood, was never very well groomed. Nana shook her head and retreated into the house to get a brush and a flannel. That face needed a wipe, too.

Sally flopped down in the kitchen chair next to Aroha and gave her an elbow in the ribs. "Not going to sit here all day, are you?" She didn't hear the forest in the same way Aroha did, but it still called with all of its whispering coolness.

Aroha twisted her feet uncomfortably. She wanted to go, but Nana had forbidden her the bush today.

Sally's grubby little hand stole over hers. "Not there, silly. Let's go into the village — there's some more strangers come in. Everyone is there."

Everyone, that was, except Nana and Aroha. Unlike the rest of their small community, Nana had never seemed interested in much beyond the hills. Maybe she didn't want to hear how bad things were in the rest of the country, maybe she didn't dare care.

"Oh come on," Sally was quick to become impatient, as usual. "We'll miss them otherwise." It remained unspoken that they had better run before Nana returned; she'd be bound to find something less interesting for two unoccupied pairs of hands to do.

The lure of the unusual finally broke Aroha's resolve. Pushing back quickly from the table, they bolted through the sun-porch, rattling the fly screen and sending the bantams scratching outside off in a squawking mass. Nana wouldn't chase after them, it was too undignified to be seen yelling at children in the street, but there would be a pile of chores waiting for Aroha when she returned. It was a small price to pay.

The street turned its back on the hills, becoming dusty and tiny as it ran down towards the small collection of shops. They were all rattling windows and peeling paint, but these were the heart of Makara. All the villagers gathered to hear the gossip and tales of woe from outside the valley here. The wind whistled down from the hilltops where the shattered remains of wind turbines resembled a broken row of teeth. Once the bane of the small town, it was universally agreed that their destruction was the only silver lining in the cloud of war.

But the girls weren't interested in woe even though it was all around them. They bounded down the road giggling. It was merely the chance to see someone that they had never seen before — a real treat in a place as small as Makara.

Jan, the store owner, was out on her verandah talking to a couple of laden men while a semicircle of villagers gawked from a respectful distance. Aroha and Sally wriggled their way to the front to catch what the grownups were saying so seriously.

"From the big smoke, then?" Jan was saying with more than a touch of distain.

The men, both tall and dark haired, laughed a little, "More smoke than there used to be in Wellington these days..."

Aroha was examining them all the while, noting their packs, but most of all the ugly black guns strapped to their backs. She was old enough to remember a time when guns had been a rarity in New Zealand. Nana still recalled that time with sadness.

Sally darted forward and ran a finger over the long muzzle at one of their backs. The child had no fear.

"Whoa," the tallest man spun around as if he'd felt that, as if the metal was part of his body. "Best leave that alone little one."

"Are you soldiers?" Sally's question was as direct as ever.

The two men scanned the little crowd, but they had seen the dug up road and perhaps sensed the air of determination. They shared the same blood, the same utu.

"Grey Wolves," they confirmed. "We got a report that there might be a cluster of enemy bots laid in this area."

The villagers murmured; there had been a lot dropped, but mostly near the big cities.

"In such circumstances, the enemy might have given them orders to give back a little vengeance of their own."

The crowd shifted a little, unsure how to take the stranger's comment.

"We're here to take care of you," the second soldier gestured in what might have been meant to be a calming way. But these were the only men that could be spared, Jan was thinking bitterly. Not much against an enemy bot that might have God knows what orders.

Jan quietly offered to equip them, so the three went into the store to conduct business. The rest of the villagers began to congeal into untidy and unhappy groups.

Aroha and Sally, with a total lack of anything else to do, followed after the soldiers. The inside of the shop was milled forest timber and even the presence of a lone light bulb and the daylight outside could not change its perpetual dimness. Jan's rangy form maneuvered about the shop with the dexterity of the night loving kiwi, though one soldier nearly knocked over a bag of flour.

They had government vouchers, which might or might not have been worth anything, but Jan was of that peculiar independent breed. A tough woman, she'd lived fifty of her years in the rugged West Coast, fiercely independent but with a wide heart. There would be no haggling, she told the men firmly. They could put their vouchers away and have whatever they needed.

While the adults measured and discussed, Sally and Aroha wandered through the store trailing bored hands over the wealth of goods. The shop carried all the things that the village couldn't provide for itself; iron goods, paint, and seeds of all kinds. It was an Aladdin's cave, Nana used to say, a New Zealand Aladdin's cave. Aroha tried not to contemplate it becoming empty and bare.

The two girls, via a rather circuitous route, eventually reached the front counter. This had been their destination all the while, for it was there that Jan kept a treasured store of boiled sweets she made in her own kitchen. Aroha stood just behind the soldier's elbow, staring longingly at the clear glass jar and the rainbow of sweetness contained within. Jan pretended not to notice. Showing a soft spot to more than two people in one day was not in her nature.

They were asking her about guides up into the hills. Jan shook her head. Most of the young men and women had signed up for the army in those few desperate days before the final decision. Not many remained who both knew the paths and could physically manage them.

Sensing her hesitation, the men exchanged glances. "We only want to go up as far as the falls."

Aroha frowned. Of all the places to go to in the bush, this was the worst. The Forest People had often found her there. It was a special place — no, more than that, a sacred place.

The adults seldom went there, undoubtedly catching the unwelcoming air.

Jan was very worried, no need to dip into her mind to sense that. "These girls know the way."

It was as if the world suddenly shrunk and spun. One of the soldiers turned to find Aroha practically ready to run.

He was not a handsome man like Seth, the village gardener, nor did he have that aura of kindness like Sally's older brother Adam, but she found herself blushing.

He ruffled her hair. She didn't like it, an entirely too familiar thing for a stranger to do. Aroha stumbled back, practically running into Sally.

"We only need to get to the falls," his companion said in a tone meant to be slow and soothing. "The bot signal came from near there. Surely you girls want to help…"

She could think of nothing worse than guiding these men to that sacred place, but what could she say?

As always, Sally rescued her. The boiled sweets on the counter made an excellent excuse. Quick as a flash, she'd grabbed a handful. On the wings of Jan's angry yelp, she pulled Aroha out of the shop. They were fugitives now, and fugitives did not have to answer uncomfortable questions, or take anyone anywhere.

They ran until they couldn't run anymore, until their chests heaved and their throats burned, near the very limits of the village. Finally, the two girls flopped down amongst the dandelions and long grasses that lined the road into town. With limbs outstretched and her face in the sun, Aroha tried to forget the bright light of the stranger's gaze.

Sally silently snapped her stolen treasure in half and handed a portion to her friend. Aroha's heart swelled with love for the other girl. They both knew there would be a scene for Sally to endure when she finally went home. Her mother was not someone who took such things lightly. But to say thanks or to even mention it would only bring a scowl. Instead they lay back and savored the sweetness while they could.

A dozen magically shaped clouds raced across the bright blue sky, and the world seemed so quiet that there could have been only the two of them in it. The call of the Forest People had not reached her today and, although Aroha did not mind it when it did come, for now it was good to feel the earth pressed into the small of her back sticky with sweat, to hear nothing but her own heartbeat in her ears.

But the Grey Wolves were an elite squad used to tracking and finding elusive enemies in deep forest, so finding two little girls in open territory was easy.

Aroha felt them arrive while the other's less sensitive senses missed them completely. She looked up through the sun and into the soldier's eyes.

He shook his head and grinned. "That shopkeeper's going to tan your hide."

Sally leapt up. "Nah, she'll just make us count buttons or something." Punishment meant little to her.

The soldier crouched down and rested on his haunches, "This is a pretty spot." He offered one hand to Aroha, "I'm Daniel Proust by the way." He gestured back to where his companion was leaning against a tree, "That's my mate Simon Hearfield."

Aroha shook the hand tentatively, as she'd been taught.

Sally still eyed him suspiciously and kept her own hands firmly tucked behind her back.

"Now, we really need to get to the falls," Daniel said seriously. "I know you might not want to take us there, but these enemy bots. They can do a lot of damage. Your friends are in danger."

"I know," Aroha whispered.

"Hey," he ruffled her hair again, and she had a flash of understanding, he'd done that with his own younger sister. "We're here to protect you."

"It's a special place," she replied, trying to make him understand.

"And you're scared..."

Well, she couldn't tell him the real truth; that it wasn't the bot that scared her, and how the Forest People would feel about adults going there. No one would understand that... and then there was the very real danger to her village.

Aroha stood up and dusted herself off. "I'll show you," she said a lot more fiercely than she felt.

And the way Daniel smiled at her made her feel grown up. Nana and her anger would just have to wait.

Ella found herself running late as usual. No matter how early she went to bed or how many times she set her alarm clock, for some reason when it came round to her shift up at the Hall everything went haywire. She'd propped her bike right next to the door all ready to go in the evening, but when she'd gone out there in the morning it had somehow developed a puncture. And the repair kit had made itself scarce, too.

At least there had been no one about to see her dissolve into a temper tantrum at the front door. Snatching up her mop cap and apron, Ella ran as best she could down the street and into the longest lane in Penherem. The view was chocolate box charming; Farmer Jones driving his red tractor, beautiful hedgerows, and the green distant hills, but Ella saw none of that. As she darted up the first turning she entered the tree lined drive of Penherem Hall. This was what drew the tourists, far more than the prettiness of the village.

The Hall had a bloodthirsty and romantic history. There had once been a castle, but it now formed the ruins that sat in a sea of well turned out gardens. While the Hall itself was a piece of far later baronial splendor, the beauty of the ruins couldn't be argued with.

As Ella ran on, she came over the slight rise and the Hall leapt out in front of her. The garden's designer had planned it that way and it worked, hitting you right between the eyes with its white columns and rising staircase. The windows gleamed and the shell drive was immaculately combed. That was what the tourists liked: the surface veneer of gentility with the rotting canker of scandal.

Ella ran through the garden to the side entrance and struggled up the stairs to the Long Gallery. When the tour did arrive, they would be much like the others; barrel through the doors, take a few snaps, download the latest promotional vid for the folks back home to prove they'd been here, and then pile onto the QuickStep to the next attraction.

Ella paused before entering. Hoping not to be noticed, she eased the concealed doorway open and peered through. Today was definitely not her lucky day. Tania Furlion was there, though she hadn't noticed her yet.

The current owner of the Hall was staring at the Holbien on the wall while chewing determinedly on her fingernails. Ella paused, amazed by this display of nerves from one who had always seemed to have none. Unobserved, she was different.

Ella had noted the ruined fingers before, but had never seen their owner actually chewing them. They were the one mark on the flawless Baroness Furlion.

With her white blonde flyaway hair confined to a severe bun, two inch black patent shoes and a conservative dark Aroldo suit sticking to her trim body, she appeared ready for today's rush of flustered tourists. At least that was the way she appeared. Something about Tania had always disturbed Ella. Sometimes she seemed to stare at nothing at all, or her eyes would dart about the room. She was not liked by the villagers, either. Tania's family had a certain reputation; bad blood, they whispered.

Ella plopped on her mop cap and began stuffing her own mess of dark curls under it while waiting for Tania to turn and acknowledge her presence. She remained still, though, eyes fixed on the painting with such attention that it made Ella's back twitch.

The Hall had more than enough of its own ghost stories: Furlion maidens locked and starved in their rooms for loving the wrong person, headless ancestors killed in feuds, or the moon-eyed dark dog that ran through the long hall when a Furlion was about to die. Could that be what was riveting Tania to the spot? Ella doubted it. Apart from her odd ways, the Baroness had never seemed to carry any stock by those stories. Money was of far more importance to her.

Whenever a tourist asked excitedly about the ghosts of Penherem Manor, she simply spun the tale out, while suggesting they might want to book into one of the more exclusive rooms to find out for themselves.

Finally, the Baroness Furlion wheeled about on her shining black heel and noticed that she was not alone.

The look she gave Ella was at first bemused, but then dropped to ill concealed anger. Tania's eagle eye took in the misaligned cap, the maid's outfit undone at the throat, and the apron ties flapping around the other woman's ankles.

Ella moved forward and self-consciously tucked her escaping hair behind her ear. "Sorry I'm late, but..."

Tania always had the effect of making Ella feel like a half made bed. Today was no different. "What was it this time?"

"I forgot to set the alarm because I was up all night working on a rewrite of my book. I got behind a little because Bakari came over...."

If Ella thought that mentioning the village librarian would cut her some slack with the Baroness, she was wrong. Tania's eyes narrowed.

The whole village knew about them, but it had been nearly a year since the icy ruler of the 'Big House' had gone slumming with the local bad boy, and people had found other things to gossip over. Still, Tania didn't help things by being so touchy about the subject — well, in Ella's opinion at least.

"No need to say any more, Ella. Knowing him, I'm just glad you turned up at all."

"Come on, I wouldn't let you down. That travel writer is on the first tour today."

Tania sighed and cast another critical eye over Ella, perhaps hoping that the writer didn't get down to the kitchen where the 'genuine Victorian maid' would be busy helping to prepare dinner. The turn of the nineteenth century hadn't been the best time for the manor, but market research had shown that it was the current tourist trend.

"Well, you'd better get to your place then." Her voice betrayed frustration.

35

Ella wasn't going to let Tania affect her that much. She knew the Baroness would have preferred droid similcas, but such things were expensive, so Tania had to rely on the local talent. Assured of that much, Ella left Tania in the Long Gallery and went down to her post.

Some might have baulked at being buried in the kitchen all day, but she loved it. She and three others ran it, and when the tourists weren't around there was the usual amount of giggling and terrible jokes flying. And the work, though difficult, was fun.

They'd make soups with the tammis. Janey, the broad shouldered daughter of a local farmer, would hold the cloth while Ella would push the thick broth through with a wooden spoon. It made your arms ache, but Maureen the cook wasn't nearly as strict as her real Victorian counterpart would have been, and they got through it with jokes and gossip.

They'd smarten up when the tourists came through. A tiny alarm would ring as the masses came down the steps towards the kitchen and immediately they'd assume their proper personas.

Visitors emerged into a kitchen full of warm smells and happy servants; perhaps not authentic but charming. Ella and Janey would offer them some baked treats from the morning and show them the delights of the kitchen, the coal range, and the gadgets. Maureen would preside over it all, contributing only her authentic presence and perhaps a gruff explanation of the recipes of the time. Maureen was a part-timer like Ella but less inclined to enjoy the contact with people.

The day passed swiftly. At the end of it, all three were tired from the combination of manual labor and forced smiles. Ella, knowing the others had families to get to, shooed them out the door and set about the cleaning. Procrastination was a fine art to a writer and she had no one waiting for her. The meditative action of cleaning was just mindless enough for her to enjoy.

As she tidied away the graters, the mincers, and other antiquated symbols of Victorian labor, Ella wondered just what she could do about Tania. She'd thought lately that she might have been tossed an offer of friendship from the strange Baroness. Perhaps she felt a connection because they were outcasts in the village; Ella because she was new and Tania just because of who she was. Though Ella missed her close friends in London, she couldn't decide if she liked the Baroness or not. Sometimes she could be sunny and fun, yet at other times she could look right through a person with a stare that could freeze you cold.

Ella might have been a stranger, but it hadn't taken her long to get the story about the Baroness.

Losing her parents as a teenager had not made anything easy for Tania Falchion. Still, plenty of people had been forced to deal with tragedy. It was weak blood, the villagers reckoned, that had let her snap. Ella had not yet moved to Penherem when the Adjusters had delivered what was left of Tania Furlion back to her ancestral home. Apparently it had not been a pleasant sight. It had taken years for Tania to reassemble her façade of normality. They were all worried that it was crumbling again. Any more 'adjustment' and there would not be anything left of the family that had lived in the Hall for six hundred years.

Tania was the last Furlion and if some whispered that it'd be a good thing to be rid of them, there were those more pragmatic ones that spoke louder about the need to have a link with the past if the village was to survive.

Being an outsider sometimes had its benefits. Ella heard all the gossip, both sides of it, but it also meant she felt obligated to do something about it. The question remained though, how could she help Tania hold onto her carefully scraped together sanity?

As she untied her starched white apron the spinebridge flickered, sending spasms of pain up her back. Experience had taught her not to give voice to the pain when others were around but the day was over so Ella allowed herself a private groan, more of annoyance than anything else. Her odd sliding walk was more pronounced when the pain came, she knew that very well. All the staff were heading to the Green Man for a drink, but she had managed to wriggle out of it. One thing she didn't need now was another distraction from writing. That deadline was only looming larger.

It was only when Ella turned around to take her coat off the hook by the door that she realised she was not alone. Dressed in light-sucking black, with his dark and faintly curled hair sticking damply to the window as he leaned against the far sill. For a moment, Ella was so shocked she didn't speak.

The stranger's hand rested lightly on the soft wood, moving a little, feeling the smoothness that only real time could give.

"They used to rub sand into it everyday." Ella commented, somehow still embedded in her tourist mode.

When he raised his eyes, they seemed to flash purple for an instant in the fading light. Ella blinked twice in confusion. How odd. It must have been a trick of the light — they were earth brown.

His voice was soft and low in the deep silence. "I take it you don't, anymore?"

Contemplating the disaster that would make of her hands, Ella grinned, "Not likely — the night bots do it with some spanking new compound."

Somehow her answer had not pleased him. With a repressed sigh he levered himself from the bench. "That's the problem with the world today — not enough people really care." He sounded older than he looked. Ella swallowed the giggle that rose to her throat. He could be one of the Treated and be in fact three times his apparent physical age. Usually, however, they went to great lengths to pretend adolescence.

The stranger made for the door and as he moved she caught a whiff of a warm musky scent that made her think of cozy fires and contentment. He said nothing about who he was or what he was doing wandering the Hall. Just as he opened the door he paused and raised an admonishing finger. "Now, young lady, aren't you supposed to be heading home?" His lips pursed together in something that might have been the beginning of a kiss, then he slipped beyond the door and was gone.

Ella breathed again, feeling her heart yammer suddenly in her chest. She couldn't quite resist running to the door. Yanking it open with its customary squeal of protest, she found the long stone hallway completely empty. How strange. She hadn't heard him arrive. She hadn't heard him leave, and the door hadn't even made a noise.

For a second Ella's brain folded itself into knots trying to think of an explanation. Was this perhaps a touch of the Furlion madness that some said haunted the Hall?

"Don't be an idiot." Being a writer sometimes meant setting aside reality, that was true, but she wasn't about to follow Tania down the path to madness. Some men made a living out of being mysterious, and the types that liked to tramp around old castles and houses were probably stranger than most. With a snort, she shut the complaining door. How could she forget that husband and wife couple last year who had insisted she personally show them the dungeon, "and perhaps the rack too?"...

But as she turned back to get her coat, Ella couldn't help thinking about those eyes and that scent he bought with him. It had been a long time since a man had interested her, and longer still since she'd been so quickly attracted.

Then she remembered that time and recalled with a shudder the consequences — consequences she still had to live with. No, on the whole it was probably better not to follow after him. For once she was going to be sensible, no matter what.

CHAPTER FOUR
Patterns

Ronan was smiling as he walked through the Hall. Something had lightened his mood in that kitchen. The tousled-haired creature with eyes of softest brown had felt a touch of his magic, he could be sure of that. What a delightful smile she had, and within he sensed something deeper. Perhaps she was a distant kin, for once his people had loved this world and had left many sleeping magics still in it.

He'd detected the slight pause in her step, almost infinitesimal. Though he might have once seen such imperfection as odd, now he loved it. It was humanity's blemishes that made them special. He'd learned that over many generations.

Ah, it was a real pity he had work to do. It would have been sweeter to make that pain pass from her, and perhaps to dance in the clouds. Ronan shook himself like a cat who'd taken an unexpected bath. Idiot. He didn't have the power to raise himself, let alone another to the clouds. It had been a very long time since he'd been that strong and he'd been quite a different person then.

Somewhere in all these hallways and rooms was the mistress of the Hall, and in her mind lay the secret of the Mask. Bakari might be content to rely on the information the Line brought him, but Ronan was not. He was curious about how the Mask had ended up here and who its keeper was.

The Hall was mercifully drained of tourists, for much as he loved the rattle and chatter of people, his senses were not what they once had been. He needed silence to hear magic.

He sensed her long before he saw her. Tania Furlion was in the Long Gallery. Ronan padded as silently as his cat form around the corner to examine the Lady of the Manor. She was standing looking out the window, beyond which could be seen the intricate knot garden. Her thoughts were laid bare, like golden carp just beneath a pond's surface. Ronan let his mind dip into the shallows.

In her mind the manor was alive with voices whispering from the dim corners and the scent of lavender wafting up from the floor. But these were no happy memories of the past; these were spirits to send anyone howling into insanity. They whispered of lost loves, departed chances, and the pain of undeath. They called from the corners and hissed from the rafters and Tania was surrounded by them.

Ronan shivered. To dwell in such constant fear was a terrible thing to contemplate. He could only respect someone who had this pain to bear and yet let not an ounce of it show from outside. She was the second intriguing creature he had met today.

"I'm not in danger of being locked in, am I?" he asked just behind her shoulder.

He could sense the pause, that moment when she judged if his voice was living or dead. Then she spun about, surprised at the results.

The woman really was an ice princess, just as Bakari had described; white blonde hair pulled back severely from a sharply exquisite face and blue eyes that impaled all they looked on. In her mind Ronan sensed the murmuring cease.

He dipped his head a little, imitating a shadow of a bow, but his fixed look never left her.

Tania sized him up, wondering at the sudden silence. "No danger of that," she replied smoothly and with a coolly professional smile. "We always make sure the Hall is clear before setting any alarms."

"Good to know." Ronan inched closer to look out at the garden. Something there had captured her interest. "I haven't quite finished taking in its..." He paused to add a little dramatic effect, "delights."

Most women would have blushed, but the Baroness' eyes merely narrowed. "We have more than our fair share, in Penherem."

"I'd say so."

Ronan could sense those floating thoughts; she'd already summed him up. Another slick man with bucket loads of charm and probably even more money. She guessed wrongly but intelligently that he had taken the Infinity virus. And Ronan did admit that he sometimes had the slick smooth features of one of those wealthy fools.

His eyes flickered to the ruined fingertips she was trying her best to hide. Her nervousness radiated from every pore, though he could be sure she was not the type to usually allow it out. Something about him was upsetting her balance and that in itself was intriguing. Most humans instinctively liked him immediately.

She smiled more forcefully. "You still have time to see the Great Hall, I could show you the way…"

"I've already seen it." He stretched, and then smiled slowly. "I hear you had some trouble there last night."

Her composure was obviously somewhat regained; she didn't even flinch. "It was just a false alarm — these old houses still have the occasional rat, you know. They are prone to setting things off."

"Oh really," he cocked his head, listening, "I don't hear any. I would have thought they had all been cleared out by humanity's relentless urge to tidy everything up."

A rapid flush of red was stealing up her cheeks, colouring the ice princess an unbecoming shade; perhaps she was in danger of melting. Her forehead twitched and her fingers locked behind her, but she said nothing.

He'd gone too far, pushing this one beyond her comfort zones. Unlike the delightful creature in the kitchen, she was not taking it well.

He tried to smooth it over. "I'm Ronan Rymour by the way. You'll probably be seeing a lot more of me about. Penherem is rather intriguing. There's a certain… something about the place."

Outside there was the hiss of the QuickStep tour departing. Having poured down the steps, they clattered and gabbed all the way to their transport. Ronan found it delightful, but to Tania's ears they grated.

42

"Well," Tania brushed invisible dust from her jacket sleeves, "As long as you stay in one of the inns, by all means enjoy the atmosphere. By the way, can I see your pass for the Manor while we're here?"

But when she looked up, Ronan made sure he was gone. Humans relied on moments to cement things into their minds, and he'd discovered an age ago that leaving them without warning was the most effective way of perking their interest.

He slipped away far more swiftly and silently than any human could manage, disappearing down the corridor. The last whisper he got from her mind was of those voices of the dead.

This town was full of surprises. Ronan had come expecting blandness and an easy job, but so far it had been neither. He'd confess to having become rather jaded with this world that had once held so many delights to him, and yet here was salvation being handed to him on a plate; a mis-stepped creature with the eyes of the Earth Mother herself and a white princess who could hear the voices of the past. This place deserved further investigation.

Ronan wended his way down the back steps, only occasionally stopping to disengage alarms on doors. Outside of the gallery, the security was rather pathetic.

He went out from the Hall into the beautifully manicured gardens. He should have really not enjoyed gardening, it was after all a confinement of the natural world, but the part of him that loved humanity loved what they did with the Mother's gifts. So he was excited by the expanse of green that leapt up to meet him.

Strictly clipped green hedges and dancing water features delighted the eye and ear. Ronan dodged the mop-haired gardener by ducking behind topiary and mixed border.

Letting his feet find their own way was the best method to find the magic in any place, he'd learnt. So he was content to merely wander for a while, basking in the lipid early spring sun. This wandering led him to that which Tania had been looking at from the Long Gallery.

Shielded behind towering yew hedges, the knot garden was like a step back in time. Ronan paused at its outer edges, admiring the optical illusion of movement in the hedge. Something curiously heavy lifted from him, and as he lowered herself into the cool marble chair overlooking the swirls and turns of the knots, Ronan could feel something unclench in his chest.

He let his eye wander along the rises and falls of the plant forms. He could taste its ancient nature. It was speaking to him as all nature spoke to his kind. The garden had always been here in some shape or form; the rise and fall of the plants echoed the deeper rise and fall of power within the earth.

The box hedges circled and ran before his eyes, dancing up and down, embracing in mind tricking ways before separating like water. As his mind traced those paths, the plants blurred until only the pattern remained and it was this that stilled everything.

Ronan could know understand why Tania had been gazing at it so long. Anyone who truly looked at this would lose themselves, and in her case lose the voices that plagued her. This small magic pool of sanity was the only part of life that mattered. It kept the mad reality away from her.

It seemed so sad that this was all she had. And even though he loved the human realm, its bitter-sweetness always broke him. Every one of their stories was a tragedy sooner or later. And in the face of that sorrow he did what he always did — he ran. As if responding to his mood soft rain began to fall, misting his dark hair with moisture.

Ronan loped across the manicured lawn in ground consuming strides, leaving that hurt behind with the odd movement of the knot. He'd wanted to tap into the power of this strange little village and the Hall was the centre of it. Now that his senses were fully attuned, Penherem reeked with that which he had lost.

For the first time in decades he felt the stirrings of something he remembered as hope. For too long had he been bogged down in this world of hard-eyed cynics and dusty scientists. He needed to feel the soft touch of his home once again. He needed it like breath. Yes indeed, it felt as though he had not breathed properly for a terribly long time.

Penherem was a whisper of that which he loved. How he could have never found it before in all the time of his roaming perplexed him. Ronan had walked, he thought, all the roads of the earth, spent at least a night in every hamlet and city, curled asleep against every mountain and ancient tree. This was especially true here in England. So how, then, could he have missed it? Thinking of the strange mask once more, he pondered whose face it had last concealed. Was it too much to hope it had been the face it resembled?

His little magics worked his bidding and now his four legs ran much faster than two. The world came alive with so many more sounds and scents that it was like moving through a heady soup. Yet he still needed somewhere to rest and get out of the rain.

The great cat flopped down under a tree heavy with mist and looked out with its yellow eyes across the moor. A quick lick to smooth fur ruffled by wet and wind, and he felt his inner calm return. It felt so much better, in fact, that he was not to be satisfied until he had completely groomed. For a while he was a flurry of activity.

His head, though, would not be silent, and memory plagued him. *My home, my Fey.* But cats don't cry, and his call remained unspoken.

Ronan waited, certain that something was afoot in the drawing night, but nothing stirred. The hill sloped away under him thick with dew-hung grass and droop headed flowers. In the hedgerows blackbirds and field mice alike hid from the rain. Every living thing was still.

It was not what he wanted. Ronan had half expected a change, perhaps a flickering of something more, but no... that was impossible! What he wanted was too far away, surely. And yet, and yet, a rogue part of him whispered, it was not to be ruled out.

The panther's perfect black sides heaved with a heavy very human sounding sigh and he licked dissolutely at his flank, thinking all the while.

Ronan felt himself stripped bare, so bare he had lost himself. That laughing, foolish creature he had once been was a stranger to him. He was a bright many-faceted jewel worn to something far more base by time and care. He felt dark and dank, and perhaps old as well. Would his dark eyed cousin recognize him now? He doubted it — even his true name was gone. After all this time, Ronan finally knew what it was to be human. And he didn't like it.

The mist was rolling in, taking with it the green hills and wrapping the world in its gray shroud. He was wrong, amusing as it had been to imagine there was no more magic in the world. Last night had merely been his wishful thinking. This place only remembered magic — it didn't have any of its own. The dark patterned hide rippled with an enormous feline sigh as Ronan's world shrank. *I am alone.*

They said never to go up into the hills, and yet people did. For Aroha and her Nana living on the very downward curve of the beech covered mountains, it was easy enough to turn their backs to the mystery, but for those soldiers there was no choice. And Aroha had yet to get up the courage to tell Nana what she had promised them.

It wouldn't be easy. A rescue party was going into the forest: not to the sacred place that was the soldiers' destination, but further east towards the sea. A group of survivalists, just recently converted to that belief by the war, had become lost there. Long Jack, who'd once been a policeman, had seen the bright red flare in the previous night's sky, and he'd organized a party of four villagers to retrieve them. Right now there was no one else. It said as much, that the only help the government could send was the two young soldiers.

Just down from Aroha's home, the men were discussing the best route in, warmly clad in bush shirts and with their packs strapped to their backs. The packs were filled mostly with first aid equipment, as they didn't expect to be long gone.

As Nana stood wrapped in her gray shawl and watched the rescue party tramp off, she shook her head.

"I hope they took their shovels," she muttered to herself. "Terribly late in the year to bring bodies back."

Aroha was curled up on the dilapidated swing that Nana had made last year out of raupo and punga log. She was trying hard not to think of cold bodies lying up amongst the trees. Their eyes would be open; cloud dew would be falling and gathering on cold cheeks. Only the birds would know where they were.

"Stop that now, Aroha," Nana's firm hand gripped her shoulder. "No use pining over lost souls." Her voice was firm as she squeezed in next to her granddaughter on the seat. It creaked alarmingly, but held.

She pulled the young girl close, enveloping her in the comforting scent of lavender, and patted her curls reassuringly. "Don't blame yourself either — we warned them."

Aroha swallowed hard on her secret. The bush did indeed hold many dangers besides the Forest People, but now how could she possibly tell Nana about her promise to the soldiers? With those people dead, there was no way she'd let her granddaughter go.

"Think about life instead, little one," Nana murmured into her granddaughter's hair. Aroha already knew what would come next. "Did I tell you about the time that seagull dropped a gift on my head?"

She had a thousand times before, but Aroha giggled, "No."

"Well then," Nana began. As she told the long and elaborate tale that involved a fine wool dress, a fancy hairstyle, and an angry bird, Aroha sighed in contentment. As always, Nana's voice drove away the dark thoughts.

"And then when I ran home to my mother, do you know what happened?" Nana tickled Aroha under the ribs.

"She said you couldn't wash it off."

"Why?"

"Because it was good luck!" The very idea of her Nana's thick dark hair being full of bird droppings was ridiculous.

Nana slapped her own knee, "But you know what? I think she might have been right. After all — here you are."

"I didn't come from bird poop!" Aroha yelled.

"No, I imagine not," Nana's eyes skittered away across the porch towards the bush, "From somewhere much better."

A little lump suddenly boarded up Aroha's throat. She'd asked about her mother and father many times, but all she ever got was that they had died not long after her birth. She couldn't even say if her curly mahogany hair was her mother's or her father's. Still, she knew better than to ask Nana again — it would only make her sad.

Her grandmother pulled herself out of the swing and went down the steps to the peeling pump. It groaned and wheezed as she worked the handle, but the water that came out would be icy cold and refreshing.

It was really difficult sometimes, knowing what to say to Nana. So many puzzles in the world, and not allowed to mention any of them! But then, Aroha had her own store of secrets.

Looking slyly out of the corner of her eye, she tried to judge if she'd be able to slip away from Nana and get into the undergrowth on the far side of the dirt track. She seemed to always know if

47

any mischief was about to enter Aroha's head. However there were the odd times when she got that funny look in her eye and went about sighing and looking at the far off hills all the time. Those were the rare moments when Nana was distracted. The question remained; was this one of those times?

Aroha couldn't help thinking of those earnest young soldiers. Nana had always said that when you gave a promise you had to stick to it.

So, really, if she had to be the tiniest bit sneaky, it was still better than breaking a promise. Aroha thought about that for a minute, weighing up Nana's outrage against the needs of her village. Even knowing how much trouble she was going to be in didn't change her mind.

When Nana sat down with a tired sigh, Aroha leapt up to furnish her with a cup of tea. The late afternoon sun helped, keeping them warm and dozy on the front porch.

You had to be careful with Nana. Any tricks had to very little ones. She'd sense it otherwise, and then there would be nothing but an afternoon of peeling potatoes to look forward to. Aroha was very quiet. Ever so gently she pushed a little — the smallest fraction of a suggestion at her guardian. Nana's head bobbed and her eyes slid shut.

Gathering her feet silently under her, Aroha crept out of the sunroom, carefully eased the fly screen door shut behind her, and left Nana snoring softly.

It wasn't as if being sneaky was part of her nature, but she perhaps enjoyed the thrill of it more than she should have. Aroha opened up the cavernous crawl space under the house, piled high and smelling faintly of rust. Nana couldn't bear to throw anything away even if there was no hope of it ever getting repaired. So there were crumbling lawn mowers and rolling piles of almost unidentifiable farm implements under here. Nana simply shoved things under the house and then refused to go near them — it made the perfect hiding place.

Aroha had already assembled her own backpack and hidden her strong walking boots under here. Jerking these on, she carefully closed the storage area and ran off through the long grass.

Few paths led into the bush, but Aroha knew them all. Once out of sight of home, there was nothing between her and the Forest People.

Sally was waiting for her just at the edge of the bush where the scrubby manuka turned into darker green of tree ferns. Her friend was also carrying a thin pack, though a much more torn and abused one. Of the soldiers, though, there was no sign.

"You got away OK, then?" Sally screwed her eyes up against the sun while emitting a jaw-breaking yawn.

"Yep — Nans always has a nap before lunch," Aroha said the lie as blandly as possible.

"That's 'cos she's getting old."

"And you?"

Sally shrugged, her eyes sliding away. It remained unspoken how easy it was for her to get lost in the crowd of children that always hovered around her mother.

"So where are the soldiers?" Aroha gazed all around, hopeful that she might be disappointed.

"Maybe they're scared," Sally replied with a giggle. "Or maybe they had such a good breakfast that they couldn't be bothered going."

"No such luck." The ferns rustled and the two Grey Wolves appeared from the edge of the bush. They had their weapons slung from their shoulders, hands clenched around the ugly muzzles, while their faces were covered with broad stripes of brown and green greasepaint. They looked just like the men in the army brochure some of the village men had been passing around at the last council meeting. Aroha shivered.

The soldiers moved closer and Daniel laid what was meant to be a reassuring hand on Aroha's shoulder. "It's going to be alright."

Adults always said that, as if they had more power in the world than a kid. It was a lie. They might have looked old to her, but she knew that they were just shy of being children themselves.

"How long will it take to reach the falls?" Simon was hanging back a little, trying to seem a bit stauncher than his mate.

"Nightfall," Aroha replied. It was not that far, directly, but the guardians of that place did like the formalities to be observed. That was why so many adults ran foul of their trickeries. Grown ups wanted to believe in their own power. They blundered in, expecting everything to be their right, but with the Forest People, that could be a deadly illusion.

They had powers to whisk away a person's mind, to pull them about in the streams of time. You approached only with great care and along the appropriate paths.

Sally nodded too. She had no touch of magic, but in her own way she understood the way things worked. Like all in the village, she'd learnt respect for the falls.

Daniel's eyes narrowed. Perhaps he'd heard different, but he was unsure, Aroha could sense that. He spared a look over his shoulder to where Simon was waiting stony faced — there was an odd adult power game going on there.

"I'll just call in." He stepped away behind the swooshing leaves of the toi toi to communicate with command.

Aroha and Sally shuffled their feet and tried not to stare at his companion.

Simon grinned, a secret little smile and walked over. "You two haven't told your folks about this..."

Aroha had images of being hauled back to Nana, of being labeled merely a child. But she was also slightly disturbed about this soldier reading them so easily.

"Nope," Sally retorted. "I mean, would you?"

A dark shadow passed over Simon's face, making Aroha think of all the warnings Nana had given her about strange men. The cloud passed though and she could see something softer.

"Maybe not," Simon smiled wryly. "We didn't want to use kids for this, but with most of the men gone... well you don't need to worry, we'll protect you."

The girls nodded quietly, not knowing what to say to that. It didn't seem like a lie, but Aroha still didn't trust it.

Daniel appeared out of the trees. "Right. Are we all set?"

Aroha tried to stand up tall like soldiers apparently did, "Yes."

The men let the girls lead. "But once we get closer you'll head back," Daniel demanded. "Things could get dangerous after that."

Aroha knew he meant the bot, but she wasn't afraid of that; what was concerning her was something far more mysterious. As they set off, she began to recite the words she would use to calm the angry hearts of the guardians of the forest.

CHAPTER FIVE

Pursuit

That evening seemed much more promising than her morning at the Hall. Ella did not have anything else to take her attention, and there could be a chance to actually get some writing done.

She'd fed Qoth and done a middling amount of procrastination-induced cleaning, all before five. Only then did she pull the couch closer to the bay window that overlooked the garden, and fish out her notepad.

The electronic stylus had just touched the screen when there came another knock. Ella dropped the device on the floor with a snort of anger. Was she going to be interrupted every day by Bakari? Did the man have nothing better to do?

But the noise was not coming from the hallway but from directly behind her. Someone was knocking on her window.

Peering over the back of the couch she could see the culprit by the dim street lighting. Penny Two Dolls' face was plastered against one windowpane while she rattled off a staccato rhythm on the next one with her fingertips. Ella sank lower in the couch and tried to judge if the girl would give up and go away.

But the little scratching and tapping went on into some version of a half remembered song. Qoth, who had taken up residence in her usual spot on the rug by the fireplace, raised her head and glared in the direction of the window, then gave Ella one of those imperious cat looks as if to say, "Well, do something about that!"

Ella struggled out of the couch and dragged the window sash up. Denied a place to play, Penny wriggled her fingers in greeting.

"What is it, Penny?"

The girl smiled enigmatically.

"You know I've got work to do," Ella tried to keep her voice hard, "and besides, it's late."

Penny rolled her eyes and poked out her tongue, though if this was directed at work or writer was hard to say.

"Where's Alice, then?" Leaning further out of the window, Ella hoped to spot her neighbor nearby. But while her attention was distracted for a moment Penny leapt forward with surprising swiftness.

Before anything could be done about it she'd snatched the notepad from Ella's fingers and darted out of sight around the corner of the house.

Ella jerked upright, smacking her head soundly on the window sash. Eyes watering, she called vainly after Penny.

"This," she reminded herself as she flicked off her slippers and replaced them with shoes, "is why I never had children."

The evening was chill, and as Ella ran down the path it began to spit with rain. "Wonderful," she grumbled, hopeful to catch the girl before she got far. However, even though she thought she'd made good time getting out the door, Penny was still nowhere to be seen. Ella stood impotently, fuming and looking up and down the street. Penherem was nearly asleep, only the muted strains of someone playing the piano down the road disturbed the night air. All was quiet. Nothing stirred in the puddles cast by the streetlights on the damp road. Then Penny peeked her head above the worn brick fence next door. She waved the notebook cheerily at Ella before disappearing once more.

"Little minx," Ella muttered before engaging in an ungainly dash up the road. "Come home before you get soaked."

It really wasn't fair. Penny was not only younger, but also she didn't have a mangled spine marring every step. Ella was sure she would've been able to catch the bright-eyed thief if she'd been having a good day, but every step was painful to her now. Though she ran through it as she'd become used to doing, it still slowed her down. By the time she reached the end of Henley Street, she was heartily sick of the chase and beginning to feel quite damp.

But, obviously, Penny Two Dolls was not. She scampered across the road without a backward glance, her most raggy doll bouncing merrily in her back pocket. Ella nearly swore as the girl ran through the wet grass of the cricket pitch and then across the village green in the direction of the church.

St. Michael's was the last place Ella wanted to visit on a chilly, wet evening. Not that she disliked the old church, but it was far too easy to get lost in the cool medieval interiors or wandering amongst the overgrown garden and leaning headstones. It was a place of contemplation, a spot to read 'Ode to Melancholy' and indulge in a little writerly sorrow. It was not a place to chase Penny around in the dark and lose her temper. But there was little choice if she wanted her Notepad back.

Penny was not hiding when Ella did catch up. She was instead standing quietly by the wrought iron gate at the rear of the church, waiting serenely in the shadows. Ella inched closer to her but not close enough to catch hold, before the girl darted through the gate and into the deeper darkness.

The trees huddled together behind the church, lacing their hands and not letting any light past — not any cast by moon or lamp.

Ella had seen this miniature wood from the street, but had never ventured in to test its depths. It seemed a place not to be dared, especially at night. But now that was exactly what she had to do if she wasn't to be a complete chicken. Sometimes it was hard being an adult.

Stepping carefully into the darkness, she called Penny's name once. The girl had vanished somewhere ahead.

Ella went further in. The trees bent reluctantly away for her, scratching her with their rough limbs as she muttered to herself in the back of her head. It was growing harder to ignore the weighty darkness around her.

She pressed on until she broke through the hovering trees. Finally she saw Penny standing against the final phalanx wood. The moon had momentarily slipped free of the veil of clouds, and its light haloed the girl as if she were on stage in the spotlight.

Turning about, Ella realised she'd been led into a thick circle. All around her was the rough bark of the same tree, mirrored over and over again.

Penny's eyes were dark and unreadable, the light of childish pranks long gone.

Ella's throat closed with an inexplicable fear. She'd heard the tour guides, like Toby from the Hall, talking about the Penherem Yew, but she'd never felt the urge to commune with those trees that had been ancient before even the birth of Christ. And despite the stories, neither did the tourists, from what she'd heard. Now, standing in the ancient circle that was one tree, she understood why.

A young tree had once occupied the earth on which she stood. But, as the millennia passed, it had expanded, the middle dying while younger growth carried on — to create this menacing circle.

Why had Penny bought her here? The girl was looking at her expectantly, like she was some hastily placed actor that knew the lines but was too stage struck to speak them. Ella's eyelids were very heavy and the circle of trees felt as though it was drawing closer. A mad thought of Macbeth's army of trees flashed across the surface of her brain.

Sanctuary, it seemed to whisper. Wrestling control of her fluttering thoughts, Ella pushed such nonsense away. She needed the notebook, she needed to meet her deadline, and most of all she needed to stop this nonsense with Penny.

The girl broke away just a moment before Ella's hand could reach her, leaving only a rare sob behind. This time she was almost glad to chase after the girl, to break away from the circle of yew and move once more into less pressing darkness.

The odd sort of race began again with Penny just ahead, sometimes moving closer as Ella's back allowed her short bursts of speed, and yet other times the girl would dawdle at corners for the woman to gain on her. By this stage Ella was too irate to even consider stopping, so they went in fits and bursts through the back meadows and fields of Penherem with only the silvered moon to guide them.

A hundred planes of beauty passed them; the rustling wildflowers of the Webb's farm, the knotted green streams between and through the light kissed woods. The solemn cry of the owl was all that Ella heard for a very long time apart from her own breathing. Finally they broke through into the gardens of the Hall and into the realm of Tania; a world of manicured lawns and well behaved mixed beds. The rain was now really beginning to fall hard, plastering Ella's hair to her forehead and sending chills through her skin.

The tourists had abandoned the calmness, and for that Ella could only be glad as she chased the child round the west wing of the Hall. Where on earth did Penny get so much energy from anyway? Ella felt more like she was chasing a unicorn than a little girl.

And then, just like that, she stopped. Once again, Penny was waiting for her; this time beside the swirls and dives of Tania's knot garden. She had the same serious look on her face and there was the same feeling in the air.

Ella found herself making a little murmur in the back of her throat as if the girl were a frightened animal. Not that Penny looked scared. The dance of the knot garden blurred as though it was moving, and Ella swayed on her feet.

Safety, the word whispered in the back of her head while the whole world shrunk to the burning darkness of Penny's eyes.

Ella swallowed the hard lump in her throat; getting her notepad back didn't feel as important now. But the girl was still not done with her. She had already turned on one foot and begun to flee again, and Ella too began to scuttle after her. Her back no longer hurt and she was no longer intent on the girl's bad behavior, she just wanted to know where she would be led next.

A dark shadow moved between Ella and Penny, something that bought her up short and snapped her clear of whatever temporary madness had taken hold.

Beneath an umbrella, Tania was all cool regard and perfectly arched eyebrow. As always, she made Ella feel like a total frump. "Not trampling on my flower beds, are you?"

She cast a despairing look over the Baroness' shoulder, but there was only a brief glimpse of Penny's flying hair as she disappeared around the taller hedges that led to the rear of the Hall. And to top it all off, a gentle rain began to fall. "Ah, I hope not," she managed. "Why didn't you stop Penny for me?"

"Penny?" Tania blinked, opening her hooded eyes as if for the first time.

Ella sighed, somewhat used to the Baroness' oddities. The little girl would not be caught now; she'd already vanished into the night. "Never mind — it's not important..."

"I hope she's not gone into the Hall," Tania was always inordinately concerned with the damage children could do — though how she'd ever had any experience with them had never been fully explained.

Ella was beginning to feel like a drowned rat, while Tania only glowed in the wet mist that surrounded her. Hoping to level the playing field, she suggested going inside. "A cup of tea would be nice?"

Tania hesitated a moment, but then showed her to the narrow door that led to her own quarters at the Hall. Ella had never been inside — indeed, she suspected none of the villagers had. Once up the curling, tight stairwell, the sanctuary was revealed to be much like Tania herself; Spartan but stylish. There was very little character anywhere in the room; no rows of books or sagging pot plants like Ella had.

"I'm just going to to hang up this umbrella and get changed; it's a bit cold tonight. Make yourself a cup of tea if you like." Tania disappeared back into the corridor while Ella hovered nervously. Tania knocked something flat on her way out of the room, it looked accidental. Her visitor wasn't fooled. Ella lifted one corner of what turned out to be an elaborate gold photo frame. A smiling Rob Claremont looked back at her.

She'd heard that gossip too: the lady from the Hall and her gardener.

Ella scuttled away from the table it stood on and went gingerly into the kitchen. Though there were enough gadgets in the cool gray and chrome room, none showed evidence of ever being used. Tania was either a neat freak or ate out every night.

With a surge of bravery, Ella made the tea. Tania returned carrying a spare towel for her guest. She'd changed into a fluffy red jumper and warm black trousers, and watched Ella try to find some marginally useful milk in her fridge.

"Sorry," she said in that husky soft voice which was so deceptive.

"No problem," Ella bluffed before shooing her into a chair and locating some biscuits and mugs.

They sat down at the kitchen table and watched each other drink like two cats deciding if they should be friends or have a dust up.

Tania stared down into her milky tea, fingers clenching around the mug.

"Did you see that strange man yesterday?" Ella finally blurted out, no longer able to bear the silence.

"The one with the dark hair — good looking?" He was probably just her type. Tania brushed back her still damp hair. "He didn't seem to be the usual tourist."

Ella hummed to herself and nodded. She wasn't used to such discussions with women who looked like Tania. Her fiercely beautiful looks must be more than capable of drawing in someone like that man.

Tania gave her a piercing look as though she had immediately seen straight to the heart of the matter. "He said his name was Ronan."

It stood to reason that he would have introduced himself to *her*. Ella cocked her head and tried to pretend the roar of the rain outside was suddenly interesting.

Still, Ella couldn't make herself get up from the table, trapped in a web of concern and fear.

Sometimes it was a mystery why she bothered at all. Perhaps it was the bond only she knew of that held the two of them together. After all, the Lady of the Manor had been down that frightening path that had recently begun to interest and frighten her. The desire to know what knowledge Tania had bought back with her, or a vain attempt to win her own salvation; Ella couldn't say which it was.

So the two women sat, quiet and still, not quite content with each other but not quite ready for the world by themselves either. Around them the manor was silent, waiting for the rain to stop and wondering if it ever would.

They found the first body the next morning.

Bakari was dragging his feet in the direction of the library while the first sluggish lines of sunlight were making their appearance. He'd spent an uncomfortable night wondering what Ronan was up to, and plagued by something else — something far less capable of being named. Unease was understandable, but this indecision wasn't. He couldn't shake it. Bakari was worried that when his moment came, he'd remain frozen.

Stick to the plan, he reminded himself, it can still work.

So engrossed was he in his own personal problems that he almost ran over the hollowed-eyed and weeping Mrs. Carew, not ten paces outside the Green Man.

It was too early for drama, Bakari thought with a sigh, but he stopped in front of the woman. At least she wasn't one of those library creatures that made his life hell. In fact, if anyone could be labeled harmless, Helen Carew could. She made her living sculpting little naked rotund earth-goddess figures and selling them in the local tourist haunts. And Bakari, looking down at her rather rubenesque figure, could see where she got her inspiration. Still, she had never harmed him, and in this world it never did to make more enemies than necessary.

The morning was chill and Helen Carew's fingers were even more so when they unexpectedly grasped hold of his. Like many Liners, Bakari didn't appreciate too much human contact, but he bore it stoically considering her distress.

"Have you heard, then?" Her voice had an edge of near panic in it, "They found him right on the Green!"

A pit of fear began drilling itself through his middle, "What do you mean?"

"Young Hamish Claremont," Helen's eyes were pink with horror and he could smell it rolling off her. "He'd been dead for only a couple of hours. They're saying its murder!"

Bakari had seen plenty of death: Liners couldn't really avoid it, but to find it turning up here in Little Penherem was a real surprise. But then again, with what was stirring here, perhaps he should have been more prepared.

And what about Ronan? He'd only been in the village for two days and already there was trouble.

Helen pressed her fullness up against his side, drawing him closer to her horror, "Ned found him this morning. Aslan ran into the bushes and there he was."

How the ancient bulldog could have located anything more than his next meal was the real question.

She would have gone on, but Ned himself emerged from the Green Man. The publican caught Helen's eye and the stern disapproval in his glance made her turn tail and scuttle back to her studio across the road.

Watching her beat a retreat, Ned shook his head and gave Bakari a compassionate look. "Told you then, did she?"

He nodded.

The publican snorted. "She'll be straight onto it, I'd say, all around the village before I've had a chance to pull my first pint." Not that Ned was adverse to the odd bit of gossip.

Bakari waited, so stunned he was not quite sure what to say. Had he not disconnected from the Line properly? Death usually came to Penherem quietly and in good order, only when invited in by those that needed it.

The other's silence perhaps inspired Ned. "Nasty looking it was, I tell you." He concealed a shudder by rolling up his sleeves. "Aslan found him in the ditch on the other side of the Green, almost in the stream. Not something that you want to see that early in the morning."

A thousand possibilities were racing through Bakari's head. The least disturbing one was that perhaps he'd been tracked to Penherem by one of his lesser friendly acquaintances. He bit back a growing dread that it might have been that little bit of work he had put Hamish's way. Surely it couldn't be that.

"Suicide?" He asked almost hopefully. These days, it was one of the leading causes of deaths.

Ned looked him straight in the eye, all movement suddenly stilled. "Not unless he reached around and filleted his own spine." He put his palms together and then opened them like miming reading a book. "If so, he's a better butcher than Harriet down the road."

Bakari whistled softly, even as his neck hair stood to attention and his heart began to yammer.

59

"Yep," Ned said, "Enough to keep me awake for a week. The cops got at it pretty fast after I called. Gotta give them that."

The mist had lifted a fraction. They could now make out movement and colour across the Green. They already had a dome over the area and droids could be seen darting about.

"Expect they'll have the killer found by lunchtime," Ned added lightly, "so I better get on and get extra sandwiches for that lot."

"Yeah," Bakari replied faintly, already doing a one-eighty and heading back to his house. Ned and the rest of the village might be able to sleep easier in their beds thinking the killer was a lone lunatic — but then they didn't have a notorious thief having breakfast in their kitchen. Coincidence was a fine thing, but something that Bakari didn't care to believe in. If Hamish had been killed for what he guessed he had been, he should at least let his latest accomplice know about it.

As Bakari retraced his steps, he could see that doors all down the street were already opening as the villagers got the news. They peered down the road to the Green, one foot in their own gardens as if this somehow proved they weren't really interested. The smell of death disturbed all animals and the inhabitants of Penherem were no different.

Bakari found himself having to put the brakes on each step back home. To be seen burning up the street at seven o'clock in the morning with a murder just behind him — now that would really set the tongues wagging.

As he wrenched open the gate and went up the path, even his little cottage looked suspicious. Was it full of assassins or armed-to-the-teeth Crew who were, even as he set palm to door lock, eviscerating Ronan on his kitchen table?

"You won't believe what's happening," he called up the hall. But when Bakari opened the door at the end of the corridor he wasn't prepared for what he saw.

"Won't believe what?" Ella's brown eyes over the teacup just raised to her lips fixed him to the spot.

Ronan was seated across the table, his face a mask of calm and his hands engaged in nothing more dangerous than spreading honey on toast.

Bakari could feel his mouth flapping in the breeze and closed it with a snap. Then his memory caught up — dammit, he'd forgotten he'd invited Ella around for French toast. This whole project was totally screwing up the remains of his real life.

"Back so soon?" He had only known the flesh world Ronan for two days, but already he could tell where he got his reputation from: he was as cold as the dead guy down the road. Those eyes looked as though they had never run against the corps, or spilled blood — both of which Panther had done numerous times. And yet the man still could sit there buttering his bread and quietly enjoying the morning sun.

Bakari shot him a burning look but tried to stay calm. "You two know each other?"

Oblivious to it all, Ella smiled a little. "We met yesterday at the Manor — except I didn't know he was one of your friends."

Ronan cocked an eyebrow at that and waited for the other's reply.

She doesn't know a thing, Bakari told himself. Sliding himself into the chair between them, he pulled the pile of buttery toast over to himself. "He's a mate from off the Line."

"Oh." Just as he knew she would, Ella lost interest.

The Line was a world she had never experienced, one of a growing minority. She stuck to the two dimensional archaic Line of messages and took what information the corps deigned to give out. She'd never felt the thrill of Third Step and the digital wind in her hair. He couldn't understand it himself, but the woman had, like everyone in Penherem, her own ghosts and reasons — it wasn't polite to ask.

The butter was good, the thick creamy kind made by Rob on his family's little farm, not the pretend kind that was ever so good for you but did nothing for the soul. Thinking of farms made him think of meat, and meat made him think of Hamish who even now was lying like prime rib roast just down the road.

"You'll never guess what's happened," he repeated before telling them the whole story straight from Ned and Helen's mouths; not choosing his words, just telling them like he'd heard it.

He got what he expected, though. Ella looked like she'd been hit in the face; she'd known Hamish pretty well from the Manor. Her hands flew up to hold her mouth on, while Ronan only seemed vaguely puzzled.

Ella's eyes were wide. "My God, Ari, I ran across the Green last night. I could have seen him… it could have…" She stopped sharply before the words, ' it could have been me' could slip out.

Ella was a friend, a good person, and when she began to cry, Bakari moved to her side and held her. He looked at Ronan defensively over her head, trying to get him to retreat and leave them alone to grieve for someone he didn't even know. But the man sat there, hands tucked under the table, not looking away either. Somehow he was curious — like he'd never seen grief before.

"I'm OK... really." Ella brushed Bakari off, not happy about showing her emotion in front of a stranger. Not that he could blame her; Ronan was so still it was pretty disconcerting. "It's just not what you expect to happen in Penherem."

Ronan raised an eyebrow. "The more sophisticated the century and the more sophisticated the crime. Seems to me the further humans go, the better they get at killing."

Bakari abruptly wished Ronan would be still again. Ella didn't need to hear anything like that. She came from a far different world than the two of them did: she couldn't imagine the places they had been, nor the nightmares they had witnessed in action.

Luckily, she was too distressed to really take much notice of anything. Getting up hurriedly, she brushed the last few crumbs off her clothes. "I better get home. Penny and Alice probably won't hear unless I tell them. They don't get out much and I wouldn't want them to wander onto the Green and see..." She bit her lip, thinking no doubt what that scene would be like.

"That's a good idea, Mouse," Bakari leant across the table and gave her hand what he hoped was a reassuring squeeze, "There'll be a lot of frightened people out there." And in here, too.

She made her way slowly to the door, her stride showing the limp she usually tried so hard to conceal. Ronan rose quietly and opened it for her. He had done it so smoothly that Ella looked up at him in surprise. Bakari shook his head. Everywhere the Panther went he stood out as different. How he ever managed to be so successful at what he did was the real puzzle.

Opening the door for Ella, Ronan touched her shoulder and, bending close, whispered something to her. She gave a little start, but also gave him a tiny smile.

Ronan took his seat opposite Bakari and resumed buttering the toast he had only half finished. "What?" he asked innocently.

"Just don't get too comfortable here."

In the pause afterwards, Ronan wolfed down his slice. "I like Penherem. Perhaps if you are so concerned with its citizens, you shouldn't have brought me here."

The odd gleam in Ronan's eye didn't make Bakari feel any better. He had no way of knowing how much the other suspected, but that look made him suddenly change his mind. Best if Ronan was kept in the dark; he might react badly if he found out about what Hamish had been doing.

"It's like this," Bakari pulled his dreads back from his face with one hand using the time to gather his thoughts. He needed to encourage trust, but not expose his real reasoning. "The mask was dug up from around here a couple of hundred years back, and it's worth a lot of money. I need that right now."

"Don't we all."

"You'll get your share."

Another silence while Ronan leaned back in his chair, eyes hooded hopefully, weighing up the evidence. "I'm not fond of games, Vortex."

"You don't need to worry," Bakari found himself snapping. "I just want the mask — that's all you're hired for."

"Well," Ronan rose abruptly like a horse from a starter's gate. "Then I better do what I'm being paid for. But I do it my own way and in my own time. Alright?"

"Of course it is." Please let that sweat stay inside him for a second longer. "Just get it done." He carefully kept his eyes on the lurid tabletop until he heard Ronan reach the door. "And be careful, there are extra cops in the village."

"I might just check in on that — might be interesting." The Crew's voice was pretty neutral but that didn't mean he hadn't made the connection.

Bakari felt as though his tongue was sticking to the roof of his mouth. "Just try not to look suspicious."

"Who, me?" Ronan ended the conversation with the banging of the door behind him.

Bakari counted evenly to twenty, all senses tuned for signs that the other was still about. Then he got up and went into the bedroom. Making himself comfortable, he pulled the hair-thin cable from the pocket in his trousers and plugged himself in, retreating to his proper world.

63

The chilly cartel might provide the money to hire Ronan, but others in his plans provided something he needed even more — information.

These people knew more of magic and the occult than he could ever find on the Line. He would never have been able to deal with a bunch of wild-eyed freaks talking about moon cycles and what type of tree he would be if he was a tree. This contact of his was cool, calm, professional and never pretended that magic was anything more than another type of power. Any romantic notions that Bakari had about magic he kept to himself.

He opened his control cube, signaled into Third Step and once more shrugged on the shape of the crow. Sending the carrier wave, he waited for a moment, scanning the deceptive rolling green hills. It felt different to him somehow, as if something were moving subtly underneath it. The real worry was that he could not immediately spot the difference — it was only pure instinct that was ringing his bells.

The crow leapt into the air, dipping and diving, feeling the power that followed in its wake. Bakari spun in Third Step, creating a basic bot of his own. It leapt into existence in the shape of a trowel fronted black beetle and, dropping to the earth with a rattle, it began digging.

Bakari diverted a minor portion of his processing power to track what it could find, while simultaneously checking on the progress of his signal wave. It had been intercepted, but knowing the level of its receiver, it would be a few nanos before he was no longer alone.

The beetle was ferreting through the local Line, searching for anything unusual. The steady stream of data it sent back was perfectly normal. And yet....

Bakari concentrated his perception. That was what had attracted his attention! The Penherem node had always been one of the more basic, a simple collection of domestic housefeeds with the Hall being the exception. But now the beetle was bringing back far more data than it would have found even a few days ago. The Penherem node was flickering like a lit up Christmas tree, pulsing with a life that didn't seem to correspond with any connections to the real world.

Exposed to this sudden influx of energy, Bakari's beetle was confused, the sheer volume of information more than such a simple bot could possibly handle.

This was strange. He'd need to load the more complex ones that he'd last used in the sprawl — unfortunately, right now there was no time for that.

It came boiling up from the ground beneath him, the blocky ill-defined avatar which could possibly be some sort of leafy vine. The quality of an avatar told a lot about the skill level of the user. Only those who were willing to risk brain surgery had the access to high quality avatars like Bakari's. It was more than likely that this second contact was using a simple carrier system, disparagingly referred to by Bakari's kind as Boxes. So whoever this contact was, they were not at home on the Line — which was perfectly fine, since their expertise lay elsewhere.

The voice too was a badly modulated concoction that could have been either sex and any age. "You need our help?"

Bakari felt at least safer with this contact, whom he had taken to calling Green in his head. He told it all about the killing in Penherem that day. Images about what had been done to Hamish were flashing in the back of his eyes. Bakari hadn't gotten a look at the crime scene, but he had seen plenty of others just like it. It was every Liner's nightmare. Though, by the time the spine was cut open, the avatar had been slain and the agony was over.

He didn't say anything to Green, but he'd already had the unnerving thought that sooner or later the helmets would figure it out, and then it would not be long before one of them was knocking at the librarian's door. The village gossips would love that.

Impossible to tell how Green took the news, but the avatar did not retreat. It was still for a moment, as if the Liner had simply walked away from the screen — likely they had.

"The method of killing suggests a certain intent." So Green might not know the Line, but they knew the methods people used against Liners. "You must come to London and meet with me. I have some...less conventional items that might move things along. Time is of the essence."

Bakari cocked his head and looked out through raven's eyes. He needed no reminding that this was dangerous.

"Panther will have to come with you — bring him."

"I'm not going to do that."

The vines curled in on themselves. "If you haven't got him under control..."

"I don't think anyone has. It can't be done."

The raven stared at the ill-rendered pixels for a long nano or two. "Perhaps not," the voice came. "Meet my messenger at Flash Point."

And then just like that, the avatar blinked out; someone had pulled the plug. Hopefully, that didn't mean anything bad.

Bakari was now going to have to convince Ronan to visit the sprawl. And although that would get them away from the trouble in the village, it would be dropping them back into the past and London — the place that had almost killed him.

Not many people in this day and age appreciated the value of a well-washed dish. Helen Carew stared down into the foam filled sink and fished out the last stubborn glass. No, there really was nothing better than taking something soiled, and with the mere application of a little time and detergent, making it sparkly and useful again. It was just a pity that the same could not be done with people.

At that grim thought, she scrubbed harder, covering the bench top with suds and water. "I am a great artist and people see my work and want to buy it." The affirmation didn't seem to be working, in all honesty, yet she muttered it five more times as she laid the glass on the opposite side of the bench. Sometimes it raised the spirits for the rest of the day, but this morning she had barely pulled the plug out of the sink before the positive feeling had drained away.

It was turning around that did it. All those sad faced goddess figures drying on the kitchen table: each one of them said *No one's interested in me*. Helen frowned, trying to hold onto her good mood.

Perhaps it was Hamish's death, or maybe that man she had seen in the village a couple of days ago. He'd been leaning on her fence staring at the birds eating from her little clay feeder in the rowan tree. At first, Helen had hoped he might have been enticed in by the notice she had only put up that very day: 'Goddess images — improve your luck, improve your life'. It was meant to encourage tourists to visit her shop, but she was quite prepared to sell them from the gate if necessary.

Still, he wouldn't have been the first man to sneer at the little women. However, this man, with the deepest brown eyes she had ever seen, hadn't sneered. Instead he smiled encouragingly when Helen brought one of the goddesses out to show him. "They're powerful," he'd said.

Ah, what a voice he'd had. Helen sighed as she wiped her hands on the tea towel.

"Yes, powerful," she reminded the quiet goddesses on the kitchen table. "But it'd also be nice if you sold."

Almost on cue, the wind whistled around the corner of the house and made the chimes hanging in the trees ring cheerfully. Helen peered out the kitchen window, wondering where on earth that had come from. She saw movement in the bushes; perhaps a peeping tom, or just another mindless vandal. With a flood of anger she didn't know she had, Helen picked up the coal shovel and dashed outside, not even thinking for a moment about Hamish's murderer.

Barreling out of the back door while waving her impromptu weapon, she couldn't have really been expecting a satyr to stand up out of the delphiniums. The coal shovel dropped out of her hands to lie rocking on the path, while satyr and artist stared at each other. Helen's first thought was that he was completely naked, not that it mattered much when his lower torso was covered in ginger brown fur — but it was the principle of the thing. Still, when she managed to pull her eyes upwards there was so much more to see. The lean tanned torso was broad with strong arms, but his face was very sweet, even with the pair of polished tan horns nestling just above his eyebrows. The satyr seemed calm enough, his head tilted to one side, his nostrils twitching like he'd smelt something unusual. Helen wasn't quite sure if she should shout and wave her hands to scare him off or to invite him in for some lunch. No one had ever mentioned the social conventions of such a situation to her and yet neither could she try and pretend she was dreaming or on drugs. The satyr was so immediately real that he simply could not be denied. Every hair, every breath proclaimed him to be more alive than anything else Helen had ever seen.

The wind rose again as the satyr's head came up. With a bound he leapt clear of the perennial border and over the tidy white fence into the farmland beyond.

"Wait!" Helen called, and not quite knowing what she was doing pushed open the gate and chased after him into the meadow. At this time of year it was full of dog roses, wildflowers and most of all thick green grass. Amongst all this the satyr's back was very hard to see, so she ran faster and harder than she'd done in a very long time. Her breath was sticking in her throat, she'd forgotten to pick up the coal shovel, but still she hitched her floral skirt up higher and ran on.

She could smell him, too, a thick musky tang that lingered in the grass and reminded her not unpleasantly of her late husband's aftershave. Another moment and Helen might have stopped, indeed her brain was already catching up with her body, but just before that moment she found him.

Normally there was no way that a slightly unfit and house bound middle-aged artist could have ever caught up with such a wild creature, if he had not wanted her to. But he had. The satyr was standing in the long grass, tufted goat's tail twitching as he held out his hand to her. The run couldn't have winded him at all, for he was breathing normally and the gloss on his skin was not sweat.

Helen looked into those huge brown eyes and forgot about the strangeness, or how her legs were aching, or about the work waiting for her on the kitchen table. Those eyes were marvelous, the colour of warm oak and totally unsullied by any white. Merely looking into them was making Helen feel at peace, but there was more. It really made no sense at all, but she was not so disconnected from her own feminine nature not to recognize what he was offering.

She should turn back and forget, maybe even find some sort of medication, but undoubtedly she shouldn't take that offered hand. Later, Helen would remind herself that at that point these were the things she would have done, had he not in turn done one thing...

The satyr smiled as if he completely understood and spoke her name. The way 'Helen' rolled from his lips was her undoing. A faint sigh escaped her. It was impossible to resist that voice. She reached out and took his nut-brown hand.

CHAPTER SIX

Consequences

Sally's breath was the loudest noise in the forest. Aroha was leading the way into the gathering darkness, trying to act as though she knew what she was doing though in truth she was frozen with fear. It was not that the People inspired such feelings in her — rather that she was afraid for her companions. Sally might not be at much of a risk but the two soldiers, trailing behind and armed to the teeth, breaking branches under their heavy boots, were in far greater danger. The smell of their army fatigues and weaponry would offend every one of the Forest folk.

Aroha pushed through a stand of Old Man's Beard, knowing they would not object to this violation of the least loved forest weed. At the same time she wove a little calmness ahead, hoping that it would carry higher and soothe any anger directed their way.

Sally inched closer. "This is taking a while, Ta." She was right. The waterfalls were not far from the village. But then, its inhabitants were not of the military nature and so the Forest People tolerated them. The stink of metal and danger were not pleasant to Aroha's allies and in bringing them to this place she had to be more careful.

"We're almost there," she hissed, looking over her shoulder to where the bush was shifting slightly.

Daniel's dark head appeared briefly, gave her a 'keep-your-chin-up-smile' and disappeared again. His less cheerful companion, however, remained hidden.

The girls went on; Sally blissful in her ignorance, Aroha tense in her knowledge.

Around them the bush was alive with the sound of birds, the liquid warble of the bellbird and the squawk of the tui. The little black bird with the tuft of white feathers at his throat was her frequent companion. They were excellent mimics and one that hung around her house had learnt to make the exact noise of the kettle boiling.

Aroha knew this one was different though, a bird of the deep bush and possibly a messenger of the Forest Folk. It would be playing no tricks for her benefit.

They worked their way upwards through the tall ferns and up the leaf covered slope. Suddenly her senses were alive. Aroha stopped and held her breath.

"What is it?" Sally was looking about her, dumb to the touch of magic.

How could she explain what she was feeling? It'd be like explaining colour to someone who had never been able to see. They were surrounded. The Folk might be invisible to the eye, but they were ready to slip through reality and into view; powerful and frightening, terrible and beautiful.

"No... nothing," Aroha whispered. "The falls are just over the next hill."

They waited there, poised at the very edge of magic until the soldiers caught up with them: Daniel as always first, Simon lingering in the background.

Sally grinned up at him. "Ta says it's just over the ridge."

"Alright. Now, you two stay here."

Sally slipped her hand into Aroha's for comfort as they stood on the ridge and watched the men pick their way down the hill, subtly moving shades of brown and green against an unfriendly background.

"Think they'll find the bot?" Sally whispered, even though the birds were loud enough to cover most sounds.

She couldn't answer; too busy weaving calmness into the ether. The Forest Folk were far angrier now, outraged at the intrusion of these men into one of their sacred spots.

Please don't hurt them, Aroha asked them. *They are my friends.*

Annoyed, yes they were very annoyed. But, restrained by her care for the men, they did not move down from the high places they occupied. Their emerald eyes watched from the trees for any signs of broken protocol.

Dimly, Aroha heard Sally's heavy sigh, but there was nothing either of them could do but wait. Buried in magic she let herself settle into the pulse of the bush; the ebb and flow of the trees in the wind, the tide of the birdcall, and the raw smell of the leaves.

The quiet of the forest was broken by the wooden thwack of bullets among the trees and the sudden smell of smoke. Aroha's chest constricted as around her the Forest People awoke fully to rage. No remote pleas for calm would do anything now.

The birds of the bush erupted from the direction of the waterfall, fleeing past Sally and Aroha and making the girls duck for cover in the flurry of their flight. No calls from them now, only the need to escape. Nor were they the only ones to feel it. Both girls were also pressed with the need to flee, but when Aroha looked across at her friend, there was also the heady brew of curiosity in her eyes.

Sally would cause more trouble down there among magic she could not see, and yet she would follow. Aroha pushed her back down when she tried to rise in the wake of the birds and bound her with a little geis to hold her to this part of the earth. It was not what her Nana had taught her; any fumbling attempt she'd ever made to make people obey her had always met with a sharp reprimand. But then, Nana was not here.

Sally's eyes glazed over a little but she hugged the ground silently, pressing her ear to the earth, listening to the calming song of the earth mother *Papatuanuku*.

Now confident that she wouldn't be followed, Aroha raced across the moist slope towards the valley floor and the sounds of conflict. It was not something that she would have done in the village, but the forest gave her power — made her something more than just a child. And it was she who had brought these two men into a domain they could never understand. She had to bargain for their lives, make excuses for their mistakes and bring them out alive as she'd been unable to do with others.

The sound of bullets thunking into wet tree-trunks stuttered to a stop. The forest descended into complete silence. Aroha used different senses now, pushing forward with her awareness. She found the tangled outrage of the Forest Folk, the horrified men, and the steel shaped deadness in the bush.

Wrapping a cloak of quiet around her shoulders, she pressed forward through the ferns and undergrowth. The mist of the waterfall gathered on her face as she drew closer. Wiping the moisture out of her eyes, she raised her head slowly out of cover to see what her mortal senses would tell her.

The mud next to the waterfall had been trampled by large soldier boots. Shrubs and bushes had been broken in haste. Such things the Folk did not tolerate and hence it was the first concern to draw her attention. Then Daniel threw up his laser shield, flooding the forest with the blue-white light. He was holding the metal strut and curved sparking shield above Simon who was lying stunned on the ground in front of him.

Not far off, a man-sized drum hovered in the air, its surface painted camouflage green. Twin turrets were aimed in the soldiers' direction while its own shield encased it in an impenetrable field.

It was obvious that this wasn't a dumb bot as the men had hoped. It might well contain any number of deadly viral agents as well as its own impressive armory. In the beginning of the conflict, bots had been dropped to cause panic among civilians — which they'd certainly done. Now that the country was lost to the enemy, would they have been told to instead seek retribution?

Daniel was shooting worried questions over his shoulder to his groggy companion, but all the time holding the shield high. It was an emergency shield, similar to the ones a few of the villagers had. It could offer only a few minutes protection from enemy fire. Nana had told Aroha how to use one, but had warned her that you shouldn't stick around thinking you were safe. The power sources on them were very unreliable and could burn out quickly.

The bot's shield was internally generated and probably able to outlast theirs. Daniel tried several times to hoist Simon over his shoulder, but the necessity of keeping the shield up made it almost impossible for them to move.

Aroha didn't know what to do. She was used to little decisions; what to eat for breakfast, when to really go to bed after Nana told her to. Not things like this.

A sharp coolness appeared at her shoulder but she did not turn. The only way to really see the Folk was not to look. Aroha inclined her head, letting her vision blur a little, and caught the glimpse of the pale hand on her skin. It had no weight, but carried thoughts clearly.

These ones intrude. These ones bring metal.

Aroha attempted not to think about time or danger — neither of which the Folk had any concept of. She showed instead images of the pain and suffering these men were trying to stop.

The scent of jasmine billowed around her nostrils and the world slowed. *They destroy.* The hint of anger.

The Folk could not discern the difference between the men and their enemy. The bot was something utterly unknown and they merely assumed the soldiers had bought it with them.

No. Aroha pushed forward images of the enemy sending it, of what it would do to the villagers.

Why should we care? The Folk's reply was like a blast from the Antarctic, a howling southerly that cared nothing for mortals and their petty concerns.

Aroha couldn't think of a quick answer. They rarely touched humanity's world, only skimming the surface of the physical realm and only in places people rarely ventured. Still, she knew one strange thing about the Folk; she was important to them. Why it was, she had not yet worked out, but she used it now.

She let them see what the village and Nana and even the two foolish soldiers meant to her. How much it would hurt to live in a broken world without other humans, even with all the mistakes they made. *Do not let me be alone*, she pleaded.

The Folk shifted and Aroha was suddenly enmeshed in a brightness, the air felt warm and thick in her throat. *Love.*

It lasted only for a moment, then the golden haze lifted and she was once more able to see the human world. Such a glimpse made her want to cry.

You understand there must be a price.

Nana had told her the rules, all unknown, tucked in her bed, murmuring fairy stories into her young ear. There were always going to be consequences for asking the Folk for aid — even to those they loved.

Yes, Aroha replied, not even voicing the consent.

But even then, the Folk were hesitant. They had not been really present in the human world for such a long time, before even Nana's birth. They did not want to take that step.

So Aroha gave them a little push, she knew the rules. *Help them.*

A slight buzz raced across the surface of her skin. The Folk stirred reluctantly.

Help them, she demanded, testing the limits of her power over them.

The air in the glade solidified, concentrating around Aroha's small tense form. And they waited...

For the third and final, magical time. *Help them!*

They could not disobey. It was one of the rules laid down between their place and the human world. And because they loved her, they played none of the games as their kind was known for. They did as bid.

The air flashed white-hot, burning itself into the back of Aroha's eyes with its power. And in that moment between breaths, when the world itself disappeared, the bot was crushed. It happened in an instant only Aroha could see. The Folk did not like metal and took this chance to vent that anger.

"Aroha!" Sally's very solid arms wrapped around her in panic, flinging her to the ground as the pieces of bot sprayed around them. Where had her friend come from? Aroha was filled with sudden love for her; she had risked it all and followed her into danger.

It was gone. She had an impression of Daniel coming towards them, startled but glad. His confusion was easy enough to read, but as always the human mind found a way to keep its world intact. It would have been the power systems overloading. He was satisfied with that.

Aroha was, however, thinking of something else: of all the Rapunzels and Hansels who had made similar bargains. What would the Folk demand of her for such intervention? Her memory danced through all the terrible prices those fairytale princesses had paid. It was a victory right now, but later would it still be?

Walking back through the rising mist, Ella couldn't stop rubbing the place on her arm where Ronan had touched her. It tingled like she'd banged her elbow against something; impossible, since he'd barely made contact with her at all.

Shaking her arm brusquely, she increased her pace, walking up Church Street and then across to Henley, which ran parallel to it.

He'd looked utterly at home when she had opened the back door of Bakari's house; such economic grace when doing something as normal as making toast. And then there was the strange fact that he'd already had a second teacup out.

Before Bakari arrived, Ronan had also said something strange, something about her needing to watch her back. He knew nothing about her or that she was in that habit anyway.

Alice Thorn was struggling with some weeds in her front garden, her bright curly hair held back with a grimy bandana and her thick woolen gloves somewhat incongruous for the heat of the day. Penny Two Dolls was nowhere to be seen. Alice waved cheerfully, pushing her hair out of her eyes. She could talk for hours about her always-in-crisis herbs and vegetables. She was one of those who believed in getting back to the earth — it was a sad indictment on this century that Penherem was the best she could do.

Ella leaned across the wall and told her the news about Hamish. Alice shook her head, her face pinching in on itself. "Thought I'd got away from all that."

It was the first hint of Alice's past she'd let slip. She was no different to the majority of Little Penherem then, fleeing an unhappy past.

"Come over for a cup of tea." It was what everyone said, a platitude and a ritual at the same time. Above all, Ella wanted to give her a reassuring hug like Bakari had, but the younger woman was already moving.

Alice began swiftly clearing up her gardening tools, not looking in her direction. "Thanks Ella, but I'd better go find Penny. I need to explain it to her — if I can....."

As always with Alice, there was a line you didn't cross, a moment where the blinds came down. Beyond that point only Penny mattered.

She should have gone after her, Ella thought, even as her neighbor's door banged and she was left staring sadly over the wall, but she was feeling decidedly odd, herself. Scuffing her boots amongst the gravel of the path, she went up the stairs and safely inside. Was this the measure of the village, then, that everyone retreated to their own concerns in crisis? She'd thought differently.

For a moment Ella just rested there, back to the door, eyes closed, waiting for the world to get itself together. The tingle had traveled up her arm, and now her whole body was vibrating, including her eyesight. Nausea blocked her throat and she dropped to her knees, contorted with such pain that it momentarily eclipsed any her back might have given her. Her hands fluttered automatically to the spinebridge but it was still in place.

Ella half crawled to her couch, feeling along the carpet with her eyes closed. God, that Ronan couldn't have palmed her some sort of pill in her tea...

She hadn't turned on her rather rudimentary HouseTalk on the way out this morning and unless she could find the console and log in manually, the ambulance wouldn't reach her. Her blind fingers skittered over delicate china and the stack of books next to the couch. A startled squawk from Qoth said she'd managed to upset some perch or other. Cats very seldom made exceptions for illness.

But just as she was beginning to panic the world seemed to right itself. Ella leaned back against the sofa gasping with relief. Her arm was only warm now, like it had been held next to a fire.

Perhaps after this, Adjustment wouldn't look so bad. Perhaps she could even get some advice from Tania. Whatever it meant, she couldn't stay here. She needed company.

Leaving Qoth to settle back and forgive her, Ella scooped up a warmer jacket and let the door bang behind her. For a moment she stood, arms wrapped around herself in the chill morning, looking up and down the street with indecision. It was early May, and it could still be cold until the sun came up properly.

The thought made her start, her head suddenly turning towards the Green and where young Hamish would be lying — cold. It was not an image she wanted to have in her head, and yet she was drawn to it. Ella's feet found their own way down Henley and onto High Street.

The Green was shedding its misty wrappings and the police could be seen, all intent and studious crawling all over Hamish's death scene. She stood locked on the scene, hearing her heart beat in her ears, bile growing hot in the back of her throat.

"Not a pretty sight, is it?" Ned Aldridge was holding the dark brown door of the Green Man open as if he had been expecting her. His blocky shape was almost indistinguishable against the dim recesses of the pub. "But I'll say this much, I've never had a better crowd for a Monday morning."

Ella's mouth twitched, uncertain if he was making a joke or being serious. One thing Ned was keen on was pulling a good crowd to his pub.

"Come in, little 'un," he stepped aside, "You're practically the only villager not here."

Once inside the Green Man, Ella could see he was right; the pub was bulging to capacity, every nook and barstool taken. Bev Aldridge could barely be seen over a steaming pile of bacon and eggs as she wielded an enormous serving spoon with admirable vigor. She managed a brief wave. Only Ari, Alice and Penny Two Dolls were missing. Poor Rob Claremont, the brother of the unfortunate Hamish, had his head bent in sorrow and his fingers were white around the obligatory pint. He was surrounded by quiet-voiced villagers, some with their hands on his arm.

And then, over by the bar, was Ronan. Ella tried not to let the idea that he was following creep into her head — but it already had. He too had a pint, but was enjoying it with what was almost unseemly zest. Leaning precariously on the two rear most legs of the bar stool, he was chatting amiably to Bev, as if unaware that she was fighting a losing battle with the bacon. Ella sighed in something that might have been irritation, and he chose that moment to look over. He grinned.

But another voice broke her concentration. "Ella, just in the nick of time." Mrs. Winslow, Penherem's oldest resident, patted a seat next to her in a vaguely commanding manner. Never one to consider Treatment, her wrinkled old face was the first one that all the tourists saw as they came into the town. She sold all the tickets from behind her battered little desk in the corner shop. Though it might take longer than Lining one from home — they liked the authenticity of it.

And authentic, Ella thought to herself as she slid gratefully into the nook, was what Mrs. Winslow was all about.

"Quite the excitement, ain't it?" The older lady took a tiny sip of the port in front of her, "Mind you, not the kind the village needs."

Ella's fingers knitted themselves together.

She was aware how the old lady's eyes dropped to her gesture; old eyes picked up everything. Mrs. Winslow took another little mouthful of port before letting fall her pearls of wisdom, "You should get out more, Ella. That cottage of yours is all very nice, but it's not the whole world."

"I do get out," Ella sounded pathetic even to herself. "All the time…" She was getting the opinion that everyone in the village gossiped about her.

"A beautiful May day like today calls for celebration. Most especially when there is so much death lurking about. Believe me, enjoy while you can." She looked up as the tall shape of Ronan appeared to the half circle of the nook. "Now, I'm sure *you* know what May is for."

The man's deep chuckle stirred the air around the women and tickled Ella's ears. "Is that an offer, Eve?" Just how he'd learnt the old lady's first name was yet another mystery. He slid into the rather cramped space next to Ella, but leaned across to take the older woman's hand, raising it to his lips.

"Goodness, no." She seemed delighted, even at the impertinent use of her first name. "These old bones are not up to that — all too much time later to lie on the earth."

"It's all a cycle." Ella was speaking before she knew it. "Even Spring has death in it, too."

Mrs. Winslow's hooded eyes popped wide with surprise. "Whatever are you talking about, girl?"

Caught out, she decided to clam up, especially when Ronan focused his attention on her.

"It's a strange little village you have here, ladies." He didn't sound at all concerned, though; in fact, quite the opposite.

A silence prevailed for a second, until Ella realised Mrs. Winslow had receded into one of her moods and wasn't going to reply. She'd slumped back into her spot and was staring morosely into her diminished glass of port.

Ella could feel her face reddening, and the more she thought about it the hotter it became. "How so?" she finally managed to blurt out.

He was looking at her askance. "Well, it seems pretty much like a tourist trap — until you dig a little deeper."

"And then?"

"Why, then," he leaned forward so that the warm hot scent of him was washing over her, "you realise there is something going on."

The air had gone so rigid that Ella thought her lungs had frozen. His words had done it, made her dreams and experiences of the last few days real. If she did not break the spell, she might not be able to take another breath.

"It's a murder, you idiot." God, had she spoken that or yelled it? Suddenly the whole pub had gone quiet and all eyes turned in her direction. Ella quavered under the attention.

Then Mrs. Winslow, who had by this stage fallen into a proper sleep, let out a booming snore. Suddenly, the spell was broken and the village enveloped Ella. They pressed around the nook, touching her shoulder, clasping her hand, telling her that it was all right. One of Bev Aldridge's tears fell on her hand, and before she could protest Rob had scooped her up in a rough hug.

"It's alright, pet," he gasped against her shoulder, "let it all out!"

Grief had them all, but even in the melee, Ella noticed that somehow Ronan had managed to slip away. Perhaps he thought himself too much the stranger — or perhaps it was all too much for him.

"Come on, love," Ned was pulling her through the crowd to the bar. "You sit yourself down and have a proper drink." He thrust a large pint of cider into her hand. "We were just remembering Hamish. I'm sure you have something to tell of him."

She certainly did, but right now that was not what they wanted to hear — so instead Ella dredged into her writer's brain for a sweet story that would make them all cry. What was needed was release and not the real memory of the lost person. She knew that better than most.

Alice had grown up knowing there weren't any monsters under the bed. Real monsters had two legs, and more often than not, they wore familiar faces. They were called friends because they wore their ugly faces only at night and because no one ever believed what one little girl said. So as soon as she was old enough to escape, she'd fled all those well-known people and the dangers, and come to somewhere that seemed like a sanctuary. Well, that's what it had seemed like until today when Ella had so flippantly told her that this was all a lie. And she hadn't even known what she'd done, because by this stage Alice had got very good at hiding.

There was one person still left in the world that she felt she didn't need to hide from, and right now she didn't want to wear her own mask. But, typically, Alice couldn't find Penny. The girl's unreliability could be relied on. She had little concept of comfort or grief, and even Alice, who had looked after her for nearly ten years, was a tenuous connection.

Just when I could do with her about. Alice sat down on the garden seat with a muffled sob. This was the rear garden, hidden from the prying eyes of those on the road or in the neighboring houses. It was her space, where none of her demons dare venture, and yet it could have had a killer running through it that night.

Alice's throat was tight and she wasn't sure if she was breathing or not. She closed her eyes, tried to get a grip on her panic. Bad idea. Those monstrous faces leered back at her from the depths of her memory. Nothing anyone had done had stopped them coming, or stopped the pain. No one had believed her when she told about how her father's friend was really a monster — a beast with an appetite for her tears.

Her fingers were straining against her palms, a habit she'd thought long gone. And now when she looked about the garden with wide despairing eyes, it all seemed changed. The garden was not full of peace, it was full of dangers and corruption just like the rest of the world. Every tree was rotten to the core, every rose was scented with vileness, for everything was already dead.

This was not a place where she could heal. It was a place she would die. They'd find her here rotting and laugh at her weakness. The despair was a heavy cloak wrapped around her, and though Alice struggled, it was hopeless. With a fatalistic groan, she knew it was a battle she was going to lose.

That pain was going to swallow her again, and yet as she prepared to sink into it, there was a light that made her raise her head. Through her sweat soaked hair, Alice glanced up, seeing something that managed to touch her curiosity.

The ferns at the back of the garden were glowing. A faint silvery gleam that seemed to dip and flutter with a breeze that was not in the garden at all.

For a moment, the panic was forgotten. Alice's brow furrowed and she blinked rapidly to clear her tears. But it was not her tears that had caused the light, for it was still there. What on earth could that be?

The monsters had always said, be still, be quiet, don't move — so it was a victory when Alice got up from the bench and went cautiously down to the bottom of the garden.

The light was still there, so she wasn't crazy, which was good. Yet, as strange as it was, it didn't make her afraid, which pretty much everything that wasn't habit in her life usually did. And it didn't hurt her eyes. It made her blink, but it also somehow warmed her.

And then a tiny hand moved aside the fern and Alice was looking into a very smooth face, almost mask-like but for its violet eyes. Behind fluttered a pair of pearl coloured wings.

Any rational person would have known this was madness, but as Alice looked into those eyes and saw herself in miniature reflected in them, she didn't think that. For, if monsters could exist, then perhaps other things could as well.

She'd taken an abrupt step into something, but oddly she didn't feel worried. As if in a dream, she found herself sitting down next to the silver-lit ferns.

A flutter of wings, the lightest of touches on her shoulder, and the voice of understanding in her ear. Without hesitation, Alice began to tell on the monsters. The winged creature listened as she laid aside her burden.

Ned pulled the cork out of the pinot slowly, and for a moment time hung on that moment, until with a half-sigh the bottle gave up its aroma. The Green Man was quiet now, the towels hung over the taps, the front door locked tightly. Instead, it now seemed to whisper of laughter and sorrow.

Ned shook his head; he was getting quite batty—a combination of the murder and his own private hell. So he didn't hurry back behind the bar, to where Bev was watching the news and eating her fish and chips off the paper on her lap. Instead, pulling out a scrupulously clean glass he poured a fraction of the pinot and took a second to savor its berry filled aroma. It reminded him of blue sky days when he and Bev had traveled the vineyards of New Zealand, sampling and falling in love with each other and the fruit of the vine.

He swirled the ruby red liquid and frowned — the pinot had been bought then, packed away with dozens of others, until now it was the last. The rest had been consumed in joy, but this one would not be. Like its homeland, it now stood for endings, and like New Zealand there would be no going back. Once those words were out of his mouth, everything would be forever different.

Despite all his earlier resolve, Ned dithered, finding an excuse in the wine to linger out in the dimness of the Green Man. Everywhere he looked, there was a memory and another sweet pain, but the murder had made him think — there wasn't enough time in this world for a person to remain unhappy. Even plain old Ned Aldridge needed and deserved to be happy. Didn't he?

Taking a small sip, Ned let the liquid roll to the back of his throat and rest there for a moment. Once upon a time, ensconced in their B & B in Blenheim, Bev had trickled pinot over her body. It had been worth the extra expense of the sheets to drink it off her.

But Bev wouldn't do that now, and he probably wouldn't have known what to do if she had. The bittersweet sting of that memory made him lurch away from the bar, swallowing the wine quickly — as bitter as medicine.

He went back into the dim corridor and up the steep steps that led to the family part of the Green Man. Bev didn't bother looking up as he dropped into the couch, but she took notice when he flicked off the vid stream.

She looked out at him from shadowed eyes, like she already knew the words he had to let loose, but she took the glass of pinot Ned offered her. So she still hadn't forgotten. Holding the glass with the tips of her lacquered fingers she swirled the liquid round and round. Ned was entranced. He found he could not look away from the dance of the wine, eyes fixed as it described lazy circles in the crystal.

The smell grew so powerful that it reached him even across the room. Bev's hair seemed to billow and grow light, as if there were a breeze coming up out of the glass.

Ned rubbed his eyes with the back of one hand, while the other didn't give up clutching the bottle of pinot. When he glanced, back Bev was looking straight at him, but there were no lurking shadows now. The violet eyes that looked back reminded him of times now lost.

The scent of the pinot could almost be seen in the air, like bunches of grapes and raspberries. It reminded them both of sunshine and laughter. Bev's hand was no longer spinning the glass and yet the contents kept moving, not slowing down but speeding up.

And now the sound of the grape came, like deep bells making Ned's spine quake. His logical brain was telling him that he must have taken a tumble back there on the stairs, or someone had slipped something into the pinot, or maybe he was mad as a hatter.

But in any case, he didn't care. Not while his wife was looking back at him like that, not while she was smiling. He deserved to be happy, but he couldn't be happy without her.

"I still love you, Bevvy," Ned said, something he hadn't uttered for years.

Her smile was wide and flashed across the wine glass at him. All their memories were in that smile; the children, the trials and tribulations, even the pain. Together, they made up a whole life.

Picking up her glass, Bev got up and held out her hand. That smile never left her lips. "Why don't you come and remind me of that, luv?"

Ned laughed loudly before following her. After that, the strange music and the unseen wind didn't seem to matter.

Tania avoided the Green Man. Everyone would be there talking incessantly about Hamish and jumping at shadows. She knew well enough what lurked in the darkness, and she didn't feel like sharing that knowledge with her fellow villagers. After the Adjustment, they had never looked at her in quite the same way. Strange, how she was still hurt by that.

No one was about on the village Green. Even the police had finished their scene examination, tidied up, and left. Tania sat on the crumbling park bench just off the cricket pitch.

Almost nothing remained to say what had happened only a few hours ago. Only a glimpse of a strip of plastic marked the cordoned off area where Hamish had breathed his last ragged gasp into the world. The poor kid was a mere blip on the statistics for the year — to everyone but herself.

She could be sure that she looked normal enough from the outside; certainly she'd had enough practice for that. Inside, however, the voices could not be escaped. Here they were different from those at the manor. The ghosts of the common folk; the murdered wives of long ago, the smothered children thrown into the ditches that had once lined the road, and hundreds of other victims of crime and accident. Now they were joined by a new voice.

Hamish. Tania ducked her head and concentrated out of the corner of her eye. His face had already faded, so that he was only a smudge of light in her peripheral vision. He spoke evenly into her ear, yet so fast that his words barely made any sense. He'd not even seen his killer, but the pain he'd endured had burned his spirit into the air. Tania pulled her chin in against the chill, feeling a few spits of rain threaten to become more.

What had possessed her to come here, where murder was freshly written and Hamish had not even had the decency yet to fade? His voice was loud enough to be confused with a still breathing person's. Perhaps she'd wanted to try and make use of her madness; perhaps if she were honest, it was the chance to help Rob.

But the confused Hamish said nothing to reveal who his killer had been. Like all the voices, he only spoke of missed chances and dreams now fallen to ashes.

A tear worked its way loose from Tania's clenched eyes. She'd grown up with him after all, and though he'd been five years younger than her and his brother Rob, she'd had a soft spot for him, even if he had ruined her early kissing experiments. She was glad she hadn't been the one to find him. Out of a sense of duty then, she sat and listened to him.

So when Bakari plopped into the seat next to her, Tania almost didn't notice. He sat a fraction too close to her — his way of reminding the lady of the manor that things had not always been cold between them.

"You're a brave one," his honeyed voice was quiet today, quieter in fact than Hamish's. "The boys aren't even playing cricket here this coming Sunday."

"It's just a place," she replied, while the moans of the dead hammered on.

"I suppose — but with the boys in blue finding nothing, it's got people a little edgy."

She shrugged in her coat, hoping that the librarian would get the hint and melt away. She could feel how tense his body was. Adjustment had taught her better control of herself than that. Bakari could have benefited from knowing how to turn off distress. It only made people suspicious — like she was now.

"So, have you seen that guy Ronan around?" Bakari really had very little experience in the real world. His voice was heavy with overdone casualness.

"Who?" What on earth did that have to do with this situation? Unless he suspected the stranger.

Tania barely restrained a jump when Hamish whispered hard against her cheek. *He knows.*

She counted three trips of her heart before Bakari got up suddenly. "Ok... well... catch you later then," and sauntered off.

Why hadn't he heard the pain in her voice? Couldn't he have asked if there was anything wrong? Had she got so good at hiding, that even he couldn't see her hurt? The answer was yes, and that was how it had to be.

It doesn't have to. Hamish sounded like he was bent over her. *There are ways you can be free.*

Tania had heard this before. In those moments before the Adjustment team arrived, when Bakari was long gone and only the lonely shades of her parents remained, she'd heard the same argument. It had been tempting, but then that scrap of her sane self had reminded her that she'd have just become one of the gray voices.

No. Hamish's voice was remarkably insistent. *You only need the Art.*

Not able to sit still and listen to anymore, Tania got quickly up from the seat and walked away. That was one advantage humanity had over the dead, they were faster to react. She outdistanced Hamish's ghost long before he tipped her over into madness.

She walked under the ash and rowan trees, already bursting with new green growth under a cloud dotted sky, scissoring her legs brusquely so that the voices were muffled as she passed them. But it wasn't as though she had anywhere to really go. She'd already knocked on Ella's door, but she was most likely in the Green Man.

Tania circled around the edge of the park past the cricket pitch, beyond sight of the pub, and reached the bridge that crossed over Lamden Stream. It partly froze in winter, but with the breath of spring the burble of water could be heard again. It was a cycle that refreshed most of humanity, but not Tania. It reminded her that she could not tell how many more springs she would see. Staring down morosely into the icy flow, watching it run over smooth rocks, she caught sight of a small pair of white feet dangling into stream.

Curious despite everything, Tania leant rather dangerously over the handrail until she could see Penny Two Dolls sitting like a content water sprite in the middle of the stream. What sort of person would let the girl get into such predicaments? Tania was scrambling down the side of the bank before she knew it, half outraged and half worried. The voices here told of drownings and suicides.

Penny's wide china-blue eyes watched with interest as Tania splashed across through the water towards her, ruining her expensive boots and at every step risking a dunking. The Two Dolls were perched on her knees and she seemed perfectly happy to remain there with them.

Tania wasn't giving her the chance. She hauled the surprised girl, who also proved rather heavy, up under one arm and waded, cursing all the while, to the bank.

Once there, she deposited her burden on her little bare feet in the mud and looked down in horror at her own ruined outfit.

"Do you have any idea how much this cost?" Tania demanded of the pale Penny.

A frown creased the tiny brow while she hugged Two Dolls closer.

Please don't start crying, Tania thought as she dragged herself out of the water. "You could have been drowned, silly girl." She could not stop herself being a little snappish.

Tiny fingers balled into what might be peeved fists, and Penny shook her head stoutly. "Wouldn't." The girl hardly ever let a word slip. It was something that Tania could identify with — they had perhaps similar demons. Penny's parents had been killed in London, in a riot just after the first bout of the Northern Water Wars. Tania knew how it felt to lose mother and father so young; her own had been killed when she was scarcely older than Penny. Even if no one spoke of those lost ones, it didn't mean they were forgotten.

Gulping down the urge to hug her, Tania pulled off her thick wool coat and wrapped it brusquely around the girl. She in turn struggled and frowned just as angrily up at her. Ungrateful little thing! Hauling a wet, shaking, grumbling eight year old up a damp and slippery slope was both undignified and unplanned. Tania's beautiful leather boots skidded in the wet leaves and dirt. The child might look like a tiny bundle of bones, but she was heavy. Finally dumping her at the top, Tania found herself scrambling to grab hold of bushes as her footwear slid back down the slope. Dress boots were not meant for this sort of punishment.

Worse still, while Tania was engaged in saving herself, Penny shot her a little bright smile from under her hair and, with a wave, ran off like a march hare. She even took the coat with her.

By the time Tania had got herself on a firm footing and recovered from the shock enough to yell furiously, the girl was completely out of sight.

Tania wanted to throw her bag in the bushes out of frustration, but she settled for whacking some offending branches instead. They snapped back and gave her a good slap in the face. No one was around, dusk was falling, and it was — at least for the moment — safe to cry. So she did.

The earth smelt good, and the tree, despite her attack on it, felt comforting against her back. She cried, and the sound of her tears and hoarse cries drowned out the dead.

Tania. Hamish was close again.

"Go away," she snarled, flinging the remains of the branches to the ground, "Leave me alone — you're dead, so shut up!"

Tania, run, it's coming. The sweet voice was twisted with horror. *Get out!* It howled in her ear.

And she suddenly didn't care if she was taking advice from the dead, for she could feel it and even see it. A knife-like wind cut through her woolen tunic, making her stumble back in shock. Her rebellious sodden boots slipped once more in the leaf litter and with a howl she slid back down the slope. The ground was not soft and as she crashed through the undergrowth every rock and branch seemed to take its chance to hurt her. The world twisted and spun, and for a moment all she heard was the roar of the dead rising around her.

Tania landed with a cry in the bottom of the stream. The breath was knocked out of her for a moment, but then the bitterly cold water snapped her alert. The voices were gone, even Hamish's, but she gladly would have had them back. The forest was being whipped up around her and the air was full of dead leaves and twigs.

Clambering to her feet, she was glad at least to feel she hadn't broken anything, though the heel of her boot was long gone. Her whole body was shaking and she squeezed her eyes shut. It made no difference. It was still there: the unmistakable noise of something coming towards her through the trees. The wind shrieked and suddenly it didn't matter to Tania if she was mad or not — she had to get away.

Pure animal instinct washed through her brain. She turned and bolted up the stream; heart trying its best to break loose from her chest. Behind, the trees snapped and gave way to the thing, but she was too afraid to look back.

The world reduced to a mad scramble through the icy water and the slippery stones. Every step was awkward and every breath a gasp.

Whatever it was, it screamed. Even as Tania scrambled over the boulders, the roar of rage and unearthliness made her glance back. Breath lodged in her throat, though her mouth managed to wrap around a howl. The thing following her was all spines and fangs. The insect-split mouth gaped wide. It was a flash from every childish nightmare she'd ever had. She wanted the voices back, she wanted that comforting madness she had almost grown accustomed to — not this!

Tania was crying now; sobbing and clawing her way through the water, the breath freezing in her lungs. The cry was the nameless prayer of the doomed.

Behind her the nightmare's long legs stretched out before it, so wide that they avoided the stream and plunged like daggers into the soft earth of the bank. From somewhere strength welled up in Tania's legs and she tore around the bend in the stream. With terrified excitement she realised that she'd reached the culvert. A crusty and rusted barely-there ladder snaked up towards the street. *I don't want to die — not to be a grey voice, not to go there and join them.*

A thousand coiled nightmares slammed into the concrete as she laid finger on her escape route, each one taking out a perfect round hole at either side of her. A mewl of terror burbled out of her as she scrambled upwards. Still she was unable to resist looking back. Just in time, she saw the tentacles draw back towards the gleaming missile shaped head of the thing. Her feet were missing vital rungs and her fingers, numb with horror, weren't helping either. She wasn't going to make it. The nightmare wasn't even going to bother climbing after her; its next strike would not miss.

And then the clouds finally parted, and the grey became white. The streambed was flooded with the most blinding spring sun, pouring over the culvert and onto the horror below. Its bellow of shock seemed like it would rupture her eardrums, and Tania could only moan and hang onto the rungs as the air around her rocked with it. Whatever it was, it could no more stand the sun than the monster under the bed could have. Her feet were running of their own accord. Skittering against slippery concrete, finally

89

they found purchase and she was moving up again. She could see the top, where sunlight covered the ground and nightmares had no place. Then sharp pain brushed her back, like a knife had suddenly plunged in. Her opponent roared again, but quieter this time. It was fleeing.

Tania reached the top and threw herself onto the wet ground. Lying there, she got her breath back. Rolling over and brushing her tears of terror away, she felt gingerly where the pain had come from. It was hard to tell without seeing, but there was only a little blood and the wound seemed small. She'd had worse playing hockey. Her attacker had caught her with one tentacle in a last desperate attempt. As Tania wiped the blood from her fingers she considered what had just happened; that thing had killed Rob and it had meant to have her too.

Whatever the voices had done to her mentally, they had never threatened violence. Either her madness had taken a frightening new turn or something else was happening in Penherem. Which ever it was, she was quite sure she didn't want to find out by herself.

CHAPTER SEVEN
Returning

Bakari took the first VFT to London before anything was open. He'd left the library door undone so that anyone who wanted to could get in. Really, he'd just thrown his job into the hands of Fate. He liked being a librarian, but in the scheme of things it was not the most important thing to him. He had more pressing things to attend to — demonstrated by the fact that he was going to London, which he hated, and in the morning, which was never his best time of day.

Every fiber of his being shrunk from cities, and in this modern world that was more than an inconvenience. Bakari had spent more than his fair share of years trawling through the underbelly of urban sprawl, where desperation and animal instinct were all anyone had to live on. He'd fought, first in the meatworld and then even harder in the lineworld, for every moment of breath. Just how hopeless that life had been, he'd never realised until he found Penherem.

Oh sure, the village was veneered and dressed up, but it still breathed. It still had a green heart and a history that wasn't steeped in human misery. Bakari had never loved anyone, never believed in such a fragile and dangerous thing as hope, until he'd become part of Penherem. The years that he'd spent in the village had been the years during which he'd learnt the meaning of the word home.

Bakari concentrated on the window, watching his old world reclaim him; first with fingers of shadow, then a stale breath, until finally the sun itself was swallowed up by the copper-gray clouds. He slid further back into his seat and glowered back at the city. The only thing that London had ever given him that was worth a damn was his Line — and even that had come at a steep price.

Bakari left the VFT and dropped effortlessly back into the sprawl. It was bad enough Lining through London, let alone having to experience it in the meatworld.

He stood for a moment on the platform and orientated himself within the vast chaos of Waterloo station. The weight of passing people buffeted him to and fro. He backed against a wall, eyes half-hooded, feigning a calmness he didn't really own.

Flicking down his shades and stuffing his hands into his worn trousers, he let the scroll of information dance across the inside of the lenses. It wasn't true Lining, often called derisively Skimming by his kind, but it did allow him to keep a foot in each world. One hand twinkled on the tiny board in his pocket and the red script on his shades responded, linking to Buzzer. If there was one constant in the London lineworld, he was it.

Buzzer had Swallowed the Line years ago, shucking off his rather porcine meatbody and stepping into what he'd always considered his true form. His finely crafted avatar, which he'd slaved years over before taking the ultimate step, was a mind-blowing gorgeous male form — one that would never age, get bad breath, or have a hair out of place. By contrast, his meatbody was securely locked away, tapping its energy off the power grid and slowly atrophying. Bakari had never heard of anyone that had met Buzzer's lost and unlamented meatbody. Buzzer would get mad with those who even hinted at its existence.

When the connection sprang to life, Buzzer's voice poured seductively into his ear.

"It's me, Vortex." Bakari cut him off.

"Well I guess that means you won't be meeting me in Line wearing rubber and carrying a paddle."

"Not until I'm down to my last dollar, Buzz."

He sniggered. "From what I hear, that isn't far off."

"There's nothing wrong with being picky about my jobs."

"Picky's one thing, but just plain dumb ain't far off. People don't like to have their employees bail out on them."

Bakari wasn't about to get into the same old argument. "Look, right now I need a heads on Flash Point."

"You back in the game, my friend?" Buzz's voice took on a note of interest.

Bakari shuddered, but managed not to snap back. He still might need his connections in this scarred town. "Might be," he tried to sound noncommittal. "I'm meeting up with a few old friends there and don't want to run into anyone... unsociable."

"Fair enough," Buzz chortled. "There are still plenty around who'd remember you — though not as many as there were."

"The business takes care of that, what with such a high turnover."

A faint distant distortion was all that marked the nano it took Buzz to check his network. Bakari held himself tightly in check; not jumping to any conclusions, waiting patiently like this was his last chance. It very well could be. "You're looking good to go. It's real quiet down there at the moment. Have a shot of tequila for me." Was that a minor note of longing in the digital voice.

"Sure thing." Bakari closed the connection and looked out once more through the smoky interior of his shades into the meatworld.

He'd thought about it once. Most Liners, at one stage or another, considered shutting up shop in the real world and swallowing the Line. But something always stopped him, no matter how close he got. Once he'd been as far as the Cutters front step; cash in hand, all his possessions sold, all his friendships severed.

He'd yet to work out what had made him turn around and begin again in a world that had lost its magic. Perhaps it was Mama's voice crooning in his memory, telling him about Mother Thunder and all the animals who made magic. It was a sound that was hard to shake, and swayed him even in the world of science.

Bakari had branded himself a fool for going on, for living on the Line without hope. Until that day over a year ago, when he'd had his epiphany. It was one of those moments on which your whole life turns, he'd known that immediately. But, it was more than that. It was also one of those times when the world itself might change. He was lucky to have seen what he'd seen, and that thought alone drove him on.

With a little sigh, Bakari pushed away from the wall into the pounding crowd and began to swim against the current towards Flash Point. It was a place Joe Average avoided unless he was a zapped up Liner, looking for a contact, or hoisting some serious weaponry. It had been Bakari's favorite haunt back in his sprawl days and even if he hated the city, now he found his feet hurrying him to get there.

Kensington had once been a fashionable place, up until about twenty years ago when a bunch of eco-terrorists had taken it into their head that it was a valid target. Perhaps it was the shop selling furs, or the up market cutter who catered to the whims of fashion, but either way, Gaia's Revenge was released there. Hundreds had died by the time the culture was discovered to have been less than perfect culture, and the outbreak had been contained.

The area never recovered, though, and by Bakari's era it had dissolved into graffiti ruins, where the descendants of those plagued victims eked out their lives amongst the pockets of the virus. Revenge was a highly manufactured plague capable of endless variations and going by a range of different channels. No one wanted to live anywhere near where it had been and might still linger. So Kensington had been transformed into the perfect place for dark dealings to take place.

Flash Point had no signs, no exterior exposure to explain what its various entrances led to. Leia and Alexis, the couple that ran the Point, made sure that their clientele always had a way out. They also had informant police by the dozen and a cracking team of Liners to keep them up to date on who was legit and who was to be watched. Bakari hoped that he was still low enough to keep under their radar. No one really wanted Leia or Alexis keeping an eye on them.

He chose the south entrance and walked down the apparently quiet oozing alleyway. Nodding to the bot cunningly disguised as a large tabby cat on top of the dumpster, he jerked open the rusted and cranky door and went in. Leia might like her tech, but she also admired the old school methods of detection.

Lights were flashing inside while the thump of the music shook his bones. It smelt of booze and ozone. Turning up the dampening effects of his shades, Bakari contemplated how much closer he should have strapped his pistol to his hand; the last thing he wanted to have to do in a firefight was untangle it from his ankle. It was too late now.

He walked the long corridor to the Point, trying not to think about how many electronic eyes were watching him, and how many weapons were capable of taking him out where he stood. Still, nothing stopped him entering and that was about as good as it got in here.

Bakari didn't pause at the doorway like some foolish first timer. He dropped into an empty, shadowy booth before checking out the lie of the land. Molly was still serving drinks, but she made no sign that she recognized him as she took his order. Both her mothers were pulling pints and chatting to the customers, neither appeared to notice him. Bakari wasn't fooled; they knew he was here. It was just that they considered him mostly harmless. He grinned to himself and refrained from waving. Leia looked a little older than last time he'd seen her, more wrinkles than there needed to be, but she was funny about that sort of thing. Alexis, on the other hand, had definitely visited a Cutter recently. She looked almost like Molly's older, blonder sister.

He threw some money down when his drink arrived and concentrated on the patrons, wondering who would be Green's messenger. They looked like just the same lot that had frequented the place in his day, mostly Liners and their hangers on. Pretty much everyone had clamped a transceiver to their Line and was shaking to the alternative music and light show that only they could see. Bakari was tempted to join them, it always made the Point far more attractive, but today he needed meat eyes and ears.

Soon enough, he picked out trouble among the crush of people and piped in smoke. A bunch of carefully concealed suit heavyweights were two booths over. Thankfully when he'd been shooting at them it was through a Line controlled bot. It had been his hardest job; attacking even a branch of the massive Infinity Rose Corporation was something not to be taken lightly. Bakari had thought himself prepared, carved by experience, ready to make the real money of cracking the top line corps. He'd been wrong. And there'd been no payout for the lack of results, but it was valuable in that he'd learnt his lesson.

Recognizing them, then, Bakari was very careful. He didn't twitch, didn't move a muscle, instead letting his eyes slide easily away from them. Should he let the ladies know? Probably best not to. Trying to throw out Infinity Rose now would be more trouble than even the Point could handle. They were probably just scoping out the Line talent.

Then Ronan grabbed hold of his shoulder and Bakari spilled his drink. The thief slipped into the booth across from him and called for Molly to get a refill. "The least I can do."

Bakari glared at him, but kept his voice level. "What are you doing here?"

"I'm just as surprised to see you, my friend." His voice was chilly. "I got a message from an old… acquaintance. If I know how she works, I'm the messenger you're waiting for. Still, I thought better of you." Ronan kept his hands under the tabletop, near his weaponry no doubt. "Because if you had any idea about who you're dealing with… well, you're stupider than I thought."

Bakari could feel his anger building up in his throat, and here was the last place he wanted to release it. It would have all been so much simpler if Ronan wasn't involved; unfortunately, he hadn't any choice in that. He refrained from sharing these thoughts with the other. Instead he smoothed his face into calmness and leaned back in the booth. "It's a simple acquisition job."

"We both know that's not true," the other replied without a hint of malice, "So perhaps we should stop lying and get to the real meat of the matter?"

Bakari's mouth went suddenly dry. Molly thankfully chose that moment to appear with her tray. It was loaded with a beer for him and something smaller and more potent for Ronan, though he'd never asked for anything. He must have had regular privileges, a thing that Bakari had lost long ago.

She darted them a sharp look from under her long fringe, slid a scrap of print paper across the table to them, and then melted back to the bar.

Ronan claimed the paper before Bakari could even reach for it. The look on his face hardened as he bundled the scrap into his hand. When he straightened up and looked Bakari in the face, it was not a pleasant experience. He opened his mouth to speak and the other was not expecting the words to be any nicer.

What Bakari had not expected was for chaos to choose that moment to break lose. The rattle of gunfire smashed into the ceiling. Liners began screaming, probably as their circuits overloaded. The lights flared once, then went out.

Ronan moved as fast in the real world as Bakari did in the virtual. In a heartbeat, he'd ripped the table free of its bolts with one hand and yanked Bakari down onto the floor behind the makeshift barricade with the other.

Against the dim light cast by the luminescent floor marking the Liners were spasming shapes, hands clutched uselessly to their heads. Cursing his slow meat reactions, Bakari clawed desperately at his leg bound gun while Ronan uncoiled his with a terrifying fluidity.

He should have taken more notice of the Rosers two booths along. Bakari propped his gun over the edge of the table. Someone had set off the sprinklers, probably by Line, and through the heavy gray drops he could make out the ugly muzzle of Leia's Grunter six hundred aimed two booths behind him.

The thud and rattle of automatic gunfire bit its way through the dull concrete floor, across a couple of twitching Liners, and smacked into the edge of the steel bar. The Point was luckily not your average pub, and Leia's gun replied angrily from behind the welded and reinforced metal plates. As paint chips flew and blood began to pool across the dance floor, someone threw a mini thermal. First came the blinding, painful white flash, and then the hiss of thick smoke that burned the eyes.

Bakari swiveled his gun, disorientated but willing to find a target never the less. The yowls of outrage from Leia rose above the sound of gunfire.

"Watch out!" Ronan roared next to his ear. Suddenly Bakari found himself lifted clear of shelter and pushed into the next booth. His head spun as he crashed into the seats. Plenty of crew were enhanced, but he was no lightweight. To be able to do that so smoothly hinted at some impressive bioware.

Where they had just been, there was a light rattle, followed by a thunderous boom that blurred his vision and made his head ring. The room shook. How in the hell had Ronan known that was coming?

The two men pumped more rounds in the direction of their attackers, though on Bakari's part it was mostly guess work. He could barely see his gun, let alone his target. Ronan's weapon was pounding in a rapid fire. It was practically the only thing Bakari could hear.

A pause, and a welcome one, as his ears finally began to settle down. Ronan shot him a smile. "Got someone," he whispered fiercely.

But then a grim voice rose out of the smoke. "Panther, why don't you just give yourself up — we can discuss this."

Bakari didn't know what was going on here, yet he was absolutely sure that this lot didn't have any interest in talking. He would have said as much, when a sound cut through the sudden stillness; Molly's young voice rising in a wail. The sound of a child crying for its mother.

His teeth ground together. This was the worst bit about the sprawl. The so called collateral damage — innocent people caught in the crossfire. It happened all too often.

"Let's get out of here," he hissed to Ronan.

"Wait." Ronan tugged him back effortlessly, and just before a second rain of gunfire came. This time it was from the direction of the hallway. Reinforcements had arrived.

While Bakari pumped his remaining rounds in the direction of the original attackers, Ronan concentrated on the newcomers. It wasn't going to last long. Whoever wanted them dead was not worried about manpower.

How typical, to die in the sprawl he hated, Bakari thought to himself as he reloaded breathlessly. I don't want to die, a part of him said, not yet. Perhaps his second epiphany was today.

Then, through all the smoke and yelling and fear, something changed. A sweet scent of jasmine enveloped the booth and Ronan's gun was suddenly silent. He must have been hit.

Bakari turned to help him up and instead looked into the golden eyes of the largest black cat he'd ever seen. It was the briefest moment. His strangled breath hadn't time to even escape his chest, yet as he looked into those ageless eyes he felt pierced through. He suddenly knew how small and young he was — how little he knew. But at the same instant he felt more alive and present than he had in years.

And then the panther sprang away into the smoke. It was so beautiful, its muscles moving gracefully under its skin, barely disturbing the air with its passing. Bakari's gun fell from his fingertips. It was inconceivable. Ronan was gone and there was only the cat. All his preconceived ideas of the world dropped away and he remembered only the childhood joy of magic revealed.

All around, however, the world had not stopped. The smoke stilled and the screaming began.

Then Ronan was at his side, gathering up the weapons where they had dropped, but not looking at him. "As you say, we'd better get out of here."

He followed him; through the heavy smoke, over the bodies of assailants and innocent Liners and out into the street. He trailed behind him wordlessly, watching and thinking but saying nothing until they had reached a nameless alley not far from the Point. They stood there staring at each other with all the comfort levels of two strange tomcats meeting for the first time.

"What the hell are you?" Bakari finally spoke.

A flash of odd violet light shone in Ronan's eye. "I think you already know the answer to that question."

"You'd be wrong."

"You might not know the name, but you surely had a clue when you asked me to steal the mask for you."

God, he'd thought he was being so clever, so mysterious; using Ronan for his own well-intentioned purposes and it seemed he'd known all along. Once again Bakari felt very young. He had no other option now. Without this man's help he might as well go back to the Point and accept Infinity Rose's kind offer of a bullet. Except he wasn't a man, was he? He'd seen the evidence today.

"I just knew you were magic."

"Did you, now?" Ronan sighed and pressed his back against the cold wall. He couldn't look old but he certainly could manage weary. "You've bought yourself a lot of trouble just for a dream, my friend."

"But... you are — aren't you?"

Bakari waited, so tense he could feel every twitch of his over-excited muscles. This was the moment in which he was sure the other would walk away, taking all their chances with him.

Something apparently switched direction in Ronan. He jerked away from the wall and began smoothly reloading his weapon. "We never called it that, but I guess perhaps I used to be... once. Now I don't know what I am. I could be nothing at all."

"But the Mask," Bakari said, "You felt it too — you can't say you didn't."

"I felt something," he replied. "But I don't know what. That's why I came to the sprawl. These days, there are people more in tune with these sorts of things than I am. And now that note...."

Those eyes suddenly ceased to be human. They widened, became darker and abruptly alien. "You're working with worrying types, Bakari. And now thanks to you, so am I." He sounded very displeased, but at the same time resigned.

He wasn't giving up, then. Bakari took a deep breath and a sigh of relief escaped.

Ronan pushed his dark hair back brusquely and adjusted his holster under the leather coat. "Since we've both gone down this path, even if I didn't know it, we're pretty much stuck. Hope you're prepared for the trouble you've made, Bakari. Or perhaps that should be, Pandora."

Bakari offered his hand and grinned with more confidence than he felt. "I bet she thought it was worthwhile, letting out those terrible things for a little hope, friend."

Ronan shook his head in acceptance, but took the offered hand in a firm clasp. "Things were getting boring anyway," he said wryly.

He spun around deeper into the labyrinth of alleyways, either supremely confident that the Liner would follow, or totally indifferent.

Bakari reminded himself of that moment, that epiphany which had set him on this path. In those flames of memory he recalled the unknown predators that had begun all of this, and the precious life that had ended so that it could begin. It still didn't seem enough, but it was all he could do to give her loss meaning. Holding his head high, Bakari followed after the man that might have been the only magic left in this sorry world. Mama would have been proud.

The Folk were never swift in their demands, Aroha knew that. She'd read the books, studied the myths, so she knew how it was supposed to go. Cinderella had her time in the sun, and even Rapunzel had a little cheer — so it wasn't like she was expecting lightning to strike that very afternoon.

They all got back to Makara just fine. Simon was alright, having taken only a slight blow from the bot's concussion grenade, but from the sideways glances that Daniel was throwing her, Aroha was not sure that he completely believed his own explanation of their miraculous survival. The villagers were happy to accept that the bot had been faulty, blown its own power supply, but for anyone that had been there, it was different.

Even Sally knew it, though she'd only seen the spectacular end results of the Folk intrusion. Hanging around Aroha, she'd come to accept a certain amount of weirdness. All she'd say to those who ran to greet them was that her friend had been very brave and the bot had exploded like a firework. She basked in their incredulity.

Things settled down. Daniel sent Simon back to base in Wellington, but he stayed on. Aroha knew he was curious, but he covered it with the explanation that he might be needed in Makara.

Nana was not such a pushover. Aroha had feared that, on the long trek home. While Nana seemed to be just as happy about the whole thing out on the street corner gossiping with all the others, as soon as she got Aroha inside, things were quite different.

"You didn't speak to Them, did you now? You couldn't have done something so foolish!"

It seemed the fact she'd run away in the first place had been overridden by other concerns. She could see there was something apart from anger in Nana's eyes, and her fingers, where they rested on the kitchen bench, were tight and white.

Aroha could feel tears clench in the back of her throat and tried to think of ways to stop them flooding out her eyes. She'd told her grandmother untruths before, but she sensed now was not the time to lie. "I did," she managed to gasp out with a little hitch in her voice.

Nana turned away, looking out the window at the smooth blue sky and the endless green of the forest. Aroha rocked on her feet; left to right, right to left, hoping for words — any words, to break the silence. Nana was usually not one to keep her thoughts to herself.

"What have you done, my darling?" she finally said, though her back remained turned. "What have you brought to this place..."

"Nan," Aroha stuttered forward a few steps, but didn't quite dare to touch her, "I couldn't let them die... could I?"

A sudden rush, and she was enveloped in her grandmother's warm thin arms and the scent of lavender. "No, you couldn't."

It was all right in that embrace — in it Aroha was totally loved. But unfortunately, she'd begun to see that in the real world these things were not necessarily so.

Nana pushed her back, holding her at arm's length. It was her face that was wet, "Don't mind me — I'm just being silly. You did what you had to. Now go get your room tidied up."

It was Nana's stalwart way of diverting her granddaughter's mind; filling it with other things, mostly chores, but this time it wasn't going to work.

Aroha obeyed, trudging off to her room as instructed, but for days after she played that little scene over in her mind. Her special gifts were hardly ever discussed. Sally obviously knew something was different, but never mentioned it. Nana knew about those differences, but only ever spoke of them in passing. The inference was that they should be ignored at all costs. and were somehow bad.

Aroha was confused. She found it hard to concentrate on day to day existence, and most of all, found it almost impossible to sleep. Every time her head met her pillow, she'd feel the Folk's breath on the back of her neck and the feeling of dread would build up in her chest, making her wake with a start. She had to be quiet; the walls were thin and Nana's bed was right up against the other side. The slightest noise and Aroha would have to explain herself.

This happened every night for nearly a week, until at last the feeling solidified into something far more concrete and far more frightening.

It had been a hard day, quiet but filled with dire portents. The sky was the colour of blood in the morning and the birds were silent in the trees. Aroha went around all day feeling like something was going to blow, with her neck itching and her nerves taunt. The warm wood cocoon of her little bedroom offered little relief after the day's strangeness.

Nana had propped open the window before shutting the door, and the breeze from off the mountains tickled Aroha's skin. No sound came from the forest. Were they ready to demand the price from her? Or had she perhaps offended them in some way? The wind gave no hint, and Aroha descended into sleep to the memory of their singing, and of long pale fingers brushing her temple.

The dreams, though, were not as sweet — a chaotic swirl of anger and sadness that threatened to drown any soul. The wounded earth was crying, reaching out unhappily for its lost self. In the myth of this land, the earth mother Papatuanuku had been wrenched away from her lover Rangi, the sky father, by their children, the gods of life. Aroha could hear the earth and the sky's anguish — it was almost unbearable; cries of such terrible loss that could wound a soul.

She awoke panting in the dark, not sure what had released her from the dreams' embrace. The wind from the hills had gone, replaced by a heavy stillness. Nothing, not even the old creaky house, made a sound. The blankets felt like lead and the air was too thick to breathe. Her chest was quiet, frozen in a between moment where life and death were both in equal amounts. Stuck in that amber moment, like one of those insects Nana had told her about, Aroha waited for the world to start again.

It released her a moment before chaos. Her feet were on the floor, running, before her brain had even fully woken. She pelted out of her bedroom and along the darkened corridor, even as the earth began to heave. The house was now shivering to the accompaniment of china falling and cupboards rattling. The sheer strangeness of the unmoving suddenly given life was more than enough to make her heart race. But Aroha kept running; bumping against the walls, dodging falling pictures. She made it to the kitchen and tumbled through the door onto the rumbling ground, still wet with dew.

The shrieks of alarmed villagers and the call of frightened sheep was the earth's orchestra. The houses all groaned and the wire and picket fences rattled. The very world itself seemed to tilt.

Aroha could feel the pain of the Mother as she buried her fingers in the wet soil; an immortal torment not meant for people to hear.

Papatuanuku, she whispered. *Great Mother,* just as the Forest People had taught her. A low hum was in the back of her throat; a call to stillness, a reminder that Papa's children needed her to be calm. *Do not destroy us, Papatuanuku.* And far away up the mountain she knew the long pale fingers of the Folk did the same, their silk soft voices repeating her call in their own mysterious language.

The world was turning and spinning on this moment. Papatuanuku could rise up and shake them all from her, as a person might rid themselves of ants at a picnic. Aroha squeezed her eyes shut and tried not to see that image before her, instead trying tried to think how much the earth should love her children — even if they were spoilt and ignorant.

But Papatuanuku listened; to the humming of the Forest People and to the whispering of one frightened daughter. The earth stilled her swaying and held her peace once more, though the pain within her had not eased at all.

Nana found Aroha lying splayed on the cool earth, fingers grubby, salty tears drying on her cheeks. Wordlessly she gathered her up very easily, even though her granddaughter was no longer small. Nestled against her warmth, smelling the lavender and rose scent she always seemed to wear, Aroha came to herself again, melting back into a skin that had for a moment not really seemed to be her own.

This was not normal. After all, Sally couldn't see the people in the forest, couldn't understand the shifting of the earth. She had it easy. Aroha half sighed and half sniffled, burrowing closer to Nana as she carried her back into the house. She'd not mentioned this to anyone — not a soul, and that was better. No one would look at her strangely; inherently, she knew her life depended on that. So she wrapped her arms around Nana and let her eyes drift shut.

It was a reminder, a forceful one at that — she belonged to the Folk and their power. The earth herself needed something, and she was a wielder of power in this time when few even acknowledged it. The Folk wouldn't forget her promise to them. The time of payment was now due — they had quite literally shaken her awake. With the sun, there would be a summoning and a price to pay.

Still, those she loved were safe and, until morning at least, she remained just a child.

CHAPTER EIGHT

Ravenous

When the cool spring evening finally wrapped itself around the village, the Seed awoke once more. It had not fed in days. Though the hunger burned, intelligence told it that the time was not right to hunt its enemies. For now it must seek other, less powerful prey. Luckily, this was their night and there would be opportunities to feast.

A coal-eyed badger stirred in her den as it passed by. Its tread was so light that not even the dead leaves rustled. The she-badger grunted fearfully while working herself deeper into her den.

Circling the woods behind the Hall, the monster felt tentatively with its other senses and sampled the ether for its enemies. A sudden surge of power reached it, and it knew they were now drawing together. This is itself suited the purposes of its master, but there was a fine line to be drawn. While the enemies were needed, it would not do to alert them to its presence just yet.

The pooka had almost caught sight of the Seed. If he had, there would have been a battle. His arrival was the greatest risk. It would have been good to eliminate him, but the time was not yet ripe.

"Soon." It hissed the promise to itself and the night drew colder.

The sharp retort of a raven's cry made the Seed hunker down into the earth once more. Fear washed over it, but it was simply a mortal bird startled from its sleep.

The raven peered down out of its nighttime perch and they eyed each other warily. Macha, the Dark Goddess' companion, would have been death for the Seed, alone and drained as it was. Luckily, this was not her.

Rising up on its hind legs, it hissed venomously at the raven. Like all mortal things, it knew danger well enough. With a snap of its wings, it flew off to another perch. Satisfied, the Seed settled down once more to wait.

Silver slices of moonlight broke through the trees and were chased by a few dark clouds. Hush had descended on the forest. The Seed lay very flat in the leaf litter; a bunch of tangled roots barely discernable in the shadows. No breath or sound gave its position away. It was the perfect ambush.

From its position on the slight rise, the Seed could see all the way down into the curve of oaks which were its target. Velvet topped mushrooms had made their home here and were nestled around vague bulges in the earth.

These protuberances were not even enough to make a human take notice unless perhaps they stubbed a toe against them. The Seed knew and saw more than they ever could. This had once been a place of worship and a place of summoning. Now it was merely one of the places of power that surrounded Penherem. The animals could feel it, and most importantly, so could the prey that the Seed was waiting for so patiently.

It didn't take long. The bright silvered moon and the whispering of the dying leaves called to them like a siren's song. Yet they had learned to be cautious. The mortal world was not as safe for them as it had once been.

They were the smallest of the Fey, barely tall enough to be seen by mortal eyes. Ever so gently, they stepped onto the earth and made no sound. Their bodies, slight and subtle things, were just held together by faint magic. Under the moon's grace they gave a soft glow.

They drifted by, very close to the Seed, so close that they almost brushed against one of its splayed limbs. It did not rise up — not yet. The moment could be sweeter still.

The Mother's Children were bolder now, seeing nothing but the moon and the forest.

Finally sure that nothing mortal lingered nearby, the sprites gave up silence. Voices of light and beauty like a thousand tiny chimes were raised in praise of the moon. They called down the ancient and powerful Mother; begging her to ring the village with her power. They scampered up the ancient oaks and raised their arms in supplication.

It was a little ritual, begun by little creatures, but it was a beginning. The Seed did not suppose that such a thing had been done in this realm for more than five hundred years.

A flood of its Master's rage and loathing smothered those thoughts. The sprites would be the ones to fail, not it.

They leapt and spun in the air, trailing silver light, weaving minor spells into this world with voice and body. It was a beginning — a beginning that the Seed could not allow to flourish.

Finally exploding out of the leaves, muscle and anger drove it swiftly among the sprites. They were such tiny things that there was barely anything for it to destroy. One snap of its mandibles, and many screamed and died. They were not fast enough, and moth wings were not going to carry them free — not when the Seed was among them. They died quickly but not easily. Their killer was cruel enough to let them live a heartbeat; long enough to realise how they'd failed.

Even when dead, there were still magics in them. The Seed swallowed, and power filled the empty crevices inside its head. The sprites might have been small, but their Art would sustain the Seed for a long while yet. As always, the Master's design was perfect economy.

Revived, it could now send its senses down the hill towards the village. More sprites and touches of magic were revealed, but stronger still was the taste of the pooka. The Seed had a particular hatred of that one. Its Master recalled great humiliation at his hand. Filled with power, it contemplated action.

Tempting as it was to grind the shapeshifter to dust, the Master's will was stronger. The way had to be secured; there was no more important matter.

Turning on its clawed feet, the Seed left the trammeled earth and turned towards the Hall.

Edmond Claremont was drunk even before he got home. As he rode his tractor back to the farmhouse, he slipped the silver hipflask out and drowned the last of the whiskey in almost one hit. He wasn't a very good drunk — people had told him as much. But it made his prison easier to bear.

As he looked out blankly at the growing dusk, Edmond could remember when the farm had been a beautiful place; full of dandelion fairies, chirping birds and the sound of laughter. That had all ceased with the end of his childhood, and now those days were just a bitter memory to trouble his sleep.

"Sleep!" He choked on a laugh — like he knew what that was anymore. The farm was royally buggered, as his father would have said. Penherem was more of a joke than ever. It was still the fat arsed shopkeepers that made the money, not a rundown family farm that hadn't been able to afford decent equipment in living memory.

Edmond raised the hipflask to his lips once more in the vain hope he'd missed something inside. He hadn't.

If only he could have got away, but everything had been against the only child of a rough-handed, bad-tempered farmer. The farm had become a prison, and before long they'd probably lay him in the cold earth of St Michael's, right next to the father who'd done the same before him. Edmond almost looked forward to that. It had to be better than this.

The tractor bumped and juddered its arthritic way down the hill. The farmhouse lights were out, except for one in the family room. Good, Jayne remembered what he'd said last time about wasting electricity, though she'd probably burnt his dinner again.

It was just something she couldn't get the hang of. What could you expect from a sprawl dweller who'd bought all her food in packets before marriage? Edmond's lips twisted. She'd been here for years, yet never seemed to make an effort, with the house, the food, or friends. She hardly ever bothered going into Penherem now.

After parking the tractor with a lurch in the tattered barn, Edmond stomped towards the house. His fingers compulsively rubbed the edge of the hipflask in his pocket. The first thing he did once inside was trip over Aaron's toy truck, left lying in wait for him. He swore and fell against the wall with a loud thump. But no query came from the family room, no 'are you all right?' Typical.

Jayne hadn't even bothered to come to Hamish's funeral and, he thought bitterly, she would probably do the same when he was pushing up the daisies. Maybe she thought he'd smashed his head and was waiting for him to bleed to death. Edmond grunted. "Yeah that'd be right!"

With a savage kick he sent the toy truck careening down the hallway to thump into the door. Only then did there come an involuntary squeak of alarm from behind it.

He needed another drink, so he turned into the darkened parlor where, like his father before him, he kept the booze. There was still enough light coming through the window for him to find his way to the cabinet without further injury. He unscrewed the sherry, which was all that was left, and drank it straight from the bottle.

Hamish and Robert had been lucky. They'd been born only a few years before their father died. They'd never had to hear that great voice booming down the hallway, never had to hear what failures they were. Lucky bastards, he thought savagely, even though Hamish was now dead. Perhaps that made him even more worthy of Edmond's jealousy.

He spun around and looked morosely out the window. You could see the lights of Penherem from here, but you might as well be a million miles away. No one ever came up to the farm. Ever since his father's, time the villagers had kept away.

The old house reeled, or at least that's how it felt to Edmund. The sound coming from the kitchen made his head throb and his hand clench on the sherry bottle. Alice was shrieking with laughter and the hallway pulsed with childish giggling. Somewhere down the hall, her brother had done something foolish — he'd probably broken something, knowing him. And then Jayne's voice came in a hushed murmur and that somehow was worse than that damn laughter. He could see her just like she was standing in front of him; eyes down cast, head bobbing up and down on her neck, fussing.

That was it! Edmond slammed the bottle down, sloshing the sweet smelling liquid on his fist. He was going to go down there and show them who the man of this house was; who was in control. He'd almost made it to the door when the bear woke up.

Alice hadn't named the ratty old creature she'd found in the attic three years ago, but she always carried it round. So it was strange to see the teddy sitting right next to the doorway. Edmond was sure it hadn't been there when he came in. Perhaps that's what made him pause for a second.

The bear hadn't been his, though he could imagine the quiet Robert with it. Still, what was it doing down here?

He made to kick it across the hallway. But there came a shift in the air; a kind of heat accompanied by a sweet smell like the roses his long dead mother had once grown at the back door. And the bear was no longer a bear, or at least not the type that his brothers had played with. It was suddenly taller, much taller than Edmond himself, standing on its rear legs with its mouth half open. The shiny brass eyes were now green and glaring down at him. That strange heat was now as strong as a blazing summer sun.

Edmond staggered back a couple of feet. The bottle dropped out of his numb fingers while his eyes remained locked on the bear's dark curved claws, as wicked looking as a pair of hay forks. That was death, right there. He didn't need to ask its name — there was oblivion waiting to suck him down.

Perhaps he was mad, or maybe it was the booze, or maybe he was about to get what he deserved, but the bear's expression somehow seemed to alter. The shocking green eyes lost their look of vengeance, and then the creature spoke. Its voice was soft, much too soft for such a large creature, but it did not alter the power of its message.

Edmond, poor boy, look at what he's made you.

The bear's head turned to the sideboard mirror and Edmond, following its gaze, looked into it as well. It felt like the first time since childhood since he'd really examined himself, and he didn't like what he saw. The face he'd somehow thought of as jovial, was a lie. What stared back at him was grey-blue and black with hatred. It was the face of a monster, but with eyes that were sad and frightened; the same eyes as his mother's.

A strangled sob erupted from his throat

He's made you hate yourself. And the bear's voice was deeply sorrowful, as if he'd seen something beautiful crushed.

A sound came from down the hall, Alice's own muffled cry. She was afraid of her father, even as young as she was. Edmond could remember being that scared, while his mother cowered in that same kitchen, trying to protect them. What would she have thought of her son now?

Edmond clawed at his face, watching in the mirror as he tried to rip that hateful expression away. "No! God, what do I do? What can I do?!"

The bear was closer now and the scent was utterly un-bearlike. It smelt of roses and warm bread and a mother's love. Edmond felt himself crying uncontrollably.

You go. The bear said. *You go and find if your heart is still alive and if the boy your mother adored is still redeemable. If he is, you come back and spend your life showing that to them.*

Edmond stood there looking at the bear. He saw no judgment in those mint green eyes, only deep sorrow and perhaps just a little hope. Something hardened in Edmond; a resolve, a chance that he never realised he had. He'd walk to Penherem and take the first VFT to his cousin's in York. Sara remembered that boy and she might know how to reach him.

While the bear watched, he wrote down a quick note, which seemed to contain a lot of apologies. Then with a nod to the creature and a sigh of relief, he left the house he'd been born into.

The bear watched him go. After the man was out of sight, he dropped his terrible form. The child's toy became just that, and the little brown figure stepped out behind it.

He was a Robin, a Goodfellow, often confused with that far more mischievous and powerful Fey, Puck. This particular Robin took a deep breath into his little lungs and looked about the house which had been his home long before Edmond Claremont had been alive. There had been Thatchers and Millers and a young Norman called Clare du Mont on this patch of land before he'd been forced to leave.

The Robin's long nose twitched. It felt good to be home and to have humans once more in his care. What had happened to young Edmond would not have been allowed in any house a Robin lived in, and he could only hope that he had shown him the right path.

For his wife and children, he was sure he had done the right thing. Terror had no place in a family. The Robin dusted off his little brown jacket. It might take a while to train the woman to put a little saucer of milk out, but the children would soon catch on — they always did. Right now, it was time for him to get to work.

Five hundred years might just never have happened.

CHAPTER NINE
Divination

It was not going to be a good day. Ella woke feeling as though she'd run a marathon, sweaty and exhausted. The dream she'd had was a jumble of jarring images, one where wings and swords had seemed to be full of dire portents. So when she staggered out of bed finally, it was made even less cheerful by the message flashing on her HouseTalk monitor.

Ella thumbed the replay button and frowned to find the visual had been withheld. It didn't matter, she recognized Doyle's voice in a split second and her heart sank predictably. First, there was the question of how he'd found her number, and then came the question she'd often asked herself: what exactly did she feel for the man after all this time?

Doyle, both real and virtual, was oblivious to the effect he had on her life. The message told her that immediately, for there was no flicker of concern for how she'd been in the nearly eleven months since he'd last seen her — no, it was straight to business.

As he spoke, she could imagine him smiling that familiar guileless smile. "El — we need to catch up."

Ella turned away while the message played, stroked Qoth, put on her dressing gown and pretended he could say what he liked.

"There's people asking about you — the sort of people you might not want to meet in a dark alley, you know. You better call me back, or I'll have to come see you in the meatworld."

It was typical of Doyle to fake Liner terms. He'd always fancied himself as one, though never had the courage to get the gear installed. Still, he knew how to make a threat sound flippant.

"Oh, Qoth," Ella scooped up the cat and pressed her face into the thick brown fur. The warm cat scent was soothing somehow. Behind her eyelids flashed images of Doyle in Penherem. The villagers would never look at her the same way again.

"Why can't he leave me alone?" she asked Qoth fiercely.

The delicate little mouth opened in a yawn, all pink gums and sharp white teeth, but if the cat recalled the 'he' in question she offered no opinion.

Ella already had the answer; if Doyle was interested in her it meant there was money involved. He'd been rebuffed by her once. He'd spent months screwing anything female that crossed his path, slept with Ella while her vulnerability was still fresh and then had the nerve to claim he wanted to 'be her friend'.

That had been a sweet moment. From somewhere still unknown, Ella had found the strength to reply. "Be your friend? To be my friend I have to at least like you, and I don't — so no, that's not going to happen." She still savored the surprised look on his face.

Perhaps the best thing was that, finally and completely, it had been true. Doyle had looked in her face and, seeing not even anger there, known it. He'd gone after that. She was left to pick up the pieces of her self respect and start a new life.

Ella went and took a long hot shower, got dressed in something a little nicer than her usual house clothes and prepared herself to find out why Doyle had crawled back into her life. It meant going back to the sprawl and that stirred up old emotions, yet she'd discovered her bravery in Penherem.

Ronan remained silent. It took all his concentration to count how many people in all his years in this world had figured him out. It couldn't be more than half a dozen. Not bad for nearly six hundred years, he supposed.

Many thought him odd or unusual. Yet there were odd and unusual people too — some even stranger to the human eye than he. He'd grown used to blending in with humans. It made the current situation even more distressing.

Glancing back, he checked to see if Bakari had given up yet; but despite the grueling pace he set through the back streets of the sprawl, the Liner was still dogging his heels. Dull rain had begun to fall on his hair and splatter onto those pitch-black shades. Perhaps Bakari thought that they afforded some protection from Ronan's regard.

The other grinned; he'd never had to rely on mere human senses. The scent rolling off his companion proclaimed his nervousness — which was good. Ronan didn't like it when people came out of a firefight as if nothing had happened.

Greer had set Ronan and the Liner up, probably to boast of her cleverness, but the explosion of violence must have put her off. Still, she was the only one who might know what was happening with this mask.

And he knew where she'd retreat to. The Greenhouse was not a place he'd wanted to revisit. In fact, the last time he'd seen Greer she had goaded him about that. "Afraid of a little greenery, mighty Ronan?"

He wouldn't put it past her to have instigated the whole mess just to get him there — she was that manipulative. It was very familiar. Her web of intrigue seemed to have caught him once again.

Greer was not the person she'd once been, but she still had more magic than even Ronan had left. She'd sacrificed a lot of herself in order to gain it: mostly her humanity but also her sight. Even now, the thought of her lost emerald eyes gave him pain. It was she who had almost convinced Ronan that humans were beyond hope. Luckily, he'd pulled back from her all-too-easy solutions and found his love of people again. Yet now, here he was walking those same muddy, sullen paths back to her door.

Ronan morosely sloshed his boots through the puddles and heard Bakari's breathing change. That slight hesitation meant he was about to do one of only two things humanity was good at. Ronan clenched his teeth but the Liner did it anyway.

He asked a question.

"So what happens to the gun and stuff when you change?" Obviously the Liner's logical mind had been whirring away as they walked. He pulled up close to Ronan's elbow.

How typical! It was always the same. Everything had to conform to some rule or other. Even with something as impossible to fathom as magic, people insisted on tying it down to rules and measurements. Sometimes Ronan wondered if it wasn't because their tiny little heads would explode if they didn't. What words could he possibly use to explain to Bakari what he was? How could he make him understand what it was to *be* magic, rather than constricted by any physical laws? Humanity was so obsessed with understanding that they insisted everything have a rule; something to be measured, something that could be replicated.

Ronan sighed and shook his head. Even the fairytales and myths were gone in this age, they had no meaning anymore and their absence left the men both struggling to find common understanding. Once he could have just *been*, and humans would have understood instinctively, but now their realm and his were as far apart as they had ever been. They had no common language anymore.

"We're here." Ronan looked dismally at the dripping silent wall that completed the alleyway.

"Here where?" His companion's voice now held something like irritation.

"For someone who is in Greer's back pocket, you certainly aren't showing much recognition of her home."

Bakari gave him such a blank look that Ronan knew he wasn't faking. He had no idea that it was Greer who had set up the whole thing. It couldn't be helped. Ronan viewed humans as children. He knew it was a fault of his, but even after so long in this world their ways still reminded him of blundering toddlers.

Nor could he help a laugh escaping. "I guess my contacts are a little better than yours, my friend. You are, in fact, just about to meet the person that hired you to hire me in the first place."

Bakari hid his annoyance pretty well for someone who spent most of his life on the Line. "In my world," he replied a little stiffly, "the real names are the ones you use on the Line."

Perhaps Bakari deserved Greer after all. Yet then again, once upon a time, he had as well.

With a sigh, Ronan flicked out his hand and gained them both entry into the witch's chamber. The palm scanner looked much like any other brick in the wall, but the childlike flower drawn on it was a clue. The docile machine contained within examined his print and a few seconds later Greer's voice seemed to float around them.

"You're slower than usual." Her voice was, as always, ice cold.

But then, his own was not much friendlier. "We have a lot to discuss. Why don't you just let us in and forget the cheap shots." With Greer it was always a dice roll. Even if she had set this whole sorry mess up, there was still a chance she could throw it all away in a fit of pique. It came with the psychopathic territory.

"I saw the mask," he added for good measure. "And I recognized the face."

She didn't reply, but the wall before them cast off its holographic skin, revealing a steel grey door with no handle. It slid aside to reveal an equally neutral corridor.

He very much didn't want to go in there — not just for the sake of his pride, either. Greer was one of the few people who could scare him. Beside him, Bakari's chin was hitting the pavement and Ronan could relate. It was certainly not the average sprawl alleyway, but Greer was not the average sprawl dweller.

Against his better instincts, Ronan stepped forward and into her domain. Bakari followed after — thankfully without asking questions. The corridor dropped steadily and steeply away and as they followed it down every step it became warmer and wetter. Greer and her charges liked it that way. It made Ronan's skin crawl.

The corridor ended finally, opening into what seemed to be a wide room. There was nothing to see of either wall or roof, for everything was covered with foliage. Everything green and vigorous was Greer's friend, perhaps because it was the very antitheses of what lay outside. Some might have found such luxuriant growth comforting, but to Ronan it was just disturbing.

A thick vine covered in garish red flowers brushed against his cheek and he flicked it away with the same enjoyment he might have felt had it been a poisonous snake.

"This is some garden," Bakari whispered, perhaps mistaken into thinking he was someplace holy. It didn't seem to affect him in quite the same way it did his companion; likely he only saw the beauty and not the beast.

"It seems your friend is more appreciative than you are, Ronan." Greer emerged out a stand of dark, club-leafed plants. She'd gotten thinner and cut her thick blonde curls to within an inch of her scalp — it didn't suit her; neither did the sewn-over eyelids which hid the caverns where once her brilliant eyes had been.

Bakari was smart enough not to say anything. He stood poised lightly between them, looking to Ronan for advice, but just as prepared to go the other way. He must have sensed the primal forces his companion and Greer represented.

The woman cocked her head, eerily mimicking what in others would have been an appraising look. "I chose well." He might have been one of her ill begotten seedlings for all the emotion in her voice.

"Don't you ever get sick of using people?" Ronan asked easily, while his eyes scanned the jungle about her; he wasn't about to count on his previous relationship with Greer for her good behavior.

Greer's lips imitated a smile. "Are you going to bring up that old chestnut again? We've got different ways of looking at things — that's all."

"Yes, I happen to think humans are more than just tools."

Greer raised her hand sharply and turned her sightless head away from him. "Enough. I didn't bring you here for this."

"Then why'd you do this at all?" Bakari's face, usually dark and calm, was almost flushed, "If you knew him — why'd you simply not get him to steal the mask for you?"

"Does he look like he'd do me any favors?"

Bakari chewed the inside of his lip and eyed the two of them, as if uncertain which one was worse.

Sensing she was losing him, Greer switched from vinegar to sugar. She walked confidently forward, hands stretched out a little. "Forgive my lying. I was afraid he'd sense if I told you the truth. We're both looking for the same thing." Even lacking her lustrous green eyes, Greer could still be charming when she thought she needed to be.

"I doubt you are, somehow," Ronan interrupted, not wanting her to sway the vulnerable Liner. "She wants power, Bakari, power from magic. Despite being a complete fool about all this — I don't think you are that selfish. You've got better reasons I hope."

Bakari's eyes were burning bright with the memory of something that Ronan could almost see. "I want magic again. I want there to be something else in this world apart from metal and death and pain."

Ronan had heard a similar cry from a thousand throats through hundreds of years; it still made him ache.

"I don't want there to be nothing else but reality in this world," Bakari's hands were clenched almost white now. "I want to make her hopes real." The memory sprung from him, so hot and painful that Ronan could at last see the beautiful old woman who had been the birth of it. Her agonizing death by fire, in a high-rise no landlord cared about, had been more reality than any young child should bear. Bakari had retreated into longing for a taste of that magic she'd fed him on.

Ronan's heart ached. Even though he'd barely known his mother, he was familiar with loss. He'd done things himself out of pain and despair. But nothing like this: nothing that could change the lives of millions.

Greer was ignorant of all this. Even if her little magics had allowed her to see, her heartless cold nature would not have understood at all.

Ronan let his tears dry against his skin. He was not afraid to show emotions; he had other weaknesses, but that was not one of them.

Greer's head tilted; perhaps she sensed something passing between the men. Her lip curled. "We all have hopes, Bakari — but only a few are strong enough to make them real."

Her sharp words cut the delicate moment in two.

"If this is your big power play, Greer, I think you were the one who chose badly. It isn't the kind of power you can use." Ronan had spent the previous night searching the musty archives of the British Library — they detailed many things the Line Mags found of little interest.

One had been the discovery of the Winter Mask, as they called it. A lot of things were dug up in Britain every year and its discovery had not raised many eyebrows. It was perhaps part of the mask's magic; part of that old magic Ronan knew as Art. It hadn't wanted to be found.

He looked at Greer and despite her lack of sight, she could feel his contempt.

Ronan couldn't have been positive, but something dark and excited seemed to move in the jungle just in the corner of his eye. He held his breath, recalling the nightmare she'd summoned at their last encounter and not wanting to visit that situation again. He looked away as conscientiously as possible; it was the only way to see Greer's Art. But even anger was hard for this consummate ice princess to manage.

Her fingers wrapped around his arm with strength her body could not possibly possess. "The world needs the magic — the Mask can bring it about."

Ronan shook his head: there was no purpose in hoping.

"But you felt it, Ronan," Bakari with his calm assertion and brimming belief reminded him of that moment, the taste of what he'd thought lost.

"I did. It was... just the same as I remember." Despite himself, his heart had strangely begun beating very fast.

Greer was pacing now, brushing impatiently at the leaves that stood in her way. "There is so little real magic left in this world. Perhaps we are all there is," a somewhat disgusted look in Ronan's direction. "Yet when we get chance to set things right, you won't!"

"Bring back the magic — I knew it!" Bakari's lips curved up in a triumphant smile.

Ronan had to grin; he would have never imagined that a Liner would want to have anything to do with the wild tides of magic, and yet it seemed that this one had set out to deliberately lure him to Little Penherem. The thought should have rankled him more than it did, but it pleased him in an odd way to see that humanity still had some surprises.

Still, it was a nice irony that it was not Greer who had succeeded. She'd spent years of their time together trying to think of ways to use Ronan's powers for her own purposes. At first very subtly, but with increasing anger and frustration as subtlety had failed. He'd tried explaining to her the futility of her attempts, tried to tell her that his home was now so very far away from here that there was no chance of that happening — but those arguments had eventually led to the scuffle. Thinking on it refreshed his nervousness, and this time he knew that the plant life around her was definitely rustling.

"You could waken more than my world, you know," Ronan said. "Not everything is as pleasant and attractive as I am."

Bakari was chewing the inside of his cheek, looking very young to the shapeshifter's old eyes. "But it's still worth the risk..."

"Magic, as you call it, isn't all fluffy unicorns and chirpy sprites — there are just as many dark creatures which would be attracted to the light," Ronan shot Greer a hard look. "You wouldn't want to be responsible for that." Her face was as sealed and remote as the mask had been, for she was already lost in a torrent of her own plans. "There is something missing — like any great spell, the right people, the right time and the right objects must be present. Obviously, we are missing something."

"Yes," Greer's ruined head nodded. "Yes, I must look, examine, find the path."

He was lost then. Ronan felt a deep weariness set into him, for she had finally got her way — he was hooked by the Winter Mask. He'd tasted the tiniest slip of his home and could no longer walk away.

Greer was smiling now, as gentle as he'd ever seen her. "We will find you a place to rest while I search for the path." The greenery around her relaxed, shuffled back into normal fauna: its mistress had other uses for her power now.

Ronan took Bakari by the shoulder and turned him to the rear of the greenhouse where, from memory, the bedroom was. "You don't want to see her in action. Believe me, it's better if we get what sleep we can."

Greer had already erased them from her consideration. Instead, her slim form cut through the deepest parts of the jungle where she kept her darkest secrets. Ronan was too tired to argue and too angry to say more. Sleep was, for now, easier.

When Greer next intruded, it was morning. Ronan levered himself off the ground, feeling the usual effects of spending too long in her domain; his throat was thick and his head was clouded. The sooner they got out of here, the better. He found Greer where they had left her, shrouded in thick fronds, but beaded with sweat as if she'd been running.

Greer's face, even without eyes, was folded with puzzlement and she seemed to sway in her place. "The way is still not clear," she said finally, "but I sense that it begins with a woman. I felt a strange and strong presence of a woman near to both of you."

Bakari got up from the ground and took a while to shake out the coat he had used as makeshift bedding. "There's only two women I'd call close in Penherem — Ella and Tania."

"You're sure this is the beginning?" Ronan would not have trusted Greer, but for his own intimate knowledge of how much she wanted this.

"You have already begun, my Fey darling." Her smile was only an imitation of ones she had once worn for him.

He gestured curtly to Bakari that now was the time to leave, but couldn't resist turning back to her. "You could come with us, Greer..."

Her flinch was so tiny that only Ronan could have possibly seen it. "You know that is impossible — but if you succeed, I may well walk with you again."

A little pain, a little remembrance made him pause. "Once that would have been grand, Greer, but even if we were to meet in my home, I would not hold your hand — not anymore."

The two men left. If there was any remorse on her face, Ronan did not turn back to find it.

CHAPTER TEN

Regret

There was to be no more lying. When Aroha woke, she knew that if she was to do as the Earth mother and the Folk had asked, it had to be done purely and without any deception. So when she went into the kitchen the next morning she told Nana exactly what she had to do.

"Go to Wellington?" Her guardian's voice broke with surprise.

She nodded. "Alone."

"You'll certainly do no such thing," Nana's lips folded in tight. "The best bits are locked down by the army and the worst," she shuddered. "It's far too dangerous."

A little piece of Aroha's confidence chipped off, but she recalled the promise and the need she'd felt in the spirit last night. It wasn't as if she was any eleven year old going off by herself, Nana might like to pretend she thought that was all she was — but it wasn't so.

"Oh, my dearest," Nana hugged her close, enveloping Aroha in lavender and fear in equal measure. "Why are you trying to grow up so quickly?"

"I've got no choice." Aroha pushed back a little and tried to look brave.

A moment, a hard look, but Nana nodded. "Being what you are means you are held to a much higher standard."

Aroha nodded. "You told me that."

Nana's shoulders slumped and she suddenly seemed tiny and frail. Was she going to cry?

Both of them jumped when the knock of the door broke the silence. Nana straightened, summoning the courage to answer. When she opened the door to Daniel, she might have been in any other day.

But the young soldier's calm face did not seem fooled. He dropped his fully loaded pack on the top of the doorstep and smiled uncertainly. "Do you know why I'm here?"

The Folk were, it seemed, not totally heartless. Aroha edged her way past Nana, meeting his blue gaze steadily. "You're here to take me to Wellington."

In the corner of one eye she saw Nana give a little shudder.

Daniel's brow furrowed, "I know it sounds odd, but…"

"You had a dream," Nana took his arm and guided him into the kitchen. "Don't get worried, it usually happens like that. Cup of tea?"

He accepted gratefully and, rather uncertainly, took a seat at the table. "It's not usual procedure for me, though."

"I dare say not," Nana was better at offering advice than taking it. She put the mug of tea into his hand and watched, amused, as he took several spoonfuls of sugar. "Not army protocol at all." She peered into his face.

Aroha had already seen it — the glimmer of magic in his eye. Perhaps he had a touch of the Folk in his family past.

He blushed a little under such close inspection, "I had an aunt who said she was psychic — the rest of the family just laughed at her. But after last night… and then this morning, I just knew I had to pack up and get over here."

"Hmm," Nana nodded. "Once you feel it yourself — you know there's a whole different world out there. It can be very frightening." She shot a glance across the room at Aroha, who was trying very hard to be very small. "But my granddaughter has a way of changing things for everyone — especially herself."

Daniel couldn't possibly understand the currents that flowed about him, but he sensed them. With a slight cough he found his way onto slightly better known ground. "So, she needs to get to Wellington. That shouldn't be difficult."

It was perhaps a day's tramp to the city. Once it had only been half an hour in the car, but the roads, though broken now, were not the greatest danger. Law was a fragmented thing in this current climate, and those who had once lurked in the shadows now strode in the daylight. Even an armed escort was no guarantee.

"But what happens then?" The soldier's eyes darted between them.

Nana's pursed her lips and waited for her granddaughter to answer.

Aroha felt her heart flutter in her chest, like the first time she'd jumped from the swing rope into the creek. The Folk had not said what had to be done. They didn't like to come close to humans, let alone tell them what to do. She only knew that she had to get to the capital.

If only she could crawl back into her bed and pretend that all the day held was weeding the garden for Nana and perhaps podding some more peas. A ragged little sigh escaped her, and only Nana's firm hand suddenly on her shoulder prevented tears.

"It'll be all right," her voice soothed. "Wellington used to be such a bonnie city — such wonderful place."

Aroha had never even seen it.

Daniel tried to smile reassuringly. "Te Whanganui a Tara— yes, a beautiful place."

But if there was one thing Aroha knew, it was that beauty could be dangerous. Her first sight of the Folk had told her that. A dry throat took away her speech.

Penherem had gone thoroughly mad since Hamish's death. It might not be apparent to the casual observer, but Ella was attuned to the pulse of the village; the hurried sounds of footsteps outside her gate, the harsh edge to gossip at the street corner, all said that the peace which once made the village so precious was gone. It made it her nervous and edgy, which combined with the conversation with Doyle into an explosive mix.

Qoth watched Ella pack that morning, the unusual event attracting the cat's attention. Ella rummaged around in the dark recesses of her wardrobe and found the large plastic bag she'd hoped never to see again.

She tipped the contents out onto her bed, her brow furrowed in concentration; ripped jeans, well worn boots, the ugly profile of a gun and the tumble of silvered fabric which was worth more than the contents of her house.

Ella picked up the shiver cloak and the coolness on her fingertips told her that it was still working. It had not really been that long — only a few months since she'd worn this. Pushing away any lingering memories Ella put it on quickly and tugged the long hood over her head and face. In the mirror it looked ridiculous, really, like some cheap Halloween costume. But once her hand was in the control glove, she could access the functions. It all came back to Ella far too easily; stillness allowed the photosensitive cloth to blend in with the background and its steady matching of heat with the ambient temperature meant even with an infrared camera there would be nothing to see.

Horrified at the memories it stirred, she tore it off and dumped it onto the bed as if it were a poisonous spider. It had been Doyle's first gift to her — not without strings, to be sure.

It remained a great tragedy to her that the very first memory she had was his face. A hard lump was forming in her throat, but for once Ella couldn't ignore reality. Qoth strolled over and sat himself down in the middle of the shiver cloak to lick her paw. Despite herself, Ella laughed.

If she'd ever had a family, she couldn't remember them; it was as if she'd never had a past before Doyle. It gave him a horrible hold over her, despite everything. All there was in her memory was a time when she'd felt wrong and dirty and lost. She'd been a good member of Doyle's crew, the best thief they'd ever had — but unlike all the rest, she'd actually managed to get away from that life.

Depending on herself to still possess some of that strength, Ella quickly dressed in her old gear, stuffed the cloak into her leather backpack and left before she could analyze the situation any more. Walking quickly to the VFT, she got on without thinking when it zipped to a halt at the station. She spent the half hour it took to reach London staring at herself in the window, practicing keeping her face calm and her eyes hard.

She got off at Victoria, still able to remember exactly how to find him. Yet she paused in the muddled chaos of the station, feeling the energies of so many people buzzing around her.

Penherem was very far away. Ella was suddenly terrified that she wasn't strong enough for all this. For sure, this time she wouldn't have the strength.

"Ella?" She nearly yelped when a firm hand grasped her elbow.

"My god, Bakari!" She wasn't sure just who she'd thought it was, but it was still a relief to see the librarian smiling at her. Then Ronan emerged at his shoulder and she felt suddenly very dim indeed.

Bakari looked troubled, and she hoped it wasn't to do with her. "I thought you hated the city worse than me, Mouse. What are you doing here?"

Once upon a time, lies had come easily to her, but seemingly Ella was out of practice. "Shopping," she blurted out.

She might as well have said she was elephant hunting. Ronan looked like he would burst out laughing, while Bakari just shook his head. Looking down, Ella realised she wasn't exactly dressed in her usual manner. She flushed bright pink and tried to hide her hot cheeks by gazing at her toes.

Bakari's hand was now guiding her out of the rush of people. "What's going on?" he demanded and the look in his eye said he wouldn't tolerate another lie.

Ella chewed the inside of her cheek and looked, really looked, at the two men. They lived and were comfortable in the world she'd tried to hide from, and what's more, she trusted them — even Ronan with his silently laughing eyes, whom she'd only known for days.

She let that trust and her own fears open the door to them. They found seats on tall metallic benches and, nursing a cup of hot chocolate, Ella told them all about Doyle, what she'd been and what she didn't want to become again.

Bakari appeared more shocked than anything. The inhabitants of Penherem complied with an unwritten code of silence; no one ever spoke of their life outside the village. And Ella was suddenly angry — the world did exist and they'd all had problems there. It was beyond stupid to pretend otherwise.

It was Ronan who finally spoke first. His hand slipped over hers and she didn't flinch from this odd gesture from a stranger.

"You can't go there alone. We'll come with you."

The offer made her both excited and afraid. They'd see where she'd come from, but then she would have more chance against Doyle with others there to show disapproval.

"Yeah," Bakari crumpled up his cup and lobbed it carelessly into the recycling can. "Can't let anyone get away with threatening you like that — especially after these last couple of days."

When Ella shot a look at Ronan, he shrugged. "We've had an interesting time in the city."

"Interesting enough to make your Doyle look like a spoilt kid."

She grinned at that. "Well, actually you're not far off."

"Then lead on," Ronan pushed back his stool.

"We can sort this guy out and be back in the Green Man for a pint by dinnertime." Bakari said.

Ella wasn't so sure, but she couldn't deny it felt much better with the two men at her back. They took the rattle bang Tube to the East. She waited until they were the only ones in the carriage before slipping on the shiver cloak, but kept it deactivated. Ronan didn't say a thing, but she caught Bakari's raised brow. He didn't need to say a word, she knew the look — not many would expect secrets to hide behind her mousey looks and quiet nature. But then again, sometimes that was the best way to hide.

The press of people assaulted them once they climbed up from the underground in the usual sprawl way, seemingly trying to walk right through everyone: they all had somewhere important to be. Bakari swam around them like a boat pushed in the ocean, while Ronan repelled them with a smile. Ella could only envy the boys that; she was shoved on all sides, too polite to thrust back or stand her ground. It was yet another reason she hated the city.

But there were good things too — the smell of curry laksas sold out of roadside stalls, the rhythmic patter of speech which owed nothing to the rural world, and the clash of colours which danced on the retina. Ella inhaled. She'd missed all this. No place was totally without merit, but the sprawl hid its dark heart beneath a veneer. She fingered the cloak's console and thought about that darkness.

Bakari and Ronan followed her without comment, content to let her lead. The Eight Bells commanded the rough little square it looked out over, and even with its peeling paint and the swinging sign that had seen better days, it was still the centre of life in the area. It also happened to be the middle of Doyle's web. Ella stood looking up at the darkened windows, remembering how welcoming this place had seemed when first she'd come here, now it held nothing but memories of broken trust.

"We'll go in the other way. See you in there." Bakari drifted past, not acknowledging he even knew her. Only Ronan shot a smile of encouragement.

That look warmed Ella, so when she shoved open the door and strolled in it was with more than a little swagger in her gait. I've changed, she reminded herself. I'm not that scared little girl Doyle found five years ago.

But apparently this didn't matter to those inside the pub; the patrons didn't even glance in her direction, too busy trying to get the hard-pressed landlady's attention. If she didn't know her, Ella might have felt sorry for her, but Doyle's mother Izzie was not one to attract sympathy: she would have dished out swift justice to anyone that offered it.

A quick scan of the Bells' interior did not reveal her son. Ella managed to slip neatly between two slightly sweaty bar flies and attract Izzie's attention. The ease with which she got it confirmed she was in trouble; Doyle's Mum had never been Ella's greatest fan. Over one shoulder, Ella caught Ronan's eye once more. He'd miraculously already secured a pint and was leaning nonchalantly on the bar, picking at the wizened peanuts on offer.

Izzie didn't smile at Ella, but her eyes narrowed even more than usual, peering at her through chunks of mascara. "He's upstairs," she jerked her head towards the door which lead to the private part of the pub. "You know the way."

Ella tried to keep her face unreadable. "I'm not going up there, Iz."

The landlady stared at her hard, looking for any sign of a crack. Then with an immense sigh of irritation, she flicked her head over her shoulder and roared, "Doyle — get your butt down here!" She turned back to her flock of patrons.

Perhaps Doyle had been waiting for that, lurking in the recesses of the upstairs, hovering in that way he had, for he appeared quickly. As if by magic he suddenly occupied the doorway, his gaze instantly locking on hers.

Ella had the uncomfortable feeling of having her past flash before her eyes. The image of the shaggy haired larrikin for an instant was all she could see of him — completely blocking reality. That old image conjured up old feelings, but once it cleared and she looked into Doyle's face, they passed, leaving only a vague sorrow.

He'd once been very beautiful to her; that was the truth, but that was all in the past. The life Doyle had been living since then had obviously caught up with him, for he was no longer that cheery, laughing boy.

He flinched, perhaps reading sympathy in her expression, but glared right back with red, glassy eyes. He'd become a man in the five years since she'd seen him, and a man she no longer wanted to know. After all, even at his worst, that old Doyle would never have sold her out.

He ducked his head and gestured her over to the stained faux leather seats of the closest snug. Ella said nothing, but slid gingerly into the corner, waiting for Doyle to say his piece.

He at least had the grace not to be able to look at her. Instead, his fingers fiddled with a crack in the ancient vinyl. It seemed a somehow lonely and vulnerable gesture to her.

Ella had to bite hard on her tongue to stop from asking inane questions like *How are you?* She reminded herself sternly that she didn't care about that.

Doyle wetted his lips. "You remember TCP?"

"Vaguely. That Liner buddy of yours?"

Unnoticed over his shoulder, she saw Bakari and Ronan slip into the booth behind them.

"Yeah. Well, he heard that there was some serious money out looking for you."

TCP wasn't much into human relationships, so Ella could imagine how long he could hold out against that lure — especially since money immediately went into his Liner gear.

Doyle smirked. "I know what you're thinking, and normally you'd have already been sold down that river, but since I knew about these guys I told him to wait."

"Caution? From you, Doyle?" That couldn't be good.

He shifted uncomfortably in his seat. "Yeah well, Infinity Rose is not to be messed with."

Bakari's large brown hand was suddenly very firmly wrapped around Doyle's shoulder and when he made to rise, Ronan slipped smoothly out from his seat and moved in next to him.

"Unfortunately, Doyle," Ronan said softly, "Neither are we."

Doyle could have made some noise; he probably had half a dozen friends in the pub right then, so Ella reached across and grabbed his hands: they were icy cold. Her eyes found his. "I don't know what you're trying to get out of me — but this is something you don't want to be in."

He remembered, she could see that he did; all those harum-scarum days when nothing had seemed impossible and nothing was too much. But they'd both learned since then. There'd been a lot of growing up and a lot of pain too.

"For what we once were," Ella said, "tell me the truth."

Sweat beaded on his brow and his hands twitched in hers. "I told them you'd come here if I asked."

Bakari's face twisted in disgust and Ronan was looking at her in a *Do I kill him now?* way. Her throat was dry, but she gave him a short shake of her head. Not today.

"How long have we got?"

Doyle wrapped his hands around his face as if he wanted to rip it off. "They're already here."

Ella managed not to look up in shock.

"Let me snap this vermin's neck," Bakari hissed. "Please, Mouse."

But Ronan had already taken her elbow. "Leave him. He's been as true to himself as he can — and we're still alive."

The three of them shouldered their way through the patrons and Ella didn't look back.

"I shouldn't have come here," she muttered. "How dumb can you get?"

Ronan's hand rested in the small of her back. "Not dumb — remember, Doyle knows all about Penherem. This way there's no nasty incident in the village."

"That's true," Bakari said. "But we'll probably not even get to see it again."

They paused for a moment at the entrance to the Eight Bells. "I have the cloak," Ella reminded them. "They're only after me, it seems."

"Nice as a shiver cloak is — I don't think these people will be fooled by it." Bakari looked uncharacteristically grim, even as he surveyed the street. "Now I know how a fish in a barrel feels."

Ella wasn't afraid — not when the threat was unknown, but her heart was pounding.

Ronan's hand found hers and she didn't flinch from it. "Now, Ari," he chided, "We might not make it to the VFT, but there is more than one way out of London." He pulled Ella off the step and down the street. Bakari became their silent shadow.

"Your friend," Ronan smiled at her, "is supposed to be one of those people who still believe in magic — what do you think about it?"

Ella somehow knew this was not a question asked lightly, and certainly not one to be laughed at. "Well, I don't know. I think perhaps there is more. I mean... there has to be..."

Ronan smiled that roguish smile that was so unsettling. "Let's just say there are some small magics left within London — still a few keepers of the old paths."

Bakari's indrawn breath whistled over the top of his teeth and Ella could taste the unrevealed things between them, like a rope of tension.

"Be quiet now," Ronan growled over his shoulder. "Magic doesn't flourish in words, but in deeds." He suddenly sounded like he was not completely from this century, an old Dickensian character perhaps, or something from Chaucer. Ella could not quite put her finger on the odd cant in his voice.

Surprisingly, Bakari hushed. In this odd little triangle they went down the busy street, isolated somewhat from the ebb and flow of the twenty-first century.

She could feel the eyes on them, not just of those they passed, but of those they did not see. Ella's finger itched to trigger the shiver cloak. She hunched her shoulders against the chill and the sudden fall of icy rain while a thousand difficult questions burned in her brain. Why would Infinity Rose want anything to do with her? She could think of nothing — nothing except the endless dark which yawned in the past before Doyle. She shuddered and almost ran into Ronan, who had stopped in the middle of the street. He had his head raised like an animal scenting the air.

Bakari pressed close, effectively sealing her between them. "What the hell is going on?" And Ella could see what he meant simply by looking down, as a thick grey mist was beginning to pool around her feet. She could feel reality slipping as it grew.

"Interesting," Ronan murmured. "Very interesting, but not very reassuring." He bundled Ella against him and pulled her faster down the street. "We'd better get off the street quickly."

"Sorry," Bakari took her other side. "This was not what I had in mind when I said we'd help."

"Just for a moment," Ronan whispered into Ella's ear, "imagine that there is magic in the world. Beneath London there are still the threads of that running, silently but strongly."

No laughter came, Ella felt it should, but it didn't feel like a fairy story — it felt real.

He squeezed her a little. "It's not easy, those paths, not as strong as they once were — but right now they may be our best hope."

"Yes," Ella said, "Ummm… magic…."

"But you said there wasn't any left," Bakari argued over the top of her head.

"The paths still work. The earth doesn't forget… now if we can just find a guardian."

Ella and Bakari looked at each other but said nothing. People still ebbed and flowed around them, oblivious to the mist rising from around their feet, while panic began to well in Ella's throat. Couldn't they feel the air?

"Ari," she clutched her friend's hand. "Can we just get out of sight — please?"

"If we do," he replied darkly, "we'll be dead within minutes. The only thing keeping us safe right now is that the Rose doesn't want to be seen."

"But this," Ella asked, "Surely…."

"Just trust us, Mouse. Don't ask any questions. Just trust us."

She had little choice, as they seemed the safest island in a swirling mass of chaos.

Ronan was craning his neck, looking over the jostling crowds, searching for something she was obviously incapable of seeing.

Yelps of annoyance began to filter forward from behind; the harsh eruption of someone pushing through the crowd towards them.

"Whatever you're looking for," Bakari hissed to Ronan, "could you please find it now."

But he needn't have whispered, for just at that moment the other shrugged forward, pulling them along. "There he is!"

When Ella could finally see his target, she still couldn't understand what was going on. The man they were making for was a dead rock in the flow of people. They never looked at the disreputable figure standing in their midst. By some magic they avoided him by feet, twisted out of his path by eddies of disgust. He carried a bucket full of rolled fabric of unknown use and he was preceded by the stench of flesh which hadn't seen water in years. The thing that marked him from the usual tatters of humanity which lived in the sprawl was the eruption on his head. It had a certain dire fascination that kept Ella from pulling her eyes away. The massive swelling on his forehead pulsed with its own life, as if there were something hidden beneath. Weirdly, she thought of a unicorn's horn.

Ronan was breaking the rules of all large cities by making straight for this man. Ella tugged on his hand, but this was no mistake. It was too late, he'd invaded the man's personal space and that monstrous head was swinging upwards. It could have been a very long time since anyone had purposely spoken to him.

Up this close, the growth on his head almost dwarfed the rest of his face.

"Someone should get this guy to a hospital," Bakari whispered to Ella.

A pair of leaf green eyes locked on them from beyond that protuberance. "Doctor once said he'd make me normal," his voice was surprisingly soft and musical, "but I wouldn't let him touch me. I don't want normal." Fierce pride suddenly burned in those eyes.

"Who does, Wiggly Joe?" Ronan actually touched the man. "We don't want anything from you, but to walk the Ways."

Surely it was her imagination, surely the swelling on the tramp's head hadn't just moved. Ella felt her skin try to crawl off her body.

"Ronan," Bakari sounded more than doubtful, "this guy's fried. He doesn't know anything."

"You're wrong," Ronan's hand tightened on the tramp's arm. "What we seek is like no train station, it moves, flexes with the earth's power — but such power has guardians, those that feel its pulse."

135

Ella tried not to snort.

The tramp's eyes flickered, revealing for a moment something aside from madness. His thick hand dipped into his pocket and removing a crusty looking handkerchief he mopped what little forehead he had. "Moves, yes... it moves."

Ronan leaned forward, surely close enough for the stench to knock him between the eyes. For that action alone Ella was convinced he'd slipped into the cracks between madness and reality. The sheer craziness of the situation had become clear. She jerked her arm free and while the men huddled around the tramp, she slipped back into the crowd.

Magic. Yeah, right. Bakari so wanted there to be more to the world that he was willing to listen to Ronan. If he could think about it for one moment, he'd realise how stupid that was. This world was all they had, and there was nothing resembling magic in it.

While they played their little games with the poor old tramp, she'd go back to the truth. The crowds that swept her away from them had no such beautiful illusions. Though that was sad, at least it was the truth.

Ella thumbed the controls of the cloak and felt the current wrap around her, cutting her off from the mindless throng. If Doyle was right, it was probably better that she escape herself: Bakari and Ronan would be safer. Her past life had taught her an unnatural nimbleness despite her back. It seemed her body hadn't forgotten, for she stepped lightly away from those that threatened to run her over. She dodged women with prams, an old man with packages and a young woman leading at least six dogs. Though the sensors bent light around her and rendered her invisible, the dogs still raised their heads and sniffed, not fooled by human trickeries.

She was going to go straight back to Penherem, pack up her bags and Qoth, and try and find somewhere else where madness didn't rule.

But somehow it wasn't done with her, for something else was hiding in the crowd. As she began to determinedly push her way back to the VFT, she saw what ultimately changed her mind.

At first it looked like another tramp, a bundle of clothes held together by string and dumped in the threshold of a boarded up doorway. But it was watching her. Its disguised head tracked her movements. Ella stopped, tried to convince herself she was wrong, but then it shifted, angled toward her.

Her heart was pounding and her hands were suddenly sticky on the controls. In that moment she had her convictions overturned. Not even if she squinted her eyes and lied to herself, could she ever imagine that flat plate of bone which was its face had ever been anything human. Thousands of bejeweled eyes were massed together like a fly's, and they were unmistakably fixed upon her. Now she knew what Dorothy must have felt, desperately clicking her jeweled slippers together, hoping for home.

It was instinct that saved her, for no matter what madness she had stepped into, there was no mistaking the fact that this alien thing was not friendly. Even as they eyed each other a nightmarish length of white mantis like claw stealthily emerged from the blankets. Calmly Ella spun on her heel and trotted back to where Ronan and Bakari were still talking to the tramp. She flicked off the shiver cloak.

Ronan gave her a look that said he'd noticed her absence.

"Well," she managed not to look over her shoulder. "Are we moving or not?"

Perhaps the tramp had been waiting for this, for he gave a long, loud sniff and fled down the concealed alleyway. London had always had a lot of these secret paths, closed in worlds of their own, and Ella had hidden in her fair share of them in the past.

Ronan and Bakari pushed her ahead, either protecting her, or urging her forward like a lamb, hard to tell which. The world contracted to the looming men behind her, the close wet walls of the alley, and the stench of the tramp scuttling in front of her. She'd expected danger when Doyle had contacted her, but not so much strangeness. The city had become an alien place all of a sudden, wreathed in purple mist which blocked out all the usual sights and sounds. Even this alley could have been from two centuries before. And here was I thinking I knew London, she thought in a cloud of icy detachment.

The tramp had just turned toward some crumbly basement steps, when Ronan made a sound awfully close to a growl. Ella didn't have time to wonder what was happening, for Bakari was suddenly shoving her hastily after Wiggly Joe, and Ronan had dropped completely away. The air was full of odd noises, like the sound of many long fingernails raking over brick. An awful image of mummified ghosts with foot-long nails flashed across her brain.

The tramp was concerned as the three of them huddled in the dripping courtyard, and Ella could feel claustrophobia setting in.

"Old lady live here," Joe was muttering as he fished in his tattered pocket. "Lived here all the time, never went out — died mad, but not mad like Joe, mad from the stream."

Ella swallowed, half an ear listening to the dreadful silence of the alleyway. "How long ago?"

Those leaf green eyes stared into the middle distance. "Three hundred years before that Roman woman killed her children here. Madness... is always near."

Closer than she'd thought, obviously, but still Ella knew better than to go back. Ronan had not reappeared and the stillness was unnerving her. When the tramp finally pulled out a key and miraculously managed to get the door opened, she almost shoved him out of the way to get inside. Whatever ancient ghosts waited there were better than the ones out here.

She and Bakari huddled in the dim, brown recesses of the room while Joe waited mildly by the open door.

"Where's Ronan?" Ella whispered.

"He'll come." Why didn't Bakari sound very sure?

She looked about. Someone might have once loved this house, but not in her lifetime. They stood in what must have been a small parlor. The roof was brown and sagging, and the sound of gently running water added to the feeling of melancholy. Ella almost gagged on the overpowering stench of mold and disuse. Usually such vacant places had squatters in them, but even the homeless must have been unable to stand the dank atmosphere and feeling of impending collapse.

Blackness engulfed the door and Ella's breath raced across her teeth, until the shape resolved itself into Ronan. He stepped smoothly through the doorway and pushed the door rapidly shut behind him. Wiggly Joe was nodding to himself, his head bouncing up and down to some rhythm that was only in his skull. The water began to run faster around them while the silence outside pressed against the door.

"Ronan," Ella found to her horror her voice was shaking, "What is going on?"

He smiled a somewhat shaky smile. "Let us just say there is a something out there that is not very friendly. We have a few moments." She knew he wasn't joking.

"Well, can we get a move on then," Bakari yelped, "cos that door isn't going to hold back a toddler with a cold."

"Normally I'd disagree," Ronan said, "as there is more than soggy wood protecting this place, but this creature is not likely to be dissuaded. What do you say Joe, shall we find the stream?"

The tramp didn't answer, instead he turned and shoved open the only sagging interior wall and led them deeper into the dripping house. Ella could help but wonder how much further into this madness she would have to go, but the outside felt more dangerous and deeper in seemed the only alternative.

Bakari surged forward, his eyes suddenly gleaming with eagerness. "Do you taste it, Mouse?"

She made a face. "You mean the damp or the mold?"

Her friend did not acknowledge her sarcasm.

Ella shook her head as they moved deeper; this could only end badly. "Where are we going, Ronan?"

He pressed against her back and his voice came smoothly to her ear. "There are many rivers beneath the sprawl, hidden by centuries of human habitation. They are the sources of power, some for good, some not. Only the guardians know one from another — with luck we have chosen the right guardian and the right place."

Ella curled her lip, as a thick drop from the ceiling above sneaked past her jacket and down her collar. "And this is how you intend to get me out of London?"

"With luck, we may ride the pulse of power to Penherem."

She could not help the giggle that arose. "Sounds very... primitive."

Ronan's breath brushed her neck. "It is."

A funny shiver ran up her back and forced her to silence. Joe had reached some significant spot, though what made it so, only he could tell. Only when she got near, could Ella tell that it was a trapdoor leading further below. Bakari reached down and pried the slime covered thing free. It gaped like an entrance into Hell itself. The stench of wet and disease made Ella gag.

Wiggly Joe dropped in like a bundle of dirty laundry and Bakari quickly followed. Ronan paused at the top step and looked back at her.

"I am not going down there."

He smiled that lopsided smile once more and held out his hand to her. The choice was obvious; she'd be left up here, or she could go down into that murky hole. She wouldn't be left alone.

Ella sighed. "You're all as mad as hell."

"True," Ronan nodded, "But I'm pretty with it."

After that comment Ella simply had to go down if just to hide her blush. She was damned if she was going to agree with him. Pushing past him bravely, she scrambled into the blackness below.

The smell was even worse down here; it hit her over the head like a hammer blow. Taking a moment to recover, Ella looked around. A dark cavern embraced them, thick with the ooze of ages. Its roof was low but broad, and there, nearly lapping at Ella's toes, was a gushing powerful river. It was not the Thames, she knew that immediately, but she could not give it a name.

Ronan came up behind and answered her unasked question. "It is the Fleet — long hidden under the city, but still a bearer of power."

Wiggly Joe was smiling like his jaw would break. "The pulse is here if you can use it."

And then the sound came from up above, a hissing rustle that drew Ella's breath from her body. An image flashed in her brain: a bone pale face and faceted eyes like a spider's, reflecting only pain and misery. And she knew, she really knew, that there was more to come, more creatures built from anger and hatred.

"Quick," she found herself saying, "Ronan. I'll live with this madness, just get us home."

"Yeah," Bakari crowded a little closer, "I think that door didn't hold for even a moment."

Ronan's breathing was heavy and those wonderful brown eyes seemed to burn in his head. Wiggly Joe was looking thoughtfully up to where they had come from, the only one not affected, his fingertips dancing on each other.

"Alright then," Ronan's hand moved and Ella suddenly found herself looking down at what he had given her, a long silver knife.

She didn't need to ask, the long flat of the blade was very familiar to her, and the curved serpentine writing cut there had a meaning that glittered on the end of her memory. The words that buzzed in her brain spun like liquid honey inside her, though what they were Ella could not have said.

"Mouse!" Bakari surged forward as she raised the hand wielding the knife and slashed her other, held high above the simmering Fleet.

The pain was intense — like the silver had cut through her brain as well as her flesh. The blood was so unexpected. God, why had she done that? What was the matter with her?

Ronan was holding the wide eyed Bakari back, but his own expression was remarkably serene, even though she was now bleeding hard. Wiggly Joe was bouncing up and down on his toes, clapping his hands together like an over-sugared child.

Ella gasped, swaying, sure that she was going to pass out, but equally sure she could do nothing but stand there bleeding. The Fleet was moving strangely. Gold light seemed to be burning her eyes. Bakari yelled, and there was a terrible sound like her ear drums bursting.

She was falling and twisting. It was madness, yet it seemed a familiar madness.

CHAPTER ELEVEN

Precipice

Makara looked very small from the top of the hill. Aroha hitched her pack higher on her back and tried to find the will to turn away. Nana had not waved her off as she usually did — even for her trips to Sally's house. She'd packed her bag with enough supplies to last for days, though Wellington was not even one day's walk away. "You never know what you'll find the city like."

Aroha felt a hard ball tighten in her throat.

"We better get going." Daniel's voice was kindly, though tense.

The tramp was easy really, for though the road might still be dangerous, it was the best way to get through the tangle of windswept hill and the broken ranks of gorse bushes with their unfriendly spines. The Folk were silent, perhaps feeling Aroha's back turned to them and knowing they had driven her on.

Daniel tramped at the front, rifle ready, his shoulders somehow showing more tension than when they were hunting the bot. Aroha felt really sorry for him, she at least could feel the call of the Folk, but he was completely blind to that world. But someone had thought that she needed him and as Nana said, don't fight the universe.

While Aroha was turning these thoughts over in her head, Daniel was circling behind her through the bush. She barely noticed, keeping her mind open, trying to sense any whiff of the Folk.

That was, until the soldier erupted out of the ferns, with a red haired bundle tucked under one arm. Sally was kicking and hissing like a feral cat, but Daniel held on regardless: perhaps he had younger sisters.

He plunked Aroha's friend down in front of her with a shake of his head. "This was supposed to be a two person outing."

"I don't like being left behind," Sally huffed and glared at Aroha, "So it's not my fault if I had to catch up."

Aroha was glad her friend wanted to be in on everything, but she also knew that this wasn't the time. Daniel at least could look after himself, but Sally was not only blind, she'd be defenseless.

"I'm not going back," Sally said when Aroha opened her mouth to say something, "Not unless you want to carry me back home."

Daniel shot her a glance. They couldn't do that either. Sally grinned, her gaze flickering triumphantly between them. "Got ya!"

Aroha flushed, partly because she didn't like losing and partly because she only had one choice if she was to avoid that happening. Once this was done, there would be no going back, her friendship with Sally would be irretrievably altered. However there was not much choice: Wellington was just too dangerous for her.

"So you did," she said and gave her friend a hug. She smelt of concealed candies and childish sweat, a good honest smell that had nothing of the Folk about it. That made Aroha's mind up. She kissed her friend gently on the side of the head and whispered a benediction into her ear.

With the way of all earth magics, it was not a command, but a wish that Sally be safe. She would wait here until safely the next morning and then go home, but Aroha had no real control over how the wild replied to her.

She stepped back and watched nervously. Sally's eyes fluttered, her face relaxing into a sleeper's calmness. When she fell, soft undergrowth caught her, lowering her gently to the ground. She curled there in a circle of warmth, like she was once more back in her mother's womb.

Daniel started forward, because this was the first real magic he had seen, but Aroha stopped him. "It's all right, wait a second."

Around Sally the earth was moving, heaving with its own primitive energy. A heartbeat later, tall furry fronds erupted from the ground. The tender shoots were curled at the tip, the symbol of eternity, but they just as quickly unfurled to become huge tree ferns, with graceful arching fronds, green on one side, silvered on the back. Daniel gasped as the ferns fluttered, bending their arms down to wrap Sally in an embrace. Each portion of the fern cradled her like a protective mother.

"She'll be safe until morning," Aroha shouldered her bag once more, "then the ferns will let her go and the bush will guide her back to Makara."

Daniel was staring. Perhaps he'd convinced himself that she was just a normal girl and he still knew more than her. Was he hurt that this wasn't so? Either way, Aroha turned away from that look, for it was too new and different. She started back on their path.

He followed after, but she could tell he kept glancing back at fern sanctuary for as long as it was visible.

"That's real power," he finally said. "Imagine what you could do..."

Aroha concentrated on walking faster.

"I mean if we could have had that when we were fighting the..."

"You don't understand," Aroha found the words leaping out of her mouth. "It's not like that at all!"

"Well, what is it like?"

But he wouldn't be able to grasp it: none of them could. It was not power. It was more than that. Aroha sighed; it was as deep as her bones and as elusive as spirit. The only explanation that she could give was one that Nana had told her.

"It's like faith."

Daniel's brow furrowed, but it silenced him. He dropped back while chewing on that concept. Faith, like Aroha's magic, could not be counted or measured, but both could be used for good or ill.

Somehow the bush seemed to have been lightened, along with Aroha's spirits, by Sally. It was good to know that she had a friend willing to break every rule to help her. Sometimes she felt so isolated by her gifts that it hurt, so it was nice to be reminded that she was still connected to humanity.

She and Daniel labored up the increasing slope, slipping through mud and dodging tiny waterfalls. The main road would have been easier but it was also far more dangerous.

At last, they broke through the trees and into the low scrub and grasses that dominated the hilltops. Aroha stopped, turned around, to look back down the valley. From here she couldn't even see the settlement, only an unbroken undulating landscape of green that ran down to the sea. The first village had been built there and had remained until a hundred years ago, but the sea rose and the people had retreated further into the security of the bush. Even from here, Aroha could see the white topped waves and smell faintly the salt and violence of the ocean.

Daniel appeared but kept his distance, watching her watch the ocean. Aroha didn't want to tell him the truth — that this was the farthest she could remember having gone in her whole life. And the last time she'd even been here Nana had carried her. Aroha was a child of the bush. She'd never seen the city and was afraid. What would she find there, and could she survive without the whispers of the Folk?

Their friendship must be paid for, and knowing that, she turned her back against the bush and the ocean.

"If we hurry we can make the outskirts of the city before nightfall," Daniel said, "and we better not try to get all the way after dark. Things are... different there now."

Aroha tried not to notice the lump in her throat. Nana had told her all about the city, or at least how it had been before. It was a small one by world standards but now those standards didn't really apply: utu had seen to that. Wellington was one of the largest cities in New Zealand.

"Are there still lots of people?" Aroha's voice sounded very small to her.

"Enough. I don't know what that magic of yours can do, but you better stick close to me." He reached under his jacket and pulled out the dayglow green badge that marked him as a Grey Wolf. He grimaced, "I'm not sure how much this thing means now, but hopefully it can't hurt."

Aroha was still a child, despite her gifts, and that scared her. Adults were not supposed to be so uncertain about anything, she knew that. This was not the first time she'd realised they were, but it still made her feel small.

The terrain changed again, becoming the treacherous broom and gorse, both foreign plants introduced in ignorance to New Zealand. As her face was scratched and legs slapped, Aroha could but wish that the rest of the road was safe enough to travel. And yet it was good to be on the land, not amongst the trappings of humanity just yet. Aroha could feel the pattern of the countryside changing around her; the quiet murmur of the Forest fading to be replaced by the restless hum of the hills and far in the distance the swirling whispers of the city.

They had come via a twisting path to avoid detection and now were approaching the suburb of Karori to the east of the city. Daniel told her as much as he could as they walked through the silent pine forest. This introduced species had no voice in this land and its silence made Aroha's nerves stand on end.

The valley in which Karori nestled was large and it had protected most people from the devastation given to the city, but still things there would not be as they once had been, Daniel warned. The suburb had been a prosperous one, but with the economy wrecked and all the rules abandoned, it had been the target of looting and revenge. Really, he didn't need to tell Aroha that, she could feel it wafting up from ahead.

They emerged from the pines into the hills of the dead: one of the city's oldest cemeteries, row upon row of tilting graves and moss covered tombs. Daniel paused a moment, within him that tremendous melancholy. People, Aroha had observed, would go to great lengths to avoid seeing their own mortality. Daniel was close now, so she managed to winkle her hand into his.

They both walked quietly past. Even though the world outside might be in a mess, this one remained the same. Aroha let her gift reach out, seeking any touch of the lives that lay about her, but there was none, only the sound of the plants growing and the wind running through the treetops.

"Look," Daniel paused by a wall strung with brass plaques and the names of loved ones lost. He pointed to the base of the wall, where a bunch of bright pink tulips lay. "No one's been buried here for at least twenty years."

She saw what he meant. Even in a time of madness, someone had still ventured out to remember one they had loved. The weight of these unusual emotions was pushing down on Aroha, until her heart was racing and bumping in her chest.

"Come on," Daniel said wistfully. "There's a safe house not far from here."

When he said that, he really meant it, the sextons old cottage leaned rather drunkenly against a crumbling wall which marked the outer edge of the cemetery, but there were several armed and uniformed soldiers outside. They welcomed Daniel, if somewhat warily.

Aroha was feeling more tired than she ever had, and her stomach was churning. Leaning wearily against Daniel, she let herself be guided into the house.

Inside was packed with sweat and organized chaos. She and Daniel were jostled round, passed from harried sergeant to grumpy captain, until at last they found themselves in front of the CO. Captain Jack Morrow was in no mood for anything out of the ordinary. Aroha could tell that just by looking at him. The irritations and complications of running a small unit in the middle of the biggest crisis the nation had ever been in, amongst civil unrest, food shortages and economic collapse, were all written on his face. Never the less, his expression softened slightly when he saw Aroha watching him warily from under Daniel's protection.

But he still snapped, "What the hell is a child doing in here?" His voice froze the air and silenced everyone. Daniel shuffled uncomfortably under such sudden scrutiny.

"I'm escorting her to Wellington, Sir."

That went down even worse than expected, and Daniel was suddenly having to explain who he was, who he was commanded by and what the hell did he think he was doing taking a child into a virtual war zone?

"There are already a lot of children there," Daniel replied quietly, "And this one has lost her parents." It was as close to a lie as Daniel was prepared to go.

Captain Morrow eyed her sternly. Aroha tried her best to look winsome, and not the least bit of a problem.

"Bloody chain of command — it's all gone to hell since Utu. Not even sure if there's anything left of your unit." He sighed, "But we can offer you a place to bunk for the night. You can camp outside with my men and the girl can sleep in my office — Hell, I never get any sleep anyway!"

Aroha smiled her thanks, which only made the commander spin around and pretend neither of them existed. But at least for that night they had safety and shelter. Aroha nestled down in the camp bed and watched the dim shapes of the commander's book case, desk, and glowing computer screen.

It felt a long way from home, even though it was only over the hills.

She hoped Sally was safe in her fern shelter and Nana was not worrying too much about her. She drifted off to sleep, thinking of those tulips and wondering of the person who had placed them there.

Bakari watched Ella fall into madness. He wasn't prepared to have magic suddenly present in his life, and the whirling stream of energy she'd called up with her blood was not what he'd expected; there was no peace in that, only raw power. He'd never say it, but he suddenly doubted his goal.

"What have you done?" he roared at Ronan as Ella disappeared into the surging gold fire.

Ronan was giving no answers now. Instead, he lunged. Bakari, already unsteady, toppled into the pulse of magic. His last glimpse of reality was into the strangely knowing eyes of Wiggly Joe.

He did not pass out, even when all points of reference disappeared and around him was only light. He didn't feel like he was falling, but there was a definite sense of movement about him and there was warmth too, cradling his body, making it impossible to be afraid.

Would have been good for Ma to see this: how she would have enjoyed this moment.

As if summoned, the light flexed and bent and there was her face; not scarred and hard like plastic as he'd last seen it, but fresh and supple, bent by only a smile.

"Boy," she whispered and the memory stirred inside him. Another warmth, this time from a Tropical sun and the feeling of utter security — he was lying in the sand leaning against Ma's side. His hands were still clumsy childish hands and his thoughts untroubled by cruelties to come. He listened to the sound of the waves licking the beach and the soft humming of his mother as she lazily plaited his hair about her fingers. There was no father, there never had been, but there was always Ma. He'd thought that would never have changed.

Bakari gasped and threw the memory clear of him. He was crying, sobbing hard, just like that night in the hospital. The fire had not left much of her to hold; only the inside of one palm remained as it had been. He'd rested his fingers there until she'd died in the early hours of the morning.

"No! No, stop it," Bakari yelled, though at who, he couldn't say. He wanted her back so painfully, wanted to stop existing in this time and go back to then — but he couldn't, no one could. "It's so unfair," he screamed.

It was then the magic released him. It was so sudden that he sat there, in the shade of the oak overlooking the Penherem Green and finished crying. Though even once he was done, he still knew he'd not truly expressed his grief. It was still lodged in his heart. He now saw Ella was lying nearby, her eyes closed but her breathing that of someone resting in deepest sleep. He touched her arm.

Bakari looked up and Ronan was there. But there was no pity in the other, only an understanding, and a knowledge that looked strange in his eyes.

"What are you?" The question leaped from him, even though he knew already that Ronan was not human.

Those brown eyes flashed, for an instant consuming all the whiteness and leaving nothing but a gleaming expanse like onyx. He smiled wryly. "We are the face behind the mask, the spirit in the tree and a baby's first dream. We are Fey."

"Nicely put," Bakari said smoothly, "Did you practice that?"

He shrugged. "It is what we say when we are asked directly."

"And you're what's missing in our world?"

Ronan reached down and offered his hand to Bakari to help him up. "You already know the answer to that, my friend, or you wouldn't have spent all that time since your mother died looking for a way to bring us back. You know how to live, but not how to appreciate living. That is what the Fey are for. Without us you would bury yourself in science."

149

Bakari paused, then took that hand. "I didn't know what I was looking for, but if you're already here, then…"

"Oh no," Ronan's lips twisted, "I'm afraid I'm not the answer. When the worlds of magic and man were separated, I chose this one. I've been here hundreds of years and I'm afraid to say it's left me with very few powers."

"Then what was that we just went through?" Both men spun about, never having realised that Ella was lying there listening to them. She rolled over in the grass and opened her hand for them to observe that there was no mark on it. She scrambled to her feet. Now Bakari could see she still had the slim silver dagger Ronan had given her. Looking down at it, Ella smiled. "For some reason I don't want to give it back."

"Then don't," the Fey replied. "It is a relic of humanity — a bit of magic they learnt from us."

"So what about that light?" Bakari tried to keep his voice steady even though he couldn't help thinking of what he had seen.

"That too is a relic, part of the old earth magic that is not Fey. Very little remains, and even fewer can use it." Ronan was eyeing Ella strangely.

Bakari shook his head, it was full of so many buzzing questions, but the ones at the forefront were concerned with survival; old instincts remained. "So what does this have to do with Infinity Rose? Why would they be after Ella, of all people?"

She shrank back at her name.

"Yes," Ronan said, his attention not wavering from her, "A good question — there's obviously something about you. I can see it and maybe that's why…"

"There's nothing about me," Ella snapped, her skin flushing scarlet. "I'm nothing — a has-been of a criminal just like most of the village."

"And your blood triggering the earth magic, was that nothing, too?"

Ella's eyes were wide and frightened, like a cornered cat. Bakari could almost see her flattened ears and stiff fur. With a hiss of frustration, she threw the silver dagger down so its blade was buried in the earth, vibrating at Ronan's feet. He didn't move and in that instant the tension sang between them.

God, they were going to thump each other in a minute. Bakari took a step forward.

Ella broke first. "Just keep the hell away from me," she snarled before running off across the Green, moving surprisingly fast for such a little person.

Ronan stood watching her for a moment.

"I hope you've got some answers," Bakari said, almost feeling sorry for the Fey.

"No more than anyone else, I'm afraid."

"But Hamish's murder, the contract out on Mouse — do you think there's a connection?"

"Maybe," Ronan said, "But how the Mask and I fit in... "

Ronan looked defeated, drained somehow of the vigor that had been his trademark.

"You know — I think there is a place where there might be some answers. How about we check out my world?"

"The Line? I'm not going to have my head carved up, my friend."

This guy might have been around for centuries, but in some things he was still naïve. Bakari chuckled. "So you've never rode shotgun, then?"

CHAPTER TWELVE

Paths

The Harbor of Tara. Aroha felt a shiver pass through her body, though it was one of wonder rather than one of fear. Her whole life she'd heard people talking about 'Welly' over the hill, and yet Nana had never allowed her to come here. It was the city, not like any of the big ones over the water, like London or New York, but still quite a deal to a young girl from the countryside.

Daniel had guided her through the fortified homes of Karori and Kelburn, where once rich suburban dwellers had now barricaded themselves in against chaos. They passed hastily welded metal fences and garage doors broken off their rails. The electricity supply held on, so the façade of survival was there, but everyone was still afraid.

They'd come to this hilltop to look down on what awaited them. The harbor was a graceful curl, almost closed on itself, but not quite — a promise not quite fulfilled, or one already broken.

"Do you really want to do this?" Daniel's hand dropped onto her shoulder.

Aroha wasn't used to anyone talking to her like that, like an adult who had a choice. "I don't want to — but I guess I have to."

"Any idea where you need to get to in the city? There's a lot to it, you know."

Aroha closed her eyes, trying to shut out the noise and confusion of the real world, trying to reach out across the valleys to where the Folk waited in silent rows, faces turned to her. *Master of water and earth.*

Aroha's mouth went dry. She'd seen a great head and eyes like fire. It was too much, they asked too much for their help; she'd never imagined that it would be like this. With a whimper, she turned and clung onto Daniel.

"Aroha," he dropped down to her level. "Why are you doing this? Was it because of me?"

He'd suspected, knowing that the bot could not have really exploded like that. Their enemy was not known for inefficiencies.

"I couldn't let you die," Aroha sniffled, "It's OK…"

Daniel was silent, he knew life was a precious gift, but Aroha could still feel the waves of guilt coming off him. He sighed, "Where do we go, then?"

In her mind a smooth-sloped green hill rose out of the sea. She told Daniel and he nodded. "I know where that is." He took her hand and they descended into the city.

They went through the canyons of the deserted university, where the taste of student energies still lingered. Aroha looked nervously up at the seeming acres of empty windows in the tall buildings, somehow expecting to catch a moving figure or a pale face, but there was nothing except the wind.

"I studied Law here," Daniel commented, in a falsely cheerful voice. "It seems a long time ago."

Aroha looked at her feet, for there'd be no university for her or any child of New Zealand at the moment. Even she, with all her gifts, couldn't tell what the future held. Her heart was beating so loudly that she was surprised Daniel didn't say something.

The city slowly resolved around them; spaces of green and concrete that in their time would have been beautiful places. Aroha could tell that from the memories that still lingered here, and her heart ached for that loss.

Now the city, from hills to the flat land full of skyscrapers, was a city of soldiers and everyone seemed to know Daniel. Their journey became a series of stops and starts. Each soldier gave new clues as to what was happening and Aroha plucked each clue up silently from each new conversation.

The people had left the city when it became a target for the enemy, but had not returned since Utu and the enemy's withdrawal. Fear remained, of their fellow man and of what might happen.

The army had moved in, both conscripts and career soldiers, one even joked to Daniel that it was, "just like WW Two but without the dances."

Everything around her said this city was not meant to be a city of war. They had stopped on the corner of two main streets, Willis and Lambton Quay from the ragged sign hanging off the tilting lamp post. Daniel was talking to a young woman, about his own age, with a tangle of golden hair that might have been her crowning glory in former times. Their voices were hushed like they didn't want her to hear. She didn't bother to tell them she could anyway.

She wandered off a few steps to peer through the broken windows into the darkened interior of what looked like it might once have been a jeweler's. The shadows there crept with frightened memories.

"Pretty," a voice like crumpled paper whispered in her ear. Aroha cautiously turned around, knowing this was not some forgotten whisper.

The old woman met her stare with one of her own. Though the face was sagging and had lost any expression, her eyes were as nimble and alive as any Aroha had ever seen. But the rest of her was another story. She'd never seen anyone made up of such a variety of clothes; a satin skirt two sizes too small, a lichen green scarf and a massive padded jacket that might have come from the Antarctic. She looked totally bogged down in the human world, but Aroha wasn't fooled, there was a taste of the Folk about her. Nana had told her about the creatures that waited at places of power; sometimes they cursed, sometimes they blessed. Aroha took a step back.

But the old woman seemed not to notice. "He's waiting for you," she said plainly in a voice that carried no emotion. "Hurry."

Aroha knew a kindly warning when she heard one. Daniel was still talking to the young woman, head bowed, when Aroha tugged on his arm.

"We've got to go."

"How sweet, Daniel," she stooped slightly to the child's level. "I didn't know you had a daughter."

Aroha frowned. Couldn't the woman see that she was far too old to be any such thing? But she wasn't going to argue. Aroha hung harder off Daniel and let her voice rise into a whine. "We've got to go — now!"

Daniel quickly said goodbye to his friend and hustled Aroha away. He didn't ask what was happening, already used to the way things were around her. They hurried on through the street, under the blue walled buildings and through the desolation to the harbor itself. Things here were better, distance concealing the emptiness of the city. There were even a small number of sailing boats moored down by the harbor. Aroha didn't really take much notice, for now she could see their real destination, the massive outcrop which filled the southern curve of the harbor.

They walked silently towards the hill, around the bay lined with elegant single pines. On one side was the narrow beach, on the other the square squat shapes of houses nestled against the hill.

"Mount Victoria," Daniel told her.

Aroha stopped, suddenly not so sure that she could do this. The images that the Folk had let her see froze her blood and made her mouth all dry. She plopped down into the only remaining park bench. It was a good spot, because she could look out to sea and not at the hill.

Daniel sat down next to her, but didn't try and hold her hand, or tell her it was going to be all right, he was smarter than that. Instead he said, "It's all changed so fast."

Most kids didn't know much about time, Aroha had observed; Sally probably hardly knew what day it was. But Aroha felt it differently. Like the time she and Nana had spent all afternoon picking blackberries. The sun had been so hot and those berries tasted warm and sticky-sweet. It was that moment she'd felt it first, real sadness knowing that the moment would be gone forever, and all she would have was memory.

It felt like that now. Once she went to that hill, all her normal child moments would be gone. Even if she got back to Nana, it would be as a different person.

Daniel sighed, "You're a quiet kid, aren't you?"

She couldn't help it; it was such a silly thing to say. She grinned. "Sometimes." But she didn't want to be quiet, or sad, or scared anymore.

Aroha slid off the bench and held out her hand to Daniel, "We better get going — he's waiting for us."

"Who?"

But she didn't want to scare him either, so she just tugged him along after her, towards the hill.

Ronan eyed the curl of metal and plastic lying in his hands doubtfully. He could feel Bakari's amused look on the back of his neck, but at this stage he didn't care. This was something totally new to him, and after nearly five hundred years he wanted to savor the feeling of newness. He admitted to more, to himself; the fact was, he was rather nervous about this whole thing.

Bakari pulled the curtains so that no one would be able to peer in his living room windows, but all the same Ronan was concerned about how he'd look once he put this contraption on. He'd never even know if he was drooling.

Bakari sat down on the floor opposite him and grinned like his face would split. "Not keen on this, are you?"

Ronan tried to look casual. "I've just never been big on this Line thing you humans are all so in love with."

"Some sort of technophobe, then?"

Ronan got the impression Bakari was deliberately trying to goad him. "I have no objection to technology — I just wouldn't cut myself open for an upgrade."

"Well, no one is asking you to," Bakari fitted the tiny monofilament cable into the back of his neck. "The piggy backer just lets you see and hear what I do. You must have used one as a kid."

Ronan gave him a wry look.

"OK... maybe you didn't." Bakari took pity on him and leaning over, uncurled the secondary wires to reveal a narrow piece of curved plastic, and then folded out a set of thin metal bands. He fitted the plastic over Ronan's head so that the two nodules rested against his ear, and then adjusted the metal pieces so they ran horizontally across his field of vision. "Now, this isn't the real thing, the quality is crap and you're not going to get any other sensory input, but hopefully it'll give you an idea."

"I don't really see what this will achieve."

"As they say, don't knock it 'til you've tried it. Besides, you asked the questions about the mask and Infinity Rose. Your way hasn't got us any answers — only more questions."

They stared at each other for a second and Ronan was somewhat pleased to find the other didn't look away. Whatever shock Bakari had got this morning hadn't turned his world completely upside down; he was prepared to accept magic. If that was true, then maybe there was hope for the rest of his kind.

"Fair enough," Ronan said. "Show me the way."

Bakari attached a double adaptor to the length of his thin cable and inserted the Line to the piggybacker, then sat back and closed his eyes. The circle of metal and plastic came alive around Ronan's head with the faintest of hums. He tried not to jump. The lengths of wire glowed white for a minute and then, with a hiss, everything went black.

Ronan yelped, and would have torn the thing off his head if Bakari's slightly amused voice hadn't reached him. "Relax. It's all just a visual feed, you're just seeing what I am. You're not really on the Line."

The man was asking a lot, though he couldn't really understand why. Ronan had seen the first faltering steps to technology; right from the first roaring, hissing steam engine through to this. And yet here was Bakari calmly asking him to relax and enjoy something that he was sure was the antithesis of everything Fey.

He twiddled his thumbs, a habit he toyed with adopting now and then. Then his vision exploded into life and he barely managed not to exclaim again. Twice would be rather undignified. Sound and image flared around him. An effortless bright blue sky, the kind he didn't think he'd seen for at least three hundred years, so beautiful it made his eyes water. It took a long time for him to catch his breath. His vision changed again, as though his head was moving, though he knew very well that it was not.

"It's me," Ronan heard Bakari like he was right behind him. Shouldn't there have been breath on his neck? "You've got no control, so just relax."

Bakari's hand appeared in view, but not his normal hand. This one ended in a broad expanse of long, dark feathers.

"Ah, yeah," Bakari said. "On the Line you can choose how you look. It's called an avatar."

"And you are?"

"A raven."

Ronan felt his insides freeze, while his distant body reacted with shock. The raven was an ancient symbol of his people, but most of all, the creature of the one Fey he loved above all others. It could not be coincidence that Bakari had chosen this bird as his form.

"Did you say something?" the human asked, perceiving some sound that Ronan had not been aware he was making, perhaps even her name.

"Ah... I just thought it was interesting that in this world you can change shape like we Fey."

"It's not real, you know," Bakari sounded perplexed. "It's just on the Line. An avatar gives you some protection here. This is one place you don't want to be yourself."

Ronan did not comment, keeping his doubts to himself. For the Fey, the real and the unreal were often interchangeable.

Bakari's odd bird-hand was moving now, sketching a strange shape in the air, and where it moved a trail of silver followed. Within a second a gleaming box hung in the air, in which odd animalistic shapes moved. Ronan blinked: one could almost have been a lion. Bakari took the cube and tossed it high and this time there was a roar, something direct from the veldt. The cube disappeared in a blaze of light but from it, in one heartbeat, Ronan saw a large feline shape speed off to the horizon. He felt his first twinge of jealousy.

"A seeker program," Bakari explained. "It's dangerous to go out on the Line without something watching your back, and that one's the best I've got. If we want to find out about Infinity Rose, then we're only going to have limited time."

The hand disappeared and suddenly with the sound of beating air, they were flying — and it was magnificent. Ronan laughed out loud with joy. He had lost many of his shapes over the years and hawk had been the first to go. Now he wished that he could feel what Bakari was feeling; the rush of air, the joyous freedom of the emptiness around him. He savored the moment.

But it changed quickly, almost as quickly as things could change in the Fey Realm. The smooth air disappeared and there were now clouds around them. In an instant Ronan felt like he was lost, unable to even see the ground. And then in the distance he saw something gleaming and glinting whiteness against all the darkness; the shape of a lion.

Bakari twisted his wings, beating against the currents that seemed bent on ripping them apart. Even though he was just an observer, Ronan's heart was beating fast.

"Is this normal?"

"Well, not unusual," Bakari dived and the sound of wind filled their ears. They were moving very fast, following the disappearing form of the lion, or rather the program, Ronan reminded himself.

The clouds thickened around them, so that all was darkness. But then it was like they had broken through a wall of some sort. The clouds evaporated into brightness and they were standing on a verdant green stretch of grass. It stretched from horizon to horizon with only one feature, directly in front of them.

The thick wall of hedges was as big as a city block, made up of a patchwork different plants which loomed large over them with what Ronan could only have described as menace. The only entrance to this ordered hedge maze was a gateway of utter darkness.

"I know I'm going to keep hearing myself saying this," Ronan found himself whispering, "But what is that?"

"Infinity Rose," Bakari replied, while his raven head craned up to where the hedges grazed the sky. "This is the Line interpretation of their system. The clouds were the outer defenses, easy for a competent operator, but this…. this is another type of defense."

Ronan was suddenly catapulted back in time to when he had ridden with his cousin, she who was both fierce and lovely and more powerful than he could ever dream of being. They had looked into the Between Worlds and even she had been awed by such strength. He heard the same angry fear in Bakari's voice, the sound of someone not used to being bested, facing something they were dwarfed by.

Ronan uttered fateful words. "There must be another way to find out these things. Let's go back..."

"Hey," Bakari snapped, "did I say I was beaten?! We just have to be careful."

Ronan sighed. He really should have known better.

The golden white lion waited at the entrance, its sides heaving slightly like it had run across the plains. There were bloody gouges in its sides.

Bakari's head shook from side to side. "My best seeker, and it has never been this beaten before. Hopefully it should still have enough juice to get us through this thing."

The lion seemed to have a proud look in its eye and Ronan felt a stirring of another ancient memory, yet every time he tried to put a finger on it, it fled like a frightened child. The answer was there in the lion's eye. Of that he was sure.

Bakari's hand appeared from his wing once more and he sketched another shape, this one curved like a sickle. It flashed out from his fingertips and hovered around the lion.

"New instructions for the program," he explained.

The lion raised its great head and turned, about to enter the maze. The air came alive, like a thousand tiny lightning bolts, and then the animal was gone.

"Crap!" Bakari hopped forward on his raven's feet to examine the entrance more closely, but not too closely. Then there was more sketching of elaborate shapes in the air, but he didn't stop to explain this lot.

"That's it," he said finally. "There's a remote killing field. Only personal avatars are getting in there."

Like all human magicians, Bakari was falling into jargon. "In something vaguely understandable to old ears, please," Ronan requested bluntly.

"Any program gets killed in there. Only a Liner has any chance of getting in, their signal is stronger."

"So, in we go."

"Easy for you to say; not your arse on the Line."

"Yes, I dare say that probably helps."

Bakari went into the maw with a soft chuckle. It was dark inside, darker than Ronan had ever seen the world, for his people were as sharp eyed as cats. Then that silver light bloomed, as Bakari sketched another cube and the lights brightened. Now he could see about with that faint grayness he experienced in cat form. Inside the gate, there was still nothing but the greenness of the dense hedges.

"Did I ever tell you about my mother?" Bakari said calmly, like they were having a pint at the Green Man, but his head was scanning to the right and left in the hedge maze. He took the right, though why was impossible to tell. Ronan remained silent, not wanting to disturb whatever precarious decisions were keeping them alive.

"She believed in magic: all the old style stuff. It used to break her heart that she lived in a run down duplex with neighbors whose favorite occupation was beating their children." Bakari had stopped at a hedge end, and the sounds of a waltz could be faintly heard. Ronan didn't know how normal or abnormal that was, but Bakari went on.

"She couldn't ignore that: couldn't bear to hear children cry. She said it was killing the earth's magic. So she always called social services. Even went round there and bailed this monster up, on his front door step." Bakari crept around the corner, bent low.

"A brave woman," Ronan commented, trying to sound as relaxed as his friend.

"The bravest and the best," Bakari's voice was rough with still powerful emotion, "and she didn't regret a thing, even when that man set fire to her unit, even when she was dying slowly in the hospital."

What could he say to that? Ronan had never really known his own mother, she'd been as distant and as loving as the moon. So he said what he really thought. "You were lucky to feel that love, my friend. Not everyone does."

"I know that," Bakari said. "But it doesn't make not having it now any easier."

The waltz had become louder, until Ronan could even identify it, Moonlight something-or-other. It reminded him of his time in Paris before the Second World War, when his powers were stronger than they were now, and he had somehow still managed to retain some of his Fey arrogance.

Bakari was standing up, looking along the open length of this part of the maze. At the end was all purple glow; a thousand glittering pinpricks of light spun and twirled around a figure that was in turn spinning and turning. It was a tiny woman, small enough so the top of her head would only reach Bakari's chest, dressed in a sparkling white dress. She was beautiful enough to make Ronan think of the dances and balls in his cousin's realm, when the Fey King ruled. Her lustrous black tresses were piled atop her head and pinned with silver bands and exquisitely made flowers. Around her ivory pale throat hung a thick string of diamonds, which served to show off her softly moving neck.

And she was dancing, gently and beautifully — her eyes never leaving Bakari. Everything about her was flawless. Ronan heard his friend sigh, for he was seeing the manifestation of his dream of magic. He took a step forward and there was a rustle. When his hand came into view, it was not covered with feathers — it was his own.

Ronan felt his distant neck prickle. Hadn't Bakari said something about the protection of an avatar...

"Bakari," Ronan hissed, "this is getting very strange."

No reply came, though his friend moved closer to the woman, who was stepping so daintily and spinning in a light of her own.

"'Tis is a place you said held danger," Ronan found he was shouting now, though he didn't know how much use that would be. "Stop!"

He could see why Bakari was attracted, even though he was a mere piggy back. The little woman was so very beautiful and the light falling around her heartbreakingly delicate. Bakari was now only a few yards from her and each step seemed to show another beauty about her; the elegant arch of her cheekbone, the dazzling black eyes which reflected the light about her, and the lips the colour of crushed berries that were almost begging to be kissed.

Ronan saw all that Bakari saw, but also more. The teeth those lips revealed when they smiled were sharply pointed and the light in those eyes was shadowy and malicious.

"Go back, Bakari!" he yelled, sure his real voice was hoarse by now, but his friend took no notice. Ronan flailed about, trying to find with his disembodied hands where his head and the piggy back device were, but nothing seemed real, only the woman and the sound of the waltz. He was going to watch Bakari die.

It was going to happen now, right at that moment when Bakari reached out for the little dark haired woman, who was nothing but a predator in disguise. For in that virtual instant she did change, as Ronan had seen many other fell creatures do in his own world. That beautiful face stretched and collapsed upon itself, becoming an arrow-like serpent head with curved teeth that dripped with poison. Bakari didn't move. He was rapt, humming the sound of that marvelous waltz.

Ronan's heart lurched and his head spun with horror. He had no power here, less even than in the human world. But his unseen hand shot forward nonetheless, remembering how much Art it had once owned, the power it had once commanded. He was not the human Ronan anymore. He reclaimed his name of power. He was once again Puck the Trickster.

Art bloomed from the end of Bakari's hand just like it was the Fey's own. It was the golden light Ronan remembered, the sign of his people's might, and there it was shining forth in the human's world of the Line. It exploded around the hissing serpent form, incinerating the menace that was leaning forward to claim the life of his friend.

Ronan felt the heat of the light burning his face and the oddest scent of all, the explosion of jasmine in his nostrils, though both of these seemed impossible within the limits of the piggyback as Bakari had explained it. He was stunned, shocked to the ancient core by this.

And yet Bakari was alive, apparently shaking his head and none the wiser. Instead he poked his toe in the dust; it was all that remained.

"Must have better defenses than I thought," he muttered proudly.

Ronan didn't say a thing, letting his pounding heart find its normal beat. Since he couldn't explain it himself, he certainly wasn't going to say anything to Bakari.

The Liner went on in the now lightening hedge maze. And suddenly he was through into a moonlight rose garden. The blooms were everywhere, climbing over the hedges, curling along the ground; great long spikes of beauty, each one glowing with a soft green light.

"This is it," he hissed to Ronan. "The core of their system."

Ronan said nothing. His mind still whirling, he didn't take much notice as Bakari set to work on the roses. Within an instant he had summoned up from nothing an army of bright purple ants. They fanned out from his hands, scrambling over the roses and chipping through their stems, while other, braver ones burrowed into the petals themselves. Some were destroyed, crushed by the innocent seeming petals, but others were getting through.

Numbers began to roll in, a constant stream of vibrant blue scrolling down Bakari's vision, but far too much for him to process now and then certainly didn't mean anything to Ronan.

"Now, we file these babies away for later," Bakari said, "and get the hell outta here while we're still in one piece."

Barely were the words out of his mouth than they both heard a hissing sound, but it was no snake this time, it was a sickly green gas starting to rise out of the ground. As Bakari backed away carefully, thousands of his inquisitive ants shriveled and died. Ronan could almost smell the death in that cloud.

"No time for anything fancy," the Liner said calmly. He sketched the shape of an open door in the air and they were gone with an abrupt snap. Ronan's head rang and even Bakari seemed suddenly breathless. He shook his head, which only made Ronan even more disorientated.

The were now inside what appeared to be a metallic bubble, all chrome and stillness, the antithesis of the hedge maze.

"Where are we?" Ronan asked.

"This is the loading chamber. It's where I work when I don't want to be at risk from the Line. I construct all my bots and programs here. It's kind of like a workshop."

A full length mirror, old fashioned and somewhat battered looking appeared in front of Bakari. It showed his raven form, with his human eyes staring out from it. Ronan felt a twinge of jealousy. Once he had been the true shapeshifter.

Bakari moved his hand over the mirror and the scrolling numbers boiled over its surface, moving like oil on water.

"Now we just have to sift through what we got." The raven peered closer. "Looks like a lot of bio med stuff. But what we really want to see is…" he stopped abruptly, "I don't believe it!"

For the figure appearing in the mirror was the knife sharp image of Greer, though not in her usual ethereal earth child outfit. She wore an immaculately tailored suit, her hair confined to a bun, and her ruined eyes were concealed by stylish eye shades.

Ronan felt comprehension beginning to dawn, but he asked the question anyway, "What's she doing there?"

"She's it, my friend, the owner and founder of Infinity Rose. Looks like we've both got the sharp end of the stick on this one."

Greer as a corporate executive? Ronan tried not to be too shocked. After all, Greer had always appeared to have enough money to do her own magical research; her lair was evidence enough of that. And he'd never seen her for great lengths of time, even when they were more friendly than now. Her wealth of knowledge on most things could spring from Infinity Rose; he'd always found it odd how very well informed she was, for someone who supposedly didn't go out at all.

"But what about Ella?" Ronan asked. "Is there any clue why Infinity Rose, or Greer, would want her?"

Bakari's fingers danced across the surface of the mirror. "Not really, only a priority one attached to finding her."

Ronan couldn't help grinning. "And she obviously doesn't know Ella is right here in Penherem or she'd have got you to help her."

"It's a massive coincidence that we're all here in the village when you think about it; the Mask, Ella, you and me."

"I'm too old to believe in coincidence my friend — something is afoot in Penherem and it's far more than we think." Ronan tried to pin down whether he was excited or afraid.

"So what have we got?" Bakari's raven cocked his head, an utterly bird like gesture. "A mask Greer wants you to steal for her, with Ella and Infinity Rose right in the middle."

"Don't forget Hamish's murder either," Ronan reminded him. "I don't see all the pieces, but I know one thing, Greer wants magic in the world, because it offers her more power than she can possibly hope to gain at the moment. Is that really something we want to happen?"

Bakari dismissed the mirror but didn't reply. He would be torn: he too wanted magic, even if for far different reasons.

"I'm going to go off Line now," he said somewhat tersely.

Ronan hadn't time to say anything, before there was another white flash and he found himself staring across the short distance at his friend's troubled face. Bakari busied himself removing the piggy back equipment and Ronan let him, his ancient mind trying to find the right path in this mess. But no matter the confusions of what was happening, he had at least gained one revelation.

He'd never seen the Line, always imagined that it was a kind of mass delusion, but Bakari had changed all that and Ronan had learned something incredible. Humanity, denied its magic for hundreds of years, had somehow managed to recreate it for themselves in the Line. It was amazing, but Ronan could think of no other explanation as to how he had managed to defend Bakari there. His ancient power had worked in the Line, where it had long ago failed in the real world. And it all fitted with what he knew about Greer. If there was magic in the Line, then she would have been one of the first to find it.

Yet, he'd always assumed that technology was the antithesis of Art, and it would take a lot of readjustment for him to fit this new reality into his world view. This was human magic, something that they'd help destroy hundreds of years ago, but recreated right here, in a world he'd never even known existed. And he could only speculate wildly how this could change things. Ronan even dared think that perhaps this new Art the humans had made, could realign the Fey world again.

The very idea that he might be able to return to the Fey made his heart race and he could not stop the mad cascade of images that followed after that thought. He ground his teeth to stop himself exclaiming.

He couldn't say anything to Bakari — for one thing, he didn't quite believe it, himself.

CHAPTER THIRTEEN

Linger

The Master of Water and Land. Aroha repeated the name to herself, trying to remember what the correct form of address would be. Nana had never told her such things, and what she had learned from the Folk had not been enough. She knew that there would be a challenge, there always had been. But what came after that? Why were the Folk sending her here, and worst of all, what would the final price of Daniel's life be.

They walked towards the hill, up deserted streets, until they reached a bare and exposed section of gorse covered rock. Laying her palm flat against the raw earth, Aroha called. It was like knocking on a stranger's door, only this was a very frightening stranger.

An almighty crack, the sound of rock torn loose from its bindings, the rumble of displaced soil, made them both leap back. Beside her, Daniel said a bad word under his breath.

A long grim passage had opened up, and if she listened closely Aroha could hear the sound of the Master's heart, a slowly playing drum; it almost drowned out the sound of her own, yammering like a tom-tom.

"In there?" Daniel growled. "You can't go in there! I've lived all my life in Wellington and I've never heard of caves under Mount Victoria."

"He's lived here longer," Aroha replied, "And we do have to go."

The look on her face must have convinced him, because he found a chem-stick, and after breaking it to produce an eerie green glow, he was first to take a step into the passageway.

Aroha followed after, ready for anything, she told herself. The walls around them were close and rich with the scent of wet earth — not a comfortable smell. Aroha tried not to think of his favor being withdrawn and them caving in, even though her imagination painted vivid pictures of it. And the further they went, the louder the sound became; the sound of his heart.

But she could not stop this, not even with the scent of danger and a man who called her friend now in peril. Especially not when they broke out of the narrow confines of the tunnel and saw the true enormous reality of the Master of Land and Sea.

It was impossible to ignore the looming head, which was curved in a great arch like some ancient gothic building. The sweeping length of bone passed between eyes the colour of bright green leaves and curved up like an enormous shovel — for in essence that was what it was. But the body could not be seen, not even if you stood open- mouthed with your head craning up, like Daniel did. The bulk of the taniwha curled away and was swallowed up into the earth.

In the time before magic had left the world, there had been no harbor here, only a lake in which two massive taniwha lived. They were brothers and rivals; the aggressive and energetic Ngake and his slower quieter brother Whataitai. One day Ngake had heard the ocean just on the other side of the mountains and his heart longed to swim there in the currents of the deep. He had curled his massive body up like a steel spring and charged across the harbor. With that powerful head and all the strength of a taniwha he had stormed his way out of the lake, plowing all the earth before him, breaking the walls that held him and the lake back.

The quieter Whataitai had suffered as the meek often do. He'd become trapped in the shallow mud created by the loss of the lake. First the water had dried up, and then in time the magic of the world withdrew as well. Whataitai finally called to the other Fey, his cousins, but there was no rescue for him. Their time had passed and their world had moved beyond the reach of the human realm. So he was stuck in every way.

But taniwhas do not die. Like the other Fey who had managed to flee, they remained immortal. So he was buried, hidden from view, still full with power, but awaiting a time when the way home was clear.

All this Aroha knew, but also she realised that this was no pet, no creature to be tamed, cuddled and made friends with. His eyes were fixed on her and she felt the regard as if pinned to the spot.

"*Ko wai e whakararuraru ana i ahau?*" He spoke in the language of the land, the language that had been born out of the mountains and lakes, Maori. Both Daniel and Aroha understood, for it was one of the two languages taught to children. This was fortunate, for taniwha could be quick to anger and not happy to give translation for the benefit of smaller beings.

"Sky dwellers, why do you break my solitude?" the thunderous voice rumbled through rock and soil.

Aroha knew this question was fraught with danger: there were a thousand wrong things to say to a taniwha. So she began carefully. "Great Whataitai, child of Taane Nui a Rangi," it never hurt to mention the taniwha's illustrious ancestry; they tended to like being reminded that they were descendants of gods, "I was sent here by the Forest Folk."

"The *patupaiarehe*? What do those pale faced meddlers want?" The taniwha shifted and its smallest claw, taller and longer than Daniel, came remarkably close.

"I don't think he likes them much," the soldier whispered in English to her. She wished he hadn't.

"Cease your twitterings," Whataitai's head lowered closer, while his breath nearly knocked them over. It grew very warm in the tunnel.

Aroha choked back panic. "I asked a favor of the Folk, and the price, they said, was to come to you."

A silence descended. All that could be heard was the monstrous breathing and heartbeat of Whataitai, but all the time that terrible green glare was fixed on Aroha.

"You are no child of this land," he finally said. "You wear the face of one like a mask, but your beginnings were not here. Perhaps that is why the *patupaiarehe* sent you to me."

"I do not know, great Whataitai, where I began. My grandmother will never speak of it."

Whataitai laughed, "A wise guardian indeed and from I, the greatest protector of all, that is high praise. But I think the time has come for your flowering, young Fey."

Aroha frowned. She'd heard that word, but only from her Nana when she thought she was alone, quietly weeping in her bedroom. It had no real meaning to Aroha, but still something stirred inside her on hearing it.

"Do you not know the story of the Three Realms?" Whataitai's head bumped against her body, the smell of salty ocean and warm earth wrapping itself around her.

She shook her head silently, too overwhelmed to speak.

"Then you have been denied your heritage. *Titiro whakamiharo ki nga tamariki a Tane.* Listen to me then, last living descendant of Taane of the forest, greatest child of Papatuanuku, Earth Mother.

"In the time before time, when the earth was new, she was not alone; for no thing is alone, like no person is alone, however much they feel it. She had two sisters, each alike in beauty; the Fey realm where all was magic and the Other Realm, where all was stillness. No one walked in that place, for it was set aside for the gods and creatures of grace. In the Fey where all magic came from, there was beauty and music and laughter. And their kind never died except by accident or murder. It was a place that humans dreamed of and could sometimes touch in their music and fair words."

Whataitai paused, his green eyes glistening with a great gleaming taniwha tear.

"But there arose in the Other Realm, that place of stillness, a great hunger and great desire for destruction that was even beyond the order of death that ruled in human realm. It was clever and quiet in the nature of that place and it was a long time before it ate that world, turning all of its beauty to darkness. But it had a terrible hunger, not sated even by a realm. It turned its intent to the other sister worlds. First of all in beauty, it looked to the Fey.

"But that realm's children wouldn't go quietly, for they had the gift of power and they fought against that which they named The Unmaker. Yet against such hate they could not triumph, so they sought help in the human world. For humans were not without their own kind of magic, wild though it was. And when the Fey mated with them, their children became masters of both magics. And so it was that only together were they able to contain the Unmaker's desire for destruction. They managed to lock away the Shattered realm from their own and for a while that was enough. And there was peace for a while, though the Fey and the humans distanced themselves from one another, fearing what they did not know.

"But the Unmaker's ways are devious and it reached across the void and filled some of the Fey with promises of glory, if they would but let it in. So once more in crisis, the Fey and the humans turned to each other, though they had grown deeply suspicious of each other by then. Yet together they found a way to push the three realms apart. Though those that did this mighty thing, your mother a great and powerful Fey and your father a gentle and good bard, finally won at great cost. The sister realms would now drift further apart. The bard had human children and would not leave them. So your mother, at the last moment, found a way for him to gain second life, reborn into the Fey world. For the Earth Mother loved him greatly."

Whataitai paused and now his eyes were swirling, taking on the hues of greenstone. "Do you know their names, little one?"

Aroha did not, and almost choked on the shame of that. What sort of child did not even know the names of her parents?

The taniwha dipped his head and nudged her almost sorrowfully. "It is not in my power to tell you. For the naming of things is a great magic in itself. When you find them out, you will be finding your own power."

"That's all very well," Daniel finally had found his voice, "but she's just a kid."

Whataitai rumbled in his chest, until their little cave began to feel like it might become a cave in. "That is not my concern, nor would I alter it if I could. The world has changed too much, and now it needs her."

"Me?" Aroha squeaked, the Folk's quest was seeming crueler by the minute.

"The two remaining Realms were not meant to be apart — they rely on each other for many things. The Fey receives energy and passion from the humans and in return the humans find beauty and magic. Without this interaction, both worlds will wither. Magic is leaving this place for good. And once it has done so, both realms will perish."

"We've done OK without it," Daniel whispered to Aroha.

"Really?" the terrible sound of rock breaking made the others jump as Whataitai shifted his tremendous bulk, "Do you think all that happens above is hidden from me? Not only here in this land, but all over the realm, is disaster happening. The earth magic has gone deep, hidden itself like I have hidden, and humanity has lost the power to wield it. The world is dying."

"And you think I can stop that?" Aroha asked quietly.

"Hey," Daniel took her hand, "You can't just lay this on her!"

"If she rejects this task, then there is no other. She must find a way to give humanity back a touch of its magic and bring the realms together, without freeing the Unmaker again."

Aroha's eyes filled with tears. Unlike Daniel, she knew the taniwha spoke the truth. It was all starting to fit in. Her gifts were unique, so they must have a purpose. But still, she'd somehow imagined once the Folk's demand was met, she'd be free to go home to Nana. Now, however, a whole vista of a different task was opening up. She didn't flinch away when Daniel's arm went around her and gave her a tight, brief hug.

"I don't believe it," he said fiercely to Whataitai over her head.

"You didn't even believe in magic until you met this child," came the thunderous reply, "And yet here you are talking to a taniwha. Wake up human!"

"It's OK," Aroha pushed away a little, "I've always known..." she paused and took a ragged breath. "I've never been the same as other children. I heard things and saw things they never did. Nana would never tell me why, so it's kinda nice to know there is a reason." She lied.

"*Ka pai*, little one there is always a reason," Whataitai's massive mouth split open in what might have been some sort of smile. The effect was spoiled by the huge teeth it revealed.

"So you don't know how she's supposed to do this?" Daniel asked somewhat rigidly.

A vast sighed rippled down the taniwha's length. "No, I see much, but not that. Yet I do have a gift that might help." He plunged his talons down into the earth and a great gash of light sprang up as though the taniwha had pierced some barrier. When he pulled free, a beautiful weapon, an ancient club made of greenstone, a *mere*, lay in his great clawed hand. For a moment Whataitai held it aloft, ancient eyes gazing on it with sadness.

He lowered it with a sigh. As the mere approached Aroha it dwindled in size, until the club was the size any Maori warrior would have used.

She took it with great reverence. It was a great toanga, a magnificent treasure. It lay in her hands, a beautifully smooth piece of greenstone crafted into an ancient weapon, yet it was different than the ones Nana had shown her pictures of, for its handle was decorated with iridescent paua shell. Aroha turned it. Even in the dim light of Daniel's army issue lantern it gleamed with a thousands shades of blue and green and pink. She looked up with amazement at Whataitai.

The taniwha blinked, "It is my power, child, the power of land and water, a fraction of the earth magic. But it is not something that can yet be taken above, for its time has not yet come. It is something you must hold within you until the right moment."

Aroha looked down at the mere and she knew what he meant. A golden light flashed out from her hands, encircling the weapon, making Daniel yelp and the taniwha hum with approval. All the fabulous veins and patterns of the greenstone leapt up and the paua reflected the light in thousands of tiny spots around the cave. The weapon was growing translucent as the light intensified, and Aroha *pushed*, inviting the power to be part of her. The mere was gone, and her hands were cupped empty around nothing.

Daniel uttered a rough expletive and turned her hands over, as if she were a street performer who had just made his watch disappear. But instead he found something else. Aroha's arm was now a mottled green colour from wrist to elbow, shining faintly and cool to the touch.

"This just gets weirder and weirder," he muttered.

"*Iti noa ana, he pito mata*. Now you must leave," Whataitai rumbled. "This cave has not long to last."

And it was not just his rumbling: the earth was remembering her true form. Aroha pressed her hand against the surprisingly warm flank of Whataitai, giving silent thanks for his wisdom and promising she would do all she could.

"*Haere ra*, then. I will rest a while," the taniwha replied, "Sleep my sleep and await your success, young Fey."

Daniel and Aroha fled up the tunnel, though she did look back once and caught a glimpse of his bulk being reclaimed. It should have made her sad, but his gift and power was really still with her. It just remained for her to find out what it all meant.

Ella ran. It felt like every fiber of her was committed to getting as far away from Ronan as possible. His words and the look in his eyes frightened her beyond anything she could remember. She was used to being unnoticed, in fact she depended on it. Ella might have thought she resented this fact, until the Fey creature had looked at her. Her mind had exploded with horror, flooding her senses with the urge to hide. Somehow it felt like a matter of life and death not to be noticed.

But where to go? If she went home, he'd be there, and Bakari's was totally out of the question. Only one other place remained. Penherem Hall seemed to have shrugged off its cloak of coldness as she ran up the crushed shell pathway. It positively glowed with late afternoon warmth. No QuickStep tour was outside and the stillness was a balm. Ella felt like she could wander through the gardens or the endless hallways and never be noticed.

Tania was waiting for her on the front entrance, dwarfed by the columns, her ivory hair almost blending in with the stone. She didn't seem at all surprised to find Ella racing up towards her, but one eyebrow did rise at the slate grey of the shiver cloak. When Ella stopped in front of her, she had no idea how to explain herself.

"You're not working today," was all Tania said.

Funny how Ella had never noticed her eyes, how wide the pupils were. Perhaps she was on some sort of medication. "No, I know I'm not. I just…" Ella paused, not quite sure how much to say. "Well, I guess I just need someone to talk to," she said in a rush.

Tania's eyebrow rose, but she turned and went into the Hall without comment. The foyer was silent except for the rhythmic tick of the grandfather clock, as quiet as it had been a hundred other times Ella had been here, but this time, for some unknown reason, a shiver ran up her spine. She followed Tania through into the small staff kitchen. Here everything was stripped bare, so it could have been any kitchen in any modern home.

Tania made her a cup of tea, which was highly unusual. After Ella took a small sip, though, she realised why Tania rarely served tea. She discretely pushed the mug of watery liquid away, trying not to offend.

Tania got herself a water and sat down opposite, hands wrapped around the chill glass. "So talk."

Ella's lips twisted. She could still feel the panic inside, but it had receded enough to make her cautious. Although she didn't want anyone to think she was mad, who better could she trust than someone who had already faced that demon?

"Do you believe in magic, Tania?"

The question didn't faze her, though her eyes did flit to the corner of the room; worried probably about someone else hearing. She licked her lips. "Yes, I guess I do."

That wasn't exactly the answer Ella had been expecting, she'd already planned her assault on Tania's skepticism. "Really?"

"Do you know why I was taken away for Adjustment, Ella?"

She shook her head, almost afraid to answer.

"I heard voices. Though I've got no proof of it, I know they are not hallucinations. They're the voices of the dead."

Ella swallowed the hard lump in her throat, "How do you..."

"Know?" Tania's calm face turned suddenly violently melancholy, as though she'd been storing up that emotion. "Because sometimes I can hear things they say — and sometimes I've acted on what I've heard. That's how I found the Winter Mask."

Ella was momentarily confused, but then she remembered the village newspaper's bit on Tania's discovery in a dusty corner of her mansion, not long after she'd returned.

The aristocrat's lips curled in a faint smile. "I don't know who it was, talking about it. All I know is that I found it there, under one hundred years of rubbish. If I'm crazy, then explain how I did that."

"I guess there is no logical explanation," Ella replied and suddenly realised that she had found an ally. "It's a kind of magic, I suppose."

"Probably," Tania said, though she shifted uncomfortably on her seat, "But it's also a curse. I can't turn it off."

"You mean you hear them all the time?"

"Pretty much. Mostly all they talk about is their deaths, and that's pretty boring."

Ella gulped, trying to imagine how that would be; like being in a room of constantly chattering people — but with the added freaky factor. So she said the first comforting thing that came to mind. "At least you're not alone."

Tania smiled a smile like a knife blade. "Why, do you know anyone else who can hear the dead?"

"No. But there are plenty of strange people in Little Penherem."

The lady of the manor raised her fingers to her mouth and began to chew determinedly on her cuticles. "So you've noticed, huh?"

Ella nodded. It had only taken her a couple of days to see that Little Penherem was overly empowered with that greatest of English virtues, eccentricity. "Do you think that means anything?"

"Everything has a meaning," Tania cocked her head, perhaps hearing something beyond Ella's recognition. "You know," she paused, "I've always wondered if it came from something about here; perhaps the hill, or the stone circle. When I go there, everything's quiet, as if…"

A sharp rap at the window made both women jump, and for an instant Ella thought she was hearing what Tania did. But it was no long, mournful ghostly face peering in through the glass, just Ronan's.

Something in Tania's expression made Ella realise that he wouldn't be welcome in the Hall. Perhaps she was feeling too fragile.

"I'll go see what he wants," Ella said, finding she would be glad to get out of the Hall's increasingly oppressive atmosphere.

Tania caught her hand before she could get very far. The gesture was so unexpected and so out of character that Ella stopped with a shudder. "Be careful," the other said somberly. "They still haven't found Hamish's killer and the ghosts are…. They're restless."

Penherem Hall was suddenly very chilly, and surely that must be her own imagination. Ella wasn't quite sure what she garbled, but she got out quickly. She was used to Tania being aloof, and if sometimes she had wished the lady of the manor would share more, Ella now profoundly wished she hadn't.

It had at least cooled her more irrational fear of Ronan. When she saw his open smiling face, she could only wonder why she'd been so afraid of him. But then she recalled the look that had skimmed Tania's face. Could she have heard something from the voices of the past? Was he dangerous?

Yet if there was anyone that Ella still trusted, it was Bakari, and his eyes were full of open and honest love: the kind of caring that had no strings attached. He held out his hand to her and even Ronan stepped aside as she went to him. Bakari's strong brown arms held her, enveloping her in his musky scent and his warmth. He didn't need to say anything; she knew with him she would always be safe.

He pushed her back a little, and gave her a little shake. "Now why'd you run off on us like that, girl? We weren't going to hurt you."

Ella's lips twisted. "I really don't know. I just... I just panicked. I can't explain it at all. I'm sorry."

"And you came here?" Ronan sounded almost offended.

"Can't explain that either. But I talked to Tania and her problems make mine seem tiny."

"Really?"

"She thinks she can hear ghosts."

They should have laughed, but so much had changed in the last couple of days, that instead they exchanged an appraising look. Neither commented.

"We better get you safe somewhere," Ronan was subtly guiding her away from the Hall. "I presume your friend Doyle knows where you live."

Ella planted her feet. She was certainly not going to let anyone else push her around, not Bakari and certainly not Ronan. Part of her flared at the thought that he was far too used to people obeying him. He just thought a little too much of himself. So she did what she usually did, avoided conflict, smoothed the waters... lied.

"Well, actually, he doesn't," she replied blandly, "I heard he was looking for me through an old friend. What sort of idiot do you take me for — as if I'd leave a forwarding address to an ex."

Ella guessed she must be quite good at this lying deal, because both men seemed to relax.

Bakari looked up at the darkening sky. "Good thing, too, El — but do you mind us walking you back to yours? Hamish's killer is still in the village."

She admitted to herself that, occasionally, it was nice to be pampered. The three of them walked companionably back to the village and no one said anything, not even Ronan. They were probably worried about her running off again if they said the wrong thing. Ella smiled secretly to herself.

As they walked down the narrow road to Penherem, the birds calling out their evening song and a chill just beginning to settle about them, Ella found her eyes drawn to the hill which was the ever-present backdrop to the village.

Raven Hill was not much of a hill in the scheme of things, but it was the tallest outcrop in the area and a good draw card for the tourists. When summer came there would be thousands of them scrambling through the remnant of forest, fording its tiny streams and climbing to the top to bathe in the awe of the stone circle which held the high ground.

Tania had said something about the Hill. Ella frowned and dropped her eyes from it. A curiosity was settling in the back of her mind, an itch that she tried to ignore. But she had never been up Raven Hill, never stood in the stone circle and after this day, of all days, her eyes were open to things she'd never thought possible.

And it couldn't be herself that was special: she couldn't even entertain that thought, so perhaps it was Penherem itself. If that were true, it could even be the village and the Hill as well. Though Ella had never engaged in any New Age experiences, she'd visited Stonehenge and Avebury and felt the places as special. Penherem Circle was surely worth a look.

And as for the men, they obviously thought they knew everything. It'd be a welcome change to lay some new information in front of them for a change — make them as surprised and shocked as she'd been today.

Ella said goodbye very quietly and politely at her doorstep and waved to them as they went on their way, all the while nursing her own plans. She watched them until they reached the end of the street.

Qoth mewed at her indignantly from under the hydrangea by the door. She'd been quite safe with the automatic cat feeder, but she was still a feline to demand personal attention. Getting over her annoyance quickly, she adoringly tried to trip Ella once the door was open.

Ella fluffed around, pulling the cushions into shape and humming to herself under her breath. She made herself a quick cup of tea and stood drinking it by the front window, content for a moment to watch Penherem life bustle past.

Helen Carew was the one person who caught her eye, though, for there was something different about her stride. The woman had annoyed Ella with her harrowed look and the way her eyes never quite seemed to catch onto you. Yet when she saw Ella standing at the window she waved cheerfully and for the first time it was possible to see what wonderful mint green eyes she had.

Ella frowned and made to go out to talk to Helen, but the other obviously had business elsewhere. She hurried off almost as quickly as she had appeared.

Qoth chirped from the window ledge in an inquisitive feline manner, rubbing her head against Ella's side.

"I don't know either, pretty lady — it beats me." Part of her filed that little change away for later examination.

The evening was pulling in, wrapping its arms around Little Penherem and muffling it with darkness and chill. She waited until the people ceased walking and the night had truly taken hold.

Ella wasn't afraid of that. She was looking forward to it, she told herself firmly — for tonight, she was going to take charge. The shiver cloak might not have been any use in the city, but it would be ideal for Raven Hill. And there was one other relic of her past that would be very useful tonight. She found the low light glasses after much swearing and throwing things about the bottom of her underwear drawer — though what had possessed her to put them there was another mystery.

She gathered her hair into a messy but utilitarian ponytail, tucked the glasses into her pocket until she was out of the village itself, and wrapped the Shiver Cloak about her for the second time in as many days.

Outside, the village was silent. The darkness, chilly but not unwelcoming, was punctuated only by the occasional street light. It felt like she had the night to herself, but who knew, perhaps she didn't.

Ella moved out of the wane light and into the shadows where her technology worked best. Putting the control glove on her right hand, she activated the cloak. It immediately warmed, not a bad thing, and when she looked down at her arm there was the reassuring shiver. Odd, how she felt so much nostalgia all of a sudden for a life that she'd been so desperate to leave behind.

She slid the glasses over her eyes, adjusted the cloak's hood and unhooked its fine veil to hide her face.

Feeling herself slipping on old habits as easily as she slipped on the cloak, Ella turned up Henley Street towards Raven Hill. Qoth watched her go from the step, golden feline eyes not fooled by man's technology.

It certainly was silent out here, but not oppressive. Ella always considered herself something of a city girl, but now as she walked through all the sights and smells of the night countryside she relished the peace there. It soothed her, made her calm, and ordered her thoughts. She could feel the stress and panic of that very strange day leeching out of her and being absorbed by the earth.

Ella twisted her lips at her own thoughts. She'd not be one of those lost souls, those crystal-waving sad-eyed people who looked for magic so very desperately. And yet — there was only one explanation for what she'd seen today. More importantly, it was the reason she was walking upwards. She shook her head and took a deep breath. She was not sad, she was not mad, and she most certainly was going to make up her own mind about things.

The wood when Ella entered it was soft and almost warm, the crescent of the moon making an appearance among the trees. Far off, a fox called into the night. She smiled and walked on.

The wood did not go on for long; it was really just a remnant of an ancient forest, more a park than anything else now. As the hill sloped further upward, it shed the trees and rose further with thin shrubs and thick grass. The shiver cloak whispered through them and Ella felt the urge to sing well up in her.

The stone circle was no grand affair, a short collection of cut rocks, half submerged in the earth. For nearly three hundred years the stones had lain buried, Ella had read all about that. Suspicious locals had first tried to break and then tried to conceal the relics of a past they didn't understand. A local historical group had resurrected the circle about fifty years ago, digging them up with amateur enthusiasm and all without notifying anyone in authority.

Ella stood just outside the ring looking in, wondering if some revelation would suddenly occur. But there was nothing but her breath rising in the cool night air and the half face of the moon. She didn't quite know what she'd been expecting, perhaps the whispering of the dead like Tania, or the white light of Ronan's earth magic. But whatever it might have been, it was obviously not.

Ella's hand went to the cloak's hood. This was ridiculous, and she was about to pull it back and throw herself down in the grass, when the sound reached her.

It was not much; the snap of a broken twig, perhaps the sound of animals retreating from feet, but her senses were heightened by the stillness and maybe even the place as well.

Heart racing, Ella moved round the other side of the stone circle, putting a good solid rock between her and whoever was coming up the hill. Now was the test if the shiver cloak really did work. Even the thought of it failing made her hand sweaty in the control glove.

The two men who emerged from the shaded wood could not have looked any more out of place. And although Ella didn't recognize them, she knew the type — corp dogs, Doyle used to call them. Operators who had once stalked the slums, but finding the going not quite plump enough, had switched allegiance to the enemy. That's how he'd seen it, and Ella right now could see his point. Their long limbed stride spoke of purpose and something about the way they carried themselves made Ella positive that under those long coats was some serious weaponry. She shrank further back against the side of the stone.

Yet if she recognized the type of man, what scuttled out from the far side of the circle defied description. The white creature stood the height of a man, but it was on eight spiked limbs and resembled nothing so much as a giant white spider, but with a head that was disturbingly human and eyes that glittered in the pale light. Ella's insides churned, her stomach cramped and for a moment her body forgot to breathe. This was the ultimate shock at the end of a day of shocks.

The men, though, were not alarmed, they did not break stride for one instant, coming into what she would have called striking distance.

One of them brushed his hair back from his face with what might have been nervousness, and the glint of metal showed all along his arm. A splicer, Ella thought to herself with a little wince. Doyle had always harbored a desire to become one, but had lacked both the funds and the complete fanaticism required to turn to technology for boosts. Some had hormone injectors, some corneal implants to enhance vision, but this one had obviously gone straight for the favoured option, partial exoskeleton.

Ella's grip tightened instinctively on the control glove. But she couldn't allow fear to drive her to stupidity. If she broke cover now, she couldn't be sure that they wouldn't spot her; some corneal implants had been specifically designed to negate the effects of shiver cloaks. Ella tried to concentrate on keeping her breathing even and her ears open.

The creature, whatever the hell it was, spoke first. The flexible bones that covered its mouth split open, revealing a shark-toothed maw. "Have you found the Child?"

"The Child has never left our care," the splicer's voice was harsh, as if he were dealing with a belligerent used car salesman and not an unearthly creature.

"Liar," it hissed, rising up on those blade-like legs and looking down at the humans. "You have the body, but nothing else. The spirit and anime are not within. You have to find them."

"Easy for you to say," the other man said in a deep melodious voice. "But that has no set form. We're onto it, though. We have leads, and almost found her in London."

"She is in no human city," came the ugly reply. "She finds no comfort there."

Ella bit her lip, managing to remain calm; they were talking about her somehow, though she could not say what this anime meant. But one thing was for sure, this creature was working with these men from Infinity Rose.

"We can only follow leads," the splicer's voice was flat, "and we don't take orders from you, either."

A soft rattle like something within the creature was moving, making Ella think of a snake. Those glittering eyes were flicking between the two men and the blade feet shuffled in the earth.

"You take orders from your mistress, that is true — but she and I have the same master. And I am hungry."

Then the air was suddenly full of movement and sound. The creature leapt in a flurry of sharpness and malevolence, realizing the potential of the menace it conveyed. The splicer stumbled back, apparently even his hardened senses terrified by the swiftness, while the other collapsed on the ground as if in obeisance to the hellish creature. But he was not bending, he was falling.

Ella's vision blurred and she felt the pulse of sudden blood on the earth as if it were coming from her own veins and not those of the startled man. Her body plunged into shock, which was the only thing that kept her from screaming aloud.

The splicer had no time to save his companion; even his revved up senses and reactions were blunt compared to this creatures. The wave of horror that seemed to flow out of it reduced him to a stunned heap.

The victim did not have more than a moment to realise his own demise, his scream of outrage brutally short. The harsh sound of bone breaking echoed around the hills and the blood flew until the stones and earth and the murderer itself were dripping with it. The man's form had not yet ceased twitching when the creature bent over him once more. The razor front claws flew like some nightmare granny knitting at terrific speed, and more cracks sounded, enough to make Ella's stomach rebel. She forced a fist into her mouth to halt the bile and looked away.

The creature finished its deadly crafts and Ella glanced back, mesmerized by the terrible power.

The man, who could have hardly known he was dead, lay butchered just as Hamish had been. The difference being that Ella had only imagined what he'd looked like, while this abrupt violence was right in front of her and horror kept her eyes open. His ribs were splayed wide open; what should have been inside, hidden and safe, was now outside and dead.

The splicer's feet finally gained purchase on the ground and those survival instincts kicked in. He leapt up with the dark barrel of an automatic pointed at the creature.

Its unimpressed stare halted him. The maw opened, the teeth now thick with blood and gristle, "This was the price agreed for my assistance. If I grow hungry, your mistress will feed me — and I will grow hungry without the Child's blood. Find her and you will not become my meat, like your friend."

The splicer watched the blood sliding off the creature's thick shell and reconsidered. His voice was no longer cocky or sure, instead thick with fear, "He... he wasn't my friend."

"Good, then, go back to your work and find what is required, if you wish to go on breathing," the monster leaned forward on those deadly legs, breathing blood and death into the man's face. "If you fail your task I will find you, and this one's death will seem but a pleasant dream."

Ella was not surprised to see this hardened warrior turn and sprint away. She wanted to do the same, but it felt as though she'd become part of the rock she hid behind. The thought that somehow the creature would be able to see beyond the shiver cloak was an overwhelming fear.

It watched the man's frantic flight, and though it had no lips of any kind, it seemed to be smirking.

Then it turned back to the dead man. Front legs dancing delicately, it arranged his internal organs to its own unknowable pattern. And Ella could almost see a pale light within its hideous carapace and had it confirmed that it indeed was feeding on the blood.

Whatever the light meant, it did not take it long to fade. The monster rose higher on its legs and turned towards the forest once more. Ella's heart started again.

But the thing turned back and those glittering eyes were not still, they darted between the stones, while the curled, feathery organs beneath its head fluttered. There was nothing else on this hillside, Ella knew that, so that could only mean one thing.

She would have to risk escape, because a chill certainty had settled on her: to stay here was to die like that man. *I am quiet*, she thought to herself, *nobody's ever seen through the cloak before.*

Keeping her head bowed and her hand firmly on the control glove, she turned away, not meeting those searching eyes. She moved as quietly as she could towards the closest edge of the wood.

However, this creature was far from human and it was full of blood and a hunger that had not been satisfied by one mortal's death. The rattle of its saber legs against stone, made Ella whirl around. No matter how much she wanted to leave the circle, she had to see.

It moved cautiously forward, those feathery organs waving in unseen breezes, the eyes scanning the ground.

Ella's bravery failed her; she managed to hold back a cry of horror, but broke into a run. Only just keeping her feet, she pelted down the slope. It was impossible to remain silent. Every footstep and gasp of breath gave her away despite the cloak. A hiss of uttermost triumph split the air and she knew that pursuit and death were just a moment behind.

Reaching the trees, she dived into their darkness, but heard the rattle of the monster's hard carapace not far off. The wood was so silent that it offered no protection. Ella would not die in the same place as the man, but she would share his pain.

I don't want to die, Ella repeated the human mantra to herself in her terrified head, but it wouldn't make any difference. She darted around a tree, a thick set oak, sure that this was it. This was the spot.

And the stallion that waited beyond reared up. He was the colour of sea foam, with huge dark eyes and a wild, tangled mane. In her terror Ella could hardly grasp what such a creature was doing here in the woods, so near her death.

The monster was close behind. The horse bent his front legs, unmistakably offering his wide back and it was such a refuge that Ella scrambled up. Barely had her fingers twined through that mane, than they were away. Clinging to his neck, Ella was bounced around. She'd never ridden before, but she was certainly not going to let herself fall off.

Trees whipped at her head, branches caught her hair and cut her skin, but she was alive. The air in her lungs seemed suddenly like a precious gift.

The creature was still there. Though the stallion wheeled about, his great haunches bunching under them, and they seemed to fly, they were still pursued. Ella felt giddy and faint; surely the forest was not this big, they should have reached the edge long before now. What was happening?

The horse stumbled beneath her, clipping his hoof against a tree root, and he almost went to his knees. Ella cried out, but he managed to spring upright and surged away once more. But she could tell he was faltering. The creature was tireless and the horse was not. The trees were forcing him to dodge and turn, and everywhere was danger.

Ella was crying now, tasting salt on her lips — not only for herself, but for the brave stallion who had meant to save her. Throwing a look over her shoulder she saw the monster scuttling on and felt the horrible weight of his desire on her.

The stallion called a challenge, a resounding whinny that made the trees shake and their enemy hiss. Then he was racing again, this time uphill, and the forest was dropping away once again but faster somehow. Ella wrapped her arms around the stallion's surging, sweaty neck and cried into it.

They were out of the trees and once more the stone circle loomed. Her rescuer galloped to the centre, past the creature's latest victim and onto the thick green grass. Here Ella slipped off, hoping that the stallion would leave, hoping that at least one of them could survive this.

But he did not. As she lay there, the air buckled around the horse like intense heat on a summer's day, his form altered and it was Ronan who bent over her, a real human hand brushing her hair back from her eyes.

His skin was cool. Ella looked up and for the first time really saw into his eyes. It was funny how she'd never noticed them before, the deepest brown she'd ever seen, but something about them suggested a dark purple, almost black. They weren't anything human, but then they weren't frightening either. The panic that had gripped her slowly eased. In this ring of stone, with Ronan's hand reaching for hers, it suddenly felt as though things weren't all that bad.

She let him pull her to her feet. "You can defeat this thing," she said confidently.

He did not let go of her hand, but he shook his head sadly. "You are too kind, Ella. I am Fey, but I have wasted all my Art in this Realm. The Seed is fresh and more powerful than I."

"The Seed?"

"The Seed of the Unmaker — his final gift to the human world, a promise of devastation to come, woken by the scent of magic."

"Then let's run."

Ronan sighed and looked down at his feet. "It has made a Loop, sealed us to the hill — we will not be able to get out until dawn and we will not live that long. I'm sorry."

And Ella suddenly noticed how tired he was, and the sweat of horse and man that was puddling at his feet. He was as pale as milk. But she wasn't afraid, just dreadfully sad for him. "I wish there was something I could do."

The Seed emerged from the woods, not hurrying, just deliberately making its way towards them, knowing that it had bought them to bay. The moonlight made its white shell gleam like bone.

Ronan raised Ella's hand to his lips and kissed it lightly. "Looks like my dance partner's arrived," and then he stepped away from her to meet the enemy. Two steps from her side he shifted again, this time a jet black panther with eyes of pure gold.

Ella wanted to cry out for him to stop, but suddenly everything was changing. The air thickened, as if the two combatants were caught in a bead of glass, each movement slow and beautiful. It felt as though she could pick up that moment, twirl it in her hand; examine the meaning and loveliness of it.

The panther leapt to meet the Seed, and the cat was all elegance and grace. A tear sprang to Ella's eye and the thought came unbidden that this second would never come again, no matter what the outcome. Every breath was precious, every action held meaning.

Then the blood came, Ronan's blood. The Seed was faster and full with its Master's power still, whereas Ronan, as he'd admitted himself, had spent the bulk of his already. Ella could see all this. They danced so close to her that she could have reached out and touched them, and when the blood flew stripes of it landed on her cheek and hair.

Ella's eyes drooped, the awareness of her body fading, as if all her concentration had forced it out. She leapt aloft, seeing her own body standing idle, the whirling chaos of the battle and the ring of stone. The only thing she could feel was the warmth of Ronan's blood and the dreadful ache of his sorrow. Even after hundreds of years, he did not want to die.

Help us, she called, though to what she couldn't have named. The warmth grew to a blinding heat, the scene blurred and dissolved and the earth rumbled.

Her body summoned her back to feel that tremor in her very bones. Swaying, she watched the stones shake and ring to some unseen power, but felt no terror. Unlike the Seed, who keened loud and high and broke from the circle to stand furious beyond the reach of its might.

The hill opened; a warmth and darkness, a sanctuary. "Come."

Ronan staggered to his feet, bleeding from a score of painful wounds, but he smiled right back. Taking her hand, feeling the rush of Art around him, he allowed her to lead them both into the heart of Raven Hill.

CHAPTER FOURTEEN
Visitation

The world that Daniel and Aroha emerged into was a far different one. The girl could feel the weight of the *ponamu mere* inside her, its power for now quiet, but with it came disturbing thoughts not entirely her own. Of this she said nothing to Daniel.

He led her down the still quiet street by the hand, sometimes so quickly that she felt dragged somehow. His palm with sweaty and he was shaking. She'd expected no less.

The words of Whataitai echoed in her head. The taniwha had spoken of her parents so easily, when Nana refused to say anything, and he had known their names though he couldn't speak them. Aroha tried to imagine the Fey and the bard, trying to picture what their faces might have been like. Would they have smiled often? Would they have loved her as Nana did? Were they even still alive?

The sudden thought bought Aroha to a stop. The taniwha had not suggested that they were dead. She'd just assumed that the reason Nana would say nothing was because their deaths hurt too much, but if her mother was Fey and immortal, and her father — he too had magic. Tears sprang to Aroha's eyes. She might even get to meet them.

"What is it?" Daniel was staring down at her, like he expected her to burst into flames then and there.

"My... my parents," she stammered. "If I can find a way to bring the Fey back — they could come here... or I could go there."

"That's just ridiculous," Daniel snapped, his good humour vanishing. "What a stupid story."

Aroha looked up at him puzzled. If you couldn't believe a story told by a taniwha, then whose could you believe? After all, Whataitai was himself enough proof of magic for even the most cynical. She was hurt that Daniel wouldn't believe what he had seen.

Seeing that look in her eye, he softened and gave her an awkward hug. "I'm sorry kid, I'm just shocked — that's all."

"I can understand that."

"Thanks," he ruffled her hair like she was little girl. "But I've got to get you back home now." He set off, without even looking back, sure she'd follow.

Aroha's lips curled a little and she smoothed down her hair. Daniel really didn't expect her to forget about the taniwha and what he'd said, did he? She might just be a 'kid', but she wasn't stupid.

If Daniel noticed that his young charge was in a huff with him, he didn't show it. He took her back through Wellington at a whopping pace, hardly speaking. But even though they went whipping through the city, Aroha still noticed something different. Smiles were everywhere, and even the crowds of homeless in their shelters near parliament seemed cheerier, as if they sensed a change in the air.

The strains of utu in her blood felt better, more at home within her. Perhaps it was the taniwha's gift, or perhaps it was the understanding of what she was. Whatever the case, others were feeling it too. People waved at her from the shattered remains of their homes and they passed several people actually pulling down the slats from their boarded up windows. Through Kelburn, they skirted a small group of residents gathered at a street corner, but not in anger. They were discussing 'getting things moving' and how they were going to cope together.

Daniel noticed none of this. His face was set in an unreadable mask, and Aroha began to feel sorry for him. She'd always been different, so it was easy for her, but he'd seen things and felt things that he couldn't have expected. She slipped her hand into his and squeezed.

"It'll be OK," she whispered.

The tramp back home was quicker somehow, perhaps because Daniel was quieter and not so jovial, and pushed them on harder. When Aroha felt herself flagging, he would lift her up in his arms and carry her. Although this was demeaning in a way, Aroha let him. It was nice to be held, and nice not to have to walk.

They left the city and its shattered suburbs and climbed over the hill. When they got to the spot where they'd left Sally, Daniel put her down with a sigh.

"You don't really have to carry me," Aroha said guiltily. "I can walk."

"It's not that," Daniel replied. "You're just a little thing, no bigger than my sister. No, I was just thinking how things are going to be different once we get back."

Aroha frowned. Whataitai had said some amazing things, and the greenstone mere was important too. But she was just a child, and somehow all that instruction about rescuing three worlds would have to wait. She was sure Nana wouldn't allow her to go running off just yet.

"After all," Daniel went on, "it's not every day you get to meet a Taniwha and find out the world's a different place to what you imagined."

It worried him. Aroha could tell the whole thing had unsettled him. He was used to uniforms and orders and duty — what he had seen under the hill had changed all that. Still, there was nothing she could do about it.

They pushed on, though the day was lengthening and clouds were rolling in from the horizon. Climbing the last curve of the land was a real effort, but at last they could see the faint line of lights of the village. Aroha looked up at Daniel, but he didn't move and his face was cast in shadow. She put her hand gently against his, only to find it curled in a fist. Something was more than just troubling him.

"Cooooeeee," the familiar voice echoed up the hill, and soon after came Nana herself. She had a thick coat on against the chill of the night and was carrying another smaller one.

Even though it had only been a couple of days, Aroha ran down the hill to greet her. She was bundled into a tight embrace that seemed to last forever. But then Nana bent down to her and those wise blue eyes met hers. She said nothing, but her granddaughter knew the silence would not keep for long.

"And what about me?" Sally's voice piped up. She was less protected against the cold, her feet still bare. "What's going on with leaving me behind like that?"

Nana held out her hand to Daniel as the children squabbled and giggled down the hill. He didn't take it, but followed the little group.

Aroha barely noticed when he left them at the village for his own home. She was far too busy listening to Sally talk nine to the dozen about all the fascinating things that had happened while she'd been away. To hear her talk, Aroha had missed out on every fun event since the beginning of time. It was like a grand conspiracy. Mrs. Lennet had kicked out her cheating husband, a pen load of lambs had escaped in the middle of town and there had been free ice cream from the store when Jan's generator finally failed.

Sally enveloped her in the human beauty of the world, and the image of the great taniwha receded a little.

At their doorstep, Nana pried Sally off and told her to go home in a mock stern voice. That didn't worry Aroha's friend one little bit, but the threat of getting her mother over did. She scampered off with a wave and a promise to give the whole story the next day.

The night was telling Aroha something, a gentle tugging at her already abused senses. She yawned until her jaw popped, trying to understand the faint vibrations of the evening.

Nana was there, tucking a warm blanket over her shoulders and guiding her back towards the house.

"We need to talk, Nan," Aroha said blurrily, thinking of the taniwha and the mere and all that she'd learned.

"Yes, my dear," a note of sadness lurked in her voice, "but not tonight, eh? There will be plenty of time tomorrow and you need to rest."

"Promise?" Aroha asked softly, leaning against the fragile warmth of her grandmother.

"I promise," came the reply, and that was enough. Nana always delivered on her promises, which was probably why she didn't make that many.

As she let herself be led inside, Aroha couldn't shake the feeling of sadness that now hung over her home, nor could she escape the thought was it was she who had brought it here.

Bakari woke with a shudder. The dream that he'd had was so vivid that his fingers went automatically to the nape of his neck. But no, he'd not left himself on the Line: it had only been his imaginings. He tried to grasp the remains of the dream but they slipped away. It had been pleasant and he could just recall the feeling of a baking sun on his back and a tickle of sensuous delight. But it had been no sex dream; it had been something more profound than that.

Shaking his head, Bakari slipped out of his bed and padded down the hallway in his underwear. It should have been colder, since England in spring was not the balmiest season, but he still felt warm and insulated. On his way to the kitchen he noticed that the sofa was empty and the rest of the house was, too. Ronan had obviously decided not to stay in. He might even be prowling around Ella's. Bakari smiled. The Fey might claim it was purely to protect her, but he'd only be half honest. There was just something about the way Ronan looked at Ella, like she was a beautiful mermaid pulling him out of the grip of the ocean.

"I'm going mad, too," Bakari whispered to himself, uncertain where such an image could have come from. He opened the fridge and fished out the half empty carton of cold milk in the back. Standing at the window by the sink, he drank it straight, letting the coldness do battle with his own lingering heat. He'd been to Jamaica once, just for his Mum's sake. Her father had come from there and before that, in the dim past, from the black heat of Africa herself. She had told him such tales about the pain and joy of that time, though she'd only heard them as stories from her own mother. Strange how he could only know the past from stories of magic.

His hunt for it had begun on a night like this one, not long after his mother's death. He could still recall the exact instant when he'd decided that she was wrong; that there was no magic in the world. That one idea had hurt so badly that the colour had drained out of life for him. He'd set out then, to get it back: desperate to prove his mother right after all.

Bakari looked out into the dimness of the garden, the wind lifting the leaves and the moon casting odd glows amongst his flowers. It was strange how that past could have brought him here, to an English village far from the home of his ancestors. And yet, he put the empty bottle down on the counter, the Fey must have walked there too. Perhaps even Ronan in his proper form.

Such odd thoughts to be having in the middle of the night.

"Something in the air," he muttered to himself. Out there in the garden a shape was moving, a cat, or a hedgehog perhaps. No, Bakari leaned closer, narrowing his eyes, it was larger than that.

Everything was so still, like he was sealed off from the world, watching an event not meant to be seen by human eyes. If Ronan had been there, he'd have called him.

And then the line of bamboo he'd planted for privacy at the end of the garden shifted and his mother stepped out onto the back lawn. Bakari's heart hammered in his chest, but after the events of the last few days he wasn't surprised.

She looked just like she always did, dressed brightly against the cruelties of the world. Her long hair was done in its usual fantastical braids which coiled about her and made her always seem so much younger than her actual years. And her face, the face that had been so destroyed at the end, was as smooth and beautiful as ever, the colour of sweet chocolate.

"Mum," Bakari pressed one hand against the glass of the window, but even that reality did not break what was right in front of his eyes.

He walked calmly to the back door and opened it just like he did most days. The grass was wet under his bare feet and he could smell the neighbor's roses in the air. All the time he never took his eyes off his mother standing so patiently at the end of the garden. She never stopped smiling.

She held out her hands to him and Bakari ran to her, just like the little boy he'd once been. He blessed every moment of magic in that night air. He sobbed into her warm shoulder, cried out in joy that which he loved above everything else had been restored to him. She'd found her way back to him from the abyss.

Whispering joy and delight, the son cried. But his mother did not speak. She pushed him back and when Bakari looked into those eyes, they were not hers. Those eyes had never looked down at a child in love, or comforted one in pain. Whatever this was, it had never birthed him or anything else.

The face shivered and became one that was familiar. The ruined eyes of Greer offered no solace, though he'd shed tears on her shoulder.

The knowledge so recently gained from the Line burned suddenly brightly in his head, images of a vast web of manipulation, all which led to Ella.

Bakari opened his mouth to speak. He had a lot to say to a woman that would impersonate his mother, and when he was done he'd send her sprawling on her arse in his garden.

But the icy white lips twitched and fire bloomed behind his eyes. He knew she wouldn't catch him when he fell.

There were no dreams this time, no pleasant images to rock him to sleep, only blackness and the awareness of danger. Bakari struggled against it, trying to find his way back. When he did, he almost longed for the blackness again.

He woke for the second time that night, knowing he was nowhere near his pleasant little cottage. He'd been to a few castles before, laughed with a couple of his boyhood friends about the racks and chains and torture instruments. It wasn't nearly so funny to wake up to find himself hanging from a wall by manacles that looked remarkably like the ones he'd tried on as a lark fifteen years ago. Life was nothing if not ironic. He was dangling, and this wasn't a vid, this hurt. His feet were at least a foot off the ground and already his shoulders were beginning to ache.

Bakari tried to take his mind of it by looking around for any clue as to where he was. But it looked just like any other set piece for a B grade horror; a rough looking rock chamber, complete with water running down the walls and a thick stench. The only light spilled from a rectangular fitting on the far wall, so at least there was electricity. Though, why that should comfort him, Bakari couldn't quite say.

He couldn't guess how long Greer had been standing at the doorway: she'd made no sound and the light barely reached her. She was wearing the same ethereal white fabric as the last time he'd seen her. The way her sightless head was turned to him gave him the creeps, and would have even in more pleasant surroundings. Eyeing her warily, he decided not to be the first one to speak — he wasn't going to give her the satisfaction. The long drawn out silence seemed to last an age, but when one of them finally broke it, it was Greer.

"Giving me the silent treatment, are you?"

"I just thought since I was the guest, I'd be polite."

She stepped down from the doorway into the room. "I see you've been learning some of Ronan's wit in your time with him." Her lips twisted on the words.

"Since you were the one that introduced us in the first place, I didn't think you'd mind."

She stopped just a few inches from him and looked up with those scarred sockets. "You haven't been a very good employee, Bakari."

His heart sank a little. She might not be very tall or powerfully built, but there was something about Greer that stank of real danger. Shutting up seemed like a very good idea.

"In fact, you've been worse than bad, you've got in my way — deliberately."

If she knew about him Lining into Infinity Rose, he was royally screwed. Right now Bakari could only hope he had absorbed a bit of Ronan's gift of the gab. "Look, I know we haven't got that Mask for you yet," he said, "but we're working on it and in the next couple of days..."

"You're not a very good liar, Bakari," she sighed, as if something upset her. Then she turned her face to the wall. "And we know it was you who broke into Infinity Rose yesterday."

Bakari bit back a denial. They would have evidence and he was damned if he was going to beg. It annoyed him, though. He thought he'd got away clean; he'd used all his best bots and tricks.

"So you must know all about me," Greer stood very still, looking like some ancient Greek sibyl. "But what I want to know is, why you risked so much. Why?"

Bakari slowed his breathing down, tried to achieve that state he reached just before entering the Line. He didn't want to show her any emotion; he, too, could be as calm as a statue.

"Why did you break into my system?" Greer whispered, and her words bounced eerily around the little chamber. "You can't have known I had anything to do with Infinity Rose. So there must be another reason."

Here it comes, Bakari thought. The torture, bribery, all those things he'd pretty much avoided in his life of so called crime.

He couldn't have been more surprised when Greer slipped from the room and returned bearing a small node connection. He recognized the dark grey cube as one of the most expensive, most sought after versions. She attached a double adaptor to the side and plugged one of the hair thin wires into his connector. She smelt like old paper, but her touch was not unpleasant. He waited for the Liner to enter the room.

But it was Greer herself who sat down at his feet, and it was she who pulled back her curling white hair and inserted the second plug into her own neck.

"But..." Bakari could hear the incredulity in his own voice, "magic and the Line... Ronan said..."

"Ronan is an unknowing fool, too long cut off from that which made him special. You will find, dear Bakari, that many things he says are wrong."

His head sunk down on his chest and he sighed. "I've been looking for magic everywhere, and it was right there all along."

Greer settled her hands about the node. "I'm very glad you've finally worked that out. But unfortunately, I don't think you'll like what the combination of magic and technology can do."

Dry fear touched him then.

"I will find out what you know, Bakari. And you can make it easy for yourself, or you can make it hard. It matters little to me which you choose."

He thought of her blank cruelty, the way she'd used the image of his dearest mother. He could only imagine what she would do to his closest friend. The warmth of his African dream had not left him, though, and the echo of it made him stronger. His mother had been brave, holding onto life as long as she could in a shattered body. He recalled her smile and her love, and knew there was no other choice for him.

"Do what you like," he said calmly. "I won't tell you anything."

Greer's hands were moving, dipping and dancing in some strange ritual that drew his eye. "Very well... Hard."

Her delicate fingertip flicked the control of the node and they fell into another world together.

CHAPTER FIFTEEN
Surrender

Ella's life had suddenly become a moving dream. She felt alive, more so than ever before. Every sound and every colour was more vivid. A single, still moment of life had ensnared her and wherever she looked there was fragile beauty, so perfect that it made her want to cry.

She'd opened Raven Hill and taken Ronan through into it — all done with something that could only have been instinct. *I don't really know myself at all anymore*, she thought, but it did not fill her with dread; rather, with a strange excitement.

Ronan said nothing, content to be led. He was slightly dazed by her sudden command: she could feel that in him. They walked down into a pale silvery light, the earth glowing with its own inner magic and brightening as she approached. And the air, even that was different, scented and heavy with the hint of jasmine. It filled Ella up and made her senses reel.

The tunnel opened into a large room, but nothing like what she might have expected. A dry stone hearth, and a stiff-backed chair big enough for two that looked as though its occupant might just have stepped out to gather herbs. Two large beds were covered with furs and bracken and the scattered remnants of someone's simple life. Ella felt she was intruding somehow.

The light had dimmed to a faint bluish haze coming from the walls.

"Is this Fey?" Her voice sounded very different, too, in here.

Ronan moved away, running his hands over the back of the chair with a dreamy gaze. He raised them to his face and drew in a great deep breath. "Yes. Not truly part of my home, but very, very close. This would have been the shelter for a simple Fey, a woodland creature, or one of the farmland."

"And they lived here?" Ella asked, uncertain how anything so homely could be otherworldly.

"It's like a hunter's cabin in the woods, a place of refuge from the wilds of the human realm."

"And all under Raven Hill?"

Ronan was bending by the hearth. He took wood stacked beside it and began to assemble a fire. "Not really under. If archeologists dug down, they'd find nothing. It's there, but not quite. Like something just out of phase. You need Art to be able to find such a place."

Ella shivered, but he said no more. She snuck closer and watched over his shoulder as he finished his task. At a soft commanding word, flames leapt up from the wood and began to burn cheerily.

"Impressive," she said.

"Not really," Ronan sat down on the seat, seemingly unconcerned for its stability, "Not compared with what you just did." He patted the spot next to him. "There's nowhere to hide this time, Ella. The Seed has the hill blocked until sunup, and we really need to discuss this."

Fighting down the lump in her throat, Ella reluctantly did as she was asked. Though she couldn't decide which was more unnerving, being questioned, or the long length of Ronan's thigh pressed against hers.

"I know what you're going to ask." God, this was her worst nightmare, what had driven her from Doyle, what she'd been fleeing for so long. This was exactly how a stag brought to bay by hounds must feel. "You're going to ask who I am, who my parents were."

"Perfectly reasonable place to start."

"Yes, all perfectly reasonable — except I don't know. I have no idea what those answers are."

She looked down at her hands, feeling the tears burning and feeling Ronan's eyes drilling into her, but she wouldn't look up. She'd done that with Doyle and the look had been the end of them — she wouldn't do it again. So Ella just said it without meeting his eye, blurting the truth into her clenched hands. "Ten years ago I woke up in a medical facility — I was in a bed, there were machines everywhere. I don't even know what my name was." The metallic, tinny taste swelled in the back of her throat, just like it had on that night. Doyle's had been the face above her, just as surprised and frightened as she was. Her mouth had been so dry she couldn't work it to say anything, so only a muffled wail communicated her plea.

And the voice in the unseen distance by the door hissed, "Doyle come on, we've got what we came for."

She'd seen his indecision then; the desire to turn a quick profit battling with the urge to do something good.

"Can't leave you in this freakin' place," he'd muttered under his breath, breaking her out of her restraints before logic kicked in.

Doyle and his crew had broken out more that night than just the equipment they'd been hired to appropriate; they'd also found their newest recruit. She'd been so glad, so very grateful when they'd whisked her away in their van, leaving the steely corridors and pain behind. Though she couldn't remember it all very precisely, only fear and panic when she thought of it.

She'd had nothing else: no name, no idea when her birthday was, what her parents had been like, or if she'd ever had a dog or a cat. The whole past was a mystery, and she was left with nothing.

So she'd called herself just that — Nill, and it had suited her and the occupation she learnt from Doyle. They'd been frightening years for sure, but they'd also been years when she'd been able to forget that place and that dreadful unknowing fear.

Ronan was silent as he took her hand in his. He said nothing when it shook and she cried. He waited until the storm had passed.

"But you didn't stay with Doyle — what happened?"

"He betrayed me." Ella shook her head. "No... that's not right — that's just what I've been telling myself. It was me. He started to get curious, started to want to know things. And every time he asked, there would be dreams. Nightmares, I guess. So I left. My gratitude only lasted five years."

Ronan's hand tightened on hers, "You should have got out sooner — he was only using you for your talents. You don't owe him anything."

"Maybe not," Ella said in a small voice, still fighting her thudding heart.

"So you came here to Penherem — and changed your name?"

"Nill didn't mean anything to me anymore, I could feel myself changing, becoming... something else. I liked it and I chose Ella because it had beauty in it — and I wanted some beauty."

Ronan seemed about to say something, but out of the corner of her eye she saw him suddenly clamp down on it, holding something in he perhaps knew she wouldn't want to hear. "And why Penherem?" he asked instead.

She shrugged, "I can't answer that either — I was on a train, passing through the sprawl and then the countryside. I got off on a whim and it was here."

"My aunt used to say, there is no such thing as a whim, there is only fate." He smiled kindly at her. His eyes looked dark violet again in the light of the cavern.

Ella could feel her pulse throb in her throat again, but not with fear this time. She knew she was blushing. "I don't believe in fate," she said in a rush. "There are paths laid down, but we decide which ones we take."

"I agree with you entirely, but such elevated discussion isn't going to fill our stomachs. I don't know about you, but after a fight I'm always ravenous." Ronan got up. "There might still be a chance for food — such places usually have something tucked away. Even after all this time, the Art might still hold."

Ella tucked her feet under her and leaned back against the chair. As she watched Ronan move about, she could only admire him. He was utterly unselfconscious, not even really caring at that moment how beautiful he was. He'd laugh if I told him that, Ella thought smugly, he'd know it but it wouldn't matter to him. Only a shape shifter could truly underestimate the value of shape.

Ella stifled a giggle.

"Well, there is some hard tack in here, though even after all this time, it's nothing to laugh about." He dropped to the floor in an elegant legs crossed position and offered a slice to Ella. "Though it might sound vain, Fey food, even stuff such as this, is still better than human fare."

Ella nibbled doubtfully on the round biscuit's corner. It tasted vaguely of lavender and sugar, and was not at all unpalatable.

"You know, if I was in my full power, I could have filled this room with flowers and a magnificent feast in an instant."

"Now you're just boasting," Ella admonished.

"No — truthfully," he wolfed down his biscuit, "But it's been a very long time since then. I was quite different, quite... unique." He grinned up at her and now those eyes were definitely the colour of violets.

Though he was smiling, in his expression were his real feelings. He was so scared and so lonely that she gasped like she'd been stabbed. Ronan looked at her and a frown creased his forehead. "Ella?" he reached out and grabbed her hand as if he thought she might fall.

Her wild gift broke free, snapping across the link into him, but it wasn't Ronan she found. It was his older, freer self.

He was a power, a cousin of the greatest Fey, born out of the wildness near the edge of their realm. Unloved by his own mother, his aunt had raised him, but it was his cousin Sive he loved. Dark haired, violet-eyed Sive the Shining had burned her way into him.

He played the fool around her, with his shapeshifting antics, but inside something like his heart yearned for her. So he traveled, entered the world of men, played tricks on them and laughed until he hurt. He took the shape of the wild pooka and broke ships and made sailors wail, but all unaware, only in it for the fun. He drank milk left out for lesser brownies and made them scamper away with little hisses. He took the shape of dark jungle cats and prowled the recesses of the wild when the mood took him to be mysterious. He dallied with dusky maidens in as many continents as he pleased, stole them from beneath their lovers' noses and made them mad for him. Even the terrifying Fey court could not alter his ways. He treated it as he did any other place, existing for his amusement. The King of the Fey, Auberon, tried many times to tame him, break him, but it never seemed to quite stick. All this he did, but none of it really touched him.

The two realms were his, and trouble seemed to roll off him like salt water off a pooka's back. He was not a fool, merely careless with the awesome power that he'd had as his birthright. But then one day he was given care of a child by Sive, a child that would change him, break his heart and remake him in another image.

Ronan cried for that loss of power, but also for the loss of innocence. For that was what he had been; the pale wicked child, the roaring tiger, the Trickster, the pooka — Puck.

Ella blinked, suddenly back in her body, aware only that her hand was still with his. She didn't let go.

"Puck?" She'd seen the plays, laughed at him in *Midsummer Night's Dream*, but what she'd felt was more wild than that, more elemental.

Ronan's eyes fell away from hers. "I used to be... no more, though. I'm only an echo of that creature now. I can recall things that happened to him — to me, I guess. But that is all, because in between him and me is the time I spent alone. The only Fey, the only one who stayed."

She knew he no longer could even find the shape of the Trickster, it had gone along with all the others. Only the cat and the pooka and the human shape remained, and she tasted the sadness in that too. He was alone and as lost as she'd felt in the hospital facility. He knew who he was, but at that moment Ella wasn't sure if that was a blessing or not.

She clasped her other hand around his, willing him to get some strength from her, hoping he could see how glad she was to know him.

Ronan's lips twitched. "I'm not sorry for it though — staying. I've learnt so much, found so many friends, seen so many things. I even found something unexpected." He leaned across and brushed his lips to hers. Time had mellowed the Trickster, for he did not nip her as Puck might have, just to see her expression. Instead, his kiss was now deep honey and power suddenly unmasked.

Their gifts, one new and great, one older and less, joined again, sweeping through them, an unexpected tide of longing. She was Ella and the frightened Nill. He was Ronan and the powerful Puck. It was good to be together, good to know each other and very good not to be alone.

Ronan's arms slid up hers. His hands cupped Ella's face, and when he pulled back, his violet eyes were wide but peaceful.

He wanted to say something, to tell her what he'd done and what he'd been for hundreds of years in this world, but there could never be enough words for that. So he just said what came first. "I'm afraid," and they were truthful words.

Ella knew that to love was to risk pain. In the human world, there would always be pain with death so close. Stroking Ronan's face, she smiled, letting her strength flow to him. They wouldn't be alone, whatever happened, and for now there was the moment to enjoy.

A gently lit cavern, a quiet space to themselves, a warm nest of ancient furs; they needed nothing more for now. Taking his hand, Ella guided it inside her shirt and against her skin.

Somewhere between nightmare and reality, Bakari found a little respite from the pain. He floated away from his body and was among that silver light he'd experienced when riding the earth magic. He could only be glad that somehow he'd managed to escape the torment of magic and Line that Greer had conjured up for him, even if only for a while.

"You shouldn't let her do that to you." The young voice seemed to have no origin. Then Bakari realised that even in this place it was still necessary to open his eyes. He looked down and there was Penny Two Dolls, standing in the disembodied wilderness of the light. She was staring up at him, but with none of the vacancy that she usually had.

In all his time in the village, he'd never heard her speak — in fact, he'd assumed she was mute. But now that seemed a ridiculous idea, for the look in her eye was the most piercing he'd ever seen. It was like she could see every part of him that had ever been; hardened street Liner, grief stricken young man, frightened child, and even loved baby.

Bakari shook his head. He was getting the strangest ideas.

"You shouldn't let her do these things," Penny repeated and her tone was not that of a child, but more of an admonishment.

Knowing it was stupid to have an argument with a kid, even if it was just a pain induced hallucination, Bakari grinned to himself. Since there was only this, or the pain of reality, he decided to choose this.

"Not much I can do about it, you know."

"There is always something to be done." Penny was looking down at the most battered of her dolls, holding it out in her hands like it was a precious pearl. "You aren't powerless, Bakari."

"Penny — she's got me locked up."

The child's eyes returned to his, and they were pools of swirling stars. He felt swallowed by them. Galaxies were turning, stars bursting to life and dying, all in the gaze of a child. But there was warmth too, a feeling of love such as he hadn't felt since the loss of his mother, and it washed over Bakari now. He wept, and she put her hand in his.

"You are strong, too. You are a warrior in your own realm. You can fight and you can win."

Those last were the words of his mother, the final words she'd said to him before he'd left on that fateful morning. Hearing them again did not plunge him into despair as they might have. He felt no gaping hole, no grasping grief, only sureness and love as if his mother and all the mothers before her were speaking to him now.

Penny was right. He wasn't powerless, and there was always hope. Greer would not break him, and he would not betray his friend. She would not get Ella's name from him.

A plan solidified in the back of his brain.

The greater part of him did not want to go back. Not because he was afraid, but because with Penny he found he could remember his mother without pain, and that was something he had never been able to do before.

"You have a task," Penny said, and turned her raggiest doll so he could see it. The face and the dark hair was familiar: it was his friend, Ella. An overwhelming urge to protect her, to shelter her from whatever Greer had planned, rose in him. Liners weren't used to being the heroes.

Penny Two Dolls smiled, and Bakari turned back to the edges of the light and to reality.

He plunged back to himself and the nightmare wrapped itself around him again, but this time there was no fear with it.

Magic burned his senses, while the Line consumed him. It was fire and pain. A forest burned around him, an ancient place. He was running, fleeing on roasting feet through it. Trees crashed and fell around him, while the sound of the fire broke against his eardrums. And she was coming. The flaming goddess of pain stalked him through the conflagration. This time, Bakari did not run from her.

Instead he turned and let the fire lick up his legs. He could smell his own flesh bubbling and burning away, the scent was enough to drive anyone mad. But the goddess coming through the smoke and heat was even worse.

Greer wore the aspect of a burning giantess. She had eyes here, soulless sucking maws, ringed in flame. No clothing could survive such a figure, her perfect breasts ran in colours of red and orange and she pushed aside crumbling trees carelessly with her hands. She was terrifying and glorious in her femaleness, enough to bring a man to orgasm and then fling him down into death.

He was the centre of her rage, he could feel it like he could feel the agony of the fire in his skin. It was as if he were the representative of everything male and foolish.

"Tell me!" She roared and the flames bent at her mighty breath, leaping towards Bakari. "Tell me why you came!" He should have crumbled then, broken up into terrified lumps of charcoal, but the memory of another warmth filled him; a love that was stronger than flame or death, and a courage he had often wanted to have.

Bakari's blackened hand reached up towards the almost unseen sky and he *called*. He demanded that this world obey him. *I am a warrior and this is my realm.*

The fire dipped, feeling a change in the atmosphere. Bakari held his breath, not taking in anymore soot and stench; he wanted cleanness and coolness.

The heavens opened as a terrific clash of thunder heralded the break of a storm above the inferno. Greer looked up and screamed in frustration and abrupt comprehension. Huge tides of rain fell into the fire and suddenly it seemed a petty thing compared to the downpour and power of the storm. The flames hissed and died abruptly. Greer the goddess was dwindling as he watched, fighting against water that was quenching her rage.

Bakari tipped back his head and let it pour over him, cooling and healing where it ran. He laughed out loud and let himself rest.

CHAPTER SIXTEEN

Gifts

Greer howled in rage and swiftly cut the connection to the Line. She felt a brief moment of disorientation, and then she was looking across the chamber at Bakari's still form, while feeling humiliation burning her cheeks. The chill of the rock had invaded her bones, and she got up carefully. Extension treatment provided her with the body of twenty year old, but somehow a lingering residue of age hung in the bones. It was as if the mind could not accept the Extension as well as the body did.

A quick finger to Bakari's throat confirmed that he was still alive, but quite beyond her now. It was puzzling, but somehow he'd managed to evade her magic.

She sighed, tapping the tips of her nails against her teeth. Her attention never left Bakari. The senses that had replaced sight saw things others could not, but still occasionally it would have been nice to 'see' things. She tucked a stray lock of Bakari's hair behind his ear and turned away.

Her mind was boiling with ideas.

She had to find Nill and unlock the secrets within that unique creature — but then she also had to get the Mask. A resolve began to form while her fingers twisted and danced, uncoupling the chains of magic she'd installed about Bakari.

If he could not be made to break, then he still could have a use. The fool Ronan had obviously fallen into friendship with the Liner — in all his incarnations Puck had a tendency to become fond of people for the oddest reasons. Not that it mattered, all that it did was afford Greer a way to manipulate the mercurial and annoying Fey — something he usually refused to allow. You could bend Ronan all you liked, try and force him to do anything, but it would be like trying to blow a wind caught feather into cup. Yet threaten that which he loved, and if he truly believed harm would happen, then he would obey.

Greer bent and opened her box of tricks, and her hands felt surely amongst the weaponry of her Art. The dull black knife, only the length of her slender hand, found its way under her fingers and slipped into her palm easily. It was an old friend. The questing fingertips of her other hand found the tiny medical kit. There'd never been any use for it before.

She stood contemplating for a second; a lock of hair did not quite convey her strength of purpose and she needed Ronan to believe, to understand that there were consequences for misbehaving. With a sigh, Greer decided that cruelty was her only choice.

A moment of profound attention, a minute of determined sawing, the crack of bone; and Bakari's right smallest finger lay in her hand. The knife was keen and glad of the blood. She staunched the wound quickly, applying the seal and antiseptic— she didn't want Bakari to die prematurely. Tucking the finger into her pocket, she smiled out of reflex. Blood dripped from the sheared stump and ran, cooling, down her leg. She didn't care.

Bakari hadn't even stirred. Perhaps the pain had dimly reached him, wherever he was, but he would be too cautious to return to a reality he couldn't control.

A faintest noise like the tips of branches dragging along the door frame, and a scent of light decay, alerted her to her ally's arrival. The Seed prompted the darkest fears in all who saw it, but her lack of vision dulled the effect. Still, when she opened the door, the warmth of its power caressed her. There were few creatures left in this realm that had such strength.

Though Greer could not see the Seed's curved claws and alien face, she knew it was dangerous. When it spoke the voice was hushed, like it came from a long way off, and each word was enunciated precisely. "The Healer is come."

"You found Nill?" Greer's heart thudded.

"No name, but it is the one. She used the earth magic to escape me, entering the underhill."

Greer's lips tightened and she could not halt the surge of jealousy. Of all the magics left, earth Art was the oldest and most powerful; it also lingered in greatest strength, hidden deep, but ready.

The chill of the Seed moved closer. "And the Fey was with her. Puck."

So, Ronan had found her — that was to be expected. Her Art would draw his, but he could not understand what she really was, he'd been too long gone from his own home.

"Can you find where they went?"

A hiss of frustration broke through the silence of the chamber. "The earth magic is not broken to the Master's will here. It conceals them."

"It doesn't matter," Greer replied as steadily as she could, feeling the blood course down her leg, reminding her of her leverage. "Ronan will come to me himself, and the Healer will follow."

The cool hardness of the Seed's carapace pressed against her leg, chilling her to the bone. "That is good, Seer, but I need to feed. Your sacrificial man was not enough: he had no Art, not even any human magics." The wheedling tone in its voice was familiar, but she needed the Seed. It, too, had its part to play.

Greer rolled up her sleeve swiftly, and the creature's bony mandibles pressed against her flesh. "Very well. Take what you need, for you will have to work hard in the next few days."

The pain was swift but bearable, as all sensory things had come to be to her. The cavern was silent for a while, but for the sound of the Seed's ravenous sucking.

Nothing much changed in Aroha's world over the next few days. Somehow, though, she and Nana never seemed to find themselves alone to discuss what had happened. It wasn't like her grandmother was being deliberately deceptive: she could hardly be blamed when the neighbor's child fell sick and she had to help, or when Sally and the rest of her siblings invaded. Still, Aroha felt a vague unease. Nana hadn't even seemed to notice her changed arm.

The truth was that the mere was beginning to weigh her down, so much so that even moving felt like an effort. She felt stronger for it, but knew that such a gift would not come without a hefty price. She was afraid to bring it up with Nana, afraid what the answer might be.

As for Daniel, he'd retreated to the old house closest to the seashore, which the villagers had cleared for him. Aroha should have gone down there, she knew, but again the feeling of disquiet made her long for the normality that Nana seemed intent on supplying.

On the third night, reality would not be delayed. Nightmares might torment her, yet there was more to be considered.

The Folk were under attack; she could hear their torn howls of agony floating down from the mountain, sliding under the bed and burrowing into her sleeping head. Her spirit answered the plea while her body remained tucked in bed. The mere came to her soul's form and the weight of it seemed the only truth, as she walked through the walls of the house and followed the cries up the hill and into the forest.

Mist enshrouded their realm, but Aroha brushed through the punga ferns and the slippery rocks unimpeded by physical limits. She reached the airy heights were the Folk made their home and came upon a sight she'd never thought to have imagined.

The Folk no longer danced away from her eye, hiding in the corner of her vision. They were in too much pain and danger for that. A true nightmare was visited on them; creatures who looked nothing more than angular assemblages of blades. The bone white creatures darted among the wisps of the Folk and forelimbs curved in ugly scimitar shapes swept among them.

The mere became even heavier, pulling down on Aroha's dream arm and making it ache with physical sensation. It would not let her leave the tree line, though she ached to. The Folk were beautiful, like jeweled sketches in the night, faint but glorious. It made her weep to see them cut down like so much unwanted grass.

It was a stark reality. She could feel their pain and their desire not to go. They had held on so tenaciously to the earth and now they were being so easily and violently severed from it.

Aroha. The Folk Lord was beside her in all his tattered glory. The echo of tears marred his pale, wispy face. *You must flee.*

No, Aroha's hand tightened on the mere, *I can help.*

There is no help for us, beloved child. We were too soon come to this realm, too rash. Our Lady always accused us of this, but we would come — because of you.

Aroha's heart sank at the look in his emerald eyes, more real than any other part of him. They had been drawn here by her? She shook her head, not wanting their deaths on her head.

Do not blame yourself. The Folk Lord's hand rested lightly on her shoulder, the softest and warmest of touches. *We, above all Fey, missed this world and its wild beauty. With your coming we were able to return.*

And this? Aroha watched with a trembling jaw, as the foul creatures finished their work. *Why is this happening? Is this my fault, too?*

Your wakening has hatched a Seed, and with it, a power that is nameless and dreadful. It has a strength that we no longer have, for we are but echoes of our former might. But do not stop, beloved light, for it is your fate and your right.

He was stepping away from her, towards the creatures as they finished their work. In the Lord's hand was a memory of a spear, something that had once made mortals tremble; now it was merely a softening in the ether.

"No," Aroha sobbed, but already she could feel her body calling her back, even as the Forest Lord was turning to his enemies. She did not want to see him go, nor to feel the strength and glee of the foul creatures. With a cry of horror she slid back to herself, awakening to the darkness of her room.

She lay gasping there for a moment, feeling the room around her but knowing it would never again feel safe. Her eyes were open in the darkness, reliving the scene, feeling the horror and resignation of it again. Despite what the Lord had said, she could not avoid the guilt. It came pressing down on her until she had to bite her lip to not cry out.

Nana pushed the door open, for a second standing in the light from the kitchen. She wasn't in her nightgown; that much Aroha could tell from her outline.

"Aroha," her voice sounded very old and very tired. Coming over, she sat down on the corner closest to the pillow and took her granddaughter's hand. "I so hoped that you would be older before this happened."

"So did I," she said raggedly through held back tears. Now that the time had come for this conversation, she suddenly just wanted to roll over and pull the covers over her head.

Nana clenched the hand she held, reading her mind. "Don't we all, my love? But even under the sheets, the monsters still exist. It's best not to lie hidden and not know when they are coming."

"And they are coming, aren't they?"

A long silence in the darkness. "Yes," the word sounded like it was being pulled out of her.

Aroha had the horrible understanding, that this was the end — the real end of what had been her childhood. It tightened her chest and made her want to scream in denial, but that wouldn't change anything. She nuzzled closer to her grandmother, curling around her knees, nestling her head on her lap, trying to store this moment up.

"What do we do?" Aroha finally asked.

She felt Nana's sigh go down the old woman's bones and into her own. Nana had always been so powerful in Aroha's life, but now she seemed as fragile as a fairy dream. It was enough to make her granddaughter screw up her eyes and only just manage to hold back a howl of despair.

Her grandmother didn't notice, and neither did she answer the question. Her voice was smooth and dreamy now, from a long way off where things weren't nearly as dire. "I was a soldier to your grandmother. We were distant relatives, ancient cousins. Her name was Anu, and back then, mine was Brenna."

"You're not my Nana, then?" a tear crept free.

A hand tightened on hers, "I will always be your grandmother, child. I was given you to look after — a sacred trust. And I have loved you as no other person in my selfish Fey life."

And the images flashed across the tiny gap: her proud ways, her duty to her Queen and a high minded distain for all that was human. She was no longer that person, that powerfully beautiful Fey, she was now totally Aroha's Nana, filled with love and concern for her above all things. She'd sacrificed everything to be that person and had found unexpected joy in it.

Aroha felt the connection between them deeper than it had ever been, right here on what was surely the brink of death. For that was what it was, coming down from the mountain, coming down to find her.

She was panicking: not knowing what to do, unable to think of a way to escape. The forest was no longer friendly and there would be no sanctuary this time. She could imagine being hunted there, and saw images of the cruel deaths of the Folk.

"What do we do?' she whispered into her Nana's pale pink dressing gown.

"We have no choice. We will fight. I will not let them have you, child." There was strength and despair in those words.

Aroha couldn't hold back her sobs.

"There, there, child. I still have power, and we still have time to make a protection circle."

"A what?"

Nana sighed again and her unguarded thought flitted through Aroha. *I should have taught you more.* However, she gave no voice to such negativity. "Get dressed quickly, child, and I'll be back."

By the time Aroha had sleepily stuffed herself into a warm jacket, jeans and boots, her grandmother had returned. Gone were the simple floral dresses and bun; instead she was wearing clothes very similar to her granddaughter's, while her silver-grey hair was tied into a long ponytail. Rather than turning on the lights, Nana instead used a small torch, daring only its limited round of brightness to show Aroha what she had in her other hand.

It was a dark box, made of some murky metal which she'd never seen before, the width of a handspan and bound in tooled leather. It looked old and mysterious.

"I could only bring what I could carry from the Fey," Nana explained in a hushed voice, "and could risk nothing that would bring the attention of the Unmaker's Seeds." She paused and lightly touched Aroha's head. "Anyway," she put the box down on the bed, "I did dare this. It has particular qualities of concealment, enough for a few essentials."

Nana opened it almost reverently. Inside, it was full of small vials and jars, packed tightly together. She ran her fingers over them. "Small stones from the Fey mountains, each with their own power, a mouthful of the water of Lake Assis," she muttered. "Valuable things, I suppose, but what I need is...ah ha!" She held aloft a twisted little bottle, pearly in colour and full of what looked like multicoloured dust.

213

"You know," Nana said with a wink to Aroha, "There is such a thing a fairy dust — like in Peter Pan. This was a gift from the sprites, before I left. You'll meet them someday, I hope. They are the creatures closest to the Mother goddess, and this is their greatest gift." She tucked the vial into her coat pocket, closed the box and put it into Aroha's hands. "You look after this for me, dear."

Her granddaughter frowned, but put the box away in her inside jacket pocket. She would have asked why, but Nana was already taking her by the hand and leading her towards the kitchen.

It was dark and cold down here tonight, something Aroha would never have thought possible of her grandmother's realm. Still they stood close together, like conspirators; the torch's light formed a puddle on the ground in front of them.

"The sprite's gift should not be used selfishly." Nana's hand grasped hers. "The Seeds will murder all the villagers, even if they have you, my dear. They enjoy fear and killing." She led Aroha out onto the porch. From here, the village was invisible. There were no lights on at this time of night, and the moon was too new to care. Aroha felt that the lump in her throat was big enough to choke her.

Nana kissed her on the top of the head. "I will stay here and begin the circle, but you must go and gather the village. Bring them all up here."

It was impossible to tell what her expression was, she kept the light from it deliberately, but Aroha knew that she was frightened. "It's all right, Nan," she said as bravely as she could. "They are not here yet — we still have time."

"Certainly we do, you clever thing," Nana's voice also played that game. "But run, all the same. I'll be waiting."

Aroha flew down the little hill, her heart thundering in her chest, tears of terror ready to break free. So little hope in the night, but she'd hold onto it as best she could. Nana had said it would be alright.

Ronan's breath running along Ella's neck woke her. Under the hill it was still warm and safe. His skin was against hers and all was right with the world.

Well, at least until she got around to opening her eyes. She stayed deliberately still and kept them shut to prolong the moment, but somehow she knew that the night was over and the sun up.

Rolling over, she looked at Ronan, to really examine him by the silver light of the cavern. It had never occurred to her before, but there were signs about him; a certain sheen to his skin and lifting of the ears that was so infinitesimal, but also very telling. Somewhere in there was Puck, a creature not of this world, who was ancient enough to be her thousand times grandfather.

And yet, Ella smiled to herself, he had been very manly just recently. Man enough to give and receive pleasure, but then there had been more. Something she'd never experienced, not even with Doyle. A moment had come when they had seemed to be only one person and not two; a seamless memory, an infinite delight. Ella had seen inside the Trickster, had *been* him and felt his pleasure. It was a heady sensation, and probably an addictive one. Stories of women enthralled by fairy folk suddenly seemed to make sense.

When had Ronan's eyes opened? He might have been lying there, watching her watching him for a while. His eyes were definitely more violet than usual, the colour of ripe plums. His fingers brushed back a strand of her tousled hair.

Ella bit her lip. It was easy for the Fey to be beautiful, but she was sure she looked awful.

"The more I know you, Ella," he said softly, "the more amazed I am. It's as if there is something about you just lurking beyond my reach."

"Do you think I'm Fey?" she joked, while snuggling closer and burying her head in his chest.

The sound of his silence was marred only by the slow thrum of his heartbeat, "No... there is something definitely not Fey about you — something I have seen but once..."

He did not elaborate, but he'd certainly spoiled a perfect moment. As if his own words had disturbed him, he slipped from the bed and back into his discarded clothes before his new lover could protest.

Ella closed her eyes; she could try to hold onto the moment a little longer, ferret it away in memory.

When she opened them again, he was doing exactly what she feared, examining her, trying to understand her, think what sort of category to sort her into. Ella shrank under that scrutiny.

Ronan's gaze softened as he sat down on the corner of the bed. His hand found hers. "Ella, there is something in you which doesn't want to be known. Remember how you ran away when we got back here?" She nodded miserably. "Well, that's not normal. People who have your kind of power, or even Fey Art, they might be shocked, but eventually they would understand. Somehow, I don't think you're ever going to get used to this by yourself."

"What do you mean?"

"I mean something, or someone, is blocking you remembering your past. Only there can you find out what sort of power you have. We shared each other, and that means you would have seen things from my past; emotions, sensations?" She nodded again. "Well, I saw nothing… not a thing. And that is not the way it's meant to be."

Once Ronan had pointed it out, she could feel what he meant. Panic was approaching her, but she could find no logical reason for it. In fact, she wanted to know herself. What did lie beyond that shocking moment? The thought that she might never know, made her angry.

"Beautiful girl," Ronan whispered, pressing his forehead against hers, "don't get frustrated. The Trickster always has a few surprises tucked away. Come on."

He got up off the bed, went to the fireplace and began stacking up the few remaining logs. Casting a look back over his shoulder, he added, "Clothing is optional."

Ella stifled a laugh, but compromised on wanting to shock him and wanting to catch his eye; she pulled on her thick jersey and padded on bare feet to see what he was doing.

Ronan whispered a word to the wood, a sharp quick phrase, said in a language that verged on familiar. Brightness leapt from that word and fire erupted where it fell. Cheeriness suddenly filled the room.

Ronan smiled wryly. "Only a few words of Art remain open to me now, let us see if they are enough." He tugged her hand, guiding her to sit between his legs and look into the crackling fire.

"Now all I need is a little more of your blood, dear heart."
Ella let out a theatrical sigh, but held out her hand. "Go ahead, but you've nearly had your limit."

"You are generous as always," Ronan used the tip of that same silver knife to prick her forefinger. Catching the tiny drop on his finger, he brought Ella's wound to his mouth and sealed it with a kiss. The bauble of blood sat elegantly on his finger, like a tiny ruby. Ronan held it aloft in the light and whispered another word to it. It was said reverently like a prayer, but it was also filled with power.

Then without further explanation, he cast the droplet into the flames. The fire surged up, shucking off reds and golds to become something else entirely. These blue-white flames made them both blink as if they had looked too hard into the sun. It took Ella a long moment to see beyond her stunned eyes.

It was like seeing into her very own nightmare. The dull dove grey walls were familiar, the muted light gave no detail, but Ella knew where they were seeing – all that was missing from this vision was the smell of disinfectant. It was the hospital complex and her first real memory. She was allowed no time to panic. The vision spun on its axis, skimming through the bland corridors with a speed that blurred all those painful memories. Now there were people in regulation white coats, people with importance and authority. Their faces though were a homogenous mass, the vision did not care to linger on them. It darted on, only to come to a sickeningly sudden halt in front of a large expanse of glass. Beyond was a figure in a hospital bed; bound to it, in fact. A dark head rested on a pure white pillow. It was a girl, no more than a young teenager really, but so motionless that it was impossible to think she'd ever thrown a tantrum, or snuck out at night. Somehow Ella knew that this girl had never stirred from her confinement. And her face was not an English one; her skin was the kind of chocolate brown that spoke of more sun than England had ever received. She was a child of the Pacific.

Her guardians were watchful — and it was not concern for the girl that made them so, but wariness. Surely they couldn't expect her to leap from the bed and hurt them, but Ella knew that was indeed what they were afraid of. The way they skirted around the bed, checked multi screened equipment, all said that. They were fascinated and terrified at the same time.

And then the girl's eyes opened, looked out into the flames. This should have made the captors excited, but it was not for them to see, it was only for Ronan and Ella.

Those eyes were deep violet, the colour of electricity. They caught and held what they saw, imparting a plea.

Come to me.

A deep pang, terrible loss and melancholy all flowed through the fire and into Ella. She was on the verge of seeing, of understanding what it all meant, when the blood burned out and the magic passed. Ronan and Ella were left staring into the ashes of the smoking hearth.

She could have sat there forever, examining the remains of that deep sorrow, but her new-found lover would not let her. He was accustomed to despair and knew it could not be allowed to dig too deep.

"Come on," he helped Ella to her feet. "The day has dawned and the Seed's trap is sprung. We can begin."

Ella looked at him and knew exactly what he meant; they had to find that girl. Whatever message she had was waiting for them back where it had all begun — the hospital where she'd woken up. But it was too scary to talk about; it was enough that she knew she could find it. Ella nodded and took Ronan's hand.

She didn't need to ask him how they would get out of the haven, for now she could feel the power moving through her. Ronan had woken an understanding in her, it seemed, shown her in his own way, how to live with Art and magic and even how to use it. She wasn't afraid of it now, and it felt more and more natural to her.

The earth was like a quiescent creature that could be felt just by the tips of her fingers. It knew her; it recognized something within her that even Ella didn't. She moved her hand as if she was pulling aside a curtain, and the hill shifted, opening the passageway that was its best kept secret.

Ronan led her out into the ring of stones, but to a scene quite different to the one last seen. The sun was sliding along the horizon, lighting up the bellies of the plump clouds. The air was sweet, cleansed of any memory of the Seed. Even the blood was gone, soaked into the forgiving earth.

And it was all real to Ella now. It was not a dream — she had changed. In one night she had discovered her power, looked into the face of her past and found an ancient lover. She could never look at things the same way again, not even at Penherem.

Ronan pulled her close to his side and kissed her lightly on the cheek, reminding her that she wasn't alone. She smiled softly, but found her eye drawn to the edge of the forest. Penny Two Dolls was standing there, almost as though she'd been there all night, leaning against a tree, swinging her most ragged doll by one arm.

Ella frowned. The child somehow looked different as well, not so wide eyed and showing no signs of running off. Ronan's breath was suddenly ragged and his fingers tightened around her.

"Who is that?" he hissed.

"It's just Penny, local kid, no one can really control her at all. She runs about all over the place."

He took a step forward, "I imagine not. There is something…"

But Penny's eyes widened, perhaps with fear, and she abruptly disappeared, swallowed into the forest as if she'd never been.

Ronan shook himself like he had just wakened. "This village just gets stranger and stranger. It's almost as if the leftovers of Fey Art have been stored here."

Ella giggled nervously, but couldn't deny her village's strangeness — it was, after all, what had drawn her to it. "Do you want to chase her?" she asked, half joking.

"Your business is more important, dear heart, so the wild children will have to wait. Let us get to this hospital."

She nodded in the affirmative, but when he took her hand and led her away, she couldn't help feeling that she should have been running in the other direction.

CHAPTER SEVENTEEN

$\mathcal{S}acrifice$

"Do they know I'm gone?" Bakari asked Penny, while his toes kept cool in the pool where Ronan and Ella's movements were being shown, like a grainy vid link. The forest which Greer had burned was as still as the grave, but no longer held any fear for him. Not with his present company.

Penny cocked her head and smiled back enigmatically. Behind her the crisped trunk of a tree suddenly found new life and sprouted a vibrant green leaf. "They have to get to the girl quickly."

It was very strange to hear Penny's voice, he thought. In all his time in Penherem, there'd never been a peep out of her. He'd assumed she was autistic or traumatized, but now, looking into her open face, it was hard to see anything but a brilliance and power he'd never seen. It could be just a weird avatar, and perhaps not even Penny herself. But then, he looked down at his own hands. He couldn't access an avatar, so most likely no one could.

Penny was abruptly at his shoulder. "There are no masks here, Bakari. Greer brought you here naked so she could hurt you more."

He shuddered. "I hate to think what she's doing to my real body then. You know I might need it again."

Penny shrugged, as if that was barely a concern. "You could do…" she tilted her face upwards to very real looking sun, "But she has gone."

"I could go back, then."

She nodded slowly, her gaze never leaving him. Bakari got the feeling she was waiting for him to say something.

"Oh, I get it," he chuckled. "But what would I do then, I'm still manacled to the wall."

"Whereas in here..."

He thought about it for a moment, using his Lining instincts, while reminding himself that this was nothing more than an elaborate construct. It was designed for one purpose, but if it was part of Greer's system, there might still be ways out to the main Line.

"Your friends are going to need help to get into the Complex," Penny said, "or they will die."

She wasn't joking, and Bakari didn't doubt she knew what she was talking about. He watched her dance her dirtiest doll along a destroyed branch. Where its little feet passed, leaves erupted from unseen buds.

If this was Greer's construct, then that shouldn't have been possible. He might have been able to do it with major cracking, but somehow this child needed none of that.

"Who are you really, Penny?"

She pouted at that, like he'd broken some sort of childish rule. "I'm the Child." Just like that, as if it was a title and needed no further explanation. She moved closer and peered down into the pool where Ronan and Ella could be seen boarding the VFT for London. "She has given up the limp."

She was right about that, too. Bakari frowned. The slight hesitation in Ella's step had been so much part of her, that without it she looked like quite a different person.

"But it doesn't matter," Penny repeated. "They'll still die. The Complex is too strong for them."

"Complex?"

"It's where she woke up. They're going there for answers."

The girl's cryptic answers were worse than no answer at all. Penny's blue eyes didn't leave his face, boring into him with dread certainty.

"Well, what do you want me to do about it?" Bakari finally demanded. "I can't get away from Greer."

She grinned back at him suddenly, but once again left it up to him to make the leap.

"You want me to leave the construct?" The thought gave him shivers. Maybe in here he could be naked without an avatar, but out on the Line, without any protection, there would be nothing to stand between him and another Liner's attack. He needed his gear.

"You defeated Greer without any of that," Penny reminded him. She was just like any other female, using a man's own pride to get around him. But while Bakari recognized that, he couldn't help feeling she was right. "But... well, you know, this construct looks pretty sturdy. How would I get out?"

She gave him a scathing look, which looked very odd on a child. "It's *your* magic, not mine."

Bakari's hand went instinctively to the spot behind his ear where the Line connection was, but there was nothing there but smooth skin; it felt very alien indeed. But perhaps what the girl meant was that he still had his Line controls inside him, even without his gear. Thrusting away all his disbelief, Bakari sketched the command cube. Even though all the logic he knew said that it shouldn't appear, it did. It hovered just under his fingertips, looking just like it had been summoned from his gear.

Bakari couldn't help letting out a little grunt of shock. Everything he'd ever known about the Line, or had ever learnt, had just gone out the window. Penny Two Dolls was grinning, hugging her dolls close and twisting about in excitement.

"You're a real know-it-all, kid," Bakari smiled back at her, "but I'm very glad you're here." She blushed and ducked her head.

"Now let's see if this thing works like a real one." He rolled the cube in his hand, playing with the intricately carved surfaces. It seemed to be exactly the same, all the symbols and depressions on it identical to the one he'd made himself. The control cube was the Liner's main tool and, like all real professionals, Bakari had spent years perfecting his to match his needs and preferences and connecting it to his various hand-constructed bots.

He couldn't spot anything that was out of place. Somehow having the reassuring weight of the cube in his hand made everything feel a lot better. It must have been the same for swordsmen in the past when they were reunited with their own sword. With the cube, Bakari was once more in control of his world.

Penny whispered something that ran up the back of his virtual neck. He turned around, "What did you say?"

"You are the Nubian prince from Abu Simbel." Her eyes were glowing, he wasn't crazy — they were two violet circles.

How on earth could he trust her? She might be the same Penny from Penherem, but then how could that be? She could just as easily be part of the system itself. Bakari could not afford to lose faith. If he couldn't accept she was here, then he couldn't be sure of anything. Liners had gone mad before, losing their grip on what was real and what wasn't — it was an easy thing to do without an avatar.

But for all that the words disturbed him, they also made no sense, so he put them behind him. For now the control cube was enough, and he had to hold onto its reality.

His fingers knew the pattern; what Bakari wanted was transport and all it took was a bit of artistry. A handful of the clear digital water was all he needed: its pattern would carry them beyond the lines of the construct. After being thrown into the air, Bakari's cube demanded change from the water, urged it to conform. In the air it spun like miniature cyclone, twisting like candy floss, and expanded into a giant sphere of water as tall as Bakari. It was confirmation that his expertise had transferred even without his gear.

Holding out his hand to Penny, he asked, "Coming?"

Without hesitation she slipped her cool hand into his and looked up, all wide-eyed confidence. "Your blood runs true."

Bakari's mind flashed back for a moment, seeing that same trust in his mother's eyes, the same belief in him. She had never had the Line, but perhaps if she had, things might have been different.

He coughed uncomfortably. "Yeah… alright then."

Another manipulation of the cube and the surface of the bubble opened to let them in. Since he wasn't quite sure if this would work, he tried to cover his worry by explaining it to Penny. "See, if this is part of Greer's construct, it might be easier to use it to get out."

Penny nodded, but gave the distinct impression that he could have been reading off the back of a cereal packet.

"Well, that's the theory. I've never actually been inside someone else's construct, especially without an avatar. If things go wrong…" He stopped before he could give voice to his vast fears.

They both stepped into the interior of the bubble and Penny began giggling again, but did not let Bakari share in the joke. Trying his best to ignore her, he concentrated on his control cube once again. A finger danced on the top and the bubble resealed itself. They were left staring at the construct through the curved wall of water. It made everything seem splayed and distorted, like some sort of Dali painting.

The urge to get out washed over him and he sent the commands through the cube as quickly as possible — before common sense could kick in.

The bubble shot up like it was really under water. Bakari was pressed back against the curve of the inside. It was so sudden that for a moment he blacked out.

No. Bakari blinked. He hadn't. It was just there was sudden and complete darkness. Waving his hand in front of his eyes didn't produce anything, and only by pinching himself could he be sure that his body was still there.

"I am black but comely, O ye daughters of Jerusalem, as the tents of Kedar, as the curtains of Solomon." Penny's voice came eerily out of the emptiness and it sent shivers up Bakari's back. He recognized the Song of Solomon from the Bible and somehow in this inky nothing it didn't feel like inane babble. It almost felt like memory.

"Where are we?" he whispered, though he wasn't quite sure why.

"Beyond the construct."

That might have been true, but this was no Line he'd ever ridden. Nothing could be felt by his questing fingertips and he was beginning to crave light with an intensity that bordered on hysteria.

Somehow Penny had found his hand; hers was small, yet comforting.

"If we're really out of Greer's world, then we should be somewhere at least. This feels like nothing at all." In here, his voice sounded young, and hers seemed to be the elder.

"Greer did not use just her Line."

Bakari knew she was right. Greer had used some sort of magic, or Art as Ronan called it, as well as technology. Could it be that magic and the Line were similar? If that was so, then anything might be possible.

Penny squeezed his hand surprisingly hard. "Ronan knows, Greer has found out, and now you have too, Bakari."

He couldn't be sure of what he'd found. Could it be that all this time he'd been looking for magic, when he was already a wizard himself?

"Humans have always had a kind of magic," Penny said calmly. "They lost it for a while, but then they found it again, just in a different shape."

Bakari said a very bad word without thinking of the child next to him — indeed he was no longer convinced she was a child. He felt such an idiot; looking all of his life for some sign of magic, and yet here it was. But the question still remained. "Then where are we, if we're not on the Line?"

The child was silent. Bakari's mind, though, was working overtime. Surely, if the Line was a kind of human magic, then perhaps the rules it obeyed could be used to do far more than he'd ever imagined.

His fingers sought out the control cube and with a quick prayer to whatever deity was watching over them at the moment, he sketched out the command for light. The sudden influx of information to his brain was a real shock. He blinked and blinked, trying to understand what he could now see through the curve of their protective bubble. They were hovering at almost cloud level above a pitted and scarred landscape that stretched beyond the limits of vision. Bakari frowned. It reminded him of a kind of Line landscape, but as he got the numbers to blur and dance before his eyes, he realised that they were fundamentally different. This was the landscape of Greer's mind.

Hidden within each slope and crater were her memories, her desires and her fears. The possibilities opened up before Bakari. He let out a long breath and leaned back in the bubble, trying not to get too excited.

Penny was smiling at him, almost as if she knew what was below her.

Having refocused, Bakari slid his hand over the cube once more and tried to comprehend what he had here. But the numbers didn't add up, there was more landscape here than there ever could have been for one human lifetime; he was able to locate memories and thoughts that must have been at least two hundred years old. Even the Infinity Virus had not been discovered back then, it was something from only the last fifty years.

"It's impossible," he muttered. What was even more confusing was he could begin to see and feel what Greer had been forced to live with all her life; the voices from the past, the great weight of sorrow and despair the ghosts carried with them. They scuttled over the landscape, narrow flashes of white that carried no weight but plenty of horror.

"What the Hell is she?" he finally asked Penny, sure now that the girl too was more than she seemed.

"She is like Ella, the hope of a power, but a plant too long grown under the darkness. She has lost her way..."

Her small voice managed to convey a great weight of sadness, more than any child could have ever known. Bakari frowned, certain that he was going to get nothing more educational out of Penny. The girl might as well have been one of those sibyls, or chattering on in tongues like some preacher.

"Well — whatever she is, if I play her like a subroutine, I might just be able to help Ella. It'll take some doing, but if I can just find the right connections and the right memories..."

Bakari grinned at the implications. There was certainly something very right about using the woman who had tortured him to help his best friend out of trouble. And she wouldn't even know that she'd done it.

It was a good thing that Nana was much loved by the other villagers, for when Aroha went banging on their doors, demanding they come up to the house, if she had been anyone else she would have been sent on her way. All she could stammer out was that there was a terrible threat to the village and her Nana needed everyone to gather her at her home. The recent war meant that anything was possible, and there must have been certain urgency about a wide-eyed, very much awake child appearing at their homes. Perhaps they too sensed something drifting down from the hills, a hint of the danger coming down on them. So all thirty villagers wrapped themselves up in blankets and what woolens came to hand, and followed Aroha back to her house; even Daniel, whom she hadn't spoken to since their return, nodded and obeyed.

When the rag-tag bunch arrived at the house on the low rise, it was to a totally different scene than Aroha had left. Nana had turned on all the lights, powering them with the remaining oil into the small generator, making the night thud with noise. The house was blazing, like a beacon against the dark night, and Nana stood there. Aroha gasped, and beside her the others also stood open-mouthed.

Nana was waiting for them, but she was no longer the normal old woman with her stained apron and knurled hands, now she was a vision of what her old glory might have been. The long hair, so often hidden in a tight bun, was freed and cast about her shoulders in magnificent silver and dark waves. It moved in unseen winds. She wore a midnight blue cloak, though where that had come from Aroha could not say. The wrinkled face, which had so often seemed careworn, now was cast in beautiful relief like that of a benevolent goddess, ancient but not diminished by its age.

Aroha thought her heart would break. It was as if all the everyday worries and concerns had been washed away to show the awe inspiring person beneath.

Her voice when she finally spoke to the shocked villagers was full of kindness and love. "My dearest friends — don't be afraid." There was magic in that voice, a kind that reminded all that heard it of the women who had loved them in their life; mothers, sisters, wives or daughters.

"Come into the circle," Nana said. And looking down they could see it, the thinnest line of silver somehow woven into the earth itself. "Step over and join me."

Unquestioningly they did so, instinctively stepping high over the circle, not breaking the endless coil that Nana had woven.

"What is it, Mrs. Bennetts?" Jan asked, her voice hushed. Even before Nana had thrown off her disguise, the villagers had always held her in a special sort of awe, never calling her by anything but her last name and never coming up to the house unless invited.

227

"We've all seen a lot recently," Nana stepped down among them, showing that she was still part of the village, even if they were too scared to touch her."The war, drones, death — but there is something else coming to these hills that is even more terrible; another world, with deadly creatures."

Aroha looked up and around her. They should have laughed and trooped back to their houses annoyed and grumpy, but the night wouldn't let them. A primitive human instinct told them that something was coming, even if they didn't acknowledge it in their modern consciences. They could feel it at the back of their necks and in the dreadful clenching of their bowels. The group swayed slightly, but no one said anything.

Sally broke free of her crowd of siblings and squeezed her way to Aroha's side. Her eyes were very wide and her face so pale that her freckles stood out like a giraffe's spots. Aroha knew the reason; in the light of her Nana's transformation, her own was revealed. Reflected in Sally's look was the knowledge of how she herself appeared, her skin the same dark brown, but her eyes were all iris and the colour of the deep night, blue-black. It was all too obvious she wasn't human.

Sally's throat bobbed but she said nothing, just snuggled in close to her friend. Aroha could only wish that she was able to understand the human fear she should be feeling. But she had seen what was coming down from the hills and her fear was more than just some ill defined mass.

Some part of her understood the fell creatures.

The humans about her were talking in hushed voices, recalling myths and legends and trying to find a way to put this night into some sort of context. But none of them doubted the silver lit figure of Aroha's Nana.

She stood calmly among them, but they avoided her touch, not out of fear but reverence. Her narrow frame was somehow more than it had ever been, thinness and frailty transformed into a type of concentrated strength. Now Aroha could almost see the Fey creature she once had been shining through the mortal shell. It made her afraid that she had lost the woman she loved.

Then Nana looked down and her eyes were not those of a distant goddess, but rather the pools of kindness they had always been. She reached out and took her granddaughter's hand.

"Are we going to die, Mrs. Bennetts?" Although Sally's body trembled her voice did not waver.

"Not if the circle stays strong, dear," Nana pulled the children closer, wrapping her other arm around Sally, "and the protection of the earth mother is within it — it shall not break."

In an instant the night changed from threatening to terrifying. The Unmaker's creatures appeared suddenly out of the darkness, sliding their knife-like bodies from the shadow to stand in the light of the house, the better to strike fear. Every human sense was repelled by them; the odd angular set of their razor limbs, the scent of death which rolled out from them, and the faintest of hums that annoyed the ear. Everything about them combined to drive the humans into hysteria.

Their sub vocal screams knocked Aroha in the chest and left her breathless, yet her grandmother was not touched by it. The silver light of her presence pushed out, encompassing all the gasping, shivering humans within its nimbus.

"Hold, my friends," she said in a voice which rose above the noise of the monsters, and every face turned to her. "Stay strong and they cannot touch us."

Though the evil beyond had power, no one doubted when they looked upon her that she spoke the truth. In the dark she glowed, holding onto Aroha and Sally and appearing to be a statue of feminine strength and determination. The villagers turned to her, filling their vision with her hope, rather than with the terror beyond the circle. As long as she kept talking, they would not panic and break the circle.

She told them of the Fey, her own world, wrapping them in words of beauty and majesty. The rolling hills beneath which they made their homes, the glittering joy of the Court of the Queen of Fey, the endless woods and bush where creatures of legend played. Each detail glowed in their minds like jewels. They were carried away beyond the danger and wrapped in her memories.

However not quite all of them were transported. Aroha could hear the words that fell from her Nana's lips, could comprehend their beauty, but it did not weave its spell around her completely, for that Art was hers as well. So she could look about her, into the astonished faces that she'd known all her life, and even beyond, if she dared.

Despite the horror, she wanted to see the face of her enemies. Those soulless eyes were ever fixed on the villagers, but they made no attempt to breach the circle. They swayed lightly on their feet, as if to say they could strike at any instant. The very shape they wore was designed to make the skin crawl, like fell spiders made of bone and poison.

Sally caught sight of their outline and clutched Aroha with a terrified whimper.

"We're safe," Aroha whispered. "Nana won't let anything happen to us."

Out of the side of her vision, it was obvious that not everyone was stricken with fear. Daniel was standing a little apart from the villagers, staring out at the monsters beyond the circle. He had his hands in his pockets and was swaying slightly from side to side.

Aroha frowned. He seemed untouched by fear at all.

Untangling Sally's hands from around her and reattaching them around Nana, she slipped away to get a closer look.

Her steps were cautious, sliding through the wet grass slowly while the weight of the greenstone mere inside her grew with each footfall. And there was heat, too, as she got towards the edge of Nana's circle, so it felt like she was drawing closer to an open oven; her skin balked at it.

She stood hesitantly a few feet from her friend. "Daniel?"

He didn't seem to hear, but all the sensations around Aroha intensified, the mere, the heat and now a faint hiss in the air from the creatures. Aroha chewed the inside of her cheek and tried not to notice that now they were congregating around the section of the circle where Daniel stood.

"I've got to thank you Aroha," Daniel was suddenly holding her by the shoulders. "You opened my eyes. I would never have guessed there was magic in the world."

She mumbled something, unsure what to say to something so unexpected.

Daniel was grinning. "But I've seen a Taniwha, and seen magic done. The world seems… bigger somehow."

"Come back to the middle," Aroha begged, feeling the heat increase and the approach of her own growing panic.

He didn't notice her. "I mean, you can do so much more with magic in your life." His eyes trailed towards the monsters beyond. "Anything is possible."

She could barely breathe now, and the hisses had changed, becoming more like whispers. Their meaning eluded her, but the threat and hunger in them was plain to feel.

"Please, Daniel," she was almost screaming now, tugging on his shirt sleeve though it felt as hot as a piece of glowing metal. Somewhere back amongst the crowd she heard Nana call her name.

"Don't be afraid," he replied softly. "It'll all be OK." Then he broke the circle.

The world dissolved into a series of horror-filled flashes. Daniel's foot kicked aside the precious powder the circle was made of. It flew out of place in an arch of silver dust.

It was the moment the monsters had been waiting for. Daniel went forward to meet them and Aroha spun away, back towards all she loved.

Nana's face was folded in fear and anger. None of the villagers had seen or felt what he'd done, but she had. Now clutching Sally to her, she raced to reach Aroha. She was quick, but not as quick as the Seeds which came pouring through the broken gap.

Daniel was standing there. Aroha caught his moment of death like a snapshot on her retina. His arms were open and he greeted the monsters with a laugh of sheer joy, as if they were his long lost brothers. That cry of happiness was cut short. He had let them in, but they held no gratitude. A long leg flashed out, and the man who had become her friend was gone in a spray of scarlet.

Aroha didn't have enough time to cry out before Nana's arms were around her and the chaos was flowing towards them. It had been terrifying to see the monsters destroying the Folk — but they had not been creatures of blood and flesh, and what the Seeds brought to the villagers was a new kind of horror.

Aroha could not close her eyes; she wanted to, but they would not obey. She, unlike Sally, saw the villagers try to flee from the broken circle. Jan was pinioned many times by dagger-like claws. She writhed under them like a terrible science dissection. Dan Flinders, who had seemed all muscle and towering strength, was cut down from behind. Even poor old Mrs. Mayhew, who had produced marvelous toffee and shown Aroha how to make hokey pokey, was in an instant turned into something unrecognizable. Sally's family was gone in a blur of whirling blades.

231

The monsters were efficient. However, around Nana, they paused. She clutched the children to her and glared back at them. The silver light was still about her. Sally was thrashing and screaming into her side while Aroha wished she could do the same.

"Old woman," the creatures had voices, which was somehow even more horrific. One spoke with an airy hiss, as orifices down its sides pumped, "You are far from home."

Nana's heart was beating fast, but she spoke without apparent fear. "As are you, Seed of the Unmaker."

"We heard. We awoke. We answered when the power stirred." They shuffled fractionally closer, trailing the debris of the villagers, like they didn't matter. "Give us the girl."

Nana laughed shortly and tightened her arms around the children, but she too was moving fractionally, turning the three of them away from the house. "You have a sense of humour, enemy mine."

The lead monster's head cocked, swiveling on its white hard neck, and the eyes which were as black as unbeing fixed on Aroha with deadly intensity. "The Child is nothing. She woke us. When she is gone, then we too will go."

Sally's cries had stilled to dry racking sobs, but Aroha could feel her own body starting to convulse with repressed horror.

Nana was stroking her head. "I am not so easily fooled as that poor boy, Seed. Nothing you can say will make me give her up."

The creatures gathered in a tight knot, stamping their feet on the earth, eager. "You are far from your home, lady Fey."

"And you, yours."

They hissed at her reply. "The difference is," came the chilling retort, "we are many, you are but one."

Aroha felt her grandmother flinch at that, but she did not speak again. Holding the girls close, she turned and guided them away from the house and the scene of desolation. Looking up, Aroha could see by the light of the moon that she was crying. Her tears were silver. She didn't look Fey and powerful now — she looked bowed and shaken.

Sally had retreated into shock and would not catch Aroha's eye. She had witnessed her family's death: an instant of profound horror that had quite possibly destroyed her. For a human there could be no healing from such a moment. Aroha was already grieving for that part of her lost friend. For both of them there would be no more carefree days. The world was wrecked.

If only she could have done something, Aroha railed at herself. The taniwha had given her power beyond her grandmother's, but she had not found the way to wield it and now the whole village was destroyed. And Daniel, the friend she'd risked everything to save, was dead.

"Don't blame yourself, child," Nana's voice was faint and strained. "The Unmaker knows all the ways to tempt, and Daniel will not be the last to give in." She caught Aroha, pushed her on ahead when it seemed she might try to look back. "Don't do that either, dear heart. They are following, and I do not know how far my power will take us."

Sally broke, crying for her mother again and again into Nana's side and shivering like a beaten animal.

"Where are we going, Nana?" Aroha asked timidly, afraid of the answer.

"To the sea, love. The land has no place for us here, and we shall only bring destruction if we stay."

The three of them, wrapped in sorrow and misery, followed the half-formed road towards the rocky beach, but always behind them came the stealthy footsteps of the killers. When the girls stumbled and Nana stopped to help them, the Seeds paused too, still too afraid of her light to dare an attack. Each time they seemed a little closer. Aroha squeezed her eyes shut and let herself be led.

If only she had power to change time. Perhaps if she imagined well enough, they could go back to podding peas on the sunporch. Sally and her brothers could be banging on the flyscreen door.

The stones twisted under their feet while the wind howled. Everything reminded them that this was real. The village was no more, and she was responsible.

They could hear the sea, though, the pounding of the grey waves on the rocks, the indrawn hiss of water running over the gravel. Nana faltered and Aroha's heart jumped.

"I don't..." her grandmother's hand tightened on her shoulder, "I don't have the strength, girls."

The sound of talons piercing the earth came from behind them. Their pursuers were eager to finish their work.

233

"Yes you do!" Aroha tugged at her sleeve, pulled at Sally, bending her determination to getting them all out of this. Sally hung like sodden washing between them, her voice and will gone.

"No," Nan's expression was drawn apart, her face smooth, like she'd already dropped her worldly cares. "They will catch us before we reach the sea. I have had my time, dear. Now it is yours."

Aroha screamed in frustration and anger. The hills echoed with her wild despair.

"No!" It felt like her insides were erupting and she would be turned inside out with grief. It was too much, too cruel. She was a wild animal thrashing against injustice.

Nana would not let her throw herself on the ground and have a tantrum. Instead she was already disentangling herself from the girls.

She grabbed the vial from inside Aroha's cardigan and before either girl could cry out, she had smashed the fragile glass. The shivering friends were engulfed in twinkling dust that smelt of roses and grass. Nana's silver light flared up again, burning white phosphorous against the night sky, a jet of flame that would burn out all too soon. She spoke a word, a summoning; a call from the past that spat like lightning into the air and demanded this last thing from the realm of humanity.

The bird came. A massive eagle, a creature from New Zealand's past, its wings thrumming with power as it dived down. The creature's shadow, its great hooked beak and powerful taloned feet, were outlined against the moon.

Its arrival was the coming of the taniwha or the moa. It had been the enemy of man when it lived, but it knew the Fey and flew out of legend for one of them now. There was not much reality to it, mostly memory held together by Fey Art, a sketch of greatness. Nearly ten feet of wing carried the eagle down in a swoop. The sound was the wail of a banshee.

Aroha knew its purpose, knew why Nana had summoned the eagle, but she cried out all the same. Too late. The two girls were caught up in the eagle's embrace, its ghostly shape bearing them aloft, even while Aroha's hands stretched back to where Nana stood in a puddle of her own dimming light.

Aroha felt herself dying with Nana, trying to hold onto those precious memories, but outraged that memory would soon be all that was left of her.

Distance softened the outline of the woman who turned back towards her attackers. In her step there was weariness but acceptance, like she was only glad to have held out that long against them. Then they seemed to blur together until her light was lost in a sudden surge of black.

The moment of her death, though not seen, felt like a steel spike driven through her granddaughter. Aroha spasmed and reached in the eagle's grasp while Sally hung like a rag doll of misery. The grip of grief was even stronger than that of the eagle's talons with claws of its own that buried into Aroha and left her weeping and feeling dead inside. Perhaps if she wept enough she could change things. Surely the gods would not be unmoved by her despair.

Nothing changed. The light was still gone, and her Nana with it. The eagle still soared on the night sky, still obeying Nana's command but not for much longer. The one who had called it out of myth had died. Memory alone could not hold the bird aloft for long.

Aroha heard the whine of Art unraveling even as the air rushed around them. She knew with a dull certainty that this, her Nan's last effort, had only a few moments left before it would begin to fade. The eagle was not meant to be, and reality demanded that it return to the realm of legends.

The tears ran cold down her cheeks. She reached out and took Sally's limp hand across the gap. Grief and guilt battled in equal measures. "I'm so sorry," she whispered to her friend. Soon both of them would join Nan beyond the bright sea of death. Her magic had brought them to this point, but she knew nothing about how to use it or save them now.

Sally's head came up and her eyes gleamed with moonlight, but she said nothing.

The friends held hands tightly, even when the eagle finally surrendered to reality with an angry cry. Somehow in the lonely abrupt descent through the air, they managed to cling to each other.

When the sea caught them below, at least it took them together. The last tumbling glimpse Aroha had of her homeland was through a mask of tears.

CHAPTER EIGHTEEN

Homecoming

Ella's hand was warm in his. Ronan looked down at it, surprised by how really good it felt. He'd never truly appreciated such a small gesture before.

The way her curves slotted against his side so easily, the soft brush of her breath on his neck, all were pleasant distractions from their destination. They were heading once more for the sprawl of London and he knew he should have been afraid, or cautious, or at least planning his assault on this fortress from Ella's past. Yet Ronan could not find a moment for any of these things.

He rolled the feeling around in the back of his head like a tasty but unidentified morsel. That was it: he was contented, happy for the first time since his powers had begun to fade. No other woman had felt so right to him. He wanted to keep her hand in his and know what was going on in her head.

He'd sampled many mortal women in his years in this realm, both before and after the Fey had slipped away. Yet fragmentary memories remained with him; a look in an eye, the sound of joyous laughter, but none had felt like this. Only one other had come close. He had not yet been Ronan then, but a dark perfect face with eyes as warm and loving as the African sun. He'd lain with a Nubian princess in the splendor of Abel Simbel. She'd been a flash of lightning in his old life, something as beautiful and incomprehensible as humanity could ever be. Puck had enjoyed his time with her; she had been the jewel of her age.

The Fey who had been Puck frowned and sat a little straighter in his chair. He recalled something familiar about that face now. In a moment of sudden clarity he saw her reflected in Bakari's features. More, he recognized something of himself. His Fey blood, which had begun stirring since he'd found Ella, told him without question that Bakari was his descendant. It was not unusual. Most Fey had gifted the human realm with their own wild seed, but as far as he had known, there had been none of his.

Until now. He frowned and looked across at Ella.

She was staring out of the window, trailing a finger down the length of the glass as she watched the last of the countryside whip past. Her mahogany curls had flopped over her eyes and she looked so young it made his chest tight.

Ronan wondered if he should tell her his revelation, but decided against it for now. Bakari should be the first to know. It might not even matter. After nearly two thousand years, Ronan was fairly sure he wasn't needed to be any sort of father figure. Yet, he felt a small measure of pride: some part of him had survived and grown in this world.

"What are you smiling about?" Ella tugged his hand.

"Nothing." Another smile would not be repressed.

"Stop it," but Ella's voice was warm somehow. "Doesn't the idea of breaking into a high-security covertly-run hospital fill you with dread?"

Ronan thought for a moment. "No... not really." It was true. A distant logical part of his brain wondered why that was. It was as if he'd been transported to that moment when he'd first stepped into the human realm, before everything had jaded him.

"I've seen a lot of bad things. What can a hospital possibly offer?" He knew he wasn't telling her the truth, but she'd probably be very scared if she knew exactly how much he felt for her.

"It's more than that," Ella paused, leaning her head back on the battered seat. "There's a taste in the air, a cloud of fear. I can't remember much about the place, but that I do recall."

"Why do you think you were there? Were you sick?"

She shook her head, eyes squeezed tightly shut, and between them the image flashed: a distorted view of the world seen through a shroud of crinkly plastic, lights blue-green and harsh, and the air which seemed to stop sound dead. And there was cold: deep, bone aching coldness.

"No…" A tear escaped the corner of her eye. "I wasn't sick, I don't think. I felt more… like an experiment. Like I was a frog tied to the school bench just waiting for the kid with the knife to arrive."

Ronan could feel her heart racing, and for once he couldn't think of the perfect words. It didn't matter how ancient he was, sometimes even the Trickster was stumped. He slipped his arm behind her and hugged her tight. In between them, the hardness of his rifle reminded them of the seriousness of the situation.

The VFT roared through the outer slums and they watched it quietly, cherishing each second. They disembarked at Victoria Station and slipped through the crowd, still silent.

Their hands found each other, as they picked a battered old mini van out of the stand outside the station and Ella told them where to go. She knew the address.

Getting out of the cab a few streets away from the facility, they stepped into a world of abandoned warehouses and peeling shops. Ronan peered into one. It seemed full of dusty remains of some ancient containers like it had taken fifty years to get from China. Immediately he began to wonder, to feel the unreality of the place. He could see no customers for this strange array of shops, and he shot Ella a piercing look.

She shrugged. "They're a front for the facility. They don't like to have visitors."

He could feel it now, the curious looks at the back of his neck.

"So just look like we're lost." She tugged him around the corner, hand raised as if looking for another cab. She led him down a maze of corridors and the sense of unreality grew. Somehow the senses he'd just recently reacquired were blurring on him already. Ronan tried to remember the feeling, but he'd been too long gone from his own magic.

Ella interrupted his train of thought. "You know," she said peering past his shoulder, "I could have done this much better by myself: I only have one shiver cloak, you know."

"I'm not going to let you out of my sight."

"Just what I wanted you to say," she kissed him briefly before turning back to the dripping wall. Her fingers danced along it, tapping out a rhythm not familiar to Ronan. The illusion wavered and then disappeared, resolving into a plain metal door. Ella grinned, expecting him to be surprised. "Never seen anything like it, right."

"Well actually," it was very like Greer's, but he tucked that observation away. Mentioning the blind witch seemed to always summon her.

Ella was obviously distracted by this journey back into her past, for her hands were running over the steel of the door. Quickly enough, she found the retina activated lock. "The back door, where they dump all their rejects and leftovers."

Ronan ran a professional eye over it. "Looks like it'll need more than a crowbar to get in. Maybe we should have brought Bakari."

A strange expression ran across her face, and he could have sworn the scent of jasmine tickled his nostrils. "This is… well, pretty personal, and besides," her muscles bunched under his fingers, "I don't think we'll need him."

Then she did it, curved her hand around the lock, and changed everything for Ronan. Blue lightning danced from her fingertips, and power that he had not seen since before he'd chosen this form suddenly reappeared in the human realm.

She was looking at him, and he couldn't read her expression. It was blank and perfect, reminiscent of another Fey he'd loved and just as powerful as she had been. Ronan felt the trickle of something that felt very much like fear. He might love Ella, but he knew only as much as she did about her background. His ancient and powerful cousin had been born to such power, and he was suddenly afraid what it might do to Ella. Could she control such Art?

Ronan held her gaze, remembering that right now she had more of the Art than he did. The thought made him flinch. Yet she smiled easily at him, and Ronan knew he didn't have to worry about what he would have done if she spun away towards the unseelie side of Art. Then she blinked, and the inscrutable goddess was gone. Only a fearful woman remained.

Ronan shook his head, trying to block out her thoughts and clear his own. It had been a very long time since he'd heard another's inner voice. While he welcomed the closeness, he needed all his concentration right now.

He said nothing about the lightning and didn't give Ella a chance to break down and cry. Whatever lay beyond the steel of the door, it was at least the truth.

"Let's go in," Ella murmured and levered open the entrance.

Inside was silent and still, a long corridor leading in and down. Their footsteps did not echo. In here, all sound was dead. Ronan tried unsuccessfully to spot any cameras.

"Curiouser and curiouser," he whispered. The corridor swallowed the words until he wished that he had not let them out at all. An even stranger feeling swirled inside him. It tickled his fingers and fluttered behind his eyelids. It was not unpleasant, but he couldn't identify it.

At his side, Ella matched him stride for stride. He could hear her thoughts if he strained his ears, but he didn't want to; her distress was already hammering in the back of his head.

When she'd last seen this corridor, she'd been running down it, naked under a battered long coat, and it had been Doyle at her side. Behind had been pain, and now here they were, walking calmly back towards it.

Greer was watching their progress. The two figures were beamed straight into her mind from the tiny silver thread which connected her to the Line. It was easy to live in two worlds if you practiced long enough, and Greer had been blessed with longer than most. It also meant that the loss of her eyes was not too onerous.

She'd somehow expected Ronan, but to see the usually quiet and unassuming Ella walking that particular corridor was a shock. Her brow furrowed and the vines of the conservatory whipped back and forth to the unseen winds of her displeasure. How foolish she'd been. Ella was Nill, and all the time she'd been right where she'd never expected — Penherem.

Steadying her breathing, Greer tried to calm herself. It was alright: in fact it was better than alright. The location was not her choice, but she had Ronan and Ella in the palm of her hand. With a short bitter smile, her hands danced across the narrow span of her gear. When the moment came, she would be ready.

Ella felt like her heart was rising up, trying to escape out of her throat. Vision flickered and blurred like she was in some badly played out corner of the Line. Yet this was real — she had to keep reminding herself that. Memories were close. She could feel them fluttering near her head like little moths, and she couldn't decide if she should crush them or invite them in.

Ronan matched her step for step, but he let her be in front, just a little, as if to let her work things out for herself. For all the emotions he could see of hers, she could feel parts of him as well. Something was stirring inside the Fey that had once been Puck: he might not even have been aware of it. He tasted like honey in her head: ripe with barely concealed power.

Ella couldn't afford to think of it now. She had to keep moving, putting one foot in front of the other, going back into her past.

Soon enough, a part of that history appeared: a steel grey uniformed guard, with a blank female corporatized face and an ugly length of gun pointed in their direction. Ella had no specific memory of the guards, but her anger, which had been simmering until that moment, erupted in an explosion. She was swifter than Ronan and not as forgiving. The air rippled and curved down the featureless corridor like the rumble of an ancient freight train, breaking with a roar over the guard, flinging her against the far wall and denying her any opportunity to raise that gun.

Ronan was staring. She could feel it, and she could even feel his thoughts: *Even I can't do that.*

"I'm not afraid anymore," Ella told him. Then she ran, not looking back to see if he was following, only knowing that now she had to find the end of the corridor. And there were others in front of her: men and women, guards and sterile-clad technicians. Those who got in her way got knocked aside, and the rest ducked back into corridors, quivering in fear from this avenging angel. Ahead Ella could hear the girl, not with her ears, but with some sense that as yet she could not name.

I'm nearly there, Ella called, and indeed it was not far now. Her feet were flying, her heart full with longing. Nothing could stand in her way. But then…

241

Ella stopped like all her strings had been cut. It was a set of double doors: thick, grey and very, very familiar. "My god," she whispered, but to herself now, because the guards had all fled and Ronan had yet to catch up. "This is it."

The girl's call went on, but Ella could not deny what was right in front of her. Her feet were doing their own thing, moving towards the door where it had all begun. She put out her hand and touched the thick surface. There was no response—the door was locked solid—but Ella was different now, and she called upon what she realised was her Art.

The power surged forward and blasted against the steel with the force of a hurricane. With an almighty tearing noise, the doors were shattered and flung across the floor to rattle like a spent tin can. Narrowing her eyes against the dimness, Ella stepped over the twisted metal and into the past. It would take a long moment to understand what she was seeing but she took it all in an instant.

Everything was sterile, clean, like the inside of some freakishly clean serial killer's wardrobe. In place of trousers, there were only beautiful bodies. Not human, though, Ella could see that. They were Skins.

For some, the Infinity Treatment came too late, or did not work — and some had been born with imperfect bodies and wanted better. Ella was grinding her teeth, for the truth was breaking over her now.

Skins, they were called, expensive repositories for the mind, made of nanobots, electronics, anything but flesh. Never flesh. Ella didn't need to turn over any of these bodies hanging like cast off jackets, but she did anyway.

Her own face was there. She'd known somehow that it would be. Ella stared back at herself. There was no movement in her features. The thing hanging there was only a doll.

But then what am I? Someone was sobbing. It was her, but who was she? Thousands of questions burbled and ran over her, and Ella crumbled. What sort of thing was she?

She was crying, sobbing and howling, and beating her hands against her head. Ronan's voice came from far off. "Ella?"

Calmness rolled over her and she looked up into his bemused face. She could only imagine what he must think of all this. After all, he'd made love to nothing more than a warm doll. It was all an illusion.

"See," she growled, tugging one of her sister-creatures around so there could be no mistaking it, "This is my history — what Doyle found. They must have been prepping me to be some pampered downloaded woman when he found me. But this," she pulled her own hair sharply, "This is nothing — I'm nothing."

Ronan couldn't say anything to that. She'd always felt hollow, empty and scared, and this was the room where all those feelings had come from.

"But this can't be," Ronan had regained his voice. "You have the Earth Magic, Fey Art, you can't be this." He turned his face away from her past.

"But I am," she shouted, holding her wrist to his eyeballs. "Do you know what is under here? Nothing but technology. No flesh, just fake skin, fake blood."

He didn't flinch from her anger and fear, but took her by the hand, pressing his flesh against whatever synthetics comprised hers. "Ella, there is more here. I can feel it and so could you if you just thought about it."

Yet, she couldn't think. Everything Ella had been sure of had been an illusion. She was, in fact, the ultimate illusion. She slumped against him and didn't resist when he scooped her up.

Where was her off switch, Ella wondered idly.

Ronan picked her up and carried her, whispering words he hoped would hold her together; lying, saying it would be all right. None of that reached Ella. She was shut away from everything, her mind spinning on herself. Didn't he know she was just a bundle of wires and vat grown tissue?

He walked through the corridors, carrying her easily, following the strains of the girl's call. The grey corridors they passed through were silent, only occasionally echoing the sounds of retreating feet. Whoever still remained in the complex was not willing to risk Ella's wrath again.

She kept her face buried in Ronan's shoulder. The world felt like it was slipping further and further away.

Until Ronan put her to her feet. Leaning heavily against him, she raised her head slowly, not really caring what was out there. When her eyes finally did focus, it was on something that persuaded her to move.

A clear sheet of plastic composite was all that separated them. Ella took a hesitant step closer. On the other side were soldiers and technicians, all buzzing around like an upset hive. She saw none of that though; all she saw was the girl.

She was just the same as in her vision: a sunkissed teenager with hair thick like night, resting as still as stone, like a sleeping Beauty. Except that she wasn't asleep — not quite. The call was stronger here. There were no words this time, just an insistence.

Ella's hand hovered nervously above the steel while her eyes darted around the room now. The people had sealed themselves in, trapping themselves in there with a girl that they were terrified of. That much was apparent from the pale faces and the guns. Ella pushed heedlessly into their minds. They had been using the child for years, draining her of power, using her to learn about magic and Art. They had kept her here, all alone, strapped to a bed, while they had taken what they needed from her.

Ella frowned. They would kill the child rather than let her in. They *knew* something about the consequences, something that terrified them to the point of madness. Rage boiled up in Ella then: a black fury that blinded her to reason, that made her want to destroy and take revenge. She didn't know what she was anymore, but she knew her enemies when she saw them.

She reached out with one finger and touched the thick layer of steel.

Ronan, who had just lately learnt fear, cried out as he sensed the flood of rising power, ready to explode. He was too late.

The world shook. Ripples ran through the steel where her finger rested. It buckled before bursting in a spray of explosive power. The guards and white suited scientists on the other side were washed away in a spray of molten metal. Human reflexes were simply not enough to cope with an explosion of Art. Ronan shifted, becoming his black feline self, and leapt through after to deal with those that remained. There weren't many.

Ella stepped through and went to the girl. The humans she had been so furious with only moments before were already forgotten. She was clean of any mortal morals, for after all, she wasn't human herself. The rules no longer applied.

The girl was still the centre of everything, and the world tightened on her. Carefully sitting on the edge of the bed, Ella took the cool hand in hers. The connection was made. A sweet rightness filled her — like coming home.

The girl was the woman, and the memories she'd lost were all there. Her heart flew as she remembered New Zealand: the sound of peas exploding from their pods, the smell of lavender when Nana hugged her, the shriek of delight Sally made at any given opportunity, the call of the bellbird, and the waving fronds of the tree ferns. All this hit her in the chest, making her cry out.

She'd fallen such a long way, the water below was not kind and the damage done to her back had been the final gift of that terrible night. Dimly she remembered her rescue, the boat that picked her up, the British cruiser which had brought her here. They had found no trace of the utu virus, and then the bone-haired woman had claimed her, proved she was a relative. It had all been a lie. They knew what she was, untrained and traumatized though she might be.

Greer had come and she'd shown them how to do this terrible thing. They couldn't control a person full of wild Art, instead they had needed her to lie still and submit. It was the scientists in their clean white coats that had broken her apart from her spirit, just so she would comply.

Her soul should have died then and there, but somehow it had strength to go on. It had found the Skin waiting for its new owner and taken that as a sanctuary. Her shattered mind had held onto the damage, both physical and mental, that the child had suffered. Doyle's arrival had been either fate or luck. Aroha had found a way to escape the walls — even if she'd had to leave her body behind.

Ella touched her face: literally her own face. It was so young. She willed her spirit to return where it belonged with all her reawakened Art. Wanting was not, however, enough. It was too late for that. The scientists had done their job well enough that little remained in the shell of the girl. They had nearly stripped her bare.

Nearly, but not quite. Ella placed her hand over her heart, knowing that something still lay within; something they had not yet succeeded in stealing. The call for the mere was as easy as breathing. Slowly, the room began to glow with a faint silver light. In it, she could glimpse swirling mists and snow-capped mountains. Home.

With a sigh, Ella looked down at the mere lying in her hand: Whataitai's gift was intact after so many trials. With it gone from the body, however, so too was the magic. The hospital bed was empty. Nothing remained of her child form, the one that had hugged Nana and leapt through the tall grasses of home. It was too much to bear. Chaos and fear were all around, there was too much information, too much loss to hold inside a single body, real or synthetic.

With a cry of incredible sadness, the woman let go, and darkness followed her.

CHAPTER NINETEEN

Traps

It was over. Greer's link allowed her to see the events happening in the compound. Ronan hovered over the woman like the protective fool he could so often be. Annoying as it was that they had broken in, it had worked out well. The spirit was back, and she had the mere. It contained all the power of land and sea that the taniwha had given Aroha. All of this could be used.

Using virtual senses and looking around her into the dark recesses of the vines and ferns of the conservatory, Greer could imagine what she would be able to do with the greenstone weapon. It was the last of the Earth Magics left in the human world. There had been many others once, symbols of a partnership between Fey and human, but people were careless creatures and all had been lost or destroyed one way or another. The taniwha's mere was now the sole repository of the old human magic. Its last owner had been wise to leave it with Whataitai. And it had been endlessly frustrating to know that the girl had it, without being able to retrieve it — even after years of trying.

Now it was here, and with Ella fallen into chaos, there remained only Ronan to best — then it would be hers. Greer's hand hovered hesitantly above her control cube. The trouble was that there were not many types of gas to use. The compound had been fitted with all sorts of cunning devices, including defenses of last resort. It mattered little that many of the remaining guards would die when she realised the cyanide gas — what mattered was that she would finally have the human magic she needed.

It was unfortunate that Ronan would perish as well, but she was fairly sure that only his blood would be required in the end. If not, there were other Fey that had escaped through the Between to the human realm. Certainly they were only of the lesser sort, but they would suffice.

Somewhere hovering over the landscape of her dreams, Bakari's brow furrowed, reading her dark intentions. Penny snuggled in against his side, but said nothing. His fingers clenched around the control cube and he whispered a word of command, though where it came from he could not say.

Greer paused. No, there would be other ways. Ronan was still needed and she still had a hold over him. Let him bring Ella out of the compound and think he had won something for her. The truth was coming out bit by bit, and soon enough he would see the whole expanse of her plans. Unfortunately for the Trickster, by then it would be too late.

The compound was a smoking ruin, full of lifeless bodies and broken dreams. Ella, slumped over, was not herself anymore. She managed to keep her feet when Ronan helped her to the exit, but she collapsed not far after and he was forced to carry her again.

She burned. His arms ached where they touched her, but they shared no words. Tucking the greenstone weapon under her shiver cloak had been her last conscious action. Her eyes did not close, but neither did Ronan want to look into them. Ella's eyes had been brown as moist earth, and these were not her eyes. Chaos was rumbling through her, and he couldn't guess what would emerge on the other side. They could have walked the ancient rivers again or taken the VFT back to Penherem, but Ronan would not risk either of those. So he called in a favor.

Leia from the Point came as quickly as he'd hoped. The long dark shape of the diesel Conqueror nudged its way down the alley, pushing aside the occasional rubbish bag and discarded shopping trolley. Leia shoved open the driver's door and looked at him with a grim twist of her mouth. "Whenever you call, how come I know it's always trouble?"

He shrugged, "I'm just that kind of person. How's Alexis?"

Leia's gaze dropped, "Damned Rosers — she didn't make it."

"Really sorry about that, Leia," he opened the back door and slid the near comatose Ella in. "She was the best."

"Yeah... maybe," the woman's hands tightened on the steering wheel. "Funny thing was, she spent so much time and money on cutters — wanted to live forever. And then look what happens."

"Life's full of irony. How's Molly coping?"

"Hey, that kid's seen it all — just never expected to lose a mother in a gunfight like that."

Ronan scooted across the front bench seat, narrowly avoiding an errant spring poking up through the leather. He didn't know what to say. Grieving was the only human emotion he had yet to get a grip on. Yet looking over his shoulder at Ella curled in a ball, he started to get some idea. To really understand grief and vulnerability, you had to love someone.

"Death's even harder to understand than life," he replied.

Leia jerked her head, turning away from him a little. There might have been the shining glint of a tear there. "I suppose. So, where are we going?"

"Can you drop us off at Little Penherem?"

Surprisingly, Leia knew where that was. While they fought their way through the traffic she told Ronan about her childhood and how her parents had taken her to that very town for the summers.

"What are the odds on that? You going there, and me knowing it for years?" she asked. One arm dangled out the window while the other twitched on the steering wheel.

"Actually... pretty good," Ronan thought of all those times which might have been coincidence. He now suspected they were more than that.

Leia dropped them off near the centre of the village, not far from the Green Man. Her eyes ran over the soft stone buildings, lush cricket pitch and poplars waving gently in the wind. "This is the kind of place Molly should have — not the sprawl."

"Maybe you should sell up and move here," Ronan joked while pulling Ella out of the backseat and into his arms.

"Maybe indeed," Leia bit her lip and smiled. "After all, what's old London town got to offer me now... nothing but memories."

Ronan caught a whiff of her grief, and even that tiniest taste broke his heart. Before he could think of any platitudes for her, Leia had shoved her foot to the floor, and the car had sped away from Penherem.

In his arms Ella stirred. It was only a twitch, a spasm to indicate the inner battle still raging. He didn't even know if she'd emerge from it at all. Looking round, he tried to decide what to do. Evening was coming on and it wouldn't be wise to take Ella back to her own house, nor to Bakari's.

"Uhhh-whooo," Helen Claremount trotted into view, swung open her garden gate and waved frantically. Ronan smiled somewhat nervously, suddenly aware how bad it looked to be lingering on a street corner with an unconscious woman. He tried to look like it was a common occurrence.

Helen took no notice. "You look lost, there." She glanced down into Ella's quiet face, "and she looks like she needs somewhere to lie down."

"I can carry her," Ronan replied gruffly.

Helen's mouth folded in, "I'm sure you could, big strapping man you are, but that wouldn't be very good for Ella, would it."

Ronan found himself being guided through the garden gate and into Helen's house. It smelt of earth and warm baking, and wild flowers were stuffed into every type of vase and pot. They couldn't possibly have all come from her garden. He raised an eyebrow.

Helen turned an interesting shade of red. "They're from an admirer."

"Everyone should have one of those."

Helen led him upstairs and insisted he hand Ella over to her care. Before Ronan knew it, Ella's shoes had been removed and she was ensconced in a huge overstuffed bed with a thick quilt over her. It was a human type of magic.

"There's just so many things going on in the village these days," Helen fussed around the room, fluffing pillows and tugging the curtains to let the dying light fall onto the bed. "An average person just has to muddle along — even when there is," she paused, looking down into her garden, "magic in the air."

It felt very odd to Ronan to hear those words come from a human mouth after so very long. He recalled those times as if they had been told to him, another person's story. He'd been Puck once. Could he be again?

He coughed uncomfortably, "Well, I think I'll go round to Ella's, pick her up a few things."

"She'd like that."

Ronan brushed a curl of her hair off her face and tried to see into what was going on inside her, but the flashes of memory and identity were too chaotic to really understand. There was a fusion going on inside Ella as the different facets of her past tried to find someway to live with each other. She would either come out or dissolve into confusion. It would do her good to have some familiar things about her.

He paused at the doorway. "You will look after her, Helen, won't you?"

"Don't worry yourself." She ushered him to the door. "You just go and do what you need to."

The street was quiet. Ronan passed a few villagers, and though he didn't know their names, they all said 'good evening' and smiled. He thought back to another village he'd spent time in, and suddenly it didn't seem that long ago. Recalling the easy joy he'd felt there, Ronan sighed. The young boy he'd been guarding had grown to be the greatest Bard in two realms. Yet he didn't even know what had happened to William. At the end of things for the Bard, Puck's own healing wounds had kept him away. He regretted that deeply. Well, things would be different this time.

Ella's cat was waiting quietly on the top step. She chirped and waved her black whip of a tail.

"I fed her," a young woman's face peered past the jasmine-covered fence, "so tell Ella not to worry."

Her name was Alice, and they stood and chatted over that fence while Qoth licked her flank. She had beautiful jewel eyes and something glowed from within. She was just like any other villager of Penherem: there was quiet strength about her and a touch of ancient Art. It was what had kept Ronan in this place.

He explained to Alice that Ella was feeling ill and might not be back to the house for a few days. She said she had no problem continuing to feed Qoth, and she'd keep an eye on the place. Smiling broadly at him, she disappeared behind the fence again.

Qoth followed him into the cottage, watching him with those golden moon eyes but not seeming offended that he was in her domain. Ronan had spent a lot of time as a cat, and he and felines generally understood each other. Still, Qoth trailed him around

251

the cottage as he collected a few clothes out of the wardrobe and retrieved shoes out from under the bed, stuffing them into a dark green bag.

He was just about to leave when a sharp mew attracted his attention. Qoth was at the French windows, yowling and digging her claws into the carpet with determination. When Ronan went over to let her out he noticed a small box on the back step. He smelt the blood as he picked it up, and his throat tightened. He snatched the brown paper from around the box and lifted the lid. It was his friend's finger. He'd noticed Bakari's hands often enough, fiddling with that damn Line thread of his, and it was wearing Bakari's thin silver band. Even if he hadn't recognized the ring, his feline senses would have identified the digit by scent.

As far as maiming went, it was not much; vat grown limbs were easy enough to get hold of, but for a threat it was clear. Thugs of all descriptions had been sending such messages for thousands of years. Somehow, it was different now that it was his friend, and possibly more than that: kin?

It was meant for Ella, but it was definitely a good thing that she had not found it. It was his burden. Bakari was his descendant, after all. The finger smelled of someone else too, someone who was his responsibility. Knowing that Greer was in Penherem did not fill him with confidence. She was annoyed that he had not stolen the Mask as asked, and hopefully she had just taken Bakari as a precaution. Still, when he caught up with her, there would be hard words exchanged. He didn't appreciate her cutting off fingers merely to make a point.

Ronan waited for night to settle over the village before setting out, but he didn't go back to Helen's. Whatever was happening to Ella would have to sort itself out; he couldn't risk bringing anymore trouble to her door. Once darkness arrived, he let himself out into her garden and shook off his human form. It was so easy that for a moment the black panther just reveled in it. For the last few years, even taking this shape had become increasingly difficult, but somehow tonight it was just as it used to be. Things had indeed changed, and it made Ronan's heart lighter.

The cat leapt over the back fence, then through the next one, and followed the smell of blood through the rest of the village. Whoever had delivered the finger had not been bothered by obstacles and as Ronan laid his nose to the scent, it too was familiar. An Unmaker's Seed; the realisation stopped the panther in his tracks.

He stood poised for a moment atop the brick wall which ran the length of the northern side of the Green. The Seed was working with Greer. The very thought made his previous hopes feel small and stupid. She'd always wanted power and magic — things the Unmaker certainly had. But even Greer couldn't imagine the sheer weight of his hatred for creation. If she had allied herself with the master of destruction, then she had gone too deep.

The panther leapt down from the wall and ran, low and silent across the open fields. Every cry of the nightbirds and every cloud that raced over him made him think of the things he had seen in the realm of the Unmaker — the Shattered world where he'd been chained for centuries. Ronan knew what would happen if that world was brought close to the human one and that foul touch reached out across the Between to this place. Not even the humans' new magic would be able to save them from that.

All the world seemed dark and unfriendly this night, but Ronan could not let that stop him. Somewhere his descendant was in deadly danger, and that came before any fears of the Unmaker. He cleared the hawthorn hedge that surrounded Penherem Hall in one fluid leap and stood panting, looking down at the lights. Unlike the last time he'd tried to break into the Hall, they'd been blazing. He could sense no life about, though the scent of Bakari's blood certainly led him here.

The Hall had seemed just like any other relic of British past before, but now he could sense far more. Old Earth magic had once run here. The patterns of the ancient rivers echoed in the stones that had been carved by human hands to make its walls. Puck's senses were coming back, and with them came a deepening dread, for now he was wondering about those voices Tania Furlion heard. What could they mean in a place of ancient magics?

This was not the time to find out. With a half voiced growl buried in his throat, the panther ran like fluid down the slight rise and across the manicured lawns. He passed the knot garden which had so interested Tania, and dimly recognized a web of Fey magic about it; one to confuse time and delay pursuers. This mystery, too, would have to wait, for the scent of blood was stronger than ever now. The rich iron taste was flooding through his feline nostrils, making his nose wrinkle and his heart beat faster.

He leapt the fence into the back garden, where kitchen herbs were grown, and found himself in utter darkness. The front was flooded with light, but the back was in darkness, with only the slimmest of moons to compensate. It was unnerving even to a panther, though there was still just enough ambient light to let his cat eyes lead him to the backdoor. It was ajar, and beyond was the smell of blood.

He paused there, settling on his paws for a moment. Once he went in there, he was sure it would be all on — there would be no time for thought. The real question was, what would he find behind these doors? Greer? Quite likely. The Unmaker's Seed? More certainly. These were dangers, but he felt he could handle them much better than he could have even a few days ago. The Seed might be a problem. As for Greer, she was powerful only in a world lacking power. She was no match for a Fey.

The great cat rose and yawned, showing his naked white fangs. With one velvet paw he batted the door open and slipped into the darkness beyond. The kitchen where he had first seen Ella was still and porcelain quiet. The cat shadow passed through, not noticing the surroundings, only smelling the taste of blood in the roof of his mouth. The panther's lip curled in a wrinkled snarl as he inhaled the smell deeply.

The Hall had layers of human scent on it: over-perfumed tourists, sweat, the bubble gum sweetness of children, but underneath there was more. His feet were silent as he went down through the maze of corridors and stairs. His eyes pierced the darkness while fear grew in his heart.

The smell stopped abruptly at a blank wall. It was nothing that a blunt dark nose could open. Ronan shifted and used his human hands to feel around the edges of the wall, palms flat against cool stone. A slight push in the right direction, a little applied pressure, and the wall slid back on itself. It was intriguing how the humans found ways with built things. Pity that they usually put them to such terrible uses.

It seemed that the Barons of Penherem had possessed certain appetites. The stones that led down into the dungeon spoke of terror old and new. Ronan walked in human form, his boots only marginally louder than paws would have. The passage grew progressively more damp as he progressed down the spiral staircase, until water was running under his hand like rusty tears. Though he had forsaken feline senses, his Fey ones were still sharper than a human's, and the smell of blood was stronger than it had ever been.

Still, Ronan would not let the worst be true, until his feet touched the bottom stair and he was faced with it. Bakari hung limp from the wall, bound with manacles. His own blood pooled around him like a dark lake. Ronan waited for a moment, letting himself take it all in, the true horror of death. For he could tell that his kin was dead, even from here: there was no sound or trace of breath, and the blood that drenched his chest could only have come from a throat wound.

A broken breath heaved through the Fey and his own throat felt constricted. His body trembled, but with grief, not anger. The sheer unfairness of it all broke over him. Bakari had seemed more alive than any other human, and he had searched so long and hard for his mother's magic. Now, at the very cusp of finding it, Bakari was dead.

Even in the face of all evidence, Ronan had to be sure. There was no way he could approach without touching the blood; his boots made little sticky splosh noises. Standing in front of Bakari, he raised his head gently and took in the cruel cut which had ended his life. On the handsome face there was no terror, no realization of death in his stilled eyes. Ronan closed them gently.

Shock had knocked the Fey. He stood there uncertain what to do, knowing that there would be no more friendly smiles, or easy friendship between them. Bakari was gone and the fact that he could never see him again was painful.

"He didn't feel a thing," Greer said from the shadows. She was wearing her luminous white gown, but its pureness was spoiled at the hem where it had dragged in Bakari's blood.

255

"That's supposed to be a comfort?" Ronan let his eyes roam past her, trying to see what horrors she'd bought with her. He would have revenge, but first he'd know her strength.

She spread her hands and smiled back at him. Concealed in the folds of her dress had been the Winter Mask. It had been so long since he'd seen it, that its sudden appearance was a shock.

He frowned. "If you could have stolen that thing yourself the whole time — why did you hire us to do it?"

The corner of Greer's mouth twitched. "You really are the most stupid Fey I've ever met."

That would have put the old Puck in a rage. Being mocked was one thing, but being underestimated was another. Ronan, though, had learned. Greer was trying to goad him, so he remained silent, edging a little away from Bakari.

Greer shook the mask at him. "It reminds you of someone, doesn't it? I would have thought that would make you want it even more."

"Well, I'm a little more cautious than I used to be."

"So I can see," Greer's eyeless face kept towards him. "A pity. Maybe your friend would still be alive if you hadn't got so clever."

"All for that mask?"

Greer shrugged and her next move was so unexpected that Ronan had only enough time for instinct to guide him: she threw it at him. It arched through the air, trailing the scent of jasmine. Ronan could hear her voice: the Queen of Fey, his cousin. Part of him still needed that. He caught it, hands going surely about the edges of the mask.

It was like touching pure ice. Coldness shot through his arms and straight into his heart. The scent of the jasmine was sickening in his nose and the voices of the dead were loud in his ears. He was trapped in Greer's world, where everything was tainted with fear. His eyes grew dark and his Fey soul trembled.

Greer sighed heavily. Now that she had him, it suddenly felt wrong. He was experiencing her own particular horrors and even though it had been necessary, it was not something she'd have willingly done to another. She glanced across at Bakari's still form. She hadn't meant to kill him either, but the Seed needed to be fed.

Now it was time. The moment to grasp her only chance at peace. She took the mask from Ronan's still hands and raised it to her face. It slid on easily, and she looked out through the goddess' eyes. It had been a clever thing for the Unmaker to do, to make a trap in the image of Ronan's greatest desire. It was only those human instincts he'd learned over the centuries that had saved him the first time. It was a good thing that he'd also picked up the human frailty of friendship along the way — without it, this moment couldn't have happened.

She almost felt sorry for Ronan. He had fought hard long ago against the Unmaker, and yet his blood would bridge the gap. Once she had the greenstone mere, the last piece would be in play and then it would all be over. For both of them.

CHAPTER TWENTY

Endings

What should she call herself? So many names whirling in her head; Aroha, Nill, Ella, and another which had never been spoken to her but was still hers — if she was willing to claim it. The woman levered herself upright in the bed. Though the memories were still settling into place, somewhere in the middle of it all, against all odds, she felt sane and complete. Her identity was slotting into this body — for she knew it was her body, even if it was made with synthetics. She'd come to see that in the whirling chaos of identity. Flesh, Fey magic, or synthetic Shell, it didn't matter, what did count was that her spirit lived.

She was in a plush pink room, tucked under a thick feather comforter, and the curtains were pulled. The light was from a small lamp and it illuminated the only decoration in the room, rows of full-bellied, full-breasted female figurines on the shelf. Something about them was familiar, though in whose life was impossible to tell. She brushed her hair back off her eyes and spent a long moment staring at the back of her own hand. It looked perfectly alright, but parts of her still expected to see a child's brown or the whiteness of Fey skin.

Suddenly feeling the weight of someone else's regard she twisted around, heart thumping. It was only Helen; she recognized her easily, by finding the mental cubbyhole where Ella's memories were stored. The plump little woman wasn't smiling, but there was something of awe in her glance.

"He said you would be fine."

The woman licked her lips experimentally. "Who?" She listened to her familiar yet alien voice in her own head. Was that her own?

"Aloshon — he's... well," Helen stuttered, "I guess you'd say he's a satyr — my satyr."

In the chaos stray thoughts started to coagulate and sort themselves out. "One of the Fey. One of my people. The little ones can cross over first."

Helen blushed. "I don't know if you'd call him 'little'."

The woman was not listening; her forehead pinched in concentration, immersed by the little floods of information that were slowly forming into an understanding. Her hands wriggled under the sheets, found the smooth coolness of the greenstone mere, and suddenly she was calm. Whatever had happened, the enemy had not taken it. The little ones would not be enough to bridge the Between. If the time of healing had begun, then it would be their only chance to bring the Shattered World close to the human one. Her addled mind began to slot the pieces together.

"He's gone, you know," Helen must have misunderstood her silence. She stepped closer to the bed. "He said he was going to get you a few things... but that was hours ago."

Dread wrapped itself around the woman's heart. The Trickster, even after all his years in the human realm, was not a creature of careful thought. Darling Ronan, he could not have known all she now did, and he had rushed off blindly, as always. He thought he knew everything, but for once he was not the most powerful Fey left in the human world. She was.

Helen took a step back, perhaps catching a glimpse of the Fey light about her. She looked suddenly uncertain of the woman she'd known for so long. Her guest put out her hand along the quilted comforter and smiled reassuringly. "Tell me the rest."

Helen sat on the edge and patted the other's hand. "Penny and Alice banged on my door. I told them you were asleep and they said for you to meet them at the Hall's main gate."

Barely were the words out of her mouth, before her guest had leapt from the bed and was stuffing her shoes on. She dragged her curls back from her face and braided them quickly. "How long ago was this?"

"About an hour ago. I would have woken you, but Ronan said..."

259

"I know. It's alright, Helen," she tried to soothe the guilty look off her face, attempting not to frighten the little woman. "But I need you to get the other villagers up and bring them to the Hall."

"At this hour?" It was true, most of them would be either tucked up in bed, or perhaps sipping a glass of port by the fireside. Helen knew this as well as anyone, and the idea of *intruding* was an awful one. Besides, the thought was easy to read: they wouldn't believe her. They all thought she was a bit of a joke.

The woman hugged Helen impulsively, giving her a little of her strength, completing the healing that the satyr had begun. "They'll come if you ask them, Helen, and I really do need you to do this. It's more important than you can imagine."

A few days before, Helen Carew would have run squeaking at the very idea, but she'd learned something of her own strength since then. She understood her own value. "You can count on me, Ella."

No time now to stop and explain, her guest decided, not when she didn't quite have all the answers, herself. Instead, she gave Helen a quick hug, then clattered down the stairs and outside. Pausing at the gate, she let her Fey Art dart ahead, testing the air for signs of the Seed.

The night was crisp and clear, the stars sparkling, the trees brushing against each other. The muffled lights in the village houses somehow conveyed a sense of calm. Nothing stirred in the night to challenge a wakened Fey, fresh and full of her own power. All she had to do now was figure out her real name.

"You know what you have to do?"

Bakari was chewing his virtual nails in what he hoped was virtual nervousness. The sheer scope of Greer's memory was becoming more daunting the longer he looked at it, and what Penny was asking was also becoming increasingly difficult.

Her lips pursed together. "You do, don't you?"

"You made yourself clear enough."

"It's pretty important that you are out of here when you do it."

"Yep, I know. If I do this right we might all get out of this alive."

Penny went quiet, suddenly childlike again. She looked at him out of the corner of her eye and chewed her lip, as if she knew something he didn't. A hollow pit opened up inside Bakari, a deep fear that all people knew — the fear of death and the unknown beyond.

Abruptly, he didn't want to know.

"Right, well, I'm sure I can find something."

She touched his hand. "I know you can."

She was just a kid, but he felt reassured all the same. "Just go, okay?" he muttered.

Just like that, she did, a slow dissolve like something from an old movie, disappearing into the ether. Now he was alone; alone in Greer's mind, with no idea how he was going to do what the girl had asked.

Penny and Alice were waiting for the woman at the gate, just as they had said they would. Around them was utter silence. The dimness of the gardens and forests felt safe and familiar, but once they set foot within the Hall, things would be different.

Alice's arm was around Penny, the child leaning in against her elder, but there was nothing frightened about the child. Her eyes were clear and dark, the velvet blue of the night sky, and in them were stars.

The woman though could see nothing more about the two. They were as much a mystery to her as they had been to Ella.

She paused, hesitant suddenly when only moments before she had been so sure. She was the healer, but she had no idea what she should do.

Alice held out her hand to her and when the woman took it, she could feel the course rub of thick scars against her palm. Alice did not pull back, merely allowed a weak smile to flutter across her face. In all her time in the village, Ella had never seen Alice's hands. They spoke of a haunted and pained past.

The woman looked down at little Penny and noticed for the first time that she had her two dolls, one jammed under each arm. She, too, was smiling.

261

"It's time to go in," Alice's voice was soft and low. "The Between is close, the chance for Healing near."

"I'm... afraid," the woman whispered hoarsely. "I'm not sure."

Penny caught her hand and pressed her face to it, and Alice tightened her grip on her other. "All will be as it should."

She was not the same girl Ella had known, the woman could tell that. Something deeper echoed in her voice and there was none of her usual reserve in that gentle smile. It was both frightening and reassuring.

"Is nothing what it seems in Penherem?" she wondered aloud.

"Hardly," Alice turned them back to their task. All three walked towards the Hall. It blazed with light, a golden star in all the darkness. Strangely, there were no security guards. The Hall had on a far different face now. In daylight, it was covered in tourists and reeked of nothing more sinister than curiosity. Now, an air of mystery and danger seeped out of every stone.

The main doors were flung wide and the silence beyond was oppressive. The woman paused at the last step. "We're expected?"

"Certainly," Alice replied, her hand guiding the other forward. "This is the Unmaker's doing, but we must go on."

The hallways were familiar. Ella had run down here in a panic only a week ago, but it felt like a century ago. Now the same body carried a lifetime of new memories.

Her two guides turned her towards the southern wing where the arts and treasures of generations of Furlions were kept. The feeling of dread grew with each step.

Something scuttled; a movement that sent shivers down the woman's spine. Her bones still recalled Ella's wound there. Movement caught her eye. One of the remote cameras situated at the entrance to the wing twisted and turned on them. Lights danced beneath it.

Penny clapped her hands together, waving madly at the camera and generally capering about like she had just seen her best friend. One of her dolls, unnoticed, fell free of her pocket.

Alice picked it up and looked down at it thoughtfully before tucking it into the waistband of her skirt, but she made no move to stop her charge's relentless leaping. "Not far now," she whispered softly. They moved on, Penny trailing in their wake, still flapping her hands madly at the camera.

If the lights were on in the main Hall, they were dimmed here amongst all the glass cases and treasures. Only grayness fell about them.

Something was different though; things had been moved, permanent displays were shifted from their usual places and shoved carelessly against the walls, all to make an open space in the centre.

"Stay here," Alice whispered and tugged the grinning Penny after her. The woman watched them duck and crawl their way through the maze of display cases and disappear into the grayness at the rear of the room.

She was not just going to sit there and wait to find out what was going to happen. The weight of the atmosphere was too heavy. She had to move. Cautiously she inched forward, straining to determine what lay ahead. What had happened here? Her thoughts darted around. Could something have happened to Tania?

She soon got her answer. Suddenly from the mezzanine floor the flood lights flicked on, and the whole central square of the room was illuminated. The woman blinked as the light reflected a thousand fold into her eyes.

That was new. A huge slab of rock that might well have come from Stonehenge, save that it was made of thick crystal like a piece of permanent ice. It lay flat, an altar of magic that had no place in this world. The sheer enormity of its presence demanded all of the woman's attention for a moment. For an instant, nothing else seemed to matter.

"The Nexus," she whispered, as another wave of understanding broke over her. It was the King Stone of the circle that stood at the centre point of the three realms. She couldn't recall having ever been there, but the image of it was burned into her brain. An image rattled through the corridors of her mind; a dark haired bard pressed against it, a spear of evil piercing through him and into the stone itself. This was the sacrifice that had moved the realms apart. The King Stone should have stood upright within the Nexus, but here it was, laid flat out in the middle of Penherem.

The stone was not empty. Shock had prevented her from seeing beyond the stone itself for a moment, but tied to its length was Ronan. His face was turned away from her, but the woman

263

could feel his pain. Standing above him, somehow taller in the flood of light. was a masked female figure, slender and dressed in flowing white robes though stained with blood on the edge. She knew the mask. Tania had called it the Winter Mask and it was her most important treasure. But who was under it?

The woman crept closer, heart racing in her chest, while knowing this was not the moment to let fear rule.

The figure before the stone also sensed her, for she stepped away from Ronan and looked straight at the other's hiding place. "Come out, Healer," she commanded.

After only a moment's hesitation, the woman rose from her hiding place. Curiosity won over her fear. It was strange to look into the face of stony perfection, a beautiful woman's face with something so welcoming about it.

"So, Healer, even you must obey the calling," the voice behind the mask was familiar, and as if to confirm it, the white clad stranger pulled the mask away. Beneath, Tania's face smiled back in that odd lopsided manner.

The woman felt her heart go suddenly cold. Tania was her friend. She'd felt sorry for her, and somehow always imagined the villagers were wrong about the poor mad lady.

"Masks beneath masks," Tania whispered and that face, too, faded. In its place was the face Ella had dreamed of days before; deep scars were all that were left where the eyes had been, but the hair was still fine and white.

"Who are you?"

"I am like you — a seed planted by my Master. You are the hope of the Fey for this realm and I am the hope of their enemy." She dangled the stone mask lightly from her fingertips. "Ronan knew me as Greer, but I have always been Tania in reality. I have been waiting a very long time for you to arrive."

"Have you?" The weight of Tania's regard was frightening.

"Yes, for without you, I cannot accomplish my task. Silly to think I had not noticed that you'd been here for so long. Perhaps I was blind. Or blinded," she chuckled to herself. "But nevertheless, you are here now, and it is time."

"Time for what?" The woman tried to filter through her still chaotic past to find answers she felt were vital.

"You really do not know? All the better." Tania pushed the mask once more over her face. Holding out her hand imperiously, she commanded, "Give me the greenstone mere." Her voice, when it came from between those stone lips, was far different. It was deeper, and echoed down the other woman's bones. The Healer could feel the Art within the voice, but had no idea how to fight it. The person who should have trained her had been killed in the green hills of Aotearoa and she'd spent her whole life in a borrowed body.

Her body twitched, and then obeyed Tania's command. She stepped up next to the King Stone and placed the still piece of greenstone into her enemy's hands.

"Ponamu," Tania's voice was full of desire, "the last gift of human magic." She smiled coyly and tugged the other woman over to look down at Ronan.

His eyes were dark and distant, focused on a far off place. Tania brushed a curl back from his eyes. "Now all the pieces are in place, dear friend: the last of the elder Fey, the gift of human magic, and even this part of the Nexus."

The woman heard her only dimly, for somewhere in her internal battle a certainty was forming, a rumble of identity.

Tania did not notice, for she was already lost in her own haze of victory. "When a Fey is slain with human magic, the ancient alliance will be destroyed, and with it the magic that has imprisoned my Master." She thrust her once-friend away from her to stumble and fall in a boneless heap on the floor. The woman who had been Ella was of no consequence now.

"The time of healing, will now be a time of destruction," Tania whispered.

Then the room was filled with a massive attack of noise; drums rattled, guitars squealed as the air was tormented fiercely enough to shake the glass in the cabinets.

Tania's mouth opened, but her scream was drowned out. Her once-friend looked out from her tangled hair and blinked. Hovering a few feet off the ground, Bakari looked down with real satisfaction. It was obvious that this was his chaos. With a theatrical gesture, he cut off the music and smiled rather thinly at Tania. She, in her turn, had pulled back the mask and was staring at him with undisguised shock. Her lip trembled as though she was going to speak.

Bakari looked down at the woman he'd known as his friend. "Are you okay, Ella?"

She managed a nod, a little jerky and uncoordinated. He looked different, two dimensional somehow.

"Ah, this?" he waved his hands. "All thanks to the display systems — I'm on the Line," he gave Greer a look of pure disgust. "Thanks to her."

Their enemy's mouth pulled back in an ugly smile. "And that's where you'll stay, too." She stepped back close to Ronan. "Now don't bother me."

The woman's legs scrambled, but found no purchase on the floor. Her nerves were still fried by whatever Greer had done. "She's going to kill Ronan. Bakari, help him."

"He can't do anything," Tania/Greer shot back, already raising the mere to strike. "He's been dead for hours. He's got no body to go back to."

From the mezzanine floor came the hiss of the Unmaker's Seed, a rattle of claws on the parquet. Such a creature would be enjoying the emotional pain as if it were a play put on for its amusement.

Bakari's digital face blanched, and a ripple of distortion passed through him. It must be a great shock to have the truth revealed in such a manner. The woman knew better than anyone that the body was an important part of identity. However, she underestimated her friend.

Perhaps it was because of the time he'd spent on the Line, or a part of the Fey nature that had brought him back, but the horror washed through him and did not carry him away.

"You know, Greer, you're really starting to annoy me."

She took no notice. Instead she raised the greenstone mere high, confident that neither of her opponents could do anything to stop her, breaking the alliance.

Then Penny's blonde head popped up above one of the display cabinets. She waved cheerily at Bakari, while the unnamed woman who had been Ella clambered to her hands and knees, sensing that something was about to happen.

Her friend's image moved, throwing back his arm, as if hurling something at Greer. She reacted as if it had been acid, dissolving into remembrance. The woman caught her agony.

The sky outside the office window was as brown as bark, but somewhat less inviting. Tania watched the sludgy movement of the clouds and through ears half closed listened to the drone of her assistant.

The view from the penthouse could have been York/Birmingham, or Sydney/Melbourne — but it just so happened, today, to be London. So much of England was now covered by this sprawling, heaving megacity that it had become synonymous with the country as a whole. This ever-hungry beast was swallowing up England. On her ruby red mouth a small smile appeared, her pointed little teeth gleaming. Tania's mind did not hear what her secretary had just told her. So long, so very long on in this world and every day longer than the last. Every single one of those days had been spent alone.

That was, until Anthony. A child, after all that time — she'd stopped expecting it. His auburn curls, his wide blue eyes had somehow made the world feel a better place. When he pointed at a racing cloud across the sky, or a squirrel chewing on an acorn, and laughed, she could feel the weight of all her days falling away. So long in this human realm and everything had long ago lost its taste, until Anthony showed her the way to enjoy it once more.

But once he was gone, darkness had closed in. Tania felt her heart shrink in her chest, her pain taking over all that he had brought her. She'd watched him grow, learn, marry and then die — it was a full life, but it was not enough!

Her fist clenched at her side while her secretary droned on.

All that was left now in this world was pain. That, and service to her Master. Why did that not bring any relief? Why was her heart so empty?

Tania fell to her knees and the world seemed to tilt with her, going suddenly crazy. The woman who had called herself Ella could finally move, and as she crawled to her feet, she saw that there were plenty of others who now could also. On the other side of the King Stone, Penny and Alice were up and running. Incredible as it was, the little girl and the woman sprinted towards Tania.

They barreled into her, catching her about the waist, knocking her to the floor and dissolving into a tumbling mass of legs and flailing hair. In between it all there were flashes of the greenstone weapon. Alice's hands wrapped about Greer's, wrestling with her for her hold on the mere. Penny had her arms wrapped around Greer's leg and was hanging on like a limpet.

Bakari hovered overhead, waving his hands frantically but unable to do anything. He called Penny's name and then the woman's. "Ella! Do something!"

Her legs were slow to recover. She felt herself scrambling to get to the fray; it felt like it took an eternity.

Then the three struggling women cried out as one. It was a sound of such infinite pain that everything froze in its tracks. The nameless woman felt that agony go through her and saw that there was now blood splattered in a fine arc across the King Stone. It took only a heartbeat for her to know that it wasn't Ronan's; it was Penny's.

The child stood up, her two dolls cast away and for the first time forgotten. She was holding her hand to her head and looking at Tania and Alice, lip trembling. The child that had barely spoken a word began to sob. Tania, who had disregarded the illusion of her perfect face, could not cry, but she dropped the Winter Mask from her fingertips. It shattered on the floor, breaking into a million sharp little pieces.

The nameless one felt time cease, replaced by nothing but golden light. It was almost like the Earth rivers she had ridden, but there was the taste of Fey about. The rest of the world had receded and there were only the three female forms. Tania was no longer fighting them, she was moving to them, taking Alice by one hand and the wounded Penny by the other. A howl ran through the world, a thrum of power that battered every sense and left the nameless one hollow and gasping.

When it cleared and there was golden light again, she was alone except for a tall dark haired woman. She looked familiar, the shape of her face echoing in some undiscovered memory. When she smiled at the nameless woman, she knew she couldn't be nameless for ever. That smile soothed all hurts and offered only infinite love.

"Where are they?" the nameless woman asked hesitantly. "Tania and Alice and little Penny?"

The other touched a spot on her flawless chest, "They are here — within me."

Realisation and remembrance helped her give this goddess a name. "Anu."

"Ah, dear child," a cool hand brushed her hair away from her eyes. "You have suffered so much — been separated from your parents, just as I have been separated from all I love."

"Grandmother," the nameless one said through a hesitant smile, as stories welled up inside her. "You were lost to the Unmaker."

She passed a hand over her grandchild's face and let her see the moment of doom. Anu, the Queen of the Fey, mother of Sive the Shining, had been lost in the distance between worlds. It was she who had bound the Unmaker in the Dawn of Time to his broken world, and when she sensed he was close to escape, it was she who had gone to make sure the breach was closed.

"But I was arrogant, vain perhaps, and thought that I could do it alone. I did not take any other Fey with me, though my sister Brigit would have gone willingly."

The Unmaker had taken her unawares, being so much stronger than she had imagined. However, Anu was the avatar of the Earth Goddess herself, and was not easily destroyed. So the Unmaker had broken her like the three realms, shattering her into her three parts; child, maiden and crone. The first two he'd scattered through time and space. The crone he had swallowed whole, before sending her to the human world to watch for the coming Fey. He knew eventually the time of Healing would occur. Poor Tania, the eternal crone, had been driven mad by it all. Unknowingly, she had worked for her enemy.

The nameless woman found herself sobbing in Anu's arms, feeling the pain and emptiness of her friend.

"You, too, have suffered," Anu said softly, "More than I would have wished for child of my child."

"And I've lost my name. I was Aroha, then Nill and finally Ella — so many names and I don't know which one is mine."

Anu kissed her forehead. "Your mother, Sive, gave you one on your birth, and it has never left you. It has always been waiting for you. Throw away the others and take it up."

The memory bubbled up from within her, a remembrance which no mortal could have had, of her first breath and her given name. Aine, her mother had whispered it into her ear, all warmth and love. It meant joy. No other had ever spoken her name. It was a gift and a weapon, the same as to all Fey, though she was half human. It would not be spoken until she was strong enough to defend it and choose who to give it to. Her father, the Bard, had kissed the top of her head before giving her to the woman she would come to call Nana.

Aine clutched the name to her. It felt more right than any other name she'd ever had.

Her real grandmother hugged her tightly, "Be proud of who you are, child of my child, but remember that it means you bear greater responsibilities than others." Her perfect forehead folded in worry. "You must go back, back to Penherem."

Aine shivered, seeing the King Stone and Ronan straining against it, but it was so distant. It was so tempting to remain here in the golden light.

"I'm sorry, dear child, but that cannot be. My maimed Tania fragment spilled the blood of a Fey with the magic of the human realm. The Nexus is weak, and the Shattered Realm will receive the Healing that is meant for another. When it is reunited with the human world, the Unmaker will be able to cross."

Aine nodded, feeling the weight of duty. If she had remained whole, and done her job properly...

"No time for that, child," Anu chided. "Regrets are for mortals."

She recognised truth. It was the task that had been set for her by her mother when she had sent her only daughter to Earth. Aine turned back to the real world and heard the ancient queen's parting words.

"I will wait for you, granddaughter, for your return."

Then the golden light melted away from her and she was back, but not the same. The women had vanished, absorbed into one, but Anu had been right. Blood on the King Stone mocked Aine, and a terrible sound in the air made her shiver deep down in her core.

"Ella," Ronan called to her, still tied to the face of the rock. He couldn't know her real name — not yet anyway. He was more glorious through her now opened eyes. He all but blazed in Aine's vision.

She ran to him, passing straight through a frantic Bakari. Her friend's form seemed more solid now, like he was mastering the electronic output required.

"Did I get it right?" His eyes were wide. "Penny told me what to do, but..."

"Yes, you did what was needed." Aine tugged at the chains wrapped tightly about Ronan.

"Tania spelled them." The Fey strained against them. "I couldn't break them." He sounded so very sorry at his own failings.

Yet the fragment that had been Tania could never match Anu's granddaughter in power. She put her hands to the chains and put forth her Art, so they became nothing more than lines of dust across Ronan's chest.

He looked up at her with a chill stillness. He had sensed her power on Raven Hill, but now there was more, a touch of the royal Fey line. It did frighten him, Aine could see that, but only in that he was afraid to lose her. He really didn't know how she felt.

Taking his hand, Aine helped him up from the King Stone. "Foolish Fey, I love you — no matter what my name is." To prove it, she bent and whispered it into his ear.

Then he was laughing aloud, hugging her, crushing her to him. Looking over his shoulder, she could feel many things changing. Her sharpened senses could discern the arrival of the villagers of Penherem. They had come, just as when she'd asked the people of Makara, bringing with them their little magics won at great cost.

Helen, Rob, Janey, Toby, Bev, Ned and all the other faces that had surrounded her while she healed in the village. In between she could also sense the presence of the little ones, the lesser Fey who had slipped through the Between or had awoken from hibernation. The weight of their attention was focused on her.

The blood on the King Stone was not to be ignored. Her own blood made of Fey and Human told her that the balance had shifted; the old pact between the two races was broken. The Hall groaned on its foundations, crying out like a stricken woman, bulging abruptly at the seams as power built within.

Bakari spat out a bitter oath as the projection equipment closest to the stone imploded in an explosion of metal and glass. His image dimmed, relying on the remaining one.

Ronan's hand tightened on her shoulder. He'd seen the last time, been in the battle in the Shattered Realm and looked into the face of darkness. "He's coming through," the Fey's voice cracked with dread.

All that Aine had been through and all that her broken selves had witnessed had been a forge for this moment. The human Bardic power of her father and the Fey energy from her mother boiled inside her, a rising tide of energy. They had sacrificed watching their child grow up to make sure she was here for this moment. Her Nana had died to preserve her. She thought of all the people who had also been lost, even unknowingly for this. Sally's cheery smile, Daniel's bravery and the ranks of her childhood friends rose in memory.

Aine's head buzzed and every ounce of her strength went into holding herself back. The world was opening. The back wall of the room was disappearing into a broken landscape, a yawning mass of low black clouds and jagged hilltops. All that occupied this place was hatred. It washed out from the chasm and rolled over the people. The strength of it was such that everyone but Aine and Ronan bent and fell to their knees. Even Bakari, somewhere on the Line, felt it and was toppled.

Above on the mezzanine floor, the Seed shrieked its delight and leapt down to alight like a giant malign spider on top of the glass case. Its jaws snapped and the bone white shell glowed with the presence of its master. Aine turned her head and glared at it. Just as it was at Makara, the Seed would serve its master by killing the villagers. It would be its gift of blood.

She gave Ronan a push. "Go. Save them."

He looked back once at the chasm, face white, eyes wide, "But..."

"This is what I was born for," she kissed him lightly on the cheek. "Serve me best by saving them."

He saw it in her, the strength of Sive and the Bard. He needed no more. He trusted in that strength as he had hundreds of years before. Ronan leapt away, shifting in the air, becoming his dangerous feline form.

Unmaker chose that moment, when Aine was alone. A huge human form of utter darkness stepped towards the chasm, ready to pass into the human world. She was all that stood before him. Aine knew she looked frail and small beside the massive thing of hatred and destruction.

She did not move.

It called out to her memories, showing her again the death of Nana, the fatal fall of Sally. She did not blink, merely remained where she was; a force of human and Fey. Like steel which derives it strength from a union of iron and carbon, she remained.

The Unmaker delved deeper, finding the memories of how it had broken her uncle Auberon and even her grandmother the great Anu. Still she did not move. A thousand forms of chaos and death it sent to her, enough to rupture any being, mortal or immortal. But she had looked into the face of destruction before, found her own horrors much earlier, and so was unmoved. It wailed and gnashed above her, unable to get past.

Aine felt the battle between Ronan the Trickster and the Unmaker's Seed at her back. Once, it would have been death for Puck. The Fey's Art had been weak before, but now it was strong. His shapeshifting had been restored with her touch. The cat moved faster than the Seed and his form was fluid, constantly changing, using all its Feyness against the Seed. Puck the Trickster was in every move and action. He was speed and glory and the fight ended quickly. The Seed was no more, a blight gone from the village. A murder was avenged.

The Unmaker was not made less by the loss of one minion. It roared as one claw of darkness found purchase in the real world, piercing the ground only a few inches from Aine. The vessel of her body was suddenly filled with understanding.

The Nexus. Stepping back only fractionally she laid her hand on the King Stone, feeling the pulse of the place where three worlds met. It had been made by great magic and it could be undone. It knew her, or rather, it knew her blood. Her father Will had once been prepared to sacrifice himself for it. He had given his life to the Nexus, part of its magic had flowed back into him in return, and from him into his daughter.

Now she called on that force, turned that power in on itself, demanding the Nexus break. The strength of its own magic could not be denied. The King Stone cried like a child, a wail of despair at such outrage. The anchor snapped like a broken harp string and the link between worlds was destroyed. Crystal shards exploded all around them, becoming a whirlwind of daggers and intense cold. The King Stone had obeyed, giving up its life at her command. The chasm began to seal, like a wound that had been waiting to be healed.

One claw of the Unmaker was buried deeply in the human realm, and even as its moment passed, it would not give up. Destruction was slowly pulling itself free of the Shattered Realm.

That was when the villagers cried out — not in horror this time, but in denial. They would not allow this to happen. Aine turned to them, looking among the crowd of people, but also seeing those that were still present but no longer alive; feeling their will being given to her. Nana. Sally.

She knelt down and touched the Unmaker, filling him with love and beauty, letting him see the will of the world. Into him flowed all the agony and joy that Aine had found in this realm. The Unmaker only knew pain and hatred — he was their avatar. Aine was filled with something far different. She had suffered here too, been broken and used, and all she loved had been killed before her. Yet there was more to the world than just pain. There was unquenched love, a touching of souls, laughter that cemented friendships, and a community of hope.

All this Aine poured into the Unmaker while tears washed down her cheeks. They were not tears of despair, not at all like the millions he had wrenched from others; they were tears of gratitude for all that she'd learned here. It was too much joy. He pulled back. With him went the Shattered Realm. It receded, hiding its broken landscape and parting from the human realm.

The chaos subsided. No more chasm, no more King Stone. The villagers stood quiet, smiling, without fear. They had felt the back wash of Aine's joy, seen themselves through her eyes. It was an experience that could not help but leave them touched. To understand your own goodness is to be surprised.

Aine sighed, but smiled at them.

Ronan slipped his hand into hers. "It's time to go, isn't it?"

He could feel it too. The thin strand of Fey that had been drawn down by her arrival in Penherem was withdrawing. Nothing remained to bind it to the human world — there was no healing for it today. Aine nodded. "We have to go back. This place is not yet ready for us."

"You can't leave us," Bakari looked like he might have been crying digital tears. He had tasted more magic in these days than any other mortal had in a long time. He did not want it to slip away now.

"Dear friend — I will miss you most of all. But I'm leaving you with something." She ached to take his hand.

"Yeah, and what would that be?" He crossed his arms and managed a glare.

"Hope," She reached out with her fingertips and almost touched him. "You know there is magic in what you do. And though the Nexus is broken, perhaps in time you could build another bridge to the Fey world. Work your own magic and find us."

A little sliver of her power leapt across to him, burying the information he would need inside his now digital brain.

"It will take so many years," he replied softly, but in awe. "What do we do until then?"

Aine smiled, "I leave a portion of my Art here in Penherem, so that the little Fey who have chosen to come back may survive. There will always be greatness here — it is a place touched by Anu." Her heart ached at the thought of leaving it. "And you of all people now have the time to master this new human magic."

He blinked, thinking of the body he'd left and what he'd become instead. "It's possible, then?"

Ronan laughed; it was a sound to lift the spirit, filled with the essence of the Puck of old. "Haven't you learned by now, Bakari? There is magic in everything you humans do. And the impossible is made possible by it."

The little Fey, satyrs and fairies, looked at her with longing eyes, peeking out from behind the humans they had taken to heart. They yearned for the Fey, but love would not let them leave.

"You are safe here, little ones," Aine whispered to them. "A time will come when Bakari finds a way, and then I will return with my mother. Take care of these, your human friends, until then."

They sighed, twittered and smiled. For immortals it would be but a heartbeat.

Aine whispered a word, a call, and out of the crowd Qoth appeared. She darted to her mistress with a chirp of delight and was scooped up. Over the feline's head Aine looked one last time at her home. "I will return when you have rebuilt the Nexus, but this time, connect only two realms. The Shattered you will leave drifting alone in the Between. It will be a new alliance."

The villagers sighed and leaned forward, as if to catch a last breath of their savior.

Bakari straightened. "I'll be waiting."

"Then care for each other until then," Aine whispered, though they all heard her. "Make the magic in your own way."

Then without further words Ronan, Qoth and Aine turned as Anu opened the pathway. They stepped forward and were gone into the Between worlds. Back home to the Fey.

EPILOGUE

Futures

The wind was blowing over the golden hills, ruffling the grass and scarlet flowers alike. The man was standing on the hill, looking down at a lake that reflected everything but the clouds. He had not quite got that part right. It was a detail, but one that was important. Bakari made a mental note to fix it as soon as possible. This construct would be complete once it was done, and then the children would be able to take over. He had limited the number of parameters that could be changed, and they would enjoy the flowers as well as the numerous small furry animals that occupied the forest by the water. He'd enjoy hearing the laughter and sensing their growing power.

"Master?" Sarah's voice was behind him. She must have been getting much better at her entrances of late, as he hadn't even heard her arrive.

He turned about and smiled. She was only a youngster, in her early twenties, but already in the blue of the Second magery. Her eyes were almond shaped and full of reverence today as they had never been before. He shook his head. "And here was I thinking you were the only one who didn't treat me like some sort of high priest."

A delicate blush spread through her cheeks. "I don't think that. I just can't help it, it's just awesome... all this," she gestured to take in the lake, the hills and the forest below. "In some of the Feeds, they are calling you the new Merlin."

Bakari ignored those last words. Thanks to his old Liner ways, he found it difficult to accept his new celebrity. "Well, this construct is nearly done," he admitted.

"We should already be onto the next one. So many more people are coming to the worlds of the Line you create." Sarah bent, picked a flower, spun it with her fingertips and examined it closely. "They all want to see what you've done, learn from you."

She thought it was all so wonderful, but Bakari wasn't completely without a clue, even if he did live solely on the Line now. In the beginning there had been plenty of people who wanted to hurt the Work, or exploit it somehow. Human beings hadn't changed that much since he'd become disembodied. But because Bakari had expected it, he'd been able to deal with it. The power of a being that lived purely on the Line could not be overcome by those who still had the limitations of a body. Not yet, anyway.

He ran the palm of his hand over the tops of the grass, enjoying the tickle of it. "We've got a long way to go, Sarah. Our task will not be easy."

"Ah, but think of the reward," she grinned, all full of the possibilities. He'd shown them to her, a taste of the magic he'd caught that day when the last great Fey had left the human world. It had been a heartbreaking moment, but one that had been heavy with hope. He could still feel Aine's eyes on him, violet eyes like the night just before dawn. Every time he remembered, the Work did not seem so onerous.

He'd kept his dream and the dream of his long dead mother. It had bound him to sanity when he'd lost his body. It would hold all of humanity together, even as they plunged into chaos in the real world. That was why the young came to him first, like Sarah — they needed his dream, too.

He took Sarah's hand, feeling its warmth and strength with senses he no longer possessed, but that were still real. "You're right, dear heart," he kissed her palm. "Thank you for reminding me."

He ached for that moment, but he was not despairing. With the help of people like Sarah, anything could be achieved, and one day he knew he would see his friends again.

PHILIPPA
Ballantine

Born in Wellington, New Zealand, Philippa Ballantine has always had her head in a book. Working with them as a librarian, reading vast numbers of them, and now writing them. Her first novel *Weaver's Web* was e-published in 2003. Her second novel, *Chasing the Bard,* earned a distinction as a nominee for the 2005 Sir Julius Vogel Award, New Zealand's version of the Hugo Awards.

Philippa has taken an active part in the podcasting community. Along with releasing her fiction as podcasts, she hosts the award-nominated *Whispers at the Edge,* a show about living and writing in New Zealand. Pip has also provided her voice to other podcast productions such as *The Metamor City Podcast, Murder at Avedon Hill,* and *MOREVI: Remastered.*

Made in the USA